The
VILLA

BOOKSPAN LARGE PRINT EDITION

G. P. PUTNAM'S SONS
NEW YORK

The VILLA

Nora Roberts

This Large Print Edition, prepared especially for Bookspan, contains the complete, unabridged text of the original Publisher's Edition.

G. P. Putnam's Sons
Publishers Since 1838
a member of
Penguin Putnam Inc.
375 Hudson Street
New York, NY 10014

ISBN 0-7394-1624-3

Printed in the United States of America

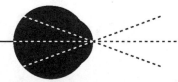

This Large Print Book carries the
Seal of Approval of N.A.V.H.

To family, who form the roots.
To friends, who make the blossoms.

The
VILLA

On the night he was murdered, Bernardo Baptista dined simply on bread and cheese and a bottle of Chianti. The wine was a bit young, and Bernardo was not. Neither would continue to age.

Like his bread and cheese, Bernardo was a simple man. He had lived in the same little house in the gentle hills north of Venice since his marriage fifty-one years before. His five children had been raised there. His wife had died there.

Now at seventy-three, Bernardo lived alone, with most of his family a stone's throw away, at the edges of the grand Giambelli vineyard where he had worked since his youth.

He had known *La Signora* since her girl-hood, and had been taught to remove his cap whenever she passed by. Even now if Tereza Giambelli traveled from California back to the *castello* and vineyard, she would stop if she saw him. And they would talk of the old days when her grandfather and his had worked the vines.

Signore Baptista, she called him. Respectfully. He had great appreciation for *La Signora,* and had been loyal to her and hers the whole of his life.

For more than sixty years he had taken part in the making of Giambelli wine. There had been many changes—some good, in Bernardo's opinion, some not so good. He had seen much.

Some thought, too much.

The vines, lulled into dormancy by winter, would soon be pruned. Arthritis prevented him from doing much of the hand work, as he once had, but still, he would go out every morning to watch his sons and grandsons carry on the tradition.

A Baptista had always worked for Giambelli. And in Bernardo's mind, always would.

On this last night of his seventy-three years, he looked out over the vines—his vines, seeing what had been done, what needed to be done, and listened as the December wind whistled through the bones of the grape.

From the window where that wind tried to sneak, he could see the skeletons as they made their steady climb up the rises. They would take on flesh and life with time, and not wither as a man did. Such was the miracle of the grape.

He could see the shadows and shapes of the great *castello,* which ruled those vines, and ruled those who tended them.

It was lonely now, in the night, in the winter, when only servants slept in the *castello* and the grapes had yet to be born.

He wanted the spring, and the long summer that followed it, when the sun would warm his innards and ripen the young fruit. He wanted, as it seemed he always had, one more harvest.

Bernardo ached with the cold, deep in the bones. He considered heating some of the soup his granddaughter had brought to him, but his Annamaria was not the best of cooks. With this in mind, he made do with the cheese and sipped the good, full-bodied wine by his little fire.

He was proud of his life's work, some of which was in the glass that caught the fire-light and gleamed deep, deep red. The wine had been a gift, one of many given to him on his retirement, though everyone knew the retirement was only a technicality. Even with his aching bones and a heart that had grown weak, Bernardo would walk the vine-yard, test the grapes, watch the sky and smell the air.

He lived for wine.

He died for it.

He drank, nodding by the fire, with a blan-ket tucked around his thin legs. Through his mind ran images of sun-washed fields, of his wife laughing, of himself showing his son how to support a young vine, to prune a mature one. Of *La Signora* standing be-side him between the rows their grandfa-thers had tended.

Signore Baptista, she said to him when their faces were still young, we have been given a world. We must protect it.

And so they had.

The wind whistled at the windows of his little house. The fire died to embers.

And when the pain reached out like a fist, squeezing his heart to death, his killer was six thousand miles away, surrounded by friends and associates, enjoying a perfectly poached salmon, and a fine Pinot Blanc.

PART ONE

The Pruning

A man is a bundle of relations, a knot of roots,
whose flower and fruitage is the world.

—RALPH WALDO EMERSON

CHAPTER ONE

The bottle of Castello di Giambelli Cabernet Sauvignon, '02, auctioned for one hundred and twenty-five thousand, five hundred dollars, American. A great deal of money, Sophia thought, for wine mixed with sentiment. The wine in that fine old bottle had been produced from grapes harvested in the year Cezare Giambelli had established the Castello di Giambelli winery on a hilly patch of land north of Venice.

At that time the *castello* had been either a con or supreme optimism, depending on your point of view. Cezare's modest house and little stone winery had been far from castlelike. But his vines had been regal, and he had built an empire from them.

After nearly a century, even a superior Cabernet Sauvignon was likely more palatable sprinkled on a salad rather than drunk, but it wasn't her job to argue with the man with the money. Her grandmother had been right, as always. They would pay, and richly, for the privilege of owning a piece of Giambelli history.

Sophia made a note of the final bid and the buyer's name, though she was unlikely to forget either, for the memo she would send to her grandmother when the auction was over.

She was attending the event not only as the public relations executive who had designed and implemented the promotion and catalogue for the auction, but as the Giambelli family representative at this exclusive, pre-centennial event.

As such, she sat quietly in the rear of the room to observe the bidding, and the presentation.

Her legs were crossed in a long, elegant line. Her back convent-school straight. She wore a black pin-striped suit, tailored and Italian, that managed to look both businesslike and utterly feminine.

It was exactly the way Sophia thought of herself.

Her face was sharp, a triangle of pale gold

dominated by large, deep-set brown eyes and a wide, mobile mouth. Her cheekbones were ice-pick keen, her chin a diamond point, sculpting a look that was part pixie, part warrior. She had, deliberately, ruthlessly, used her face as a weapon when it seemed most expedient.

Tools, she believed, were meant to be used, and used well.

A year before, she'd had her waist-length hair cut into a short black cap with a spiky fringe over her forehead.

It suited her. Sophia knew exactly what suited her.

She wore the single strand of antique pearls her grandmother had given her for her twenty-first birthday, and an expression of polite interest. She thought of it as her father's boardroom look.

Her eyes brightened, and the corners of her wide mouth curved slightly as the next item was showcased.

It was a bottle of Barolo, '34, from the cask Cezare had named Di Tereza in honor of her grandmother's birth. This private reserve carried a picture of Tereza at ten on the label, the year the wine had been deemed sufficiently aged in oak, and bottled.

Now, at sixty-seven, Tereza Giambelli was a legend, whose renown as a vintner had overshadowed even her grandfather's.

This was the first bottle of this label ever offered for sale, or passed outside the family. As Sophia expected, bidding was brisk and spirited.

The man sitting beside Sophia tapped his catalogue where the photograph of the bottle was displayed. "You have the look of her."

Sophia shifted slightly, smiled first at him—a distinguished man hovering comfortably somewhere near sixty—then at the picture of the young girl staring seriously out from a bottle of red in his catalogue. "Thank you."

Marshall Evans, she recalled. Real estate, second generation Fortune 500. She made it her business to know the names and vital statistics of wine buffs and collectors with deep pockets and sterling taste.

"I'd hoped *La Signora* would attend today's auction. She's well?"

"Very. But otherwise occupied."

The beeper in her jacket pocket vibrated.

Vaguely annoyed with the interruption, Sophia ignored it to watch the bidding. Her eyes scanned the room, noting the signals. The casual lift of a finger from the third row brought the price up another five hundred. A subtle nod from the fifth topped it.

In the end, the Barolo outdistanced the Cabernet Sauvignon by fifteen thousand, and she turned to extend her hand to the man beside her.

"Congratulations, Mr. Evans. Your contribution to the International Red Cross will be put to good use. On behalf of Giambelli, family and company, I hope you enjoy your prize."

"There's no doubt of it." He took her hand, lifted it to his lips. "I had the pleasure of meeting *La Signora* many years ago. She's an extraordinary woman."

"Yes, she is."

"Perhaps her granddaughter would join me for dinner this evening?"

He was old enough to be her father, but Sophia was too European to find that a deterrent. Another time, she'd have agreed, and no doubt enjoyed his company. "I'm sorry, but I have an appointment. Perhaps on my next trip east, if you're free."

"I'll make sure I am."

Putting some warmth into her smile, she rose. "If you'll excuse me."

She slipped out of the room, plucking the beeper from her pocket to check the number. She detoured to the ladies' lounge, glancing at her watch and pulling the phone from her bag. With the number punched in, she settled on one of the sofas and laid her notebook and her electronic organizer on her lap.

After a long and demanding week in New York, she was still revved and, glancing through her appointments, pleased to have time to squeeze in a little shopping before she needed to change for her dinner date.

Jeremy DeMorney, she mused. That meant an elegant, sophisticated evening. French restaurant, discussion of food, travel and theater. And, of course, of wine. As he was descended from the La Coeur winery DeMorneys, and a top account exec there, and she sprang from Giambelli stock, there would be some playful attempts to pry corporate secrets from each other.

And there would be champagne. Good, she was in the mood for it.

All followed by an outrageously romantic

attempt to lure her into bed. She wondered if she'd be in the mood for that as well.

He was attractive, she considered, and could be amusing. Perhaps if they both hadn't been aware that her father had once slept with his wife, the idea of a little romance between them wouldn't seem so awkward, and somehow incestuous.

Still, several years had passed. . . .

"Maria." Sophia neatly tucked Jerry and the evening to come away, when the Giambelli housekeeper answered. "I've a call from my mother's line. Is she available?"

"Oh, yes, Miss Sophia. She hoped you would call. Just one moment."

Sophia imagined the woman hurrying through the wing, scanning the rooms for something to tidy when Pilar Giambelli Avano would have already tidied everything herself.

Mama, Sophia thought, would have been content in a little rose-covered cottage where she could bake bread, do her needlework and tend her garden. She should have had a half dozen children, Sophia thought with a sigh. And had to settle for me.

"Sophie, I was just heading out to the

greenhouse. Wait. Catch my breath. I didn't expect you to get back to me so quickly. I thought you'd be in the middle of the auction."

"End of it. And I think we can say it's been an unqualified success. I'll fax a memo of the particulars this evening, or first thing in the morning. Now, I really should go back and tie up the loose ends. Is everything all right there?"

"More or less. Your grandmother's ordered a summit meeting."

"Oh, Mama, she's not dying again. We went through that six months ago."

"Eight," Pilar corrected. "But who's counting? I'm sorry, baby, but she insists. I don't think she plans to die this time, but she's planning something. She's called the lawyers for another revamp of the will. And she gave me her mother's cameo brooch, which means she's thinking ahead."

"I thought she gave you that last time."

"No, it was the amber beads last time. She's sending for everyone. You need to come back."

"All right, all right." Sophia glanced down at her organizer and blew a mental kiss goodbye to Jerry DeMorney. "I'll finish up here and be on my way. But really, Mama, this new habit of hers of dying or revamping every few months is very inconvenient."

"You're a good girl, Sophie. I'm going to leave you my amber beads."

"Thanks a bunch." With a laugh, Sophia disconnected.

Two hours later, she was flying west and speculating whether in another forty years she would have the power to crook her finger and have everyone scrambling.

Just the idea of it made her smile as she settled back with a glass of champagne and Verdi playing on the headphones.

Not everyone scrambled. Tyler MacMillan might have been minutes away from Villa Giambelli rather than hours, but he considered the vines a great deal more urgent than a summons from *La Signora.*

And he said so.

"Now, Ty. You can take a few hours."

"Not now." Ty paced his office, anxious to get back into the fields. "I'm sorry, Granddad. You know how vital the winter pruning is, and so does Tereza." He shifted the portable phone to his other ear. He hated the portables. He was always losing them. "MacMillan's vines need every bit as much care as Giambelli's."

"Ty—"

"You put me in charge here. I'm doing my job."

"Ty," Eli repeated. With his grandson, he knew, matters must be put on a very basic level. "Tereza and I are as dedicated to MacMillan wines as we are to those under the Giambelli label, and have been for twenty years. You were put in charge because you're an exceptional vintner. Tereza has plans. Those plans involve you."

"Next week."

"Tomorrow." Eli didn't put his foot down often; it wasn't the way he worked. But when necessary, he did so ruthlessly. "One o'clock. Lunch. Dress appropriately."

Tyler scowled down at his ancient boots and the frayed hems of his thick trousers. "That's the middle of the damn day."

"Are you the only one at MacMillan capable of pruning vines, Tyler? Apparently you've lost a number of employees over the last season."

"I'll be there. But tell me one thing."

"Of course."

"Is this the last time she's going to die for a while?"

"One o'clock," Eli responded. "Try to be on time."

"Yeah, yeah, yeah," Tyler muttered, but only after he clicked the phone off.

He adored his grandfather. He even adored Tereza, perhaps because she was so ornery and annoying. When his grandfather had married the Giambelli heiress, Tyler had been eleven years old. He'd fallen in love with the vineyards, the rise of the hills, the shadows of the caves, the great caverns of the cellars.

And in a very real sense he'd fallen in love with Tereza Louisa Elana Giambelli, that whip-thin, ramrod-straight, somewhat terrifying figure he'd first seen dressed in boots and trousers not so different from his own, striding through the mustard plants between the rising rows of grapes.

She'd taken one look at him, lifted a razorsharp black eyebrow and deemed him soft and citified. If he was to be her grandson, she'd told him, he would have to be toughened up.

She'd ordered him to stay at the villa for the summer. No one had considered arguing the point. Certainly not his parents, who'd been more than happy to dump him for an extended period so they could fly off to parties and lovers. So he had stayed, Tyler thought now as he wandered to the window. Summer after summer until the vineyards were more home to him than the house in San Francisco, until she and his grandfather were more parents to him than his mother and father.

She'd made him. Pruned him back at the age of eleven and trained him to grow into what he was.

But she didn't own him. It was ironic, he supposed, that all her work should have formed him into the one person under her aegis most likely to ignore her demands.

Harder, of course, to ignore the demands when she and his grandfather unified. With a shrug, Tyler started out of the office. He could spare a few hours, and they knew it as well as he. The MacMillan vineyards employed the best, and he could easily have absented himself for most of a season with confidence in those left in charge.

The simple fact was he hated the big, sprawling events the Giambellis generated. They were invariably like a circus, with all three rings packed with colorful acts. You couldn't keep track, and it was always possible one of the tigers would leap the cage and go for your throat.

All those people, all those issues, all those pretenses and smoky undercurrents. He was happier walking the vineyards or checking the casks or plunking down with one of his winemakers and discussing the qualities of that year's Chardonnay.

Social duties were simply that. Duties.

He detoured through the charming ramble of the house that had been his grandfather's into the kitchen to refill his thermos with coffee. Absently he set the portable phone he still carried on the counter and began rearranging his schedule in his head to accommodate *La Signora.*

He was no longer citified, or soft. He was just over six feet with a body sculpted by fieldwork and a preference for the outdoors. His hands were wide, and tough with calluses, with long fingers that knew how to dip delicately under leaves to the grape. His hair tended to curl if he forgot to have it trimmed, which he often did, and was a deep brown that showed hints of red, like an aged burgundy in the sunlight. His rawboned face was more rugged than handsome, with lines beginning to fan out from eyes of clear and calm blue that could harden to steel.

The scar along his jaw, which he'd earned with a tumble off a stand of rocks at age thirteen, only annoyed him when he remembered to shave.

Which he reminded himself he would have to do before lunch the following day.

Those who worked for him considered him a fair man, if often a single-minded one. Tyler would have appreciated the analysis. They also considered him an artist, and that would have baffled him.

To Tyler MacMillan, the artist was the grape.

He stepped outside into the brisk winter air. He had two hours before sunset, and vines to tend.

Donato Giambelli had a headache of outrageous proportions. Her name was Gina, and she was his wife. When the summons from La Signora had come, he had been happily engaged in eye-crossing sex with his current mistress, a multitalented aspiring actress with thighs strong enough to crack walnuts. Unlike his wife, all the mistress required was the occasional bauble and a sweaty romp three times a week. She did not require conversation.

There were times he thought Gina required nothing else.

She babbled at him. Babbled at each of their three children. Babbled at his mother until the air in the company jet vibrated with the endless stream of words.

Between her, the baby's screaming, little Cezare's banging and Tereza Maria's bouncing, Don gave serious thought to opening the hatch and shoving his entire family off the plane and into oblivion.

Only his mother was quiet, and only because she'd taken a sleeping pill, an airsickness pill, an allergy pill and God knew what else, washed them all down with two glasses of Merlot before putting her eye mask in place and passing out.

She'd spent most of her life, at least the portion he knew of it, medicated and oblivious. At the moment, he considered that superior wisdom.

He could only sit, his temples throbbing, and damn his aunt Tereza to hell and beyond for insisting his entire family make the trip.

He was executive vice president of Giambelli, Venice, was he not? Any business that needed to be conducted required him, not his family.

Why had God plagued him with such a family?

Not that he didn't love them. Of course he loved them. But the baby was as fat as a turkey, and there was Gina pulling out a breast for its greedy mouth.

Once, that breast had been a work of art, he thought. Gold and firm and tasting of peaches. Now it was stretched like an over-filled balloon, and, had he been inclined to taste, flavored with baby drool.

And the woman was already making noises about yet another one.

The woman he'd married had been ripe, lush, sexually charged and empty of head. She had been perfection. In five short years she had become fat, sloppy and her head was full of babies.

Was it any wonder he sought his comfort elsewhere?

"Donny, I think *Zia* Tereza will give you a *big* promotion, and we'll all move into the *castello.*" She lusted for the great house of Giambelli—all those lovely rooms, all the servants. Her children would be raised in luxury, with privilege.

Fine clothes, the best schools and, one day, the Giambelli fortune at their feet.

She was the only one giving *La Signora* babies, wasn't she? That would count for quite a bit.

"Cezare," she said to her son as he tore the head off his sister's doll. "Stop that! Now you made your sister cry. Here now, here, give me the doll. Mama will fix."

Little Cezare, eyes glinting, tossed the head gleefully over his shoulder and began to taunt his sister.

"English, Cezare!" She shook a finger at him. "We're going to America. You'll speak English to your *zia* Tereza and show her what a smart boy you are. Come, come."

Tereza Maria, screaming over the death of her doll, retrieved the severed head and raced up and down the cabin in a flurry of grief and rage.

"Cezare! Do as Mama says."

In response, the boy flung himself to the floor, arms and legs hammering.

Don lurched up, stumbled away and

locked himself in the sanctuary of his in-flight office.

Anthony Avano enjoyed the finer things. He'd chosen his two-story penthouse in San Francisco's Back Bay with care and deliberation, then had hired the top decorator in the city to outfit it for him. Status and style were high priorities. Having them without having to make any real effort was another.

He failed to see how a man could be comfortable without those basic elements.

His rooms reflected what he thought of as classic taste—from the silk moiré walls, the Oriental carpets, to the gleaming oak furniture. He'd chosen, or his decorator had, rich fabrics in neutral tones with a few splashes of bold colors artfully arranged.

The modern art, which meant absolutely nothing to him, was, he'd been told, a striking counterpoint to the quiet elegance.

He relied heavily on the services of decorators, tailors, brokers, jewelers and dealers to guide him into surrounding himself with the best.

Some of his detractors had been known

to say Tony Avano was born with taste. And all of it in his mouth. He wouldn't have argued the point. But money, as Tony saw it, bought all the taste a man required.

He knew one thing. And that was wine.

His cellars were arguably among the best in California. Every bottle had been personally selected. While he couldn't distinguish a Sangiovese from a Semillon on the vine, and had no interest in the growing of the grape, he had a superior nose. And that nose had steadily climbed the corporate ladder at Giambelli, California. Thirty years before, it had married Pilar Giambelli.

It had taken that nose less than two years to begin sniffing at other women.

Tony was the first to admit that women were his weakness. There were so many of them, after all. He had loved Pilar as deeply as he was capable of loving another human being. He had certainly loved his position of privilege in the Giambelli organization as the husband of *La Signora*'s daughter and as the father of her granddaughter.

For those reasons he had, for many years, attempted to be very discreet about his particular weakness. He had even tried, a number of times, to reform.

But then there would be another woman, soft and fragrant or sultry and seductive. What was a man to do?

The weakness had eventually cost him his marriage, in a technical if not a legal sense. He and Pilar had been separated for seven years. Neither of them had made the move toward divorce. She, he knew, because she loved him. And he because it seemed like a great deal of trouble and would have seriously displeased Tereza.

In any case, as far as Tony was concerned, the current situation suited everyone nicely. Pilar preferred the countryside, he the city. They maintained a polite, even a reasonably friendly relationship. And he kept his position as president of sales, Giambelli, California.

Seven years they had walked that civilized line. Now, he was very afraid he was about to fall off the edge of it.

Rene was insisting on marriage. Like a silk-lined steamroller, Rene had a way of moving toward a goal and flattening all barriers in her path. Discussions with her left Tony limp and dizzy.

She was violently jealous, overbearing, demanding and prone to icy sulks.

He was crazy about her.

At thirty-two, she was twenty-seven years his junior, a fact that stroked his well-developed ego. Knowing she was every bit as interested in his money as the rest of him didn't trouble him. He respected her for it.

He worried that if he gave her what she wanted, he would lose what she wanted him for.

It was a hell of a fix. To resolve it, Tony did what he usually did regarding difficulties. He ignored it as long as humanly possible.

Studying his view of the bay, sipping a small vermouth, Tony waited for Rene to finish dressing for their evening out. And worried that his time was up.

The doorbell had him glancing over, frowning slightly. They weren't expecting anyone. As it was his majordomo's evening off, he went to see who was there. The frown cleared as he opened the door to his daughter.

"Sophie, what a lovely surprise."

"Dad."

She rose slightly on her toes to kiss his cheek. Ridiculously handsome, as ever, she thought. Good genes and an excellent plastic surgeon served him well. She did her best to ignore the quick and instinctive tug of resentment, and tried to focus on the equally quick and instinctive tug of love.

It seemed she was forever pulled in opposing directions over her father.

"I'm just in from New York, and wanted to see you before I headed up to the villa."

She scanned his face—smooth, almost unlined and certainly untroubled. The dark hair wisped attractively with gray at the temples, the deep blue eyes were clear. He had a handsome, squared-off chin with a center dimple. She'd loved dipping her finger into it as a child and making him laugh.

The love for him swarmed through her and tangled messily with the resentment. It was always so.

"I see you're going out," she said, noting his tuxedo.

"Shortly." He took her hand to draw her inside. "But there's plenty of time. Sit down, princess, and tell me how you are. What can I get you?"

She tipped his glass toward her. Sniffed, approved. "What you're having's fine."

She scanned the room as he walked over to the liquor cabinet. An expensive pretext, she thought. All show and no substance. Just like her father.

"Are you going up tomorrow?"

"Going where?"

She tilted her head as he crossed back to her. "To the villa."

"No, why?"

She took the glass, considering as she sipped. "You didn't get a call?"

"About what?"

Loyalties tugged and tangled inside her. He'd cheated on her mother, had carelessly ignored his vows as long as Sophia could remember, and in the end had left them both with barely a backward glance. But he was still family, and the family was being called to the villa.

"*La Signora.* One of her summits with lawyers, I'm told. You might want to be there."

"Ah, well, really, I was—"

He broke off as Rene walked in.

If there was a poster girl for the trophy mistress, Sophia thought as her temper sizzled, Rene Foxx was it. Tall, curvy and blonde on blonde. The Valentino gown showcased a body ruthlessly toned, and managed to look understated and elegant.

Her hair was swept up, slicked back to leave her lovely, pampered face with its full, sensuous mouth—collagen, Sophia thought cattily—and shrewd green eyes.

She'd chosen diamonds to marry the Valentino, and they flashed and shimmered against her polished skin.

Just how much, Sophia wondered, had those rocks set her father back?

"Hello." Sophia sipped more vermouth to wash some of the bitterness off her tongue. "Rene, isn't it?"

"Yes, and it has been for nearly two years. It's still Sophia?"

"Yes, for twenty-six."

Tony cleared his throat. Nothing, in his opinion, was more dangerous than two sniping females. The man between them always took the bullet.

"Rene, Sophia's just in from New York."

"Really?" Enjoying herself, Rene took Tony's glass, sipped. "That explains why you're looking a bit travel-frayed. We're about to leave for a party. You're welcome to join us," she added, hooking her arm through Tony's. "I must have something in my closet that would work on you."

If she was going to go claw to claw with

Rene, it wouldn't be after a coast-to-coast flight and in her father's apartment. Sophia would choose the time, and the place.

"That's so considerate, but I'd feel awkward wearing something so obviously too large. And," she added, coating her words with sugar, "I'm just on my way north. Family business." She set her glass down. "Enjoy your evening."

She walked to the door, where Tony caught up with her to give her shoulder a quick, placating pat. "Why don't you come along, Sophie? You're fine as you are. You're beautiful."

"No, thank you." She turned, and their eyes met. His were full of sheepish apology. It was an expression she was too accustomed to seeing for it to be effective. "I'm not feeling particularly festive."

He winced as she shut the door in his face.

"What did she want?" Rene demanded.

"She just dropped by, as I said."

"Your daughter never does anything without a reason."

He shrugged. "She may have thought we could drive up north together in the morning. Tereza's sent out a summons."

Rene's eyes narrowed. "You didn't tell me about that."

"I didn't get one." He dismissed the entire matter and thought of the party and just how he and Rene would look making their entrance. "You look fabulous, Rene. It's a shame to cover that dress, even with mink. Shall I get your wrap?"

"What do you mean you didn't get one?" Rene slapped the empty glass on a table. "Your position at Giambelli is certainly more important than your daughter's." And Rene meant to see it remained that way. "If the old woman's calling the family, you go. We'll drive up tomorrow."

"We? But—"

"It's the perfect opportunity to take your stand, Tony, and to tell Pilar you want a divorce. We'll make it an early night, so we'll both be clearheaded." She crossed to him, slid her fingers down his cheek.

With Tony, she knew, manipulation required firm demands and physical rewards, judiciously melded.

"And when we get back tonight, I'll show you just what you can expect from me when we're married. When we get back,

Tony . . ." She leaned in, bit teasingly at his bottom lip. "You can do anything you want."

"Let's just skip the party."

She laughed, slipped away from his hands. "It's important. And it'll give you time to think of just what you want to do to me. Get my sable for me, won't you, darling?"

She felt like sable tonight, Rene thought as Tony went to comply.

She felt rich tonight.

CHAPTER TWO

The valley, and the hills that rose from it, wore a thin coat of snow. Vines, arrogant and often temperamental soldiers, climbed up the slopes, their naked branches spearing through the quiet mist that turned the circling mountains to soft shadows.

Under the pearly dawn, the vineyard shivered and slept.

This peaceful scene had helped spawn a fortune, a fortune that would be gambled again, season after season. With nature both partner and foe.

To Sophia, the making of wine was an art, a business, a science. But it was also the biggest game in town.

From a window of her grandmother's villa, she studied the playing field. It was pruning season, and she imagined while she'd been traveling vines had already been accessed, considered, and those first stages toward next year's harvest begun. She was glad she'd been called back so that she could see that part of it for herself.

When she was away, the business of the wine occupied all her energies. She rarely thought of the vineyard when she wore her corporate hat. And whenever she came back, like this, she thought of little else.

Still, she couldn't stay long. She had duties in San Francisco. A new advertising campaign to be polished. The Giambelli centennial was just getting off the ground. And with the success of the auction in New York, the next stages would require her attention.

An old wine for a new millennium, she thought. Villa Giambelli: The next century of excellence begins.

But they needed something fresh, something savvy for the younger market. Those who bought their wine on the run—a quick impulse grab to take to a party.

Well, she'd think of it. It was her job to think of it.

And putting her mind to it would keep it off her father and the scheming Rene.

None of her business, Sophia reminded herself. None of her business at all if her father wanted to hook himself up with a former underwear model with a heart the size and texture of a raisin. He'd made a fool of himself before, and no doubt would again.

She wished she could hate him for it, for his pathetic weakness of character, and his benign neglect of his daughter. But the steady, abiding love just wouldn't shift aside. Which made her, she supposed, as foolish as her mother.

He didn't care for either of them as much as he did the cut of his suit. And didn't give them a thought two minutes after they were out of his sight. He was a bastard. Utterly selfish, sporadically affectionate and always careless.

And that, she supposed, was part of his charm.

She wished she hadn't stopped by the night before, wished she wasn't compelled to keep that connection between them no matter what he did or didn't do.

Better, she thought, to keep on the move as she had for the past several years. Traveling, working, filling her time and her life with professional and social obligations.

Two days, she decided. She would give her grandmother two days, spend time with her family, spend time in the vineyard and the winery. Then it was back to work with a vengeance.

The new campaign would be the best in the industry. She would make sure of it.

As she scanned the hills, she saw two figures walking through the mist. The tall gangly man with an old brown cap on his head. The ramrod-straight woman in mannish boots and trousers with hair as white as the snow they trod. A Border collie plodded along between them. Her grandparents, taking their morning walk with the aging and endlessly faithful Sally.

The sight of them lifted her mood. Whatever changed in her life, whatever adjustments had been made, this was a constant. *La Signora* and Eli MacMillan. And the vines.

She dashed from the window to grab her coat and join them.

At sixty-seven, Tereza Giambelli was sculpted, razor-sharp, body and mind. She had learned the art of the vine at her grandfather's knee. Had traveled with her father to California when she'd been only three to turn the land of the ripe valley to wine. She'd become bilingual and had traveled back and forth between California and Italy the way other young girls had traveled to the playground.

She'd learned to love the mountains, the thatch of forest, the rhythm of American voices.

It was not home, would never be home as the *castello* was. But she had made her place here, and was content with it.

She had married a man who had met with her family's approval, and had learned to love him as well. With him she had made a daughter, and to her lasting grief, birthed two stillborn sons.

She had buried her husband when she was only thirty. And had never taken his name or given it to her only child. She was Giambelli, and that heritage, that responsibility was more vital and more sacred even than marriage.

She had a brother she loved who was a priest and tended his flock in Venice. She had another who had died a soldier before he had really lived. She revered his memory, though it was dim.

And she had a sister she considered foolish at best, who had brought a daughter more foolish yet into the world.

It had been up to her to continue the family line, the family art. She had done so.

Her marriage to Eli MacMillan had been carefully considered, scrupulously planned. She had considered it a merger, as his vineyards were prime and nestled below hers in the valley. He was a good man and, more important in her calculations, a good vintner.

He had cared for her, but other men had cared for her. She enjoyed his company, but she had enjoyed the company of others. In the end, she'd thought of him as the Merlot, the softer mellowing juice blended to her stronger, and admittedly harsher, Cabernet Sauvignon.

The right combination could produce excellent results.

Her acceptance of his marriage proposal had been contingent on complex and detailed business arrangements. The arrangements had benefited both their companies, and had contented her.

But Tereza, who was rarely surprised, had been so, to find comfort, pleasure and simple satisfaction in a marriage now approaching its twentieth year.

He was a fine-looking man still. Tereza didn't discount such matters, as they spoke of genes. What made up a man was as important, to her mind, as what that man made of himself.

Though he was ten years her senior, she saw no sign of him bowing to age. He still rose at dawn every day, and would walk with her, regardless of the weather, every morning.

She trusted him as she had no man since her grandfather, and cared for him more than she had any man not of her blood.

He knew all of her plans, and most of her secrets.

"Sophia arrived late last night."

"Ah." Eli laid a hand on her shoulder as they walked between the rows. It was a simple gesture, and habitual for him. It had taken Tereza some time to grow used to this casual touching from a man, from a husband. A longer time still to come to depend on it. "Did you think she wouldn't come?"

"I knew she would come." Tereza was too

used to being obeyed to doubt it. "If she'd come straight from New York, she would have been here sooner."

"So, she had a date. Or did some shopping."

Tereza's eyes narrowed. They were nearly black and still sharp in distance vision. Her voice was sharp as well, and carried the exotic music of her homeland. "Or stopped off to see her father."

"Or stopped off to see her father," Eli agreed in his slow, comfortable way. "Loyalty's a trait you've always admired, Tereza."

"When it's earned." There were times, much as she cared for him, when Eli's unending tolerance infuriated her. "Anthony Avano has earned nothing but disgust."

"A pitiful man, a poor husband and a mediocre father." Which made him, Eli mused, very like his own son. "Yet he continues to work for you."

"I let him into Giambelli too intimately in those early years." She'd trusted him, she thought, had seen potential in him. Had been deceived by him. That she would never forgive. "Still, he knows how to sell. I use whatever tools perform their task. Firing him long ago would have been a personal satisfaction and professionally unwise. What's best for Giambelli is what's best. But I don't like to see my granddaughter cater to the man. *Uh.*"

She tossed aside thoughts of her son-in-law with an impatient wave of the hand. "We'll see how he takes what I have to say today. Sophia will have told him I called her home. So, he'll come."

Eli stopped, turned. "And that's exactly as you wanted it. You knew she'd tell him."

Her dark eyes glinted, and her smile was cool. "And if I did?"

"You're a difficult woman, Tereza."

"Yes. Thank you."

He laughed and, shaking his head, began to walk with her again. "Your announcements today are going to cause trouble. Resentment."

"I should hope so." She stopped to examine some of the younger vines supported by trellis wires. Cane-pruning would be required here, she thought. Only the strongest of them would be permitted to grow and to be trained.

"Complacency becomes rot, Eli. Tradition must be respected, and change explored."

She scanned the land. The mist was raw and the air damp. The sun would not burn through it that day, she was certain.

Winters, she thought, grew longer with every year.

"Some of these vines I planted with my own hands," she continued. "Vines my father brought from Italy. As they grew old, the new was made from them. The new must always have room to sink their roots, Eli, and the mature are entitled to their respect. What I built here, what we've built in our time together, is ours. I'll do as I think best with it, and for it."

"You always have. In this case, as in most, I agree with you. It doesn't mean we'll have an easy season ahead of us."

"But a vintage one," she said. "This year . . ." She reached over to turn a naked vine in her fingers. "A fine and rare vintage. I know it."

She turned, watched her granddaughter run up the slope toward them. "She's so beautiful, Eli."

"Yes. And strong."

"She'll need to be," Tereza said and stepped forward to catch Sophia's hands in hers. *"Buon giorno, cara. Come va?"*

"Bene. Bene." They kissed cheeks, hands tightly linked. *"Nonna."* Sophia eased back, studied her grandmother's face. It was a handsome face, not soft and pretty as the girl on the label made so long ago, but strong, nearly fierce. Carved, Sophia always thought, as much by ambition as time. "You look wonderful. And you."

She shifted to throw her arms around Eli. Here, it was all very simple. He was Eli, just Eli, the only grandfather she'd ever known. Safe, loving and uncomplicated.

He gave her a little lift with the hug, so her toes just left the ground. It made her laugh, and cling. "I saw you from my window." She stepped back as her feet hit the ground again, then lowered to pat and stroke the patient Sally. "You're a painting, the three of you. *The Vineyard,* I'd call it," she continued, straightening to button Eli's jacket at his throat against the chill. "What a morning."

She closed her eyes, tipping her head back and breathing deep. She could smell the damp, her grandmother's soap and the tobacco Eli must have secreted in one of his pockets.

"Your trip was successful?" Tereza asked.

"I have memos. My memos have memos," she added, laughing again as she hooked her arms through theirs so they could walk together. "You'll be pleased, *Nonna*. And I have some brilliant ideas, she says with due modesty, on the promotion campaign."

Eli glanced over, and when he saw Tereza wasn't going to comment, patted Sophia's hand. The trouble, he thought, would start very quickly now.

"The pruning's begun." Sophia noted the fresh cuts on the vines. "At MacMillan as well?"

"Yes. It's time."

"It seems a long way till harvest. *Nonna,* will you tell me why you've brought us all here? You know I love to see you, and Eli, and Mama. But preparing the vines isn't the only work that's required for Giambelli."

"We'll talk later. Now we'll have breakfast before those monsters of Donato's are up and driving us all insane."

"*Nonna.*"

"Later," Tereza said again. "We're not all yet here."

. . .

Villa Giambelli sat on a knoll above the center of the valley and beside a forest that had been left to grow wild. Its stones showed gold and red and umber when the light struck them, and its windows were many. The winery had been built to replicate the one in Italy, and though it had been expanded, and ruthlessly modernized, it was still in operation.

A large, attractively outfitted tasting room, where patrons could, by appointment, sample the products along with breads and cheeses, had been added to it. Wine clubs were welcomed to lavish affairs four times a year, and tours could be arranged through the offices there or in San Francisco.

Wine, bought from the winery itself on those occasions, could be shipped anywhere in the world.

The caves, with their cool, damp air, that pocketed the hills were used for storage and the aging of the wine. The fields that had built Villa Giambelli and its facilities stretched for more than a hundred acres, and during harvest the very air smelled of the promise of wine.

The central courtyard of the villa was tiled in Chianti red and boasted a fountain where a grinning Bacchus forever hoisted his goblet. When the winter cold had passed, dozens and dozens of pots would be set out so that the space was alive with flower and scent.

It boasted twelve bedrooms and fifteen baths, a solarium, a ballroom and a formal dining room that could accommodate sixty. There were rooms dedicated to music, and rooms celebrating books. Rooms for work and for contemplation. Within its walls was a collection of Italian and American art and antiques that was second to none.

There were both indoor and outdoor pools, and a twenty-car garage. Its gardens were a fantasy.

Balconies and terraces laced the stone, and a series of steps afforded both family and guests private entrances and exits.

Despite its size, its scope and its priceless treasures, it was very much a home.

The first time Tyler had seen it, he'd thought of it as a castle, full of enormous rooms and complicated passages. At the moment, he thought of it as a prison, where he was sentenced to spend entirely too much time with entirely too many people.

He wanted to be outside in the raw air

tending his vines and drinking strong coffee out of a thermos. Instead he was trapped in the family parlor sipping an excellent Chardonnay. A fire was snapping gaily in the hearth, and elegant little hors d'oeuvres were set around the room on platters of colorful Italian pottery.

He couldn't understand why people wasted the time and effort on bits of finger food when slapping a sandwich together was so much quicker and easier.

Why was it food had to be such a damn event? And he imagined if he uttered such heresy in a household of Italians, he'd be lynched on the spot.

He'd been forced to change out of his work clothes into slacks and a sweater—his idea of formal wear. At least he hadn't strapped himself into a suit like . . . what was the guy's name? Don. Don from Venice with the wife who wore too much makeup, too much jewelry and always seemed to have a shrieking baby attached to some part of her body.

She talked too much, and no one, particularly her husband, appeared to pay any attention.

Francesca Giambelli Russo said little to

nothing. Such a contrast to *La Signora,* Ty mused. You'd never make them as sisters. She was thin and drifty, an insubstantial little woman who stayed glued in her chair and looked as though she'd jump out of her skin if anyone addressed her directly.

Ty was always careful not to do so.

The little boy, if you could call a demon from hell a boy, was sprawled on the rug smashing two trucks together. Eli's Border collie, Sally, was hiding under Sophia's legs.

Great legs, Ty noted absently.

She was looking as sleek and polished as ever, like something lifted off a movie screen and dropped down in three dimensions. She appeared to be fascinated by whatever Don was saying to her, and kept those big, dark chocolate eyes of hers on his face. But Ty watched as she discreetly slipped Sally hors d'oeuvres. The move was too slick and calculated for her to have had her full attention on the conversation.

"Here. The stuffed olives are excellent." Pilar stepped up beside him with a small plate.

"Thanks." Tyler shifted. Of all the Giambellis, Tyler was most comfortable with Pilar. She never expected him to make endless, empty conversation just for the sake of hearing her own voice. "Any idea when we're going to get this business rolling?"

"When Mama's ready, and not before. My sources tell me lunch is set for fourteen, but I can't pin down who we're waiting for. Whoever it is, and whatever this is about, Eli seems content. That's a good sign."

He started to grunt, remembered his manners. "Let's hope so."

"We haven't seen you around here in weeks—been busy," she said even as he uttered the words, then she laughed. "Naturally. What are you up to, other than business?"

"What else is there?"

With a shake of her head, she pressed the olives on him again. "You're more like my mother than any of us. Weren't you seeing someone last summer? A pretty blonde? Pat, Patty?"

"Patsy. Not really seeing. Just sort of . . ." He made a vague gesture. "You know."

"Honey, you need to get out more. And not just for . . . you know."

It was such a mother thing to say, he had to smile. "I could say the same about you."

"Oh, I'm just an old stick-in-the-mud."

"Best-looking stick in the room," he countered and made her laugh again.

"You always were sweet when you put your mind to it." And the comment, even from a man she considered a kind of surrogate son, boosted the spirits that seemed to flag all too easily these days.

"Mama, you're hoarding the olives." Sophia dashed up, plucked one off the plate. Beside her lovely, composed mother, she was a fireball, crackling with electricity. The kind that was always giving you hot, unexpected jolts if you got too close.

Or so it always seemed to Ty.

For that single reason, he'd always tried to keep a safe and comfortable distance.

"Quick, talk to me. Were you just going to leave me trapped with Don the Dull forever?" Sophia muttered.

"Poor Sophie. Well, think of it this way. It's probably the first time in weeks he's been able to say five words at the same time without Gina interrupting him."

"Believe me, he made up for it." She rolled her dark, exotic eyes. "So, Ty, how are you?"

"Fine."

"Hard at work for MacMillan?"

"Sure."

"Know any words with more than one syllable?"

"Some. Thought you were in New York."

"Was," she said, mimicking his tone as her lips twitched. "Now I'm here." She glanced over her shoulder as her two young cousins began to shriek and sob. "Mama, if I was ever that obnoxious, how did you stop yourself from drowning me in the fountain?"

"You weren't obnoxious, sweetie. Demanding, arrogant, temperamental, but never obnoxious. Excuse me." She handed the plate to Sophia and went to do what she'd always done best. Make peace.

"I suppose I should have done that," Sophia said with a sigh as she watched her mother scoop up the miserable young girl. "But I've never seen a pair of kids less appealing in my life."

"Comes from being spoiled and neglected."

"At the same time?" She considered, studied Don ignoring his screaming son, and Gina making foolish cooing noises to him. "Good call," she decided. Then be-

cause they weren't her problem—thank Jesus—she turned her attention back to Tyler.

He was such a . . . man, she decided. He
looked like something carved out of the
Vacas that guarded the valley. And he was
certainly more pleasant to contemplate
than the four-year-old temper tantrum behind her.

Now if she could just pry a reasonable
conversation out of him, she could be nicely
occupied until lunch was served.

"Any clues about the theme of our little
gathering today?" Sophia asked.

"No."

"Would you tell me if you knew?"

He shrugged a shoulder and watched
Pilar murmur to little Tereza as she carried
her to the side window. She looked natural,
he thought. Madonnalike, he supposed was
the suitable word. And because of it, the irritable, angry child took on an attractive,
appealing look.

"Why do you suppose people have kids
when they're not going to pay any real attention to them?"

Sophia started to speak, then broke off as
her father and Rene walked into the room.
"That's a good question," she murmured

and, taking the glass from his hand, finished off his wine. "Damn good question."

At the window, Pilar tensed, and all the simple pleasure she'd gotten from distracting the unhappy little girl drained away.

She felt instantly frumpy, unattractive, old, fat, sour. Here was the man who had discarded her. And here was the latest in the long line of replacements. Younger, lovelier, smarter, sexier.

But because she knew her mother would not, Pilar set the child on the floor and walked over to greet them. Her smile was warm and easy and graced a face much more compelling than she thought. Her simple slacks and sweater were more elegant, more feminine than Rene's slick power suit.

And her manner carried an innate class that held more true sparkle than diamonds.

"Tony, how good you could make it. Hello, Rene."

"Pilar." Rene smiled slowly and trailed a hand down Tony's arm. The diamond on her finger caught the light. She waited a beat, to be certain Pilar saw it, registered the meaning. "You look . . . rested."

"Thank you." The backs of her knees dissolved. She could feel the support going out from under her as completely as if Rene had rammed the toe of her hot red pump into them. "Please, come in, sit. What can I get you to drink?"

"Don't fuss, Pilar." Tony waved her off, even as he leaned down to give her an absent peck on the cheek. "We'll just go say hello to Tereza."

"Go to your mom," Ty said under his breath.

"What?"

"Go, make an excuse and get your mom out of here."

She saw it then, the diamond glint on Rene's finger, the blank shock in her mother's eyes. She shoved the plate at Ty and strode across the room. "Mama, can you help me with something for a minute?"

"Yes . . . just let me . . ."

"It'll only take a second," Sophia continued, quickly pulling Pilar from the room. She just kept moving until they were well down the hall and into the two-level library. There, she pulled the pocket doors closed behind her, leaned back against them.

"Mama. I'm so sorry."

"Oh." Trying to laugh, Pilar ran an unsteady hand over her face. "So much for thinking I pulled that off."

"You did beautifully." Sophia hurried over as Pilar lowered to the arm of a chair. "But I know that face." She cupped her mother's in her hands. "Apparently so does Tyler. The ring's ostentatious and obvious, just like she is."

"Oh, baby." Her laugh was strained, but she tried. "It's stunning, gorgeous—just like she is. It's all right." But already she was turning the gold band she continued to wear round and round her finger. "Really, it's all right."

"The hell it is. I hate her. I hate both of them, and I'm going back in there and telling them right now."

"You're not." Pilar got up, gripped Sophia's arms. Did the pain she could see in her daughter's eyes show as clearly in her own? And was that her fault? Had this endless limbo she'd lived in dragged her daughter into the void? "It solves nothing, changes nothing. There's no point in hate, Sophie. It'll only damage you."

No, Sophia thought. No. It could forge you.

"Be angry!" she demanded. "Be furious and bitter and crazed." Be *anything,* she thought. Anything but hurt and defeated. I can't bear it.

"You do it, baby." She ran her hands soothingly up and down Sophia's arms. "So much better than I could."

"To walk in here this way. To just walk in and shove it in our faces. He had no right to do that to you, Mama, or to me."

"He has a right to do what he wants. But it was poorly done." Excuses, she admitted. She'd spent nearly thirty years making excuses for Anthony Avano. A hard habit to break.

"Don't let it hurt you. He's still your father. Whatever happens, he always will be."

"He was never a father to me."

Pilar paled. "Oh, Sophia."

"No. No." Furious with herself, Sophia held up a hand. "I am obnoxious. This isn't about me, but I just can't help making it about me. It's not even about him," she said, winding down. "He's oblivious. But she's not. She knew what she was doing. How she wanted to do it. And I hate her coming into our home and lording that over you—no, damn it, over us. All of us."

"You're ignoring one factor, baby. Rene may love him."

"Oh, please."

"So cynical. I loved him, why shouldn't she?"

Sophia whirled away. She wanted to kick something, to break something. And to take the jagged shards of it and swipe them over Rene's perfect California face. "She loves his money, his position and his goddamn expense account."

"Probably. But he's the kind of man who makes women love him—effortlessly."

Sophia caught the wistfulness in her mother's voice. She'd never loved a man, but she recognized the sound of a woman who had. Who did. And that, the hopelessness of that, emptied her of temper. "You haven't stopped loving him."

"If I haven't, I'd better. Promise me one thing? Don't cause a scene."

"I hate to give up the satisfaction, but I suppose chilly disinterest will have more impact. One way or the other, I want to knock that smug look off her face."

She walked back, kissed both her

mother's cheeks, then hugged her. Here she could, and did, love without shadows and smudges. "Will you be all right, Mama?"

"Yes. My life doesn't change, does it?" Oh, and the thought of that was damning. "Nothing really changes. Let's go back."

"I'll tell you what we're going to do," Sophia began when they were in the hall again. "I'm going to juggle my schedule and clear a couple of days. Then you and I are going to the spa. We're going to sink up to our necks in mud, have facials, get our bod ies scrubbed, rubbed and polished. We'll spend wads of money on overpriced beauty products we'll never use and lounge around in bathrobes all day."

The door of the powder room opened as they walked by, and a middle-aged brunette stepped out. "Now that sounds wonderfully appealing. When do we leave?"

"Helen." Pilar pressed a hand to her heart even as she leaned in to kiss her friend's cheek. "You scared the life out of me."

"Sorry. Had to make a dash for the john." She tugged at the skirt of her stone-gray suit over hips she was constantly trying to whittle, to make certain it was back in place. "All that coffee I drank on the way up. Sophia, aren't you gorgeous? So . . ." She shifted her briefcase, squared her shoulders. "The usual suspects in the parlor?"

"More or less. I didn't realize she meant you when Mama said the lawyers would be coming." And, Sophia thought, if her grandmother had called in Judge Helen Moore, it meant serious business.

"Because Pilar didn't know, either, nor did I until a few days ago. Your grandmother insisted I handle this business personally." Helen's shrewd gray eyes shifted toward the parlor.

She'd been involved, one way or another, with the Giambellis and their business for nearly forty years. They never failed to fascinate her. "She keeping all of you in the dark?"

"Apparently," Pilar murmured. "Helen, she's all right, isn't she? I took this latest business about changing her will and so on as part of this phase she's been in this past year, since *Signore* Baptista died."

"As far as I know, healthwise, *La Signora* is as hale as ever." Helen adjusted her black-rimmed glasses, gave her oldest friend a bolstering smile. "As her attorney, I can't tell you any more about her motivations, Pilar. Even if I completely understood them. It's her show. Why don't we see if she's ready for the curtain?"

CHAPTER THREE

La Signora never rushed her cue. She had planned the menu personally, wanting to set the tone for the lavish, and the casual. The wines served were from the California vineyards, both Giambelli and MacMillan. That, too, was meticulously planned.

She would not discuss business at the meal. Nor would she, much to Gina's annoyance, allow three ill-mannered children at the table.

They had been sent to the nursery with a maid who would be given a bonus, and Tereza's considerable respect if she lasted an hour with them.

When she deigned to speak to Rene, it was with chilly formality. Because of it, she felt a grudging admiration for the woman's spine. There had been others, many others, who had withered visibly under that frost.

Along with family, and Helen, whom she considered one of her own, she had invited her most trusted winemaker and his wife. Paulo Borelli had been with Giambelli, California for thirty-eight years. Despite his age, he was still called Paulie. His wife, Consuelo, was a plump, cheerful woman with a big laugh who had once been a kitchen maid at the villa.

The final addition was Margaret Bowers, the head of sales for MacMillan. She was a divorced woman of thirty-six who was currently being bored senseless by Gina's chatter and wishing desperately for a cigarette.

Tyler caught her eye and gave her a sympathetic smile.

Margaret sometimes wished desperately for him, too.

When the food was cleared and the port passed, Tereza sat back.

"Castello di Giambelli celebrates its centennial in one year," she began. Immediately conversation stopped. "Villa Giambelli has been making wine in the Napa Valley for sixty-four years. MacMillan has been doing so for ninety-two. That is two hundred and fifty-six years combined."

She scanned the table. "Five generations have been vintners and wine merchants."

"Six, *Zia* Tereza." Gina fluttered. "My children give you six."

"From what I've seen your children are more likely to be serial killers than vintners. Please, don't interrupt."

She lifted her port, nosing the wine, sipping slowly. "In those five generations we have earned a reputation, on two continents, for producing wine of quality. The name Giambelli *is* wine. We have established traditions and have blended them with new ways, new technology, without sacrificing that name or what it means. We will never sacrifice it. Twenty years ago, we established a partnership of sorts with another fine vintner. MacMillan of Napa Valley has run side by side with Giambelli, California. The partnership has aged well. It's time for it to be decanted."

She felt rather than saw Tyler tense. She gave him high marks for holding his tongue, and met his eyes now. "Changes are necessary, and for the good of both. The next hundred years begin today. Donato."

He snapped to attention. "*Sì*, yes," he corrected, remembering she preferred English at her California table. "Yes, Aunt Tereza."

"Giambelli Italy and California have been run exclusive of each other. Separate. This will no longer be the case. You will report to the chief operating officer of the newly formed Giambelli-MacMillan company, which will have bases in both California and Venice."

"What does this mean? What does this mean?" Gina exploded in Italian, shoving awkwardly from the table. "Donato is in charge. He is next in line. He carries the name. He is your heir."

"My heir is who I say is my heir."

"We give you children." Gina slapped a hand on her belly, then waved an arm in disgust at the table. "Three children, and more will come. No one gives the family children but me and Donato. Who will carry on the name when you're gone if not my babies?"

"Do you bargain with your womb?" Tereza said evenly.

"It's fertile," she snapped back even as her husband tried to pull her back into her chair. "More than yours, more than your daughter's. One baby each, that's all. I can have a dozen."

"Then God help us all. You'll keep your fine house, Gina, and your pocket money. But you will not find yourself mistress of the *castello.* My *castello,*" she added coolly. "Take what you're given, or lose a great deal more."

"Gina, *basta!* Enough," Don ordered and had his hand slapped for his trouble.

"You're an old woman," Gina said between her teeth. "One day you'll be dead and I will not. So we will see." She swept out of the room.

"*Zia Tereza, scusi,*" Donato began and was cut off by a sharp gesture.

"Your wife does you no credit, Donato, and your work falls short of my expectations. You have this year to correct those matters. You will remain in your position with Giambelli until the time of the next pruning. Then we will reassess. If I am pleased, you will be promoted, with a salary and the benefits that apply. If I am not, you will remain with the company on paper only. I will not see one of my blood removed, but you will not find your life so easy as you have. Is this understood?"

His tie was suddenly too tight, and the meal he'd just eaten threatened to revolt in his belly. "I've worked for Giambelli for eighteen years."

"You worked for twelve. You have put in appearances for the last six, and even those appearances have been inconsistent recently. Do you think I don't know what you do, or where you spend your time? Do you think I'm not aware of what your *business* is when you take trips to Paris, to Rome, to New York and California at Giambelli expense?"

She waited for this blow to land, saw the faint sheen of sweat skin his face. And was disappointed in him yet again. "Your wife is foolish, Donato, but I am not. Have a care."

"He's a good boy," Francesca said quietly.

"He might have been. Perhaps he'll be a good man yet. Margaret, you'll pardon the family histrionics. We're temperamental."

"Of course, *La Signora.*"

"You will, if you choose to accept, oversee and coordinate the heads of sales of Giambelli-MacMillan, California and Venice. This will require considerable travel and responsibility on your part, with the appropriate salary increase. You'll be needed in

Venice in five days to establish your base there and familiarize yourself with the operation. You have until tomorrow to decide if you want to consider this arrangement, and if so we will discuss the details."

"I don't need time to decide, thank you." Margaret kept her voice brisk and even, and her heart pounded like wild surf. "I'll be happy to discuss the details at your convenience. I'm grateful for the opportunity." She shifted to Eli, nodded. "Grateful to both of you for the opportunity."

"Well said. Tomorrow then. Paulie, we've already discussed our plans, and I appreciate your input and your discretion. You'll assist in coordinating the operation in the fields, the winery. You know the best men here, and at MacMillan. You'll serve as foreman."

"I have nothing but respect for Paulie." Ty's voice was calm, even if temper and frustration had twin grips on his throat. "His skills and his instincts. I have nothing but admiration for the operation here at the villa, and the people involved in it. And the same from what I know of Giambelli, Venice. But we have a top-flight operation, and people, at MacMillan. I won't see that operation or those people overshadowed by yours, *La Signora.* You're proud of what you and yours have accomplished, of the legacy you've inherited and intend to pass on. So am I of mine."

"Good. So listen. And think." She gestured to Eli.

"Ty, Tereza and I didn't come to this decision overnight, nor do we do it lightly. We've discussed this for a long time."

"You're not obliged to bring me into those discussions," Ty began.

"No." Eli interrupted before the heat he saw building in his grandson's eyes could flash. "We're not. We've worked out, with Helen, how the legalities and formalities should and must be met. We've strategized how to implement this true merger to the benefit of all involved—not just for this season, but for the season a hundred years from now."

He leaned forward. "Do you think I want any less for MacMillan than you? Any less for you than you want for yourself?"

"I don't know what you want. I thought I did."

"Then I'll make it clear, here and now. By doing this, we'll become not only one of the biggest winemakers in the world, but the best in the world. You'll continue to oversee MacMillan."

"Oversee?"

"With Paulie as foreman, and you as operator, as vintner. With some addendums."

"You know the fields, Ty," Tereza said. She understood his resentment. It pleased her. That hot, choking anger meant it mattered to him. It would have to matter a very great deal. "You know the vines, and the casks. But what you do, what you learn stops at the bottle. It's time to go on from there. There's more to wine than the grape. Eli and I intend to see our grandchildren blended."

"Grandchildren?" Sophia interrupted.

"When is the last time you worked in the fields?" Tereza demanded of her. "When is the last time you tasted wine that wasn't uncorked from a pretty bottle taken from a cabinet or a chilled bucket? You've neglected your roots, Sophia."

"I've neglected nothing," Sophia shot back. "I'm not a winemaker. I'm a publicist."

"You'll be a winemaker. And you," she said, pointing at Ty, "you'll learn what it is to sell, to market, to ship. You'll teach each other."

"Oh, really, *Nonna*—"

"Quiet. You have the year. Pilar, Sophia won't have as much time to devote to her usual duties. You'll fill that gap."

"Mama." Pilar had to laugh. "I don't know anything about marketing or promotion."

"You have a good brain. It's time you used it again. To succeed we'll need all the family." Tereza shifted her gaze to Tony. "And others. You will remain in sales, and will, for now, keep your title and privileges there. But you will report, as does Donato and all department heads and managers, to the COO. From this time on we have a business relationship only. Do not come to my house or to my table again uninvited."

It was a downslide. His title was one matter. His salary, and long-term benefits, another. She had the power to strip him clean. He used the single shield he had. "I'm Sophia's father."

"I know what you are."

"I beg your pardon, *signora*." Rene spoke with meticulous politeness, underlined by steel. "If I may speak?"

"You are, invited or not, a guest under my roof. What do you wish to say?"

"I realize that my presence here isn't particularly welcome." Her tone never varied, her eyes never left Tereza's. "And that my relationship with Tony doesn't meet with your approval. But he is, and has been, an asset to your company. As I intend to be one to him, that can only benefit you."

"That remains to be seen. You'll excuse us." She scanned the table. "Helen, Eli and I must speak with Sophia and Tyler. Coffee will be served in the parlor. Please enjoy."

"You say it," Sophia began, trembling with anger as the rest filed out of the room, "and it's done. Have you gotten so used to that, *Nonna,* that you believe you can change lives with a few words?"

"Everyone has a choice."

"Where is the choice?" Unable to sit, she surged to her feet. "Donato? He's never worked outside the company. His life is absorbed by it. Tyler? He's given all his time and energy to MacMillan since he was a boy."

"I can speak for myself."

"Oh, shut up." She rounded on him. "Five words in succession tie your tongue in knots. And I'm supposed to teach you how to market wine."

He got to his feet and, to her shock,

grabbed her hands, jerking her forward as he turned them palms up. "Like rose petals. Pampered and soft. I'm supposed to teach you how to work?"

"I work every bit as hard as you do. Just because I don't sweat and stomp around in muddy boots doesn't mean I don't give my best."

"You're off to a hell of a start, both of you." Eli sighed and poured more port. "You want to fight, fight. It'll be good for you. The problem is neither of you has ever had to do anything that didn't suit you down to the ground. Maybe you'll fail, maybe you'll both fall flat on your asses trying to do something else. Something more."

Sophia tossed up her chin. "I don't fail."

"You have a season to prove it. Would you care to know what you'll have at the end of it? Helen?"

"Well, this has been fun so far." Helen lifted her briefcase onto the table. "Dinner and a show, for one low price." She took out files, laid them down and set her briefcase back on the floor. Adjusted her glasses. "In the interest of brevity and comprehension, I'll keep this simple and in layman's terms. Eli and Tereza are merging their respective companies, streamlining them, which will cut some costs and incur others. I believe it's a very wise business decision. Each of you will carry the title of vice president, operations. Each of you will have varied tasks and responsibilities, which are set down in the contracts I have with me. The contract term is one year. If at the end of that year your performances are unacceptable, you will be shifted back to a lesser position. Those terms will be negotiable at that time and in that eventuality."

As she spoke she slid two thick contracts from the files. "Ty, you will remain in residence at MacMillan, the house and its contents will continue to be available for your use. Sophia, you will be required to move here. Your apartment in San Francisco will be maintained by Giambelli during this year, for your use when you're required to do business in the city. Ty, when you're required to do business there, accommodations will be provided. Travel to other destinations for the company will, of course, be arranged and paid for by the company. The *castello* in Italy is available to either of you, whether your travel there is business, pleasure or a combination of both."

She glanced up, smiled. "So far, not so bad, right? Now the carrot. If at the end of this contract year, Sophia, your performance is acceptable, you will receive twenty percent of the company, one-half interest in the *castello* and the title of co-president. Reciprocally, Tyler, should your performance be acceptable, you will receive a like twenty percent, full interest of the house where you now reside and the title of co-president. You will both be offered ten acres of vineyards, to develop your own label if you wish, or the market value thereof should you prefer."

She paused, and added the final weight. "Pilar receives twenty percent as well, if she agrees with her own contract terms. This gives like shares to everyone. In the event of Eli's or Tereza's death, their respective share passes, spouse to spouse. On that unhappy day when neither of them are with us, their forty-percent share will be disbursed as follows: Fifteen percent to each of you, and ten percent to Pilar. This will give each of you, in time, thirty-five percent of one of the biggest wine companies in the world. All you have to do to earn it is adhere to the contract stipulations during this year."

Sophia waited until she was certain she could speak, and kept her hands tightly gripped together in her lap. She was being offered more than she'd ever imagined or would have asked for. And was being slapped down like a child at the same time. "Who decides on the acceptability of our performances?"

"In the interest of fairness," Tereza said, "you will rate each other on a monthly basis. Eli and I will also give you performance evaluations, and these will be added to the evaluations generated by the COO."

"Who the hell is COO?" Tyler demanded.

"His name is David Cutter. Recently of Le Coeur, and based in New York. He'll be here tomorrow." Tereza got to her feet. "We'll leave you to read your contracts, to discuss, to consider." She smiled warmly. "Helen? Coffee?"

Rene refused to budge. There was one thing she'd learned in her modeling career, during her brief stint as an actress and in her lifelong social climb. The only right direction to move is up.

She'd tolerate the old woman's insults, the estranged wife's distress and the daughter's killing glares as long as it meant winning.

Despising them didn't stop her from tolerating them, as long as it was necessary.

She had the diamond on her finger, one she'd selected personally, and intended the wedding band to follow quickly. Tony was her entrée into the world of the ridiculously rich, and she was sincerely fond of him. Nearly as fond as she was of the idea of the Giambelli fortune.

She'd make certain he did whatever was necessary in the next year to solidify his position with Giambelli, and she intended to do so as his wife.

"Tell her now," she ordered and picked up her coffee cup.

"Rene, darling." Tony moved his shoulders. He could already feel the weight of the shackles. "This is a very awkward time."

"You've had seven years to deal with this, Tony. Get it done, and get it done now." She sent a significant look toward Pilar. "Or I will."

"All right, all right." He patted her hand. He preferred awkward to ugly. With a pleasant smile on his face, he got to his feet and crossed over to where Pilar sat trying to calm a mildly distressed and obviously confused Francesca.

"Pilar, could I have a word with you? A private word."

A dozen excuses ran through her head. She was, in her mother's absence, hostess. The room was full of guests. Her aunt needed her attention. She should order more coffee.

But they were only that, excuses, and would do nothing but postpone what had to be faced.

"Of course." She murmured soothing words in Italian to her aunt, then turned toward Tony.

"Shall we use the library?" At least, Pilar thought, he wasn't bringing Rene with him. Even as they passed, Rene shot her one look, hard and bright as the stone on her finger.

A victor's look, Pilar thought. How ridiculous. There'd be no contest to win, and nothing to lose.

"I'm sorry Mama chose to make this announcement, and have this discussion, with so many people in attendance," Pilar began. "If she'd told me beforehand, I'd have urged her to talk to you privately."

"Doesn't matter. Her personal feelings for me are very clear." As his feathers were rarely ruffled, those feelings had rolled off him for years. "Professionally, well, I might have expected better. But we'll smooth it over." Smoothing things over was what he did second best. Ignoring them was his strong point.

He stepped into the room, sat in one of the deep leather chairs. Once he'd thought he would live in this house, or at least maintain a base there. Fortunately, as things had turned out, he preferred the city. There was little to do in Napa but watch the grapes grow.

"Well, Pilar." His smile was easy, charming as always. "How are you?"

"How am I, Tony?" Hysterical laughter wanted to bubble into her throat. She suppressed it. That was one of her strongest points. "Well enough. And you?"

"I'm good. Busy, of course. Tell me, what do you intend to do about *La Signora's* suggestion you take a more active part in the company?"

"It wasn't a suggestion, and I don't know what I intend to do about it." The idea of it was still buzzing through her head like a swarm of hornets. "I haven't had time to think it through."

"I'm sure you'll be fine." He leaned forward, his face earnest.

That, she thought with a rare flare of bitterness, was part of his skill and his deception. This pretense of caring. This veneer of interest.

"You're a lovely woman, and certainly an asset to the company in any capacity. It'll be good for you to get out and about more, to be occupied. You may even find you have a talent for it. A career might be just what you need."

She had wanted a family. Husband, children. Never a career. "Are we here to talk about my needs, Tony, or yours?"

"They're not exclusive of each other. Not really. Pilar, I think we should look at this new direction Tereza has plotted out as an opportunity for both of us to start fresh."

He took her hand in the easy way he had

with women, cupping it protectively and provocatively in his. "Perhaps we needed this push. I realize that the idea of divorce has been difficult for you."

"Do you?"

"Of course." She was going to make it sticky, he thought. What a bore. "The fact is, Pilar, we've led separate lives for a number of years now."

Slowly, deliberately, she pulled her hand from his. "Are you speaking of the lives we've led since you moved to San Francisco, or the lives we led while we continued to maintain the pretense of a marriage?"

Very sticky, he thought. And sighed. "Pilar, our marriage failed. It's hardly constructive to rehash the whys, the blames, the reasons after all this time."

"I don't believe we ever actually *hashed* them, Tony. But maybe the time's past where doing so would make any difference."

"The fact is by not ending things legally I've been unfair to you. You've been clearly unable to start a new life."

"Which hasn't been a problem for you, has it?" She rose, walked over to stare into the fire. Why was she fighting this? Why did it matter? "Let's at least be honest here. You came here today to ask me for a divorce, and it had nothing to do with my mother's decisions. Decisions you knew nothing about when you put that ring on Rene's finger."

"Be that as it may, it's foolish for either of us to pretend this wasn't long overdue. I put off the divorce for your sake, Pilar." Saying it, he believed it. Absolutely believed it, which made his tone utterly sincere. "Just as I'm asking for it now, for your sake. It's time you moved on."

"No," she murmured. She didn't turn yet, not yet, to look at him. Somehow when you looked at him, into those quietly sincere eyes, you ended up believing the lie. "We can't even be honest here. If you want a divorce, I won't stop you. I doubt I could in any case. She won't be as easily handled as I was," she added, turning back. "Maybe that's good for you. Maybe she's right for you. I certainly wasn't."

All he heard was that he would get what he wanted without trouble. "I'll handle the details. Quietly, of course. After all this time, it won't interest the press. Actually, it's hardly more than signing a few papers at this point. In fact, I'm sure all but our most intimate friends think we're already divorced."

When she said nothing, he got to his feet. "We'll all be happier once this is behind us. You'll see. Meanwhile, I think you should speak with Sophia. It's best coming from you—woman to woman. No doubt that when she sees you're agreeable, she'll feel more friendly toward Rene."

"Do you underestimate everyone, Tony?"

He held up his hands. "I simply feel that we'll all be more comfortable if we can keep this friendly. Rene will be my wife, and as such will be part of my professional and social life. We'll all see each other now and then. I expect Sophia to be polite."

"I expected you to be faithful. We all live with our disappointments. You got what you came for, Tony. I'd suggest you take Rene and leave before Mama finishes her port. I think there's been enough unpleasantness in this house for one day."

"Agreed." He started for the door, hesitated. "I do wish you the best, Pilar."

"Yes, I believe you. For some reason, I wish you the same. Goodbye, Tony."

When he closed the doors behind him, she walked carefully to a chair, sat slowly as if her bones might shatter at too sharp a move.

She remembered what it was like to be eighteen and wildly in love, full of plans and dreams and brilliance.

She remembered what it was like to be twenty-three and sliced through the heart by the stab of betrayal and the true loss of innocence. And thirty, fighting to cling to the shreds of a disintegrating marriage, to raise a child and hold a husband who was too careless to pretend to love you.

She remembered what it was like to be forty and resigned to the loss, empty of those dreams, those plans with the brilliance dulled dark.

Now, she thought, she knew what it was to be forty-eight, alone, with no illusions left. Replaced, legally, by the new, improved model, as she'd been replaced covertly so often.

She lifted her hand, slid her wedding ring up to the first knuckle. She'd worn that simple band for thirty years. Now she was being told to discard it, and the promises

she'd made before God, before family, before friends.

Tears burned at her eyes as she slipped it
from her finger. What was it, after all, she
thought, but an empty circle. The perfect
symbol for her marriage.

She had never been loved. Pilar let her
head fall back. How lowering, how sad, to
sit here now and accept, admit what she
had refused to accept and admit for so
long. No man, not even her husband, had
ever loved her.

When the doors opened, she closed her
fingers around the ring, willed the tears to
wait.

"Pilar." Helen took one look. Her lips tightened. "Okay, let's forget the coffee section
of today's entertainment."

At home, she crossed to a painted cabinet, opened it and selected a decanter of
brandy. She poured two snifters, then
walked over to sit on the footstool in front of
Pilar's chair.

"Drink up, honey. You look pale."

Saying nothing, Pilar opened her hand.
The ring glinted once in the firelight.

"Yeah, I figured that when the slut kept
flashing the rock of ages on her finger. They

deserve each other. He never deserved you."

"Stupid, stupid to be shaken like this. We haven't been married for years, not in any real sense. But thirty years, Helen." She held up the ring and, looking through that empty circle, saw her life. Narrow and encapsulated. "Thirty goddamn years. She was in diapers when I met Tony."

"That's the big ouch. So she's younger and got bigger breasts." Helen shrugged. "God knows those reasons alone are enough to hate her fucking guts. I'm with you there, and so's the crowd. But think of this. If she sticks with him, by the time she's our age, she'll be feeding him baby food and changing *his* diapers."

Pilar let out a moaning laugh. "I hate where I am, and I don't know how to get someplace else. I didn't even fight back, Helen."

"So you're not a warrior." Helen rose to sit on the arm of the chair, wrapped an arm around Pilar's shoulder. "You're a beautiful, intelligent, kind woman who got a raw deal. And damn, honey, if this door finally closing isn't the best thing for you."

"God, now you sound like Tony."

"No need to be insulting. Besides, he didn't mean that, and I do."

"Maybe, maybe. I can't see clearly now. I can't see through the next hour much less the next year. God, I didn't even make him pay. Didn't have the guts to make him pay."

"Don't worry, she will." Helen leaned over, kissed the top of Pilar's head. No man like Tony should slip through life without paying, she thought.

"And if you want to scald him a bit, I'll help you outline a divorce settlement that will leave him with permanent scars and one shriveled testicle."

Pilar smiled a little. She could always count on Helen. "As entertaining as that might be, it'd just drag things out, and make it more difficult for Sophie. Helen, what the hell am I going to do with the new life that's been dumped in my lap?"

"We'll think of something."

Sophia was doing a lot of thinking herself. She was already getting a headache from reading the pages of the contract. She got the gist of it, even mired in the legalese.

And the gist was *La Signora* maintained control as she always had. Over the next year Sophia would be expected to prove herself, which she'd thought she had. If she did, to her grandmother's satisfaction, some of that much-desired control would be passed to her hands.

Well, she wanted it. She didn't much care for the way she'd have to go about getting it. But she could see the reasoning.

The hardest part was in nearly always being able to see her grandmother's reasoning. Perhaps because, under it all, they thought so much alike.

She had not taken a deep and intimate interest in the making of wine. Loving the vineyards for their beauty, knowing the basics wasn't the same as investing time, emotion and effort into them. And if she would one day step into her grandmother's place, she needed to do so.

Maybe she preferred boardrooms to fermenting tanks, but . . .

She glanced over at Tyler, who was scowling down at his own contract.

This one took the tanks over the boardroom. That would make them a good business match, or contrast, she supposed.

And he had every bit as much at stake as she did.

Yes, *La Signora* had, once again, been as brilliant as she'd been ruthless. Now that her temper had cleared away to allow for cool common sense, she could see not only that it could work, but that it would.

Unless Ty mucked things up.

"You don't like it," she said.

"What the hell's to like about it? It was a goddamn ambush."

"Agreed. That's *Nonna*'s style. Troops fall in line more quickly and in a more organized fashion when you order them to right before the battle. Give them too much time to think, they might desert the field. Are you thinking of deserting the field, Ty?"

His gaze lifted, and she saw the steel in his eyes. Hard and cold. "I've run MacMillan for eight years. I'm not walking away from it."

No, he wouldn't muck it up. "Okay. Let's start from there. You want what you want, I want what I want. How do we get it?" She pushed to her feet, paced. "Easier for you."

"Why is that?"

"I essentially give up my apartment and

move back home. You get to stay right where you are. I have to take a crash course in winemaking, and all you have to do is socialize and go to a few meetings now and then."

"You think that's easier? Socializing involves people. I don't like people. And while I'm going to meetings about things I don't give a rat's ass about, some guy I don't even know is going to be looking over my shoulder."

"Mine, too," she snapped back. "Who the hell is this David Cutter?"

"A suit," Ty said in disgust.

"More than that," Sophia murmured. If she'd believed that, she wouldn't have been concerned. She knew how to handle suits. "We'll just have to find out how much more." That was something she could take care of very shortly, and very thoroughly. "And we're going to have to find a way to work with him, and each other. The last part shouldn't be that hard. We've known each other for years."

She was moving fast where he preferred to pace himself. But damned if he wasn't going to keep up. "No, we haven't. I don't know you, or what you do or why you do it."

She put her palms on the table, leaned forward. Her magnificent face moved close to his. "Sophia Tereza Maria Giambelli. I market wine. And I do it because I'm good at it. And in one year, I'm going to own twenty percent of one of the biggest, most successful and important wine companies in the world."

He rose slowly, mimicked her pose. "You're going to have to be good at it, and a lot more for that. You're going to have to get your hands dirty, and get mud on your designer boots and ruin your pretty manicure."

"Do you think I don't know how to work, MacMillan?"

"I think you know how to sit behind a desk or on a first-class seat on a plane. That superior ass of yours isn't going to find life so cozy for the next year, Giambelli."

She saw the red haze at the edges of her vision, a sure sign temper was taking over and she was about to do something foolish. "Side bet. Five thousand dollars says I'm a better winemaker than you are executive at the end of the season."

"Who decides?"

"Neutral party. David Cutter."

"Done." He reached over and gripped her

slim hand in his big, hard one. "Buy yourself some rough clothes and some boots that were made for work instead of fashion. Be ready to start your first lesson tomorrow, seven A.M."

"Fine." She set her teeth. "We'll break at noon, head down to the city for your first lesson. You can take an hour out to buy some decent suits that have been tailored in the last decade."

"You're supposed to move here. Why do we have to go to the city?"

"Because I need a number of things in my office, and you need to be familiarized with the routine there. I also need things from my apartment. You've got a strong back and your ass isn't bad, either," she added, smiling thinly. "You can help me move."

"I've got something to say."

"Well, goodness. Let me prepare myself."

"I don't like your mouth. Never did." He jammed his hands in his pockets because when she smirked, as she was doing now, he really just wanted to pop her one. "But I've got nothing against you."

"Oh, Ty. That's so . . . touching."

"Look, just shut up." He dragged a hand through his hair, jammed it back in his pocket. "You do what you do because you're good at it. I do what I do because I love it. It's all I've ever wanted to do. I got nothing against you, Sophia, but if it looks like you're going to cost me my vines, I'll cut you out."

Intrigued, and challenged, she studied him from a new angle. Who'd have thought the boy next door could be ruthless? "All right, so warned. And same goes, Ty. Whatever I have to do, I protect what's mine."

Blowing out a breath, she looked down at the contracts, then lifted her gaze back to his. "I guess we're on the same page here."

"Looks that way."

"Got a pen?"

"No."

She walked to a server, found two in a drawer. She offered him one, flipped through her contract to the signature page. "I guess we can witness each other's." She drew a deep breath, held it. "On three?"

"One, two. Three."

In silence, they signed, slid contracts across the table, witnessed.

Because her stomach was churning, Sophia topped off their glasses, waited for

Tyler to lift his. "To the new generation," she said.

"To a good season."

"We won't have one without the other." With her eyes on his, she clinked glasses. "*Salute.*"

CHAPTER FOUR

The rain was razor-thin and mean with cold, a miserable drizzle that sliced through the bones and into the spirit. It turned the light blanket of snow into a mire of mud and the dawn light into a gloomy smear on the sky.

It was the sort of morning when a reasonable person snuggled in bed. Or at the very least lingered over a second cup of coffee.

Tyler MacMillan, Sophia discovered, was not a reasonable person.

The phone woke her, had her sliding a hand reluctantly out of the covers, groping for the receiver, then dragging it under the warmth with her. "What?"

"You're late."

"Huh? I am not. It's still dark."

"It's not dark, it's raining. Get up, get

dressed, get out and get over here. You're on my time now."

"But . . ." The drone of the dial tone made her scowl. "Bastard," she muttered, but she couldn't drum up enough energy to put any punch into it.

She lay still, listening to the hiss of rain on the windows. It sounded as if it had ice around the edges. And wouldn't that be pleasant?

Yawning, she tossed back the covers and got out of bed. She might have been on his time now, she thought, but before long he'd be on hers.

The rain dripped off the bill of Ty's cap and occasionally snuck under his collar to slide down his back. Still, it wasn't heavy enough to stop the work.

And a rainy winter was a blessing. A cool, wet winter was the first crucial step toward a rare vintage.

He would control what he could control— the work, the decisions, the precautions and the gambles. And he would pray that nature got on board with the team.

The team, he thought, hooking his thumbs

in his pockets and watching Sophia trudge through the mud in her five-hundred-dollar boots, that had increased by one.

"I told you to wear rough clothes."

She puffed out a breath, watched the rain dissolve it. "These are my rough clothes."

He studied her sleek leather jacket, the tailored trousers, the stylish Italian boots. "Well, they will be before it's over."

"I was under the impression rain delayed pruning."

"It's not raining."

"Oh?" Sophia held out a hand, palm up, and let the rain patter into it. "Isn't that strange, I've always defined this wet substance falling out of the sky as rain."

"It's drizzling. Where's your hat?"

"I didn't wear one."

"Jesus." Annoyed, he pulled his own cap off, tugged it over her head. Even its wet, battered ugliness couldn't detract from her style. He imagined it was bred into her, like bones.

"There are two primary reasons for pruning," he began.

"Ty, I'm aware there are reasons for pruning."

"Fine. Explain them to me."

"To train the vine," she said between her teeth. "And if we're going to have an oral lesson, why can't we do it inside where we'd be warm and dry?"

"Because the vines are outside." And because, he thought, here he ran the show. "We prune to train the vines to facilitate their shape for easier cultivation and harvesting, and to control disease."

"Ty—"

"Quiet. A lot of vineyards use trellising techniques instead of hand pruning. Here, because farming's an unending experiment, we use both. Vertical trellising, the Geneva T-support and other types. But we still use the traditional hand-pruning method. The second purpose is to distribute the bearing wood over the vine to increase its production, while keeping it consistent with the ability to produce top-quality fruit."

When he told her to be quiet, he did so like a patient parent might to a small, irritable child. She imagined he knew it and fluttered her lashes. "Is there going to be a quiz, Professor?"

"You don't prune my vines, or learn trellising, until you know why you're doing it."

"We prune and trellis to grow grapes. We grow grapes to make wine."

Her hands moved as she spoke. It was like a ballet, he'd always thought. Graceful and full of meaning.

"And," she continued, "I sell the wine through clever, innovative promotion and marketing techniques. Which, I'll remind you, are as essential to this vineyard as your pruning shears."

"Fine, but we're in the vineyard, not in your office. You don't take an action here without being aware of the cause and the consequence."

"I've always thought it more being aware of the odds. It's a gamble," she said, gesturing widely. "A high-stakes game, but a game at the core."

"You play games for fun."

She smiled now and reminded him of her grandmother. "Not the way I play them, sweetheart. These are older vines here." She studied the rows on either side of them. The rain was dampening his hair, teasing out those reddish highlights, the color of a good aged Cabernet. "Head pruning here, then."

"Why?"

She adjusted the bill of the cap. "Because."

"Because," he continued, taking his pruners out of their sheath on his belt, "we want the bearing spurs distributed evenly on the head of the vine."

He turned her, slapped the tool in her hands. He pushed a cane aside, exposing another, then guided her hands toward it and made the cut with her. "We want the center, the top, left open. It needs room to get enough sun."

"What about mechanical pruning?"

"We do that, too. You don't." He shifted her to the next cane. She smelled female, he decided. An exotic counterpoint to the simple perfume of rain and damp earth.

Why the hell did she have to splash on perfume to work in the fields? He nearly asked her, realized he wouldn't like or understand her reasons, and let it go.

"You work by hand," he told her, and did his level best not to breathe her in. "Cane by cane. Plant by plant. Row by row."

She scanned the endless stream of them, the countless vines being tended by laborers, or waiting to be tended. The pruning, she knew, would run through January, into

February. She imagined herself bored senseless with the process before Christmas.

"We break at noon," she reminded him.

"One. You were late."

"Not that late." She turned her head, and her body angled into his. He was leaning over her, his arms around her so that his hands could cover hers on cane and tool. The slight shift was uncalculated. And potent.

Their eyes met, irritation in his, consideration in hers. She felt his body tense, and the tingle of response inside her own. A slightly quickened pulse, a kind of instinctive scenting of the air, and the resulting stir of juices.

"Well, well." She all but purred it, and let her gaze skim down to his mouth, then back again. "Who'd have thought it?"

"Cut it out." He straightened up, took a step back as a man would on finding himself unexpectedly at the edge of a very long drop. But she simply continued her turn so that their bodies brushed again. And a second step back would have marked him a coward. Or a fool.

"Don't worry, MacMillan, you're not my type." Big, rough, elemental. "Usually."

"You're not mine." Sharp, slick, dangerous. "Ever."

If he'd known her better, he'd have realized such a statement wasn't an insult to her. But a challenge. Her mild, and purely elemental, interest climbed up another level. "Really? What is?"

"I don't like cocky, aggressive women with fancy edges."

She grinned. "You will." She turned back to the canes. "We'll break at twelve-thirty." Once again she looked over her shoulder at him. "Compromise. We're going to have to do a lot of it to get through this season."

"Twelve-thirty." He pulled off his gloves, held them out to her. "Wear these. You'll get blisters on those city-girl hands."

"Thanks. They're too big."

"Make do. Tomorrow you bring your own, and you wear a hat. No, not there," he said as she started to clip another cane.

He moved in behind her again, put his hands over hers and angled the tool correctly.

And didn't see her slow, satisfied smile.

· · ·

Despite the gloves, she got the blisters. They were more annoying than painful as she did a quick change for the afternoon in the city. Dressed and polished, she grabbed her briefcase and called out a goodbye as she dashed out the door. During the short drive to MacMillan she ran over her needs and obligations for the rest of the day. She was going to have to pack quite a bit into a very short amount of time.

She zipped up to the front entrance of the sprawling cedar-and-fieldstone house, gave two quick toots of the horn. He didn't keep her waiting, which pleased her. And he had changed, she noted, so that counted for something. Though the denim shirt and comfortably faded jeans were a long level down from what she considered casual office wear, she decided to tackle his wardrobe later.

He opened the door of her BMW convertible, scowled at her and the ragtop. "You expect me to fold myself into this little toy?"

"It's roomier than it looks. Come on, you're on my time now."

"Couldn't you have driven one of the four-wheels?" he complained as he levered himself into the passenger seat.

He looked, she thought, like a big, cranky Jack in a very small, spiffy box. "Yes, but I didn't. Besides, I like driving my own car." She proved it, the minute his seat belt was secured, by punching the gas and flying down the drive.

She liked the glimpses of mountain through the rain. Like shadows behind a silver curtain. And the row upon row of naked vines, waiting, just waiting for sun and warmth to lure them into life again.

She sped past the MacMillan winery, its faded brick upholstered with vines, its gables proud and stern. It was, to her, a romantic and lovely entrance to the mysteries of the caves it guarded. Inside, as inside the winery at Giambelli, workers would be lifting, twisting the aging bottles of champagne or readying the tasting room if there was a tour or wine club scheduled for the day. Others might be transferring wine from vat to vat as it cleared and clarified.

There was work, she knew, in the buildings, in the caves, in the plants, even as the vines slept.

And, she thought, there was work for her in San Francisco.

She was racing out of the valley like a

woman breaking out of jail. Ty wondered if she felt that way.

"Why is my seat warm?"

"Your what? Oh." She glanced over, laughing. "Just my little way of warming your ass up, darling. Don't like it?" She clicked the button, turned off the heated seat. "Our top priority," she began, "is the centennial campaign. There are a lot of stages, some of which, like the auction earlier this week, are already implemented. Others are still on the drawing board. We're looking for something fresh but that also honors tradition. Something classy and discreet that appeals to our high-end and/or more mature accounts, and something kicky that catches the interest of the younger and/or less affluent market."

"Yeah, right."

"Ty, this is something you have to understand the causes and consequences of as well. Selling the wine is every bit as essential as what you do. Otherwise, you're just making it for yourself, aren't you?"

He shifted, tried to find room for his legs. "Sure would be easier that way."

"Look, you make different levels of wine. The superior grade that costs more to produce, more to bottle, more to store and so on, and your middle of the line right down to the jug wine. More goes in the process than the wine."

"Without the wine, nothing else matters."

"Be that as it may," she said with what she considered heroic patience, "it's part of my job, and now yours, to help sell those grades to the consumer. The individual consumer and the big accounts. Hotels, restaurants. To pull in the wine merchants, the brokers, and make them see they must have Giambelli, or what will now be Giambelli-MacMillan, on their list. To do that, I have to sell the package as well as what's inside the bottle."

"The packaging's fluff," he said, eyeing her deliberately. "It's what's inside that tips the scales."

"That's a very clever, and subtle, insult. You get a point. However, packaging, marketing, promotion are what up the product on the scale to begin with. With people, and with wine. Let's stick with wine for the moment, shall we?"

His lips twitched. Her tone had gone frigid and keen, a sure sign he'd indeed scored a point. "Sure."

"I have to make the *idea* of the product intriguing, exclusive, accessible, substantial, fun, sexy. So I have to know the product and there we're on even ground. But I also have to know the account, and the market I'm targeting. That's what you have to learn."

"Surveys, statistics, parties, polls, meetings."

She reached over and patted his hand. "You'll live through it." She paused, slowed down slightly. "Do you recognize that van?"

He frowned, squinting through the windshield as a dark, late-model minivan turned on the road up ahead into the entrance to Villa Giambelli. "No."

"Cutter," Sophia muttered. "I just bet it's Cutter."

"We could put off the trip to San Francisco and find out."

It was tempting, and the hope in Ty's voice amused her. Still, she shook her head and kept on driving. "No, that would make him too important. Besides, I'll grill my mother when I get home."

"I want in that loop."

"For better or worse, Ty, you and I are in

this together. I'll keep you in my loop, you keep me in yours."

It was a long way from coast to coast. It was, in some ways, another world, a world where everyone was a stranger. He'd ripped out the roots he'd managed to sink into New York concrete with the hope he could plant them here, in the hills and valleys of northern California.

If it had been that, only that, David wouldn't have been worried. He'd have found it an adventure, a thrill, the kind of freewheeling gamble he'd have jumped at in his youth. But when a man was forty-three and had two teenagers depending on him, there was a great deal at stake.

If he'd been certain remaining with La Coeur in New York was what was best for his kids, he'd have stayed there. He'd have stifled there, trapped in the glass and steel of his office. But he'd stopped being sure when his sixteen-year-old son had been picked up for shoplifting, and his fourteen-year-old daughter had started painting her toenails black.

He'd been losing touch with his kids, and

in losing touch, losing control. When the offer from Giambelli-MacMillan had fallen in his lap, it had seemed like a sign.

Take a chance. Start fresh.

God knew it wouldn't be the first time he'd done both. But this time he did so with his kids' happiness tossed into the ante.

"This place is in the middle of nowhere."

David glanced in the rearview mirror at his son. Maddy had won the toss in San Francisco and sat, desperately trying to look bored, in the front seat. "How," David asked, "can nowhere have a middle? I've always wondered that."

He had the pleasure of seeing Theo smirk, the closest he came to a genuine smile these days.

He looks like his mother, David thought. A young male version of Sylvia. Which, David knew, neither Theo nor Sylvia would appreciate. They had that in common as well, both of them bound and determined to be seen as individuals.

For Sylvia, that had meant stepping out of marriage and away from motherhood. For Theo . . . time, David supposed, would tell.

"Why does it have to be raining?" Maddy slumped in her seat and tried not to let her eyes gleam with excitement as she studied the huge stone mansion in front of the car.

"Well, it has something to do with moisture gathering in the atmosphere, then—"

"Dad." She giggled, and to David it was music.

He was going to get his children back here, whatever it took. "Let's go meet *La Signora.*"

"Do we have to call her that?" Maddy rolled her eyes. "It's so medieval."

"Let's start out with Ms. Giambelli and work from there. And let's try to look normal."

"Mad can't. Geeks never look normal."

"Neither do freaks." Maddy clumped out of the car on her ugly black boots with their two-inch platforms. She stood in the rain, looking to her father like some sort of eccentric princess with her long pale hair, pouty lips and long-lashed blue eyes. Her little body—she was still such a little thing— was draped and swathed in layers of black. There were three silver chains dangling from her right ear—a compromise, as David had been terrified when she'd started campaigning to have her nose, or somewhere even more unsanitary, pierced.

Theo was a dark contrast. Tall, gangly, with his deep brown hair a curling, unkempt mass around his pretty face, straggling toward his still bony shoulders. His eyes were a softer blue, and too often for his father's taste, clouded and unhappy.

He slouched now in jeans that were too baggy, shoes nearly as ugly as his sister's and a jacket that sagged past his hips.

Just clothes, David reminded himself. Clothes and hair, nothing permanent. Hadn't his own parents nagged him into rebellion about his personal style when he'd been a teenager? And hadn't he promised himself he wouldn't do the same with his kids?

But God, he wished they'd at least wear clothes that fit.

He walked up the wide fan of steps, then stood in front of the deeply carved front door of the villa and dragged a hand through his own thick, dark blond hair.

"What's the matter, Dad? Nervous?"

There was a smirk in his son's voice, just enough of one to strain the wire holding David's composure together. "Give me a break, okay?"

Theo opened his mouth, a sarcastic retort

on the tip of his tongue. But he caught the warning look his sister gave him and saw his father's strained expression. "Hey, you can handle her."

"Sure." Maddy shrugged. "She's just an old Italian woman, right?"

With a half-laugh, David punched his finger to the buzzer. "Right."

"Wait, I gotta get my normal face on." Theo put his hands on his face, shoving, pulling at the skin, drawing his eyes down, twisting his mouth. "I can't find it."

David hooked an arm around his neck, and the other around Maddy's. They were going to be all right, he thought, and held on. They were going to be fine.

"I'll get it, Maria!" Pilar dashed down the foyer, a spray of white roses in her arms.

When she opened the door she saw a tall man holding two children in headlocks. All three of them were grinning.

"Hello. Can I help you?"

Not an old Italian woman, David thought as he hastily released his children. Just a beautiful woman, with surprise in her eyes and roses lying in the crook of her arm. "I'm here to see Ms. Giambelli."

Pilar smiled, scanned the faces of the boy

and girl to include them. "There are so many of us."

"Tereza Giambelli. I'm David Cutter."

"Oh. Mr. Cutter. I'm sorry." She held out a hand for his. "I didn't realize you were expected today." Or that you had a family, she thought. Her mother hadn't been forthcoming with details. "Please come in. I'm Pilar. Pilar Giambelli . . ." She nearly added her married name, a force of habit. Then determinedly let it go. "*La Signora*'s daughter."

"Do you call her that?" Maddy asked.

"Sometimes. When you meet her, you'll see why."

"Madeline, my daughter. My son, Theodore."

"Theo," Theo mumbled.

"I'm delighted to meet you. Theo. And Madeline."

"Maddy, okay?"

"Maddy. Come into the parlor. There's a nice fire. I'll arrange for some refreshments if that suits you. Such a nasty day. I hope it wasn't a terrible trip."

"Not so bad."

"Endless," Maddy corrected. "Awful." But she stared at the room when they entered. It was like a palace, she thought. Like a pic ture in a book, where everything was in rich colors and looked old and precious.

"I bet it was. Let me have your coats."

"They're wet," David began, but she simply plucked them out of his hand and draped them over her free arm.

"I'll take care of them. Please, sit, make yourselves at home. I'll let my mother know you're here and see about something hot to drink. Would you like coffee, Mr. Cutter?"

"I absolutely would, Ms. Giambelli."

"So would I."

"No, you wouldn't," he said to Maddy and had her sulking again.

"A latte, perhaps?"

"That's cool. I mean," she corrected when her father's elbow reminded her of her manners, "yes, thank you."

"And, Theo?"

"Yes, ma'am, thank you."

"It'll just take a minute."

"Man." Theo waited until Pilar was safely out of the room, then plopped into a chair. "They must be mega-rich. This place looks like a museum or something."

"Don't put your boots up on that," David ordered.

"It's a footstool," Theo pointed out.

"Once you put feet into those boots they cease to be feet."

"Chill, Dad." Maddy gave him a bracing, and distressingly adult, pat on the back. "You're like COO and everything."

"Right." From executive vice president, operations, to chief operating officer, in one three-thousand-mile leap. "Bullets bounce off me," he murmured, then turned toward the doorway when he heard footsteps.

He started to tell his kids to stand up, but he didn't have to bother. When Tereza Giambelli walked into a room, people got to their feet.

He'd forgotten she was so petite. They'd had two meetings in New York, face-to-face. Two long, involved meetings. And still he'd walked away from them with the image of a statuesque Amazon rather than the fine-boned, slim woman who walked toward him now. The hand she offered him was small and strong.

"Mr. Cutter. Welcome to Villa Giambelli."

"Thank you, *signora.* You have a beautiful home in a magnificent setting. My family and I are grateful for your hospitality."

Pilar stepped into the room in time to hear the smooth speech and see the practiced formality with which it was delivered. It was not, she thought, what she'd expected from the man holding two travel-rumpled teenagers in playful headlocks. Not, she decided, noting the sidelong glances from his children, what they were used to from him.

"I hope the trip wasn't tedious," Tereza continued, shifting her attention to the children.

"Not at all. We enjoyed it. *Signora* Giambelli, I'd like to introduce you to my children. My son, Theodore, and my daughter, Madeline."

"Welcome to California." She offered her hand to Theo, and though he felt foolish, he shook it and resisted sticking his own in his pocket.

"Thanks."

Maddy accepted the hand. "It's nice to be here."

"You hope it will be," Tereza said with a hint of a smile. "That's enough for now. Please, sit. Be comfortable. Pilar, you'll join us."

"Of course."

"You must be proud of your father," Tereza began as she took a seat. "And all he's accomplished."

"Ah . . . sure." Theo sat, remembered not to slouch. He didn't know much about his father's work. In his world, his dad went to the office, then came home. He nagged about schoolwork, burned dinner, sent for takeout.

Or, mostly during the last year, had called home and said he'd be late and Theo or Maddy should call for takeout.

"Theo's more interested in music than wine, or the business of wine," David commented.

"Ah. And you play?"

This was his father's deal, Theo thought. How come he had to answer so many questions? Adults didn't get it anyway. "Guitar. And piano."

"You must play for me sometime. I enjoy music. What sort do you prefer?"

"There's just rock. I go for techno, and alternative."

"Theo writes music," David put in, and surprised a blink out of his son. "It's interesting material."

"I'd like to hear it once everyone's settled. And you," Tereza said to Maddy. "Do you play?"

"I had piano lessons." She shrugged a

shoulder. "I'm not really into it. I want to be a scientist." Her brother's snort had her temper rising.

"Maddy's interested in everything." David spoke quickly before blood could be shed. "The high school here, from what I've been told, should speak to both her and Theo's specific interests very well."

"Arts and science." Tereza leaned back. "They take after their father then, as wine is both. I assume you'll want a few days to settle in," she continued as a cart was wheeled in. "A new position, a new location, new people. And, of course, a new school and routine for your family."

"Dad says it's an adventure," Maddy said and earned a stately nod from Tereza.

"And we'll try to make it so."

"I'm at your disposal, *signora,*" David said, and watched Pilar as she rose to serve coffees and cakes. "I appreciate, again, the use of your guest house. I'm sure settling in will be a pleasure."

Because he was watching her, he caught the quick widening of Pilar's eyes. So, he thought, that one comes as a surprise to you. I wonder why. "Thanks."

"Enjoy," Pilar murmured.

When the coffee was served, they fell into light conversation. David followed Tereza's lead and left business out of it. Time enough, he concluded, to get to the meat.

In precisely twenty minutes, Tereza got to her feet. "I regret my husband was unavailable to see you today, and meet your charming children. Would it be convenient for you to meet with us tomorrow?"

"At your convenience, *signora.*" David rose.

"At eleven then. Pilar, will you show the Cutters the guest house, and see they have all they need?"

"Certainly. I'll just get our coats."

What the hell was this? Pilar wondered as she retrieved jackets. Normally she had her finger on the pulse of the household. Yet her mother had managed to slip an entire family in on her without sending up a single alarm.

So many changes, and practically overnight. It was time she paid more attention, she decided. She didn't care for the order of things to change when she wasn't prepared for it.

Still, she conversed easily when she returned and geared herself up to play gracious hostess. "It's a short drive. An easy walk really, in good weather."

"Winter rain's good for the grapes." David took her jacket, helped her into it.

"Yes. So I'm reminded whenever I complain about the wet." She stepped outside. "There's a direct line from house to house, so you've only to call if you need anything or have a question. Our housekeeper's Maria, and there's nothing she can't do. Thank you," she added when David opened the side door of the van for her.

"You'll have wonderful views," she added, shifting around to speak to the children when they climbed in the back. "From whichever bedrooms you choose. And there's a pool. Of course, you won't be able to enjoy that just now, but you're welcome to use the indoor pool here at the main house whenever you like."

"An indoor pool?" Theo's mood brightened. "Cool."

"That doesn't mean you drop in wearing your bathing trunks whenever you feel like it," his father warned. "You don't want to give them the run of the house, Ms. Giambelli. You'll be in therapy in a week."

"Hasn't worked for you," Theo shot back.

"We'll enjoy having young people around. And it's Pilar, please."

"David."

Behind their backs, Maddy turned to her brother and fluttered her lashes wildly.

"David. Just take the left fork. You can see the house there. It's a pretty place, and the rain gives it a bit of a fairy-tale aspect."

"Is that it?" Suddenly interested, Theo leaned up. "It's pretty big."

"Four bedrooms. Five baths. There's a lovely living room, but the kitchen/great room is friendlier, I think. Anybody cook?"

"Dad pretends to," Maddy said. "And we pretend to eat it."

"Smart-ass. Do you?" David asked Pilar. "Cook?"

"Yes, and very well, but rarely. Well, perhaps your wife will enjoy the kitchen when she joins you."

The instant and absolute silence had Pilar cringing inside.

"I'm divorced." David pulled up in front of the house. "It's just the three of us. Let's check it out. We'll get the stuff later."

"I'm very sorry," Pilar murmured when the kids bolted from the van. "I shouldn't have assumed—"

"Natural assumption. A man, a couple of kids. You expect the full family complement. Don't worry about it." He patted her hand casually, then reached across to open her door. "You know, they're going to have to fight over the bedrooms. I hope you don't mind screaming scenes."

"I'm Italian," was all she said and stepped out into the rain.

CHAPTER FIVE

Italian, David thought later. And gorgeous. Aloof and gracious at the same time. Not an easy trick. In that area, she was her mother's daughter.

He knew how to read people, an invaluable trick of the trade in the climb up the slippery executive ladder in any major corporation. His read of Pilar Giambelli was that she was as accustomed to giving orders as she was to taking them.

He knew she was married, and to whom, but since she hadn't been wearing a ring he assumed the marriage to the infamous Tony Avano was over, or in serious trouble. He'd have to find out which before he let himself consider her on a more personal level.

There was a daughter. Anyone in the business had heard of Sophia Giambelli. A firecracker by reputation who had style and ambition in spades. He'd be meeting her along the way, and wondered just how she'd taken to his induction as COO. Might have to play some politics there, he mused, and reached for the cigarettes in his pocket. Only to remember they weren't there because he'd quit three weeks and five days earlier.

And it was killing him.

Think about something else, he ordered himself, and tuned in to the music played at a brutal volume in his son's new room. Thank God it was at the other end of the hall.

There'd been the expected combat over bedrooms. Still, his kids had been fairly restrained all in all. He put that down to reluctant manners in front of a stranger. In any case the squabble had been out of habit and without real heat as every room in the house was appealing.

Damn near perfect, he thought, with its gleaming wood and tile, silky walls and lush furnishings.

The perfection, the casually elegant style, the absolute order of things gave him the willies. But he expected the kids would soon put that to rights. Tidy they weren't. So however polished the box, the contents would soon be jumbled and they'd all feel more at home.

Already weary of unpacking, he wandered to one of the windows and stared out over the fields. Pilar was right. The view was stunning. This was part of his turf now. He intended to leave his mark.

Down the hall Maddy wandered out of her room. She'd tried to act casual about it after arguing with Theo over who got what. The fact was she was thrilled. For the first time in her life she didn't have to share a bathroom with her idiot brother. And hers was done in this cool pattern of dark blues and deep reds. Big splashy flowers, so she imagined taking a bath there would be like swimming in some weird garden.

Plus she had a huge four-poster bed. She'd locked the door so she could roll all over it in privacy.

Then she'd remembered that she wouldn't see New York when she looked out the windows, or be able to call one of her friends and hang out. She wouldn't be able to walk to the movies whenever she felt like it. She wouldn't be able to do anything she was used to doing.

Homesickness had settled so hot and heavy in her belly it ached. The only person she could talk to was Theo. It was the poorest of choices, in her opinion, but the only one left.

She pushed open his door to a blast of the Chemical Brothers. He was lying on his bed, his guitar across his chest as he tried to match the guitar riff blasting on his stereo. The room was already in chaos, as she imagined it would stay until he moved out to go to college.

He was such a pig.

"You're supposed to be unpacking."

"You're supposed to mind your own business."

She flopped, stomach down, on the foot of his bed. "There's nothing to do here."

"You just figuring that out?"

"Maybe Dad'll hate it, and we'll go home."

"No chance. Did you see how he slicked up for the old lady?" Because he felt homesick, too, he set his guitar aside and opted to speak to the bane of his existence. "What's up with that?"

"He sounded like something out of a

movie. You know how he looks when he puts on one of his suits for a meeting?" She rolled over on her back. "He sounded like he looks then. Nothing's going to be the same now. He was looking at that woman."

"Huh?"

"The Pilar woman. What kind of a name is that?"

"I guess it's Italian or something. What do you mean looking at her?"

"You know. Scoping her out."

"Get out."

"Man, guys don't notice anything." Feeling superior, she sat up, tossed back her hair. "He was checking her out."

"So what?" Theo gave a little jerk of the body, a horizontal shrug. "He's checked out women before. Hey, I bet he's even had sex with some of them."

"Gee, you think?" While the sarcasm dripped, she pushed off the bed to pace to the window. Rain and vines, vines and rain. "Maybe if he has sex with his boss's daughter, he'll get caught, he'll get fired, and we'll go back home."

"Home where? He loses his job, we've got no place to go. Grow up, Maddy."

She hunched her shoulders. "This sucks."

"Tell me about it."

Ty was thinking the same thing about life in general as Sophia whipped him into a meeting—a brainstorming session, she called it. She'd rattled off names at him as she'd zipped through the advertising section. Gesturing, calling out orders and greetings, snatching up messages as she went.

He remembered none of the names, of course, and the faces had all been a blur as he'd kept pace with Sophia. The woman moved like a linebacker with an intercepted ball in her hand. Fast and slick.

There were three other people in the room now, all what he thought of as Urban Warriors with their trendy clothes and trendy hair and little wire-rim glasses and electronic palm books. Two were female, one was male. All were young and handsome. He couldn't for the life of him remember who was who, as they'd all had androgynous names.

He had some kind of fancy coffee in his hand he hadn't wanted and everyone was talking at once and munching on biscotti.

He was getting a killer headache.

"No, Kris, what I'm looking for is subtle but powerful. A strong image with an emotional message. Trace, quick sketch: couple—young, casual, late twenties. Relaxing on a porch. Sexual, but keep it casual."

Since the man with the blond choppy hair picked up the pencil and sketch pad, Ty assumed he was Trace.

"It's sunset," Sophia continued, rising from her desk to wander the room. "End of day. This is a working couple, no kids, upwardly mobile, but settled."

"Porch swing," the perky black woman in a red vest suggested.

"Too settled. Too country. Wicker love seat, maybe," Sophia said. "Strong color in the cushions. Candles on the table. Fat ones, not tapers."

She leaned over Trace's shoulder, made humming noises. "Good, good, but do it this way. Have them looking at each other, maybe have her leg swung over his knees. Friendly intimacy. Roll up his sleeves, put her in jeans, no, in khakis."

She sat on the edge of her desk, lips pursed as she pondered. "I want them to be having a conversation. Relaxed, having a moment. Enjoying each other's company after a busy day."

"What if one of them's pouring the wine. Holding the bottle."

"We'll try that. You want to sketch that one out, P.J.?"

With a nod perky P.J., as Ty now thought of her, picked up her pad.

"You should have water." The second woman, a redhead who looked bored and annoyed, stifled a yawn.

"I see we've interrupted Kris's nap," Sophia said sweetly, and Ty caught the quick, simmering glare under the redhead's lowered lashes.

"Suburban scenes bore me. At least water adds an element, and subliminal sexuality."

"Kris wants water." Sophia nodded, pushed to her feet to wander the room while she considered. "Water's good. A pond, a lake. We can get good light from that. Reflections. Take a look, Ty. What do you think?"

He did his best to tune back in and look intelligent as Trace turned his sketch around. "I don't know anything about advertising. It's a nice sketch."

"You look at ads," Sophia reminded him.

"All the time, whether you consciously take in the message or not. What does this say to you?"

"It says they're sitting on the porch drinking wine. Why can't they have kids?"

"Why should they?"

"You got a couple, on a porch. Porch usually means house. Why can't they have kids?"

"Because we don't want young kids in an ad for an alcoholic beverage," Kris said, with a hint of a sneer in her voice. "Advertising 101."

"Evidence of kids then. You know, some toys on the porch. Then it says these people have a family, have been together awhile and are still happy to sit on the porch together and have a glass of wine at the end of the day. That's sexy."

Kris started to open her mouth, then noted the gleam come into Sophia's eyes. And wisely closed it again.

"That's good. That's excellent," Sophia said. "Even better for this one. Toss toys on the porch, Trace. Keep the wine bottle on the table with the candles. Here's our cozy yet hip suburban couple.

"Celebrate the sunset," she murmured.

"It's your moment. Relax with Giambelli. It's your wine."

"More cozy than hip," Kris muttered.

"We use an urban setting for hip. Two couples, friends getting together for an evening. Apartment scene. Keep them young, keep them slick. Show me the city out the window. Lights and silhouettes."

"Coffee table," P.J. put in, already sketching. "A couple of them sitting on the floor. The others lounging on the couch, everybody talking at once. You can almost hear music playing. Food scattered on the table. Takeout. This is where we pour the wine."

"Good, perfect. Celebrate Tuesday. Same tags."

"Why Tuesday?" Ty wanted to know in spite of himself.

"Because you never make big plans for Tuesday." Sophia slid onto the edge of the desk again, crossed her legs. "You make plans for the weekend. You fall into plans otherwise. Tuesday night with friends is spontaneous. We want people to pick up a bottle of our wine on the spur. Just because it's Tuesday. Your moment, your wine. That's the pitch."

"The wine's Giambelli-MacMillan."

She nodded. "Correct. We need to identify that as well within the campaign. A wedding. Celebrate our marriage. Champagne, flowers, a gorgeous couple."

"Honeymoon's sexier," Trace commented as he refined his other sketch. "Same elements, but in a snazzy hotel room. Wedding dress hanging on the door and our couple in a lip lock with champagne on ice."

"If they're in a lip lock, they're not going to be thinking about drinking," Ty said.

"Good point. Hold the kiss, but the rest is great. Show me . . ." Her hands began to move. "Anticipation. Silk, flowers, and put the flutes in their hands. Give me eye lock instead of lip lock. Go, my children, and create magic. See what you can get me in the next few hours. Think: Moments. The special and the ordinary."

She recrossed her legs as her team headed out, talking over one another. "Not bad, MacMillan. Not bad at all."

"Good. Can we go home now?"

"No. I've got a lot of stuff to deal with here, and more to pack up in order to set up an office at the villa. Can you draw?"

"Sure."

"That's a plus." She scooted off the desk to cross over and dig a sketch pad from a wall of shelves.

There were a lot of things on the shelves, Ty noted. Not just business junk, but the knickknacks people, particularly female people, in his opinion, seemed to collect. Leading the pack of the dust catchers were frogs. Little green frogs, larger bronze frogs, dancing frogs, fashionably dressed frogs and what appeared to be mating frogs.

They didn't seem to jibe with the sleekly dressed woman who bulleted down office corridors on high heels and smelled like a night in the forest.

"Looking for a prince?"

"Hmm?" She glanced back, following his gesture. "Oh. No, princes are too high-maintenance. I just like frogs. Here's what I see. A kind of montage. The vineyards, the sweep of them in the sunlight. Vines pregnant with grapes. A solitary figure walking through the rows. Then close up, enormous baskets of grapes, just harvested."

"We don't use baskets."

"Work with me here, Ty. Simplicity, accessibility, tradition. Gnarled hands holding the basket. Then on to the casks, rows and rows of wooden casks, dim light of the caves. The mystery, the romance. A couple of interesting-looking guys in work clothes drawing out the free flow. We'll use red, a lovely spill of red wine out of a cask. Then different workers tasting, testing. Then finally a bottle. Maybe two glasses and a corkscrew beside it.

"From vine to table. A hundred years of excellence. No, from *our* vines to *your* table." Her brow furrowed as she pictured the ad in her mind. "We lead with the hundred years of excellence, then the montage, and below: From our vines to your table. The Giambelli-MacMillan tradition continues."

She turned back to him, looked over his shoulder, then let out a snort. He'd been sketching while she talked, and the result was circles and stick men and a lopsided column she supposed was a bottle of red.

"You said you could draw."

"I didn't say I could draw well."

"Okay, we're in some trouble here. Sketching isn't my strong suit, though compared to you, I'm da Vinci. I work better when I have some visual aides." She blew out a breath, paced. "We'll make do. I'll have the team fax me sketches as we go. We'll coordinate schedules so that we can hold a weekly session either here or at my office in the villa."

She dropped down on the arm of his chair, frowned into space. She was tuned in to her team, and had sensed the undercurrents. It was something she needed to deal with right away. "I need a half hour here. Why don't you head over to Armani, and I'll meet you there."

"Why am I going to Armani?"

"Because you need clothes."

"I have plenty of clothes."

"Honey, your clothes are like your drawing. They meet the basic definition, but they aren't going to win any prizes. I get to outfit you, then you can buy me the proper vintner attire." She gave his shoulder an idle pat, then rose.

He wanted to argue, but didn't want to waste time. The sooner they were finished and driving north, the happier he'd be.

"Where's Armani?"

She stared at him. The man had lived an hour out of San Francisco for years. How could he not know? "See my assistant.

She'll point you in the right direction. I'll be right behind you."

"One suit," Ty warned as he walked to the door. "That's it."

"Mmm." They would see about that, she thought. It might be fun to dress him up a bit. Sort of like molding clay. But before the fun started, she had work. She walked back to her desk and picked up the phone. "Kris, can I see you a minute? Yeah, now. My time's pretty tight."

With a roll of her shoulders, Sophia began gathering files and disks.

She'd worked with Kris for more than four years, and was very aware there had been considerable resentment when the fresh-out-of-college Sophia had taken over as head of the department. They'd come to terms, delicately, but she had no doubt that Kris's nose was now seriously out of joint.

Couldn't be helped, Sophia thought. Had to be dealt with.

There was a brisk knock, and Kris stepped in. "Sophia, I've got a pile of work."

"I know. Five minutes. It's going to be rough shuffling things around between here and Napa for the next several months. I'm in a pinch, Kris."

"Really? You don't look pinched."

"You didn't see me pruning vines at dawn. Look, my grandmother has reasons for what she does and how she does them. I don't always understand them, and I very often don't like them, but it's her company. I just work here."

"Right. Um-hmm."

Sophia stopped packing up, laid her palms on her desk and met Kris's eyes dead-on. "If you think I'm going to enjoy juggling my time between the work I love and mucking around the vineyards, you're crazy. And if you think Tyler is gunning for a position here in these offices, think again."

"Excuse me, but he now *has* a position in these offices."

"And one you believe should be yours. I'm not going to disagree with you, but I'm telling you it's temporary. I need you here. I'm not going to be able to drive down here every day, I'm not going to be able to take all the meetings or delegate every assignment. Essentially, Kris, you've just been promoted. You don't get a new title, but I will do everything I can to see that you get the financial compensation for the extra responsibilities that are about to be dumped on you."

"It's not about the money."

"But money never hurts," Sophia finished. "Ty's position here, and his title, are titular. He doesn't know anything about promotion and marketing, Kris, and isn't particularly interested in either."

"Interested enough to make comments and suggestions this morning."

"Just a minute." She could be patient, Sophia thought, but she would not be pushed. "Do you expect him to sit here like a moron? He's entitled to express an opinion, and it so happens he made very decent suggestions. He's been tossed off the cliff without a parachute, and he's coping. Take a lesson."

Kris set her teeth. She'd been with Giambelli nearly ten years and was sick to death of being passed over for their precious bloodline. "He has a parachute, and so do you. You were born with it. Either one of you screw up, you bounce. That doesn't go for the rest of us."

"I won't go into personal family business

with you. I will say you're a valued member of the Giambelli, and now the Giambelli-MacMillan, organization. I'm sorry if you feel your skills and talents have been over-looked or undervalued. Whatever I can do to correct this, will be done. But these ad-justments must be made, and over the next several months it would pay all of us to make sure we don't screw up. I have to be able to depend on you. If I can't, I need you to let me know so that I can make other arrangements."

"I'll do my job." Kris turned to the door, yanked it open. "And yours."

"Well," Sophia murmured when the door slammed smartly. "That was fun." On a sigh, she picked up her phone again. "P.J., I need a minute."

"No, we want classic. This very subtle chalk stripe to start."

"Fine, great. I'll take it. Let's go."

"Tyler." Sophia pursed her lips and patted his cheek. "Go try it on, like a good boy."

He snagged her wrist. "Mom?"

"Yes, dear?"

"Cut it out."

"If you'd done more than brood for the last thirty minutes on your own, we'd be practically out the door. This one," she said, handing him the rich brown with narrow stripes, "and this." She selected a classic black three-piece.

To cut off any complaints, she wandered away from him to ponder the shirts. "Shawn?" She gestured to one of the associates she knew by sight. "My friend Mr. MacMillan? He's going to need guidance."

"I'll take good care of him, Ms. Giambelli. By the way, your father and his fiancée were in just this morning."

"Really?"

"Yes, shopping for their honeymoon. If you're looking for something special for the wedding, we have a fabulous new evening jacket that would be smashing on you."

"I'm a little pressed for time today," she managed. "I'll come back and see it first chance I get."

"Just let me know. I'll be happy to send some selections to you for approval. I'll just check on Mr. MacMillan."

"Thanks." She picked up a dress shirt blindly, stared hard at the cream-on-cream pattern.

Not wasting a minute, she thought. Shopping for the honeymoon before the divorce is final. Spreading the word far and wide.

Maybe, maybe it was best she'd be out of her usual loop in the city for a while. She wouldn't be running into people chatting about her father's wedding every time she turned around.

Why was she letting it hurt her? And if it did, this much, how much worse was it on her mother?

No point in raging, she told herself, and started through the shirts like a woman panning for gold in a fast stream. No point in sulking.

No point in thinking.

She moved from shirts to ties and had a small mountain of choices when Ty came out of the dressing room.

He looked annoyed, faintly mortified and absolutely gorgeous.

Take the farmer out of the dell, she mused, and just look what you got. Big, broad shoulders, narrow hips and long legs in a classic Italian suit.

"My, my." She angled her head, approving. "You do clean up well, MacMillan. Leave fashion to the Italians and you can't go wrong. Call the tailor, Shawn, and let's get this show on the road."

She walked over with two shirts, the cream-on-cream and a deep brown, held them up to the jacket.

"What's the matter?" Ty asked her.

"Nothing. Both of these will do very well."

He took her wrist again, holding it until she shifted her gaze to his. "What's wrong, Sophie?"

"Nothing," she repeated, troubled that he could see the worry brewing inside her. "Nothing important. You look good," she added, working up a smile. "All sturdy and sexy."

"They're just clothes."

She pressed a hand to her heart, staggered back a step. "MacMillan, if you can think that, we have a long way to go before we get close to middle ground." She plucked up a tie, draped it over the shirt. "Yes, definitely. How do the pants fit?" she began and reached down to check the waistband.

"Do you mind?" Flustered, he batted her hand away.

"If I was going to grope, I'd start lower.

Why don't you put on the black suit? The tailor can fuss with you."

He grumbled for form, but was relieved to escape to the privacy of the dressing room. Nobody was going to fuss with him for another minute or two.

He wasn't attracted to Sophia. Absolutely not. But the woman had been studying him, touching him. He was human, wasn't he? A male human. And he'd had a perfectly natural human male reaction.

Which he was not going to share with some tailor or a skinny clerk named Shawn.

What he would do was calm himself back down, let them measure whatever needed to be measured. He'd buy everything Sophia pushed on him and get the ordeal over with.

He wished he knew what had happened between the time he'd gone into the dressing area the first time and come out again. Whatever it was had put unhappiness into those big, dark eyes of hers. The kind of unhappiness that made him want to give her a shoulder to lean on.

That was a normal reaction, too, he assured himself as he stripped off the chalk-striped and put on the black. He didn't like to see anything or anyone hurting.

Still, under the circumstances he was going to have to stifle any and all normal reactions to her.

He glanced at himself in the mirror, shook his head. Who the hell were either of them going to fool by dressing him up in some snappy three-piece suit? He was a damn farmer, and happy to be one.

Then he made the mistake of looking at the tag. He'd never realized a series of numbers could actually stop the heart.

He was still in shock, and no longer remotely aroused, when Shawn came chirpily into the dressing room with the tailor in tow.

"Consider it an investment," Sophia advised as she drove out of the city and north. "And darling, you did look fabulous."

"Shut up. I'm not talking to you."

God, he was cute, she thought. Who knew? "Didn't I buy everything you told me to buy? Even that ugly flannel shirt?"

"Yeah, and what did it cost you? Shirts, some trousers, a hat and boots. Under five hundred bucks. My bill came to nearly twenty times that. I can't believe I got hosed for ten thousand dollars."

"You'll look every inch the successful executive. You know, if I met you when you were wearing that black suit, I'd want you."

"Is that so?" He tried to stretch out his legs in the little car, and failed. "I wasn't wearing it this morning and you wanted me."

"No. I had a momentary lust surge. Entirely different. But there's something about a man in a well-cut three-piece suit that does it for me. What does it for you?"

"Naked women. I'm a simple man."

She laughed and, pleased to be on the open road, punched the gas. "No, you're not. I thought you were, but you're not. You did well in the office today. You held your own."

"Words and pictures." He shrugged. "What's the big deal?"

"Oh now, don't spoil it. Ty, I didn't say anything before we went in because I didn't want your impressions to be colored with my opinions, or my experience, but I think I should give you a basic personality rundown of the people you'll work most closely with on my end."

"The guy goes along. He's got a good brain for what he does and likes the work. Probably single so he doesn't have someone pushing him in the ambition department. And he likes working around attractive women."

"Close enough." Impressed, she glanced over at him. "And a good thumbnail for someone who claims not to like people."

"Not liking them much doesn't mean I can't read them. Perky P.J. now . . ." He trailed off as she glanced his way and laughed. "What?" he said.

"Perky P.J. That's perfect."

"Yeah, well, she's got a lot of energy. You intimidate her, but she tries not to let it show. She wants to be you when she grows up but she's young enough to change her mind about that."

"She's easy to work with. She'll take whatever you toss at her and make it shine. She's good at finding fresh angles, and she's learned not to be afraid to squash an idea one of us lobs that doesn't hit the mark with her. If you run into snags that I'm not around to untangle, you should go to her."

"Because the redhead already hates my guts," Ty finished. "And doesn't think much of yours, either. She doesn't want to be you when she grows up. She wants to be you now, and she wouldn't mind if you had a sudden, bloody accident that took you out so she could step into your shoes and run the show."

"You did get a lot out of your first day in school. Kris is good, really good with concepts, with campaigns and, when it's something she believes in, with details. She's not a good manager because she rubs people wrong and tends to be high-handed with other members of the staff. And you're right, at the moment she hates you just because you exist in what she considers her space. It's not personal."

"Yeah, it is. It's always personal. It doesn't worry me, but if I were you, I'd watch my back. She'd like to leave her heel marks all over your ass."

"She's tried, and she's failed." Idly, Sophia tapped her fingernails on the steering wheel. "I'm a great deal tougher than people think I am."

"I got that already."

Ty settled back as best he could. They'd see how tough she was after a few weeks in the field.

It was going to be a long, chilly winter.

CHAPTER SIX

Pilar was nearly asleep, finally, when the phone rang at two A.M. She shot up in bed, snatching at the phone as her heart slammed into her throat.

An accident? Death? Tragedy?

"Hello. Yes?"

"You ignorant bitch. Do you think you can scare me off?"

"What?" Her hand trembled as she raked it through her hair.

"I'm not going to tolerate you or your pitiful attempts at harassment."

"Who is this?" She groped for the light, then blinked in the sudden flash.

"You know damn well who it is. You got a fucking nerve calling me, spouting off your filth. Shut up, Tony. I'll say what I have to say."

"Rene?" Recognizing her husband's placating voice in the background, Pilar struggled to clear her head, to think over the wild drumming of her heart. "What is this? What's the matter?"

"Just cut the goddamn innocent act. It might work with Tony, but it doesn't with me. I know what you are. You're the whore, sweetheart, not me. You're the fucking liar, the fucking hypocrite. If you ever call here again—"

"I didn't call." Fighting for calm, Pilar dragged the covers up to her chin. "I don't know what you're talking about."

"Either you or your bitch of a daughter, and it's all the same to me. Get this straight. You're out of the picture, and you have been for years. You're a frigid, dried-up excuse for a woman. Fifty-year-old virgin. Tony and I have already seen the lawyers, and we're making legal what everyone's known for years. There isn't a man out there who wants you. Unless it's for your mother's money."

"Rene, Rene. Stop. Stop now. Pilar?"

Pilar heard Tony's voice through the rush of blood in her head. "Why are you doing this?"

"I'm sorry. Someone called here, said perfectly vile things to Rene. She's very upset." He had to shout over the shrieks. "Of course, I told her you'd never do such a thing, but she . . . she's upset," he repeated, sounding frazzled. "I have to go. I'll call you tomorrow."

"She's upset," Pilar whispered, and began to rock as the dial tone buzzed in her ear. "Of course she has to be soothed. What about me? What about me?"

She hung up the phone, tossed back the covers before she gave in to her first instinct and curled into a defensive ball under them.

She was trembling as she yanked on a robe, as she dug deep into her lingerie drawer for her secret emergency pack of cigarettes. Stuffing them in a pocket, she pushed through the French doors and rushed out into the night.

She needed air. She needed a cigarette. She needed, Pilar thought as she ran across her terrace and down the stone steps, peace.

Wasn't it enough that the only man she'd loved, the only man she'd ever given herself to hadn't cherished her? Hadn't respected her enough to keep his vows? Did she have to be plagued now by her latest replacement? Awakened in the middle of the night and screamed at, sworn at?

She strode away from the house, through the gardens, keeping to the shadows so that if anyone in the house was awake they wouldn't see her through the windows.

Pretenses, she thought, furious to find her cheeks were wet. We must maintain pretenses at all cost. Wouldn't do to have one of the servants see Ms. Giambelli smoking in the shrubbery in the middle of the night. Wouldn't do for anyone to see Ms. Giambelli doing her best to stave off a nervous breakdown with tobacco.

A dozen people might have called Rene, she thought bitterly. And she very likely deserved the abuse tossed out at her by each and every one. From the tone of Tony's voice, Pilar knew he had a pretty good idea just who'd made the call. Easier, she supposed bitterly, to let Rene believe it was the discarded wife rather than a more current lover.

Easier to let the long-suffering Pilar take the slaps and the insults.

"I'm not fifty," she muttered, fighting with her lighter. "Or a goddamn virgin."

"Me neither."

She whirled, dropping the lighter with a little crash of metal on stone. Temper warred with humiliation as David Cutter stepped from shadow to moonlight.

"I'm sorry I startled you." He bent down for her lighter. "But I thought I should let you know I was here before you continued your conversation."

He flicked the lighter on, studying her tear-stained cheeks and damp lashes in the flare. Her hands were shaking, so he steadied them.

"I couldn't sleep," he continued. "New place, new bed. Took a little walk. Want me to keep on walking?"

It was breeding, she supposed, that prevented her from a fast, undignified retreat. "I don't smoke. Officially."

"Neither do I." Still he took a deep, appreciative sniff of the smoke-stung air. "Quit. It's killing me."

"I've never smoked officially. So I, occasionally, sneak outside and sin."

"Your secret's safe with me. I'm very discreet. Sometimes venting to a stranger works wonders." When she only shook her head, he tucked his thumbs into the pockets of his jeans. "Well, it's a nice night after the rain. Want to walk?"

She wanted to run back inside, bury herself under the covers until this new mortification passed. She had plenty of reason to know embarrassments faded quicker when you stood up and moved on.

So she walked with him.

"Are you and your family settling in?" she asked as they fell into step together.

"We're fine. Period of adjustment. My son got into some trouble in New York. Kid stuff, but there was a pattern to it. I wanted to change the canvas."

"I hope they'll be happy here."

"So do I." He dug a handkerchief out of his jeans, silently passed it to her. "I'm looking forward to getting a good look at the vineyards tomorrow. They're spectacular now, with a bit of moon and a hint of frost."

"You're good at this," she murmured. "At pretending you didn't come across an hysterical woman in the middle of the night."

"You didn't look hysterical. You looked

sad, and angry." And beautiful, he thought. White robe, black night. Like a stylized photograph.

"I had an upsetting phone call."

"Is someone hurt?"

"No one but me, and that's my own fault." She stopped, stooped to crush the cigarette and bury it under the mulch on the side of the path. Then she turned, took a long look at him.

It was a good face, she decided. A strong chin, clear eyes. Blue eyes, she remembered. Deep blue that looked nearly black in the night. The faintest smile on his lips now told her he knew she was examining, considering. And was patient and confident enough to let her.

And she remembered the way he'd been grinning when he'd had his arms around his children. A man who loved his children, understood them enough to point out their interests to strangers as he had to her mother, inspired Pilar's trust.

In any case, it was difficult to maintain pretenses when you were standing in your robe with that man in the middle of the night.

"Make up your mind?" he asked her.

"I suppose. In any case, you're all but living with the family, so you'll hear things. My husband and I have been separated for a number of years. He informed me recently, very recently, that we are getting divorced. His bride-to-be is very young. Beautiful, sharp-edged. And . . . very young," she said again with a half-laugh. "It's ridiculous, I suppose, how much that part bothers me. In any case, it's an awkward and difficult situation."

"It'll be more awkward and difficult for him if he ever takes a good look at what he let go."

It took her a moment to adjust to the compliment. "That's very kind of you."

"No, it's not. You're beautiful, elegant and interesting."

And not used to hearing it, he realized as she simply stared at him. That, too, was interesting. "That's a lot for a man to let go. Divorce is tough," he added. "A kind of death, especially if you took it seriously to begin with. Even when all you've got left of it is the illusion, it's a hell of a shock to watch it shatter."

"Yes." She felt comforted. "Yes, it is. I've just been informed that the lawyers will legalize the end of my marriage very shortly. So I suppose I'd better start picking up the pieces."

"Maybe you should just sweep a few of them out of the way." He touched her shoulder, leaving his fingers there, lightly, when he felt her tense and shift slightly away. "It's the middle of the night. Some of the daylight rules don't apply at three in the morning, so I'm going to tell you straight out. I'm very attracted to you."

She felt a little clutch in her belly. Whether it was pleasure or anxiety, she hadn't a clue. "That's very flattering."

"It's not flattery, it's fact. Flattery's what you get from a guy at a cocktail party who's thinking about making a move on you. I ought to know."

He grinned at her now, wide and easy, the way he'd been grinning when she'd first seen him. The clutch came again, harder and deeper this time. She realized, stupefied, that it was pure, animal attraction.

"I've scooped out plenty of flattery along the way. Just as I imagine you've deflected plenty. So I'm telling you straight." Now the grin faded, and his eyes, dark in the shadows, went quiet, serious. "The minute you opened the door today, it was like I was hit by a thunderbolt. I haven't felt that in a long time."

"David." She took another step back, then came up short when he reached for her hand.

"I'm not going to put any of those moves on you. But I thought about it." He continued to watch her, steady, intense while her pulse began to sprint. "Which is probably why I couldn't sleep."

"We barely know each other. And I'm . . ." *A fifty-year-old virgin.* No, she thought, she damn well wasn't. But close. Close enough.

"True enough. I didn't intend to bring this up quite so soon, but it seemed the moment. A beautiful woman in a white robe, a sprinkle of moonlight in a garden. You can't ask a man to resist everything. Besides, it gives you something to think about."

"Yes, it certainly does. I should go."

"Will you have dinner with me?" He brought her hand to his lips—it seemed like the moment for that, too. Enjoyed the light tremor of it, the subtle scent. "Soon?"

"I don't know." She tugged her hand from

his and felt like a foolish and fumbling young girl. "I . . . good night."

She rushed back down the path and was breathless by the time she reached the steps. Her stomach was fluttering, her heart skipping in her chest. They were sensations she hadn't experienced in so long, it was almost embarrassing.

But she no longer felt angry. And no longer felt sad.

It was just midnight in New York when Jeremy DeMorney took the call. He considered the person on the other end of the phone no more than a tool. One to be wielded as necessary.

"I'm ready. Ready to move to the next stage."

"Well." Smiling, Jerry poured himself a snifter of brandy. "It's taken you a considerable amount of time to make up your mind."

"I have a lot to lose."

"And more to gain. Giambelli's using you, and they'll toss you out without a flinch if it suits their purposes. You know it, I know it."

"My position is still secure. The reorganization hasn't changed that."

"For the moment. You'd hardly be calling me if you weren't concerned."

"I'm tired of it, that's all. I'm tired of not being appreciated for my efforts. I don't care to be watched over and evaluated by strangers."

"Naturally. Sophia Giambelli and Tyler MacMillan are being groomed to step into the traditional shoes, whether they earn it or not, they'll wear them. Now there's David Cutter. A smart individual. La Coeur is sorry to lose him. He'll be taking a serious look at all areas of the company. A serious look that could very well turn up certain . . . discrepancies."

"I've been careful."

"No one's ever careful enough. What do you intend to bring to the table now? It's going to have to be more than the ante we discussed previously."

"The centennial. If there's trouble during the merger, bleeding over to the next, banner year, it will eat at the foundation of the company. There are things I can do."

"Poisoning an old man, for instance?"

"That was an accident."

The panic, the hint of whine in the tone made Jerry smile. It was all so perfect. "Is that what you call it?"

"It was your idea. You said it would only make him ill."

"Oh, I have a lot of ideas." Idly, Jerry examined his nails. La Coeur paid him for his ideas—his less radical ideas—as much as they did because his name was DeMorney. "You implemented it, friend. And bungled it."

"How was I to know he had a weak heart?"

"As I said, no one's ever careful enough. If you were going to kill someone, you should have gone for the old woman herself. With her gone, they couldn't plug the holes in the dike as fast as we could drill them."

"I'm not a murderer."

"I beg to differ." You're exactly that, Jerry thought. And because of it you'll do anything, everything, I want now. "I wonder if the Italian police would be interested enough to exhume Baptista's body and run tests if they happened to get an informative and anonymous call. You've killed," Jerry said after a long pause. "You'd better be prepared to do whatever's necessary to back yourself up. If you want my help, and my financial backing to continue, you'll start showing me what you can do for me. You can begin by getting me copies of every-thing. The legal papers, the contracts, the plans for the ad campaign. Every step of it. The vintner's logs, Venice and Napa."

"It'll be risky. It'll take time."

"You'll be paid for the risk. And the time." He was a patient man, a wealthy one, and could afford both. Would invest both, to bury the Giambellis. "Don't contact me again until you have something useful."

"I need money. I can't get what you ask without—"

"Give me something I can use. Then I'll give you payment. COD, friend. That's how it works."

"They're grapevines. Big deal."

"They're going to be a big deal for us. The grapevines," David informed his sulking son, "are what's going to buy your burgers and fries for the foreseeable future."

"Are they going to buy my car?"

David glanced in the rearview mirror. "Don't push your luck, pal."

"Dad, you can't live out here in Nowheresville without wheels."

"The minute you stop breathing, I'll check out the nearest used-car lot."

Three months before—hell, David thought—three weeks before that comment would have resulted in his son's frozen silence or a snide remark. The fact that Theo's response was to clutch his throat, bug out his eyes and collapse gasping on the backseat warmed his father's heart.

"I knew we should've taken those CPR classes," David said absently as he turned into MacMillan Wineries.

"It's okay. He goes, it's more fries for us."

Maddy didn't mind being out early. She didn't mind driving around the hills and valleys. What she did mind was having nothing to do. Her greatest hope at the moment was that her father would break down and buy Theo a car. Then she could nag her brother to drive her somewhere. Anywhere.

"Pretty place." David stopped the van, got out to look over the fields and the workers steadily pruning vines in the frosty morning. "And this, all this, my children," he continued, sliding an arm around each of them when they joined him, "will never be yours."

"Maybe one of them has a babe for a daughter. We'll get married, then you'll work for me."

David shuddered. "You're scaring me, Theo. Let's go check it out."

Ty spotted the trio heading down through the rows, and swore under his breath. Tourists, he thought, hoping for a tour and a friendly guide. He didn't have time to be friendly. And he didn't want outsiders in his fields.

He started to cut over to head them off, stopped and studied Sophia. This, he decided, was her turf. Let her deal with people, and he'd deal with the vines.

He crossed to her, noted grudgingly she was doing the job, and doing it well. "We got some tourists heading down," he told her. "Why don't you take a break here and steer them to the winery, the tasting room? Someone should be around to give them the standard tour."

Sophia straightened, turned to scope out the newcomers. The father and son were pretty much out of L.L. Bean, she concluded, while the daughter had taken a left turn into Goth-land.

"Sure, I'll take them." And get a nice hot cup of coffee for the trouble. "But a quick look at the fields, and a brief, informative explanation of the pruning phase, would lead nicely into the winery and make Dad more inclined to pop for a couple bottles."

"I don't want civilians tromping through my fields."

"Don't be so territorial and cranky." She put on a bright smile, deliberately grabbed Ty's hand and dragged him toward the family.

"Good morning! Welcome to MacMillan Vineyards. I'm Sophia, and Tyler and I would be happy to answer any questions you might have. It's winter pruning time at the moment. An essential, even crucial part of the winemaking process. Are you touring the valley?"

"In a manner of speaking." She had her grandmother's eyes, David thought. The shape and the depth of them. Pilar's were softer, lighter, hinted of gold. "Actually, I was hoping to meet both of you. I'm David

Cutter. These are my children. Theo and Maddy."

"Oh." Sophia recovered quickly, taking David's offered hand even while her mind leaped forward. Checking us out, she thought. Well, that would work both ways.

Thus far, her research had only unearthed that David Cutter was a divorced, single parent of two who'd climbed the corporate ladder at La Coeur with a steady, competent hand over two decades.

She'd determine more in a face-to-face. "Well, welcome again. All of you. Would you like to come into the winery or the house?"

"I'd like to take a look at the fields. Been a while since I've seen a pruning in process." Gauging the mood, caution and resentment, David turned to Tyler. "You've got a beautiful vineyard, Mr. MacMillan. And a superior product from them."

"You got that right. I've got work to do."

"You'll have to excuse Tyler." Setting her teeth, Sophia wrapped her arm through his like a rope to hold him in place. "He has a very narrow focus, and right now all he sees are the vines. Added to that, he has no discernible social skills. Do you, MacMillan?"

"Vines don't need chitchat."

"All growing things do better with audio stimulation." Maddy didn't flinch at Ty's annoyed expression. "Why do you prune in winter?" she demanded. "Instead of in the fall or early spring?"

"We prune during the dormant season."

"Why?"

"Maddy," David began.

"It's okay." Ty took a closer look at her. She might dress like an apprentice vampire, he thought, but she had an intelligent face. "We wait for the first hard frost that forces the vines into dormancy. Pruning then prepares for the new growth in the spring. Pruning over the winter decreases the yield. What we're after is quality, not quantity. Overbearing vines produce too many inferior grapes."

He glanced back at David. "I guess you don't have a lot of vineyards in Manhattan."

"That's right, and one of the reasons I accepted this offer. I've missed the fields. Twenty years ago, I spent a very cold, wet January in Bordeaux pruning vines for La Coeur. I've done some fieldwork off and on over the years, just to keep a hand in. But nothing like that very long winter."

"Can you show me how to do it?" Maddy asked Tyler.

"Well, I . . ."

"I'll start you off." Taking pity on Tyler, Sophia radiated cheer. "Why don't you and Theo come with me? We'll get a close-up look at how this is done before we go into the winery. It's a fascinating process, really, though this phase appears to be very basic. It requires precision and considerable practice. I'll show you." She herded the kids out of earshot.

"Theo's going to trip over his tongue." David let out a sigh. "She's a beautiful woman. Can't blame him."

"Yeah, she looks good."

The warning tone had David struggling with a grin. He nodded soberly. "And I'm old enough to be her father, so you've got no worries in that direction."

From his viewpoint, Cutter was just the type Sophia usually went for. Older, slicker, classier. Under the rough gear, there was class. Being a farmer didn't mean he couldn't spot it.

But that was beside the point.

"There's nothing between me and Sophia," he said, very definitely.

"Either way. Let's just clear the air here, okay? I'm not here to get in your way, or interfere with your routine. You're the vintner, MacMillan, and I'm not. But I do intend to do my job, and to keep abreast of every step and phase of the vineyards."

"You've got the offices. I've got the fields."

"Not entirely, no. I was hired to coordinate, to oversee, and I was hired because I know the vines. I'm not just a suit, and frankly, I was tired of trying to be one. Mind?"

He plucked the pruners out of Tyler's belt sheath and turned to the near row. Gloveless, he lifted canes, studied and made his cut.

It was quick, efficient. And correct.

"I know the vines," David repeated, holding the tool out to Tyler. "But that doesn't make them mine."

Irritated, Tyler took back the tool, shoved it into its sheath like a sword into a scabbard. "All right, let's clear some more air. I don't like someone looking over my shoulder, and knowing he's going to be giving me grades like I was in high school. I'm here to make wine, not friends. I don't know how they did things at La Coeur, and I don't care. I run this vineyard."

"You did," David said evenly. "Now we run it, whether we like it or not."

"We don't like it," he said shortly and strode away.

Hardheaded, inflexible, territorial, David mused. It was going to be an interesting little battle. He glanced over to where Sophia entertained his children. Theo's throbbing hormones were all but sending out bolts of sex-crazed red light. And that, David thought wearily, was going to be complicated.

He strolled over, watched with approval as his daughter cut through a cane. "Good job. Thanks," he said to Sophia.

"My pleasure. I assume you'll want to meet with me to be briefed on my promotional campaign plans. I'm setting up an office at the villa. Would this afternoon work for you? Maybe two o'clock."

Clever girl, he thought. Make the first move, establish turf. What a family. "Sure, that works for me. I'll just get these two out of your hair."

"I want to see the rest," Maddy said.

"There's nothing to do at home anyway. It's boring."

"We haven't finished unpacking."

"Are you in a hurry for that?" Sophia laid a hand on Maddy's shoulder. "If you're not you can leave Theo and Maddy with me. I have to go back to the villa in an hour or so, and I can drop them off. You're in the guest house, right?"

"That's right." He glanced at his watch. He had some time before his meeting. "If they're not in the way."

"Not at all."

"Fine. I'll see you at two. You guys stay out of trouble."

"You'd think we look for it," Maddy muttered under her breath.

"If you don't," Sophia said as David walked away, "you're not having enough fun."

She liked the kids. Maddy's intense questioning was entertaining, and kept her on her toes. And it was sweet to find herself the object of a teenage boy's crush-at-first-sight.

Also, who knew more about a man, how he behaved, how he thought, how he planned, than his children? A morning with

David Cutter's teenagers would be interesting and, she believed, informative.

"Let's go drag Ty away," Sophia suggested, "and make him take us through the winery. I'm not as familiar with MacMillan's operation as I am with Giambelli's." She tucked her tool away. "We'll all learn something."

Pilar paced the chambers of Judge Helen Moore and tried not to fret. Her life, she thought, seemed to be tumbling out of her control. She wasn't at all sure how to grab it back. Worse, she was no longer sure how much of it she wanted to keep.

Steps had to be taken, of that she was sure. She was so sick of feeling used and useless.

Most of all, she needed a friend.

She'd barely seen her mother or her daughter that morning. Purposely. It was cowardly, she supposed, to avoid those closest to her. But she needed time to shore up the damage, to make her decisions, to coat over the ridiculous hurt that still scraped inside her gut.

Instinctively she reached down to toy with

her wedding ring and felt the quick jolt when it wasn't there. She'd have to get used to that naked finger. No, damned if she would. She was going to go out today, this afternoon, and buy some ridiculously expensive, knock-your-eyes-out bauble to go on the third finger of her left hand.

A symbol, she told herself. Of freedom and new beginnings.

Of failure.

On a sigh of defeat, she dropped into a chair just as Helen rushed in.

"Sorry, we ran a little over."

"It's all right. You always look so distinguished and terrifying in your robes."

"If I ever lose this extra fifteen pounds, I'm going to start wearing a bikini under them." She stripped the robe off, hung it up. Rather than a bikini, she wore a quiet brown suit.

Too matronly, Pilar thought. Too boxy. And very Helen.

"I really appreciate your making time for me today. I know how busy you are."

"We've got two hours." Helen flopped into the chair behind her desk, pulled off her shoes and curled her toes. "Want to go out for lunch?"

"Not really. Helen . . . I know you're not a

divorce lawyer, but—Tony's moving to finalize things quickly. I don't know what to do."

"I can handle it for you, Pilar. Or I can recommend someone. I know several sleek sharks who'd do the job."

"I'd feel a lot more comfortable if you handled it, and if it was kept as simple as possible. And as clean."

"Well, that's disappointing." With a frown, Helen pushed up her glasses. "I'd love to leave Tony bleeding from the ears. I'll need your financial papers," she began, pulling over a yellow legal pad for notes. "Fortunately, I browbeat you into separating your finances from his years ago. But we're going to keep your ass covered. He may very well make demands, monetary ones, real estate and so on. You are *not* going to agree to anything."

She tipped down her glasses to stare at Pilar over the rims with a look that terrified lawyers. "I mean that, Pilar. He gets nothing. *You* are the injured party. He's petitioning for the divorce. He wants to get remarried. He walks out with what he walked in with. I'm not going to allow you to let him profit from this. You got that?"

"It's not a matter of money."

"Not for you. But he lives high, and he's going to want to continue living high. How much have you funneled to him over the last decade or so?"

Pilar shifted uncomfortably. "Helen . . ."

"Exactly. Loans that are never repaid. The house in San Francisco, the house in Italy. The furnishings in both."

"We sold—"

"He sold," Helen corrected. "You wouldn't listen to me then, but you will now or you find another lawyer. You never recouped your fair share of the real estate, which your money paid for in the first place. And I know damn well he slid plenty of your jewelry and personal property into his pocket, too. That stops cold."

She pushed up her glasses, sat back. The gesture, the body language changed her from judge to friend. "Pilar, I love you, and that's why I'm going to say this to you. You've let him treat you like a doormat. Hell, you all but stitched 'Welcome' on your tits and invited him to step all over you. And I, and others who love you, hated watching it."

"Maybe I did." She wasn't going to cry now; just absorb the fresh hurt. "I loved him, and part of me thought that if he needed me enough, he'd love me back. Something happened last night, and it's changed things. Changed me, I suppose."

"Tell me."

Rising, Pilar wandered the office and told Helen of the phone call. "When I listened to him making those careless apologies, cutting me off to placate Rene after she'd attacked me, I was disgusted with all of us. And later, after I'd calmed down again, I realized something. I don't love him anymore, Helen. Maybe I haven't for years. That makes me pitiful."

"Not anymore, it doesn't." Helen picked up the phone. "Let's order in. I'll explain what needs to be done. Then, sweetie, we're going to do it. Please." She held out a hand. "Let me help you. Really help."

"Okay." Pilar sighed. "Okay. Will it take more than an hour?"

"Doesn't have to. Carl? Order me two chicken clubs, with side salads, two cappuccinos and a big bottle of fizzy water. Thanks." She hung up the phone.

"Perfect." Pilar sat again. "Is there a good, overpriced jeweler near here?"

"As a matter of fact there is. Why?"

"If you've got time before you have to don your robes again, you could help me buy something symbolic and gaudy." She held up her left hand. "Something that'll make Rene crazy when she sees it."

Helen nodded with approval. "Now we're talking."

CHAPTER SEVEN

Sunday slid into the week like a balm on a mild, nagging itch. She wouldn't be spending her morning hours covered in wool and flannel and pruning vines. She wouldn't have Ty breathing down her neck just waiting for her to make a mistake.

She could drive into the city, do some power shopping, see people. She could remember what it was like to have a life.

With this in mind, Sophia considered calling one of her friends to set up a few hours of socializing. Then she decided she'd rather spend that frivolous time with her mother.

Next free day, she decided, she'd make plans with friends. She'd spend a weekend in San Francisco, have a dinner party at her apartment, go to a club. Now she was going to nag her mother into taking a girl day.

Sophia knocked briskly on her mother's bedroom door, then pushed it open without waiting for an answer. She'd never had to wait for her mother.

The bed was already made, the curtains open to the wavering sunlight. As Sophia stepped inside, Maria walked in from the adjoining bath.

"Mama?"

"Oh, long up and about. I think she's in the greenhouse."

"I'll find her." Sophia stepped back, hesitated. "Maria, I've barely seen her all week. Is she all right?"

Maria's lips tightened as she fussed unnecessarily with the yellow roses on Pilar's dresser. "She doesn't sleep well. I can tell. Eats like a bird, and then only if you insist. I scolded her just yesterday, and she says it's holiday stress. What stress?" Maria threw up her hands. "Your mama, she loves Christmas. It's that man who troubles her. I won't speak ill of your father, but if he makes my baby sick, he'll answer to me."

"Get in line," Sophia murmured. "We'll

look after her, Maria. I'll hunt her down now."

"See that she eats!"

Christmas, Sophia thought as she jogged downstairs. It was the perfect excuse. She'd ask her mother to give her a hand with some last-minute Christmas shopping.

She scanned the house as she hurried through. Her mother's poinsettias, red and white stars in dozens of silver pots, were mixed with miniature hollies in lush arrangements throughout the foyer. Fresh greenery twined with tiny white lights and glossy red ribbon swagged doorways.

The three Giambelli angels were displayed on the long refectory table in the family parlor. Tereza, Pilar and Sophia, she thought, the carved faces reflecting each of them at the age of twelve.

How alike they looked. It was always a little jolt, a little tug of amused pleasure to see them. The continuity, the undeniable blood tie of those three generations. She'd been thrilled when she was given her angel all those years ago. Thrilled to see her own features on the graceful, winged body. And, she realized as she trailed a fingertip over the trio, she was still.

One day it would fall to her to commission an angel for a child of her own. What an odd thought, she mused. Not unpleasant, but certainly odd. The next generation, when the time came, was hers to begin.

Measured by those who'd come before, she was falling a bit behind on that particular family duty. Then again, it wasn't something she could pencil in on her monthly calendar. Fall in love. Get married. Conceive child.

Nope, such things didn't schedule neatly into a life. She imagined she'd enjoy those things with the right man at the right time. But it was so easy, too easy, to make a mistake. And love, marriage, children couldn't be casually crossed off the slate like an inconvenient dentist appointment.

Unless you were Anthony Avano, she corrected, annoying herself with the automatic snap of resentment that accompanied the thought. In that area she had no intention of following in her father's footsteps. When she made the choice, and the promises that went with it, she would keep them.

So for now, three angels would have to be enough.

She turned to study the room. Candles in

spears and chunks of silver and gold, more greenery artfully arranged. The grand tree, one of four that would traditionally stand in the villa, dripping with crystal garland, laden with precious ornaments brought over from Italy, stood regally by the windows. Presents were already tucked under it, and the house smelled of pine and candle wax.

Time had gotten away from her, she thought guiltily. A great deal of it. Her mother, grandmother and the staff had worked like trojans to dress the house for the holidays while she'd buried herself in work.

She should have taken the time, *made* the time to help. Didn't put it on your appointment calendar, did you, Sophia? she thought with a wince. The annual Christmas party was nearly on them, and she'd done nothing to help with the planning or preparations.

She'd amend that immediately.

She went out the side door, instantly regretting she hadn't stopped for a jacket, as the wind had a bite. As a result she ran down the winding stone path, cut left and sprinted to the greenhouse.

The warm, moist heat felt so inviting. "Mama?"

"Down here. Sophie, wait until you see my paperwhites. They're spectacular. I think I'll take them and the amaryllis into the parlor. Very festive."

Pilar stopped, looked up. "Where's your jacket?"

"Forgot." Sophia leaned over and kissed her mother's cheek, then took a good, long look.

Her mother's ancient sweater was pushed up at the elbows and bagged at the hips. Her hair was tied back at the nape of her neck. "You're losing weight."

"Oh, I am not." Pilar waved that away with hands covered in stained gardening gloves. "You've been talking to Maria. If I don't gorge myself three times a day she's convinced I'm going to waste away. As it is, I stole two sugar cookies on the way out here and expect them to pop out on my hips any moment."

"That should hold you till lunch. Which I'll buy. I'm so behind on my shopping. Help."

"Sophia." With a shake of her head, Pilar shifted her long trough of narcissi and began to fuss with the tulips she was forcing.

They would bloom, she thought, and bring color to the dreary days of winter. "You started your holiday shopping in June and finished it in October. Just as you always do to make the rest of us hate you."

"Okay, caught me." Sophia boosted herself up on the work counter. "Still, I'm dying to go into the city and play for a few hours. It's been a brutal week. Let's run away for the day."

"I was just there a couple of days ago." Frowning, Pilar set the tulips aside. "Sophie, is this new order of things your grandmother's set up too much for you? You're up at dawn every day, and then you spend hours in your office here. I know you're not seeing any of your friends."

"I thrive on pressure. Still, I could use an assistant, and I believe you're supposed to fit that bill."

"*Cara,* we both know I'd be useless to you."

"No, I don't know that. Okay, we move to Plan B. I'm putting you to work. You've done all the decorating in the house and it looks beautiful, by the way. I'm sorry I didn't help."

"You've been busy."

"I shouldn't have been too busy. But now it's office time, and that'll segue into party-planning time. You need to bring me up to date on that, which is part of an assistant's duty. Now, which flowers do you want to take in? I'll help you with them, then we start the clock."

The girl, Pilar thought, made the head spin. "Sophie, really."

"Yes, really. You're the trainee. I'm the boss." She scooted off the counter, rubbed her hands together. "I get to make up for all the years you bossed me around. Especially between the ages of twelve and fifteen."

"No, not the hormone years. You couldn't be so cruel."

"Bet me. You asked if this new system was too much for me. It's not. But it's damn close. That's a fact. I'm not used to doing all my own filing and phone tags and typing. Since I'm not about to admit to *Nonna,* or to MacMillan, that I'm feeling the least bit squeezed, you could help me out."

Pilar blew out a breath, tugged off her gloves. "You're doing this to keep me busy, just as Maria hounds me to eat."

"Partially," Sophia admitted. "But that

doesn't change the fact that I spend time every day doing basic office work. If I could pass that over, I might actually begin to date again in this decade. I miss men."

"All right, but don't blame me if you can't find anything in your files." Pilar pulled the thin band out of her hair, scooped her fingers through it. "I haven't done basic office work since I was sixteen, and then I was so miserable at it, Mama fired me."

She turned, started to laugh, then noticed Sophia was gawking at her hand.

Embarrassed, Pilar nearly stuck her hand, and the five-carat square-cut ruby on her finger, behind her back. "It's a little much, isn't it?"

"I don't know. I think I've been struck blind by the glare." Sophia took her mother's hand, examined the stone and the stunning channel-set diamonds around the square. "Wow. *Magnifico.*"

"I wanted something. I should have told you. You've been so busy. . . . Damn it." Pilar tried to explain. "I've used your schedule to avoid talking to you. I'm sorry."

"You don't have to apologize to me for buying a ring, Mama. Except I believe that one might be considered a small monument."

"I was angry. You should never do anything when you're angry." To give herself something to do, Pilar picked up her gardening tools, began to replace them. "Baby, Helen is handling the divorce for me. I should've—"

"Good. She won't let you get scalped. Don't look at me like that, Mama. You've been careful, all my life you've been careful never to speak against my father. But I'm not blind, and I'm not stupid."

"No." Overcome by sadness, Pilar set her little trowel aside. "No, you've never been either." And had seen, had understood so much more than a child should.

"If you let him, he'd take your money and anything else that wasn't nailed down. He wouldn't be able to help himself. I feel better knowing Aunt Helen's looking out for your interests. Now let's get these flowers into the house."

"Sophie." Pilar laid a hand on her daughter's arm as Sophia picked up a pot of amaryllis. "I'm so sorry this hurts you."

"You've never hurt me. He always has. I don't suppose he can help that, either." She picked up a second pot. "Rene's going to swallow her tongue when she gets a load of that rock."

"I know. That was the idea."

For over fifty years, Giambelli, California had held lavish Christmas parties for family, friends, employees and associates. As the company had grown, so had the guest list.

Following the tradition set by the Italian branch of the company, the parties were held simultaneously on the last Saturday before Christmas. The house was open to family and friends, and the winery to employees. Associates, depending on their position on the feeding chain, were placed in the proper location.

Invitations to the main house were prized like gold and often used as a symbol of status or success. Still, the Giambellis didn't stint on the festivities in the winery. Food was elegant and plentiful, wine flowed freely, and both the decorations and the entertainment were top-notch.

Every member of the family was expected to make an appearance at both venues.

Having done so since her fifteenth year,

Sophia was well aware that the winery party was a great deal more entertaining. And less full of irritating relations.

She could hear one of her cousin Gina's progeny shrieking at the other end of the hall. Her hopes that Don and his herd would remain in Italy had been dashed the evening before when they'd arrived.

Still even their presence wouldn't be as annoying as that of her father and Rene. Her mother had stuck firm on their being invited, going head to head with *La Signora* on the issue. The consolation was their invitation had been to the winery.

That, she thought as she fastened on her diamond teardrop earrings, would stick sharply in Rene's craw.

She stepped back, studied the results in her cheval glass. The shimmering silver gown with its short, fitted jacket worked well. The scooped neck was a nice frame for the diamond necklace. Both it and the earrings had been her great-grandmother's.

She turned, checked the line of her skirt, then called out an invitation at the knock on her door.

"Look at you!" Helen came in, pretty and plump in frosty pink. "You sparkle all over."

"It's great, isn't it?" Sophia took another turn, for the fun of it. "I bought it in New York, thinking of New Year's, but I had to press it into duty tonight. Not too much with the diamonds?"

"Diamonds are never too much. Honey." She shut the door. "I wanted a minute. I hate to bring this up now, right before you have to socialize with hundreds of people, but Pilar told me Tony and Rene will be here."

"What is it?"

"The divorce is final. Yesterday. It was really no more than a formality after all these years. Since Tony was in a hurry and didn't complicate matters with financial negotiations, it was really just a matter of filing the papers."

"I see." Sophia picked up her evening bag, opened and closed the catch. "Have you told Mama?"

"Yes. Just now. She's fine. Or she's holding up. I know it's important to her you do the same."

"Don't worry about me, Aunt Helen." She crossed the room, took Helen's hands. "You're a brick. I don't know what she'd have done without you."

"She needs to move on."

"I know."

"And so do you." She squeezed Sophia's hands. "Don't let Rene have the satisfaction of seeing this hurts you, on any level."

"I won't."

"Good. Now I've got to go down and run herd on my husband. If I leave James alone down there this early, he'll sneak canapés and ruin the caterer's presentation." She opened the door, glanced back. "Tony didn't do many admirable things in his life. You're one of them."

"Thanks." Alone, Sophia let out a long breath. Then she straightened her shoulders, marched back to her mirror. Opening her bag she took out her lipstick. And painted her lips bloody-murder red.

David sipped a full-bodied Merlot, mingled with the crowd packed into the towering stone walls of the winery, tried to tune out the hot licks from the band that was currently thrilling his son, and scanned the area for Pilar.

He knew the Giambellis would put in an appearance. He'd been well schooled on

the pomp and protocol for the holiday festivities. He'd be expected to split his time
between parties, which—though it hadn't
been put precisely that way—was both a
privilege and a duty.

He was learning fast that nearly every assignment in this organization came under
the heading of both.

He could find no complaint with it. He'd
been given a challenge, which he needed.
He was being well compensated financially,
which he appreciated. And he was associated with a company he respected. And
that he valued.

Everything he'd seen in the past weeks
had confirmed that Giambelli-MacMillan
was a tight, family-oriented ship, run with
efficiency and little sentiment. It wasn't
cold, but it was calculated.

Product was king and queen here. Money
was respected and expected, but it was not
the goal. Wine was. He'd found the opposite true in his later years with La Coeur.

Now, seeing his son actually enjoying
himself, watching his daughter interrogate
some poor winemaker over some point of
procedure, he was content.

The move had been exactly what all of them had needed.

"David. Good to see you."

He turned, surprise registering briefly as he looked into Jeremy DeMorney's smiling face.

"Jerry, I didn't know you'd be here."

"I try never to miss an annual Giambelli bash and always hit the winery before the villa. Very democratic of *La Signora* to invite reps from the competition."

"She's quite a lady."

"One of a kind. How are you taking to working for her?"

"It's early days yet. But the move's gone well. I'm glad to get the kids out of the city. How are things back in New York?"

"We're managing to grope along without you." The little sting in the statement wasn't softened by the smirk. "Sorry, we're still a little sore. Hated losing you, David."

"Nothing lasts forever. Anyone else here from La Coeur?"

"Duberry flew in from France. He's known the old lady for a hundred years. Pearson's representing the local group. A few top levels from other labels. Gives us all a chance to drink her wine and spy on each other. Got any gossip for me?"

"Like I said, it's early days yet." He spoke casually, but he'd become wary. Jerry's policy of gossip and corporate backstabbing had been one of the reasons it had been so easy to leave La Coeur. "Great party though. Excuse me, there's somebody I've been waiting for."

Maybe all my life, David thought as he left Jerry without a backward glance and worked through the crowd to Pilar.

She wore blue. Deep blue velvet with a long rope of pearls. She looked warm and regal, and he would have said utterly confident if he hadn't noticed the quick flicker of panic in her eyes.

Then she shifted her head, just a little, and focused on him. And God help him, she blushed. Or at least more color came into her face. The idea that he'd put it there drove him crazy.

"I've been watching for you." He took her hand before she could do anything about it. "Like a kid at a school dance. I know you have to mingle, but I want a minute first."

It was like being swept away by a single warm wave. "David—"

"You can't mingle without wine. It won't do." He tugged her forward. "We'll talk about business, about the weather. I'll only tell you you look beautiful five or six dozen times. Here." He plucked a flute of champagne from a tray. "I don't see how you can drink anything else looking the way you do."

That same flutter was back in her stomach. "I can't keep up with you."

"I can't keep up with myself. I'm making you nervous." He touched his glass lightly to hers. "I'd say I was sorry for that, but I'd be lying. It's best to start out a relationship with honesty, don't you think?"

"No. Yes. Stop." She tried to laugh. He looked like some sort of sophisticated knight in his formal black with his rich blond hair glinting in the shimmer of light. A foolish thought, she told herself, for a middle-aged woman to have. "Are your children here?"

"Yeah. They whined about being dragged here, and now they're having the time of their lives. You're beautiful. I did mention I was going to tell you that, didn't I?"

She nearly giggled before she reminded herself she was forty-eight, not eighteen, and supposed to know better. "Yes, I believe you did."

"I don't suppose we could find a dark corner and neck."

"No. That's a definite."

"Then you'll just have to dance with me, and give me a chance to change your mind."

It staggered her that she thought he could change it. That she wanted him to. Inappropriate, she told herself firmly. Ridiculous. She was years older than he.

God, what was she supposed to do? Say? Feel?

"There are a thousand thoughts going through your head," he murmured. "I wish you'd tell me all of them."

"Jesus." She pressed a hand to her belly where a soft, gooey ball slid in among the flutters. "You're awfully good at this."

"I'm glad you think so because I start feeling clumsy every time I see you."

"Fooled me." She drew in a breath, steadied herself. "David, you're very attractive—"

"You think so?" He touched her hair, couldn't help himself. He loved the way it curved against her cheek. "Could you be more specific?"

"And very charming," she added, struggling to keep her voice firm. "I'm very flattered, but I don't know you. And besides . . ." She trailed off, her smile freezing. "Hello, Tony. Rene."

"Pilar. You look lovely." Tony leaned over to kiss her cheek.

"Thank you. David Cutter, Tony Avano and Rene Foxx."

"Rene Foxx Avano," Rene corrected with a purr. She lifted her hand, wiggled her fingers to send the diamond circlet wedding ring flashing. "As of today."

It wasn't a stab in the heart, Pilar realized, as she'd thought it would be. But more of a burn, a quick shock that annoyed as much as it hurt. "Congratulations. I'm sure you'll be very happy together."

"Oh, we already are." Rene slid her arm through Tony's. "We're flying out to Bimini right after Christmas. It'll be lovely to be out of this cold and rain. You really should take time for a little vacation yourself, Pilar. You're looking pale."

"Strange. I was thinking how vital she looks tonight." Gauging the ground, David lifted Pilar's hand, kissed her fingers. "Delicious, in fact. I'm glad I had a chance to meet you, Tony, before you left the country."

Smoothly, David slid an arm around Pilar's waist. "I've had considerable trouble reaching you the last few days." He gave Rene a glance, just a few degrees short of polite. "Now I see why. Let my office know your travel plans, won't you? We've business to discuss."

"My people know my plans."

"Apparently mine don't. You'll excuse us, won't you? We need to make the rounds before heading up to the villa."

"That was unkind," Pilar whispered.

"So what?"

Gone was the flirtatious charm. In its place was power of the cold and ruthless sort. It wasn't, she thought, any less appealing on him.

"Over and above the fact that I didn't like him on principle, I'm COO and should have been informed if one of the VPs was going out of the country. He's been dodging me for days, avoiding my calls. I don't care for it."

"He's just not used to having to report to you, to anyone."

"He'll have to adjust." Over her head, David spotted Tyler. "So will others. Why don't you help clear the way a little and introduce me to some of the people who are wondering what the hell I'm doing here?"

Ty was trying to be invisible. He hated big parties. There were too many people to talk to, and too few who had anything to say. He'd already calculated his plan. One hour in the winery, one hour in the main house. Then he could slide away, go home, catch a little ESPN and go to bed.

As far as he was concerned, the music was too loud, the winery too crowded and the food too rich. Not that he minded looking at people, especially when they were all slicked up and polished and trying to look better than the people they were talking to.

It was kind of like watching a play, and as long as he could stay safely in the audience he could manage for a while.

He'd watched the little drama between Pilar and Rene. Tyler was fond enough of Pilar that he'd have sacrificed his corner and gone to her side if David Cutter hadn't already been there. Cutter irritated him on principle, but Tyler had to give him points for quick action. The little hand kiss had been a good move, one that seemed to annoy Rene and Avano.

And whatever he'd said had wiped that idiot smile off Avano's face in a hurry.

Avano was an asshole, Tyler thought, sipping his wine. But with Rene prodding at him, he could be a dangerous one. If Cutter could keep him in line, it was almost worth having him in the mix.

Almost.

"Why are you standing over here all by yourself?"

Tyler looked down, frowned at Maddy. "Because I don't want to be here."

"Why are you? You're an adult. You can do what you want."

"You keep thinking that, little girl, you're doomed to disappointment."

"You just like being irritable."

"No, I just *am* irritable."

She pursed her lips at him, nodded. "Okay. Can I have a sip of your wine?"

"No."

"In Europe, children are taught to appreciate wine."

She said it so grandly, standing there in her layers of black and dead-ugly shoes, Ty wanted to laugh. "So, go to Europe. Around here it's called contributing to the delinquency."

"I've been to Europe, but I don't remember it very well. I'm going to go back. Maybe I'll live in Paris for a while. I was talking to Mr. Delvecchio, the winemaker. He said wine was a miracle, but it's really just a chemical reaction, isn't it?"

"It's both. It's neither."

"It has to be. I was going to do an experiment, and I thought you could help me."

Tyler blinked at her, a pretty, badly dressed girl with an inquiring mind. "What? Why don't you talk to your father?"

"Because you're the vintner. I thought I would get some grapes, put them in a bowl and see what happens. I'd have another bowl, with the same type and weight of grapes, and I'd do stuff to it. The kind of things you do."

"I eat grapes in a bowl," he said, but she'd caught his interest.

"See, one bowl would be left alone, Mr.

Delvecchio's miracle. The other I'd process, using additives and techniques. Pushing the chemical reaction. Then I could see which worked best."

"Even if you use the same type of grapes, you'll have variations between your tests."

"Why?"

"You're talking store-bought this time of year. They may not have come from the same vineyard. Even if they do, you get variations. Soil type, fertility, water penetration. When they were picked. How they were picked. You can't test the grapes on the vine because they're already off the vine. The must in each bowl could be considerably different even if you left them both alone."

"What's must?"

"Juice." Bowl wine, he thought. Interesting. "But if you wanted to try it, you should use wooden bowls. The wood'll give the must some character. Not much, but some."

"A chemical reaction," Maddy said with a grin. "See? It's science, not religion."

"Baby. Wine's that and a whole lot more." Without thinking, he offered her his glass.

She sipped, delicately, her gaze shifting

just in case her father was nearby. Experimentally she let the wine roll around on her tongue before she swallowed. "It's pretty good."

"Pretty good?" With a shake of his head, he took the glass back from her. "That's vintage Pinot Noir. Only a barbarian would call it 'pretty good.'"

She smiled, charmingly now because she knew she had him. "Will you show me the big wine barrels and the machines sometime?"

"Yeah. Sure."

"Mr. Delvecchio said you do the white in stainless steel and the reds in wood. I didn't get a chance to ask him why. Why?"

Didn't he look cute? Sophia thought. Big, grouchy MacMillan deep in what seemed to be a serious conversation with the miniature Morticia. And if things were as they appeared, he was enjoying himself. He even looked good doing it.

The fact that he did made her even more pleased she'd decided against bringing a date. Having a date meant her attention would have to be focused. Being loose gave her much more room to circulate and enjoy whoever's company intrigued her the most.

At the moment, she thought Tyler fit the bill.

It would take her a little while to work her way over to him. After all, she had social obligations to dispense. But she kept him at the corner of her vision as she began to work the crowd.

"Sophia. Stunning as always."

"Jerry. Happy holidays." She leaned in, kissed both of his cheeks. "How's business?"

"We've had a banner year." He slipped an arm around her shoulders, steering her through the groups in the tasting room and toward the bar. "And expect another. A little bird tells me you're planning a brilliant promotion campaign."

"Those little birds chatter entirely too much, don't they?" She beamed at the bartender. "Champagne, please. Another from the flock was singing about you launching a new label. Mid-market, with an American target."

"Someone's going to have to shoot those

birds. I saw the write-up in *Vino* on your Cabernet '84."

"An excellent vintage."

"And the auction went quite well for you. Shame on you, Sophia, for standing me up when you were in New York. You know I'd looked forward to seeing you."

"Couldn't be helped. But I'll cash in my rain check next trip."

"I'm counting on it."

She lifted her wine, sipped.

He was an attractive man, smooth, almost silkily attractive. The faintest sprinkling of silver at the temples to add distinction, the slight dip in the chin to add charm.

Neither of them would mention her father, or the poorly kept secret of Jerry's wife's infidelity. Instead, they would keep it light, mildly flirtatious, friendly.

They understood each other, Sophia thought, very well. The competition between Giambelli and La Coeur was high, and often exhilarating. And Jeremy DeMorney was not above using whatever means came to hand to push his edge.

She admired that.

"I'll even spring for dinner," she told him.

"And the wine. Giambelli-MacMillan wine. We'd want the best, after all."

"Then perhaps some La Coeur brandy, back in my apartment."

"Now, you know how I feel about mixing business with . . . business."

"You're a cruel woman, Sophia."

"You're a dangerous man, Jerry. How're your kids?"

"The children are fine. Their mother has them in Saint Moritz for the holidays."

"You must miss them."

"Of course. I thought I might spend a day or two in the Valley before heading home. Why don't you and I mix pleasure with pleasure?"

"That's tempting, Jerry, but I'm swamped. I don't think I'll come up for air until after the first of the year." She caught a movement out of the corner of her eye, watched her mother slip off toward the ladies' room. With Rene a few feet behind.

"Speaking of swamped, I have something I have to deal with right now. Lovely to see you."

"And you," he replied as she worked her way through the crowd. It would be even lovelier to see her, he thought, when she and the rest of her family were ruined.

Helping bring that about would be mixing business with business, he thought. And pleasure with pleasure.

Rene pushed through the door of the cozy, wood-walled ladies' lounge one step behind Pilar. "Managed to land on your feet, didn't you?" Rene leaned against the door, to discourage anyone from joining them.

"You got what you wanted, Rene." Though her hands wanted to tremble, Pilar opened her evening bag and pulled out her lipstick. She'd intended to steal two private minutes before making her last rounds and heading up to the villa. "I shouldn't be an issue for you anymore."

"Ex-wives are always an issue. I'll tell you this, I won't tolerate you calling me, or Tony, and spewing out your neurotic abuse."

"I didn't call."

"You're a liar. And a coward. Now you're going to hide behind David Cutter." She grabbed Pilar's hand, jerked it up so the ring fired in the lights. "What did you have to do to wheedle this out of him?"

"I don't need a man to buy me jewelry, Rene, or anything else. That's an elemental difference between us."

"No, I'll tell you the difference between us. I go after what I want, in the open. If you think I'm going to let Tony slink away because you've gone whining to your family, you're wrong. You're not going to shove him out, your David Cutter isn't going to shove him out. And if you try . . . just think of all the interesting information he could pass along to your competitors."

"Threatening the family, or the business, isn't going to help secure Tony's position. Or yours."

"We'll see about that. I'm Mrs. Avano now. And Mr. and Mrs. Avano will be joining the family, and the other top-level executives, at the villa tonight. I'm sure our invitation was misdirected."

"You'll only embarrass yourself," Pilar told her.

"I don't embarrass easily. Remember this. Tony has a piece of Giambelli, and I have a piece of him. I'm younger than you, and a hell of a lot younger than your mother. I'll still be here when you're gone."

"Will you?" Deliberately, Pilar turned to

the mirror, slowly, carefully painted her lips. "How long do you think it will take for Tony to cheat on you?"

"He wouldn't dare." Secure in her own power, Rene smiled. "He knows if he does, I'll kill him. I'm not the passive, patient wife. Tony told me what a lousy lay you were. We laugh about it. My advice? If you want to keep Cutter on the string, pass him down to your daughter. She strikes me as someone who knows how to entertain a man in bed."

Even as Pilar whirled, Sophia opened the door. "Oh, what fun. Girl talk? Rene, how brave of you to wear that shade of green with your coloring."

"Fuck you, Sophia."

"Erudite, as always. Mama, you're needed at the villa. I'm sure Rene will excuse us. She'll want plenty of room and privacy to fix her face."

"On the contrary, I'll just leave the two of you alone so you can hold your mother's hand while she dissolves into helpless tears. I'm not finished, Pilar," Rene added as she opened the door. "But you are."

"That was entertaining." Sophia studied her mother's face. "You don't look like you're about to dissolve into tears, helpless or otherwise."

"No, I'm done with them." Pilar dropped her lipstick back in her bag, closed it with a snap. "Sophie, honey, your father married her today."

"Well, hell." On a long sigh, Sophia stepped over, put her arms around her mother, laid her head on Pilar's shoulder. "Merry Christmas."

CHAPTER EIGHT

Sophia bided her time. She needed to catch her father alone to say what she had to say, and not when Rene was draped all over him like poison ivy on a tree trunk. She promised herself she'd be calm, mature and crystal clear. Losing her temper was not an option.

She worked the crowd as she waited, danced once with Theo, who'd been so entertaining he'd nearly cured her sour mood.

When she spotted Rene on the dance floor with Jerry, she made her move.

It didn't surprise her to see her father tucked into a corner table flirting with Kris. It revolted her slightly, but didn't surprise her he'd turn on the charm for another woman on his wedding day.

But as she approached, she caught the

subtle signals—a light touch, a promising glance—that told her it was more than flirtation. And that did surprise her.

Her father, she was certain, was cheating on Rene with Kris. Still, it was so like him, so ridiculously like him, it barely put a hitch in her stride.

She didn't know which of the three of them in that sticky triangle was the biggest fool, and at the moment, it wasn't her problem.

"Kris, I'm sorry to break up this tender moment, but I need to speak with my father. Alone."

"Nice to see you, too." Kris got to her feet. "It's been so long since you've bothered to come by the office, I nearly forgot what you look like."

"I don't believe I report to you, but I'll be sure to send in a photo."

"Now, princess," Tony began.

"Don't push it." Sophia kept her tone quiet, level, but the look she sent her father had his color going up and his mouth closing. "Let's just put this entire situation down to Christmas-party insanity. We'll have a meeting, Kris, in my office, when my schedule permits. For tonight, let's put business aside for personal matters. You can consider yourself lucky I saw you before Rene did. Now I need to speak to my father on family business."

"With you at the wheel, your family's not going to have much of a business." Deliberately Kris leaned down, skimmed a fingertip over the back of Tony's hand. "Later," she murmured and strolled away.

"Sophie, you have the entirely wrong impression. Kris and I were just having a sociable drink."

Her gaze cut like a blade. "Save it for Rene. I've known you longer. Long enough not to have the slightest interest in your bimbos. Please don't interrupt," she said before he could sputter out a protest. "This won't take long. I hear congratulations are in order. Or if not in order, required by elemental manners. So fucking congratulations."

"Now, Sophie." He stood, reached for her hand, but she snatched it out of reach. "I know you're not fond of Rene, but—"

"I don't give a damn about Rene, and at the moment, I don't give much of one about you."

He looked sincerely surprised, sincerely

hurt. She wondered if he practiced the expression in his shaving mirror. "You don't mean that. I'm sorry you're upset."

"No, you're not. You're sorry I've cornered you about it. You were married today, and you didn't bother to tell me. That's one."

"Princess, it was a small, simple ceremony. Neither Rene nor I felt—"

"Just be quiet." His answer had been quick and smooth, but she knew the truth. He hadn't so much as thought of telling her. "You came to a family function, and under the business cloak, this is a family function, flaunting yourself and your new wife and a side piece for good measure. That's insensitive enough, but it goes up a considerable number of levels as you didn't have the decency to tell Mama about the marriage first. That's two."

Her voice had risen, just enough to turn some heads. Uneasy, Tony moved in closer. He took her arm, stroked it, tugged gently. "Why don't we go outside and I'll explain. There's no need to cause a scene in here."

"Oh, there is. Every need. I'm desperately trying to resist the temptation to do just that. Because here's the kicker, you son of a bitch. You pushed that woman in my mother's face." She jabbed a finger into his chest as her temper reared up and took over. "You let Rene corner her, let her spew all over her, let her make scenes and cause pain while you sit over here and slobber over yet another woman—and one young enough to be your daughter, if you ever remembered you have one. That's three, goddamn you. That's three and you're out. You stay away from her, and you stay away from me. You keep your distance, and see that your *wife* does the same. Or I'll hurt you, I promise you, I'll make you bleed."

She whirled away before he recovered, caught the amused smirk on Kris's face. She took a step in that direction, then another, not entirely certain what she intended to do. Then her arm was gripped and she was being swept away into the crowd.

"Bad idea," Ty said quietly as he slid his grip from her arm to her waist to keep her close. "Really bad idea to murder staff members at the company Christmas bash. Let's go outside."

"I don't want to go outside."

"You need to. It's cold. You'll cool off. So far you only entertained a handful of people who were close enough to hear you rip into Avano. Nicely done, by the way. But with the steam puffing out of your ears, you're going to end up putting on a show for the whole party."

He all but pushed her out the door.

"Stop shoving, stop dragging. I don't like being manhandled." She jerked free, rounded and nearly, very nearly struck him.

"Go ahead. First shot's free. After that, I hit back."

She sucked in a breath, blew it out, sucked in another while she continued to glare at him. With every breath her glittery gown threw out sparks in the moonlight.

She was, Ty thought, outrageous and magnificent. And dangerous as a handful of dynamite with the fuse already hissing.

"There you go," he said with a nod. "A few more and you might be able to see past the blood in your eyes."

"The bastard."

She stalked away from the ivy-covered stone walls of the winery, its shrubberies draped in festive lights. Away from the laughter, the music that pulsed against the tall, narrow windows. Into the shadows of the old cypress trees where she could rant privately until she was calm again.

He heard her muttering in Italian, some of which he understood, none of which sounded particularly pleasant.

"I couldn't help it." She turned back to where he stood, waiting while she worked it off. Her busy hands dropped to her sides.

"No, I don't guess you could. Always were a brat." Because it was cold, and she was starting to shiver, he stripped off his jacket, dropped it over her shoulders.

Her temper had fizzled, left her feeling raw and empty inside. "I don't care about him and Kris, even though it complicates my department. I can deal with that, with her. But he hurt my mother."

"She's handling it, Sophie. She's going to be okay." He jammed his hands in his pockets before he gave in to the urge to stroke and pet. She looked so damn miserable. "I'm sorry he hurt you."

"Yeah. Well, what else is new?" The blast of anger had left her with a dull headache and a raw stomach. "I guess I should thank you for getting me out of there before I cut loose on bystanders."

"If you mean Kris, she doesn't strike me

as a bystander. More an operator. But no thanks necessary either way."

She turned back, saw by his face he was beginning to be embarrassed. Because she found that endearing she rose on her toes, lightly kissed his cheek. "Still. Thanks. I wasn't shouting, was I? I lose track when I'm in a tantrum."

"Not very much, and the band was loud."

"That's something then. Well, I believe my work is done here. Why don't you walk me up to the villa? You can make sure I don't throw another tantrum."

"I guess. You want your coat?"

"That's all right." She smiled and pulled his jacket a little closer. "I've got yours."

The gardens of the villa sparkled with thousands of fairy lights. The heated terraces were decked with flowers and ornamental trees. Table groupings invited guests to spill out into the starlight, enjoy the night and the music that slipped through the doors and windows of the ballroom.

Pilar used it as an excuse to have a moment in the air before returning inside to circulate among the guests and do her duty.

She considered sneaking in an emergency cigarette.

"Hiding out?"

She jumped in her shadowy corner, then relaxed when she saw it was her stepfather. "Caught me."

"I was sneaking out myself." In an exaggerated move, he craned his neck, looking side to side, then whispered, "You carrying?"

The laugh felt marvelous. "Just one," she whispered back. "We can share it."

"Light it up, partner. Your mother's busy. We've got enough time to suck one down."

She lit the cigarette, and they stood in the shadows, companionably, conspiratorially passing it between them.

Relaxed in his company, she leaned back on the wall of the house, looked out. Lights were glowing in the fields, highlighting the naked twists and fingers of the vines. Behind them, the glamour of the music swelled.

"It's a beautiful party."

"As always." With enough regret for both of them, Eli stubbed out the last of the cigarette. "You and your mother and Sophia have outdone yourselves this year. I hope

Tereza let you know how much we appreciate all the work you put into this event."

"She has. In her way."

"Then let me thank you in mine." He slipped his arms around her, guided her into a dance. "A pretty woman should never be without a dance partner."

"Oh, Eli." She laid her head on his shoulder. "What would I do without you? I'm such a mess."

"Not you. Pilar, you were a grown woman with a child of your own when I married your mother. I've tried not to interfere in your life."

"I know."

"Tereza does enough of that for both of us," he said and made her chuckle. "However," he continued, "I'm going to speak my mind. He was never good enough for you."

"Eli—"

"Never would have been good enough. You wasted a lot of years on Tony Avano, but you managed to get a wonderful daughter out of it. Treasure that, and don't waste the rest of your life wondering why it didn't work out."

"He married Rene. Just like that."

"All the better." He nodded when she jerked back to stare at him. "For you, for Sophia, for everyone involved. They suit, such as they are. And their marriage simply takes him one step further out of your life. If I had my way, he'd be out of the business as well. Completely out. And I suspect that's what's going to happen within the next year."

"He's good at his job."

"Others will be equally as good, and won't give me indigestion. Your mother's had her reasons for keeping him on. But those reasons aren't as important as they once were. Let him go," Eli said, kissing her forehead. "He'll sink or he'll swim. Either way, it's no longer your problem."

From the terrace below, Tony listened, and his mouth hardened. He was still stinging from what he continually told himself had been a completely uncalled-for and inappropriate attack by his own daughter. He'd have been able to shrug it off, but it had been in public. In public at a business event.

And business, he thought, wasn't what it had been.

He didn't believe, not really, that the Giambellis would cut him loose. But they were going to make his life difficult.

They thought he was stupid, that he was careless. But they were wrong. He already had a plan in place to ensure his financial security held. God knew he needed money, and plenty of it. Rene was already draining the resources he had.

Of course he'd been unwise to become involved with Kris. He was doing his best to break that off, delicately. So far that had been a bit more problematic than he'd anticipated. It was flattering, really, that a lovely young woman like Kris would be so attached, so reluctant to part ways. And angry, he recalled, angry enough to call Rene in the middle of the night.

Still, he'd handled that. Rene had assumed the caller was Pilar, and he hadn't corrected her. Why should he have?

He sipped his wine, enjoyed the starlight and, as was his way, began to put trouble aside before it could take root.

He was handling Kris as well, he decided. Promising to help her move into Sophia's position with Giambelli had stemmed that flood, just as a nice little bauble generally stemmed floods from Rene.

It was all, he thought, knowing your quarry's weakness.

And knowing it, using it, maintained the status quo.

He intended to continue living his life as he believed he deserved. It was time to tap his sources, a little more here, a little more there. And look toward the future.

Sophia moved through her circle of friends and did her best to avoid her cousin Gina. The woman was becoming more than a pest. She'd moved up the scale to embarrassment. Not only was she dressed in what appeared to be a Christmas-red tent with fifty pounds of sequins, but she was busily chirping to anyone she could corner about her husband's brilliance.

Don, Sophia noted, was keeping very close to the bar. He was easily half-drunk and trying to make himself invisible.

"Your mother all right?"

Sophia stopped to smile at Helen. "Last time I saw her. Hello, Uncle James." She turned to give Helen's husband a hard hug.

James Moore had been one of the constants in her life, and often more a father to her than her own.

He'd let himself go pudgy, had lost more hair than he'd kept, but behind his silver wire glasses, his eyes twinkled green at her. He looked like everyone's favorite uncle and was one of the top, and most devious, criminal defense attorneys in California.

"Prettiest girl in the room, isn't she, Helen?"

"Always."

"You haven't been by to see me in weeks."

"I'll make up for it." She gave his cheek a second kiss. "*La Signora* has been keeping me busy."

"So I hear. We brought you a present."

"I love presents. Gimme."

"It's over there, making time with that redhead."

Sophia glanced over and gave a quick yip of pleasure as she spotted Lincoln Moore. "I thought Linc was still in Sacramento."

"He'll fill you in," James told her. "Go on over. Talk him into marrying you this time."

"James." Helen arched a brow. "We're going to find Pilar. Go enjoy yourself."

Lincoln Moore was tall, dark and handsome. He was also the closest thing Sophia had to a brother. At various stages of their lives, her two-month seniority had been used to advantage—by both of them. Their mothers' friendship had been a bond that had ensured they'd grow up together. Because of it, neither of them had ever felt like an only child.

She walked up behind him, slid an arm through the crook of his and asked the redhead, "Is this guy coming on to you?"

"Sophie." With a laugh, he picked her off the floor, gave her a quick turn. "My surrogate sister," he told the redhead. "Sophia Giambelli, Andrea Wainwright. My date. Be nice."

"Andrea." Sophia offered a hand. "We'll talk."

"No, you won't. She lies about me. It's a hobby."

"It's nice to meet you. Linc's told me a lot about you."

"He lies, too. Did you both come in from Sacramento?"

"No, actually, I'm an intern at Saint Francis, the emergency-medicine rotation."

"Basketball injury." Linc held up his right

hand, showed off the splint on his right finger. "Dislocated it trying to jam. Andy took a look at it, fixed me up. Then I hit on her."

"Actually, he hit on me before I fixed him up. But since I couldn't dislocate the rest of his fingers, here I am. And it is a great party."

"I'm living in San Francisco again," Linc told Sophia. "I decided to take my father up on a job with his firm. I want some real law experience before I get too deep in the political thing. I'm a glorified law clerk, and not that glorified, but it's going to give me what I want until I pass the bar."

"That's great! Linc, that's fabulous. I know your parents must be thrilled to have you home again. We'll make time to catch up, okay?"

"Absolutely. I heard you've got your hands full right now."

"Never too full. When do you take the bar?"

"Next month."

"He's brilliant, you know," she told Andy. "It can be a real pain in the butt."

"Don't start, Sophie."

"Enjoy yourselves." She spotted Ty coming in, looking miserable. "Duty calls. Don't sneak out without seeing my mother. You know she dotes on you." Sophia brushed at his jacket. "God knows why."

"I won't. I'll call you."

"You'd better. Nice meeting you, Andrea."

"You, too." Andy glanced up at Linc. "So, are you brilliant?"

"Yeah. It's a curse." Grinning, he drew her onto the dance floor.

"Smile, MacMillan."

Ty looked down at Sophia. "Why?"

"Because you're going to dance with me."

"Why?" He bit back a sigh as she took his hand. "Sorry. Been hanging around with Maddy Cutter too long. The kid never stops asking questions."

"The two of you seemed to be hitting it off. We'd dance better if you actually touched me."

"Right." He laid a hand at her waist. "She's an interesting kid, and bright. Have you seen my grandfather?"

"Not for a bit. Why?"

"I want to see him, and *La Signora*. Then I figure I'm done with this and can go home."

"You're such a party animal." She slid her hand over his shoulder and tugged playfully at his hair. There was so much of it, she thought. All thick and unruly. "Live a little, Ty. It's Christmas."

"Not yet. There's still a lot of work to be done before Christmas, and to be done after."

"Hey." She tugged his hair again so that he stopped scanning the crowd for his grandfather and looked at her. "There's no work to be done tonight, and I still owe you for coming to my rescue."

"You weren't in trouble. Everyone else was." It wasn't gratitude he was looking for, but distance. A safe distance. She was always dangerous, but pressed up against a man, she was lethal. "And I have some charts and some grafts I want to go over. Why is that funny?" he demanded when she chuckled.

"I was just wondering what you'd be like if you ever loosened up. I bet you're a wild man, MacMillan."

"I get loose," he muttered.

"Tell me something." She skimmed her fingers down the nape of his neck, enjoyed the way those lake-blue eyes flared with annoyance. "Something that has nothing to do with wine or work."

"What else is there?"

"Art, literature, an amusing childhood experience, a secret fantasy or desire."

"My current fantasy is to get out of here."

"Do better. Come on. The first thing that pops into your head."

"Peeling that dress off you, and seeing if you taste like you smell." He waited a beat. "Good, that shut you up."

"Only momentarily, and only because I'm assessing my reaction. I find myself a great deal more intrigued by the image than expected." She tipped her head back to study his face. Oh yes, she liked his eyes, especially now, when there were sparks of heat in them. "Why do you suppose that is?"

"I've answered enough questions for one night." He started to step back, but she clamped her hand on his shoulder.

"Why don't we fulfill our duty here, then go to your place?"

"Is it that easy for you?"

"It can be."

"Not for me, but thanks." His tone turned careless and cold as he looked away from her again and around the room. "But I'd say you've got plenty of alternates here if you're up for a quick one-night stand. I'm going home."

He stepped back, walked away.

It took her nearly ten seconds before she had her wind back, and another three before the fury spurted up and scored her throat. The delay allowed him to get out of the room and down the first flight of stairs before she came after him.

"No, you don't." She hissed it under her breath, then stalked past him. "In here." She strode into the family parlor, banged the pocket doors closed.

"*Cazzo! Culo!* You son of a bitch." Even now her voice was quiet, controlled. He couldn't know how much that cost her.

"You're right." He cut her off before she could spew all the venom. "That was out of line, and I'm sorry."

The apology, quietly given, turned temper to tears, but she held them back by sheer raw will. "I'm a whore, in your opinion, because I think of sex the way a man does."

"No. Jesus." He hadn't meant that, only to get under her skin the way she got under his. Then get the hell away from her. "I don't know what I think."

"It would be all right, wouldn't it, if I pretended reluctance, if I let you seduce me. But because I'm honest, I'm cheap."

"No." He gripped her arms now, hoping to steady them both. "You got me worked up. You always have. I shouldn't have said what I did. Anything that I did. For God's sake, don't cry."

"I am *not* going to cry."

"Good. Okay. Look, you're beautiful, outrageous and over my head. I've managed to keep my hands off you up till now, and I'm going to keep them off."

"You've got them on me now."

"Sorry." He dropped his arms to his sides. "Sorry."

"You're saying you insulted me because you're a coward?"

"Look, Sophie. I'm going home, soak my head. We'll get back to work tomorrow and forget this happened."

"I don't think so. I get you worked up, do I?" She gave him a little shove, moving in, and he stepped back. "And your answer to that is to take a slap at me."

"It was the wrong answer. I said I was sorry."

"Not good enough. Try this."

She was on him before he could act. All that was left was reaction.

Her mouth was hot, and soft and very

skilled. It fed ravenously on his. Her body was lush and smooth and very female. It pressed intimately against his.

His mind blanked. He could admit that later—just snapped from on to off like a switch, giving him no shield against the panther leap of arousal. She tasted like she smelled; he learned that much.

Dark and dangerous and female.

He'd jerked her closer before he could stop himself, responded to the sharp nip of her teeth even as his system went to fast overload.

One minute she was wrapped around him like some exotic, strangling vine, and the next he was cut loose with every ounce of blood drained from his head.

"Deal with it." She ran a finger lightly over her own bottom lip, then turned to shove the doors open again.

"Just a damn minute." He had her arm, spun her around. He wasn't sure what he planned to do, but he didn't plan for it to be pleasant.

Then he saw the utter shock on her face. Before he could react she was shoving him aside, racing across the room to the refectory table.

"Dio! Madonna, who would do such a thing?"

He saw it then, the three Giambelli angels. Red ran down the carved faces like blood from slash wounds. Written across the chest of each, in that same violent hue, were vicious messages.

BITCH #1

BITCH #2

BITCH #3

"Sit down, Sophie. I'll get them out before your mother or grandmother sees them. Take them home, clean them up."

"No, I'll do it. I think it's nail polish. A nasty girl trick," she said quietly. Temper would do no good, she thought as she gathered the three figures. And she couldn't find her anger under the sadness. "Rene, I suppose. Or Kris. They both hate the Giambelli women at the moment."

"Let me take care of it for you." He laid his hands on her shoulders. "Whoever did it knew it would hurt you. I can get them cleaned up and put back before anyone notices."

She wanted to push the angels into his

big, strong hands, and herself along with them. Because she did, she stepped away from him. "I take care of my own, and you're in a hurry to go home."

"Sophie."

His tone was so patient, so kind, she sighed. "I need to do it myself. And I need to be angry with you a little while longer. So go away."

He let her go, but once he was outside, he turned and climbed the stone steps to the ballroom. He'd hang around awhile, he decided. Just to be sure the only thing anyone hurt that night were wooden angels.

In her room, Sophia carefully cleaned off the figures. It was, as she suspected, smears of bold red nail polish. A petty vandalism, and an ugly one, but not permanent.

You can't destroy the Giambellis so easily, she thought. We're tougher than that. Tough enough, she thought, for her to ignore the nastiness of the act and leave the perpetrator of it disappointed.

She took them back downstairs, replaced

them and found that single act steadied her again.

Easier, she realized, than steadying herself against what had passed between her and Tyler.

Moron, she thought, wandering to an antique mirror to add a fresh dusting of powder to her nose. The moron could certainly kiss when he put some effort into it, but that didn't make him less of a moron. She hoped he suffered. She hoped he spent a long, sweaty, uncomfortable night. If he looked haggard and miserable the next day, she might, just might let him off the hook.

Then again.

She watched herself in the mirror as she traced a finger over her lips.

Dropped her hand quickly to retrieve her lipstick when the doors opened.

"Sophia."

"*Nonna.*" She glanced toward the three angels. All was as it should be. "Just doing some repairs. I'll be right back up."

Tereza closed the doors behind her. "I saw you go out after Tyler."

"Mmm." Keeping it at that, Sophia carefully painted her lips.

"Do you think, because I'm old, I don't recognize the look in your eye?"

"What look is that, *Nonna*?"

"Hot blood."

Sophia gave a little shrug, recapped her lipstick. "We had an argument."

"An argument didn't require you to replace your lipstick."

Laughing now, Sophia turned. "What sharp eyes you have, Grandma. We did have an argument, and I solved it my way. It's both legal and moral for me to kiss Ty, *Nonna*. We're not blood kin."

"I love you, Sophia. And I love Tyler."

Sophia softened. The words came rarely from Tereza. "I know."

"I didn't put the two of you together so you would hurt each other."

"Why did you put us together?"

"For the good of the family." Because the day had been long, Tereza gave in and sat. "Hot blood can cloud the judgment. This is a pivotal year, and already before it begins, we have upheaval. You're a beautiful young woman."

"Some say I look like my grandmother."

Tereza allowed herself a small smile. She, too, glanced toward the three carved figures, and her eyes softened. "A little, perhaps. But more you favor your grandfather. He was beautiful, like a painting. I married for duty, but it wasn't a hardship. And he was kind. Beauty is a weapon, *cara.* Take care how you use it, for without that kindness, it will turn and strike back at you."

Sophia sat. "Am I . . . hard, *Nonna*?"

"Yes." Tereza reached over, touched her hand lightly to Sophia's. "That's not a bad thing. A soft woman is too easily molded, and too easily bruised. Your mother's been both. She's my daughter, Sophia," she added coolly, when Sophia stiffened. "I will speak my mind there. You're not soft, and you go your own way. I'm pleased with you. I say only that hard can become brittle, without care. Take care."

"Are you pleased with me, *Nonna,* because in going my own way, I go yours?"

"Perhaps. You're Giambelli. Blood tells."

"I'm also Avano."

Tereza inclined her head, her voice turned fierce. "You're proof, aren't you, of which line is stronger? Your father's in you. He's a sly man, and you can be sly. He's ambitious, and so are you. But his weaknesses have never been yours. His lack of heart has ruined him as much as his lack of courage. You have both heart and courage, and so you can be hard and not brittle."

"I know you hate him," Sophia said softly. "Tonight, so do I."

"'Hate' is a strong word. You shouldn't use it against your father, whatever he is, whatever he's done. I have no hate for Anthony Avano." Tereza got to her feet again. "I have no feelings toward him now. He's made his last choice that concerns me. We'll deal with each other one final time, then he'll no longer exist for me."

"You mean to cut him loose."

"He made his choice," Tereza repeated. "Now he'll deal with the consequences of it. It's not for you to worry over." She held out a hand. "Come, you should be at the party. We'll find your mother and show them three generations of Giambelli women."

It was very late when Tony let himself into the apartment. He wondered if anyone knew he had the key, after all this time.

He'd brought his own bottle of wine, a choice from his personal cellar. The Barolo would keep things civilized. Business discussions, and the word "blackmail" never entered his mind, should always be conducted in a civilized manner.

He uncorked the bottle in the kitchen, left the wine on the counter to breathe and selected two glasses. Though he was disappointed not to find fresh fruit in the refrigerator, he made do with the wheel of Brie.

Even at three in the morning, presentation mattered.

It was lucky he'd made the appointment so late. It had taken quite some doing to wind Rene down. She'd spent over an hour, even after the drive back to the city, haranguing him about the Giambellis, their treatment of her, his future with the company. And money.

Money was the main matter, of course.

He could hardly blame her for it.

Their lifestyle required a great deal of money. Unlike Pilar, Rene didn't bring unlimited funds to the table. And unlike Pilar, Rene went through money like it would shortly become unfashionable to have any in your pocket.

No matter, he thought, arranging crackers with the cheese. It would be a simple and civilized matter to increase their cash flow.

The Giambellis intended to cut him loose. He was certain of that now. Neither Pilar nor Sophia would stand up for him. He'd known that was a possibility, but had chosen to ignore it and hope for the best. Or rather, he admitted here, in private, he'd allowed Rene to push him into a corner.

But he had options. Any number of options. The first of which should be coming along any minute.

This first business deal would be a stopgap, buy him time. He had other avenues, and they could be widened if necessary. He had contacts, and prospects.

Tereza Giambelli would be very sorry she'd underestimated him. A great many people would be sorry.

In the end he would land on his feet, as he always had. He had no doubt of it.

The knock on the door made him smile. He poured two glasses of wine, set them and the bottle on a tray with the cheese and crackers. He set the tray on the coffee table in the living room.

He shot his cuffs, smoothed his hair, then walked to the door prepared to begin negotiations.

PART TWO

The Growing

Not a having and a resting, but a growing and a becoming, is the character of perfection as culture conceives it.

—MATTHEW ARNOLD

CHAPTER NINE

"I don't know why we had to come back here."

"Because I needed a few more things." She could have put it off, Sophia admitted. But no reason to waste a trip into San Francisco without stopping by her apartment. Hadn't she taken pity on Ty and driven Eli's SUV instead of her convertible?

"Look," she continued. "I explained that at the beginning I'm going to have to spot-check the offices. Kris is going to continue to resist the new feeding chain. She needs to see you and me together, a team."

"Some team."

"I'm managing." She pulled into her parking slot, set the brake. "I think we should call a holiday truce. At the moment, Ty, I just don't have the time to fight with you."

She climbed out, slammed her door, jammed her keys in her briefcase.

"What's the problem?"

"I don't have a problem. You're the problem."

He walked around to her side, leaned on the fender. She'd been edgy for two days, he thought. Long enough for anybody to stew. He didn't think it was about their incident at the Christmas party. She'd come out on top of that one.

"A team, remember? Are you still upset about the angels?"

"No. I took care of them, didn't I? Good as new."

"Yeah, you deal, all right. So what's the problem now?"

"You want to know the problem? Fine. I hate getting up at the crack of dawn every day, tromping around the fields in the cold. But I'm doing it. Then I go back and do the work I'm trained to do. But I'm obliged to juggle it from the villa and the offices here, where I have a second-in-command who's not only slept with my father but is ready to mutiny."

"Fire her."

"Oh, that's an idea." She tapped a finger

to her temple, while her voice dripped disdain. "Why hasn't that occurred to me?
Could it be because we're weeks into a reorganization, in the middle of a huge and intense and vital promotional campaign and I
have no one qualified to take over her
work? Yes, you know, I think that might be
the reason I haven't kicked her bitchy,
cheating ass out."

"Look, brat, you got sand in your shoe,
you shake it out."

"I don't have time," she snapped and, to
prove it, yanked out her Filofax. It bulged.
"Would you like to take a look in here, see
my schedule for the next six weeks?" She
jammed it back in her briefcase.

"So you're pressed." He gave a little
shrug. "Take the mornings off to do what
you have to do. I'll carry you in the vineyard."

The look she gave him shot like a bullet.

"Nobody carries me, MacMillan. But
you're damn right I'm pressed. I'm supposed to be training my mother, who has little to no interest in public relations. I've had
to cancel three dates with three very interesting men because I'm buried in work. My
social life is going down the toilet. I haven't

been able to get through goddamn Rene for two days to contact my father, who hasn't been to *his* office. And it's imperative I speak with him about one of our top accounts within the next forty-eight hours as someone—who unfortunately won't be me—is going to need to fly to San Diego for a meeting in approximately forty-*nine* hours."

"What about Margaret? I thought she was taking over most of the major accounts."

"Do you think I didn't try that? Do I look stupid?" Tired, frustrated and fed up, she stalked to the garage elevator and stabbed the button. "She left for Italy yesterday afternoon. Neither she nor her office is fully updated on the Twiner account because it's always been my father's baby. Since I don't want the people at Twiner to know we've got a hole in the loop, I've been tap-dancing with them for days."

"Nobody carries you," Ty pointed out. "But you're carrying Avano."

"No, I'm through carrying him. But I'll carry Giambelli, and that's why I'm covering for him as long as I can. I don't like it, I'm pissed off and I have a stupid headache."

"Okay." He surprised them both by reaching up to rub her stiff shoulders when they stepped onto the elevator. "Take some aspirin, then we'll work it through a step at a time."

"She's got no right to block me from speaking to my own father. Not on a personal level or a business one."

"No, she doesn't." That, Ty assumed, was the real headache. "It's a power play. She won't get her kicks unless you let her know it steams you. Work around him."

"If I work around him, it makes him look like a . . . damn it. He *is* a fool. I'm so angry with him for putting me into this spot. If I don't clean it up by end of day—"

"You'll clean it up by end of day."

"Yeah." She let out a breath, stepped off the elevator on her floor. Turned to study him. "Why are you being nice to me?"

"It throws you off. Plus, Twiner is a big stake. I don't spend all my time in the fields," he said when she lifted her eyebrows at him. "If you'd told me you were trying to track down your father, I'd have given you a hand with it. You haven't gone to Cutter."

She pressed her lips together. "No. But I

figure he knows something's up. He'll pin-point the target soon enough."

"Then we'll just have to be faster. Team-work, remember?"

"That's only because you dislike him more than you dislike me."

"And your point is?"

It made her laugh as she put the key in the lock. "As good a reason as any. I just need to grab a few things, including some old files I want my mother to study. And I think I might have some notes on Twiner that'll partially plug this hole. I'll have you back home by dinner."

She stopped, turned. "Unless," she said, adding a slow smile, "you'd like to order in and try out a different kind of teamwork."

"Cut it out."

"You liked kissing me."

"When I was a kid I liked green apples. I found out they're hell on the system."

"I'm ripe."

He reached past her to turn the knob. "You're telling me."

She gave his arm a friendly squeeze as she turned. "I'm starting to like you, MacMillan. What the hell will we do about that?" She pushed open the door, took one step inside, froze.

"Dad?"

She had a brief impression, no more than a blur, before Ty was shoving her out the door again. But that blurred image stayed in her mind, was all she could see.

Her father, slumped in her chair, the side of his face, the glinting silver at his temples, the front of his shirt all crusted and dark. And his eyes, his handsome, clever eyes, filmed over and staring.

"Dad. He's . . . I have to . . . My father."

She was pale as a sheet and already beginning to shudder when Ty pushed her against the wall outside her apartment. "Listen to me, Sophia. Listen. Use your cell phone. Call nine-one-one. Do it now."

"An ambulance." She fought her way through the fog that wanted to slither over her brain, and began to fight Tyler. "He needs an ambulance. I have to go to him."

"No." He gripped her arms, gave her one brisk shake. "You can't help him." He tabled the idea of going back in to check on Tony himself. Sophia couldn't be left alone. And he'd already seen enough to be certain there was nothing to be done.

He pulled Sophia to the floor, opened her briefcase himself and dug out her cell phone. "I need the police," he said.

Sophia lowered her head to her knees as Tyler gave the emergency operator the necessary information. She couldn't think. Wouldn't think yet. Somehow she had to steady herself and get through.

"I'm all right." Her voice was quiet, almost calm, even if her hands couldn't be. "I know he's dead. I have to go in to him."

"No." He settled down on the floor beside her and draped an arm over her shoulders as much in restraint as comfort. "You don't. You're not. I'm sorry, Sophia. There's nothing you can do."

"There's always something." She lifted her head. Her eyes were dry. Burning dry. "Someone killed my father, and there has to be something I can do. I know what he was." Her voice broke there, and the tears that were scalding her throat poured up and out. "He's still my father."

"I know it." He tightened his grip until she laid her head on his shoulder. There was something to do, he thought as she wept. Even if it was only to wait.

· · ·

He didn't leave her. Sophia told herself to remember that whatever happened between them—or didn't—when things had been at their very worst, Tyler had stayed with her.

She sat on the sofa in the apartment across the hall from her own. She'd been to a couple of parties there, she recalled. The gay couple who lived there threw delightful parties. And Frankie, a graphic artist who often worked at home, had opened the apartment to her, and the police. And bless him, had discreetly closed himself in the bedroom to give them privacy.

No doubt the story would make its way like an electric fire through the building. But for now, he was being a pal. She'd remember that, too.

"I don't know what he was doing in my apartment," Sophia said, again. She tried to study the face of the man who questioned her. Like his name—Detective Lamont? Claremont?—his features kept slipping out of focus.

"Did your father, or anyone else, have a key?" The name was Claremont. Alexander Claremont.

"No, I . . . Yes." Sophia lifted a hand, pressed a fingertip against her temple as if to loosen the thought. "My father. I gave him a key not long after I moved in. He was having some decorating work done on his place, and I was going to be out of the country. I offered to let him use my place while I was gone. I don't think I ever got the key back. I never thought of it again."

"Did he often use your place?"

"No. He didn't use it when I offered, but stayed at a hotel." Or said he had, she thought. Had he used her apartment then, and since? Hadn't there been times she'd come back from a trip and felt someone had been there in her absence?

Little things out of place.

No, that was stupid. It would have been the cleaning service. Her father would have had no reason to use her apartment. He'd had his own, with Rene.

He cheated on your mother, a voice murmured in her brain. He cheated on Rene.

"Ms. Giambelli?"

"I'm sorry. What did you say?"

"You want some water? Something?" Tyler interrupted, to give her a moment to tune back.

"No, no thanks. I'm sorry, Detective. I keep losing the thread."

"It's all right. I asked when was the last time you had contact with your father."

"Saturday night. There was a party at our vineyard. It's an annual event. My father was there."

"What time did he leave?"

"I couldn't say. There were a great many people. He didn't say goodbye to me."

"Did he attend alone?"

"No, his wife was with him. Rene."

"Your father is married?"

"Yes, he was married the day of the party. Rene Foxx. Hasn't she been contacted?"

"I was unaware of her. Can I reach her at your father's address?"

"Yes, I . . . Yes," she said again, biting back what had nearly tumbled off her tongue.

"Do you own a gun, Ms. Giambelli?"

"No."

"You had no handgun in your apartment?"

"No. I don't like guns."

"Did your father own a gun?"

"I don't know. Not to my knowledge."

"When was the last time you were in your apartment?"

"Over a week ago. As I told you, I'm stay-ing primarily in Napa for the next several months. I came here today, after Mr. MacMillan and I left the offices downtown, to pick up a few more things."

"What was your relationship with your father?"

She toughened up. Sitting beside her, Tyler felt it. "He was my father, Detective. Why don't I save you the trouble of asking me if I killed him. No, I didn't. Nor do I know who killed him, or why."

Claremont's voice remained steady. "Did your father have any enemies?"

"Obviously."

"That were known to you," he added with-out skipping a beat.

"No. I don't know of anyone who would have killed him."

Claremont looked down at his pad, ap-peared to study some notes.

"How long have your parents been di-vorced?"

"They've been legally separated over seven years."

"Separated?"

"Yes. They haven't lived together, in any real sense, since I was a child."

"Would this Rene Foxx be your father's second wife?"

"That's correct."

"Just married a couple days ago."

"So I was informed."

"When were your parents divorced, Ms. Giambelli?"

There was a cold ball in her belly now. She wouldn't let him see the nerves. "I believe the decree was final the day before my father married Rene. It was only a legality, Detective."

Though her knees shook, she got to her feet. "I'm sorry, I have to go to my family. I don't want them to hear about this on the evening news, or from a stranger. I need to go home. Can you tell me . . . what happens with my father now? What arrangements need to be made?"

"We'll continue our investigation. My partner is working across the hall with the crime-scene unit. I'll discuss arrangements with next of kin."

"I'm my father's only child."

"His wife is his legal next of kin, Ms. Giambelli."

Her mouth opened, closed. When her hand fluttered up, Tyler simply took it in his and held it. "I see. Of course. I have to go home. Ty."

"We're going."

"Mr. MacMillan, I have some questions for you."

"I gave you my address." Tyler shot a look over his shoulder as he led Sophia to the door. "You know where to find me."

"Yeah." Claremont tapped his pad as the door closed. "That I do." He had a feeling he and his partner were going to take a ride into the country, very soon.

He walked to the bedroom door, sure if he opened it, the neighbor would tumble out, ear first. Instead he knocked. Might as well keep things friendly while he asked more questions.

Alexander Claremont liked French wine, Italian shoes and American blues. He'd grown up in San Francisco, the middle son of solidly middle-class parents who'd worked hard to ensure a good life and good educations for their three boys.

His older brother was a pediatrician, his younger a professor at Berkeley. Alex Claremont had planned to be a lawyer.

He'd been born to be a cop.

The law was a different entity in the hands of a cop than it was in the hands of a lawyer. For a lawyer it was there to be bent, twisted, manipulated and tailored to fit a client's needs.

He understood that and, on a very basic level, respected that.

To a cop it was the line.

It was the line Claremont worshiped.

Now, barely two hours after walking onto the crime scene, he was thinking about the line.

"What do you think of the daughter?"

He didn't answer at first, but his partner was used to that. She was driving because she'd gotten to the car first.

"Rich," he said at length. "Classy. Tough shell. Didn't say anything she didn't want to say. Thought it, lots of thinking going on, but she watches her words."

"Big, important family. Big, juicy scandal." Maureen Maguire braked at a light. Tapped her fingers on the wheel.

She and Claremont were polar opposites, which was, in her opinion, why they'd found their rhythm after the initial bumps three years back, and worked well together.

She was as white as a white woman could be. Irish and freckled and strawberry-blond with soft blue eyes and a dimple in her left cheek. At thirty-six, she was four years Claremont's senior, comfortably married where he was radically single, cozily suburban where he was uptown urban.

"Nobody sees the guy go in. No vehicle. We're running the cab companies to see if they had a drop-off here. From the looks of the body, he'd been dead at least thirty-six hours. Key to the place was in his pocket, along with three hundred and change in cash and plenty of plastic. He had a gold Rolex, gold cuff links with pretty little diamonds in them. The apartment had plenty of easily transported items. No robbery."

He shot her a look. "No kidding."

"Just crossing off the list. Two glasses of wine, one full, one half-full. Only one with prints—his prints. He got plugged where he sat. No tussle, no signs of struggle. From the angle of the shots, the killer was sitting on the sofa. Nice little wine-and-cheese party and oh, excuse me, bam, bam, bam. You're dead."

"Guy was divorced and remarried within a day. Romantic interlude gone bad?"

"Maybe." Maguire pursed her lips. "Hard to say from the scene. Three shots, twenty-five-caliber, I'd say, and close range. Not much of a pop, but it's surprising nobody heard anything in a snazzy building like that."

She parked, glanced up at the next snazzy building. "Funny, huh, how a new husband doesn't come home and the new bride doesn't report him missing."

"Let's find out why."

Rene had just gotten in from a three-hour session at her salon. Nothing smoothed her feathers better than a long bout of pampering. Unless it was shopping. But she'd taken care of that as well with a quick foray into Neiman's, where she'd treated herself lavishly.

Tony, she thought, as she poured herself a small vermouth, was going to pay and pay dearly for this little bout of the sulks.

He'd gone off like this before, a couple of days at a time, when she'd pressured him over some matter. The good part was, he always came back, always with some very attractive trinket in hand, and naturally agreed to do whatever she'd demanded he do in the first place.

She didn't mind so much, as it gave her a little time to herself. Besides, now it was all legal and tidy. She lifted her left hand, studied the glitter of her rings. She was Mrs. Anthony Avano, and intended to stay that way.

Or scalp him bald in a divorce.

When the bell rang, she smiled. It would be Tony, come crawling back. He knew better than to use his key when he'd been gone. The last time he'd done so, she'd pulled a gun on him.

One thing about her Tony, he learned fast.

She opened the door, prepared to make him beg, then frowned at the couple holding up badges.

"Mrs. Avano?"

"Yes. What's this about?"

"Detective Claremont, and my partner, Detective Maguire, San Francisco PD. May we come in?"

"Why?"

"Please, Mrs. Avano, may we come in?"

"Is Tony in jail?" she hissed through her teeth as she stepped back. "What the hell did he do?"

"No, ma'am, he's not in jail." Maguire

moved in. "I'm sorry, Mrs. Avano. Your husband is dead."

"Dead?" Rene let out an annoyed huff of breath. "That's ridiculous. You've made a mistake."

"There's no mistake, Mrs. Avano," Claremont said. "Could we sit down?"

Rene felt a little jerk in her stomach, stepped back. "You expect me to believe Tony's dead. Just dead?"

"We're very sorry, ma'am. Why don't we sit down?" Maguire started to take her arm, but Rene yanked away.

She'd lost some of the color in her face, but her eyes were alive. And angry. "Was there an accident?"

"No, ma'am. Could you tell us the last time you saw your husband, or had contact with him?"

Rene stared hard at Claremont. "Saturday night, early Sunday morning, I guess. What happened to Tony?"

"You weren't concerned when you didn't hear from him?"

"We had an argument," she snapped. "Tony often goes off on little sulks afterward. I'm not his mother."

"No, ma'am." Maguire nodded. "His wife. You were married recently, weren't you?"

"That's right. What happened to him? I have a right to know what happened."

"Anthony Avano was shot and killed."

Her head jerked back, but almost immediately the color rushed back into her face. "I knew it! I warned him she'd do something crazy, but he wouldn't listen. She was harassing us, wasn't she? Those quiet types, you can't trust them."

"Who is that, Mrs. Avano?"

"His wife." She sucked in a breath, turned and stalked over to pick up her drink. "His *ex*-wife. Pilar Giambelli. The bitch killed him. If she didn't, his little tramp of a daughter did."

He didn't know what to do for her. She sat in the passenger seat, her eyes closed. But he knew she wasn't sleeping. Her composure was a thin and tensile veneer, and he wasn't certain what he'd find if he managed to crack it.

So he gave her silence on the long drive north.

The energy, the vitality Sophia owned like

breath was gone. That concerned him most. It was like having a doll sitting beside him. Maybe it was a kind of bubble, a void between the shock and the next stage of grief. He didn't know about such things. He'd never lost anyone important to him. Certainly never lost anyone so brutally and suddenly.

When he turned into the drive, she opened her eyes. As if she sensed home. In her lap her fingers linked together.

The bubble's burst, Ty thought, watching her knuckles go white.

"I'll come in with you."

She started to refuse, that knee-jerk I-can-do-it-myself response. It was hard to admit she wasn't sure she could do anything herself just yet. And he was family. She needed family.

"Thanks. My mother." She had to swallow as he stopped the four-wheel at the base of the steps. "It's going to be very hard for my mother."

"Sophia." He laid his hand over hers, tightening his grip when she would have shifted away. "Sophia," he said again until she looked at him. "People always think they have to be strong. They don't."

"Giambellis do. I'm numb, Ty. And I'm afraid of what's going to happen inside me when I'm not. I'm afraid to start thinking. I'm afraid to start feeling. All I can do is the next thing."

"Then we'll do the next thing."

He got out of the car, came around to her side. And in a gesture that made her throat burn, took her hand.

The house was warm, and fragrant with her mother's flowers. Sophia looked around the grand foyer like a stranger. Nothing had changed. How could it be that nothing had changed?

She watched Maria come down the hall. Everything moves like a dream, Sophia thought. Even footsteps echo like a dream.

"Maria, where is my mother?"

"Upstairs. She's working in your office. Miss Sophia?"

"And *La Signora*?"

Uneasy, Maria looked toward Tyler. "She is in the fields, with Mr. Mac."

"Would you send someone for them, please. Send someone out for my grand-parents?"

"Yes, right away."

She went quickly, while Sophia turned

toward the stairs. Her hand tightened on Tyler's. She could hear music coming from her office. Something light and frothy. When she stepped into the doorway, she saw her mother, her hair scooped back, bent over the keyboard of the computer.

"What do you mean I've committed an illegal function? Damn it, I hate you."

Another time the baffled frustration would have amused Sophia. Now it, and everything, made her want to weep.

"Mama?"

"Oh, thank God! Sophia, I've done something. I don't know what. I've been practicing for an hour and still I'm useless on this thing."

She pushed back from the desk, glanced up—and froze.

"What is it? What's wrong?" She knew every line, every curve, every expression of her daughter's face. Her stomach twisted painfully as she rushed across the room. "What's happened?"

"Mama." Everything changes now, Sophia thought. Once it was said, nothing was ever going to be the same again. "Mama, it's Dad."

"Is he hurt? Is he ill?"

"He . . ." She couldn't say the words. Instead, she released Ty's hand and wrapped her arms tight around her mother.

The twisting in Pilar's stomach stilled. Everything inside her stilled. "Oh God. Oh my God." Pressing her face to Sophia's hair, she began to rock. "No. Oh, baby, no."

"I'm sorry. I'm so sorry, Mama. We found him. In my apartment. Someone . . . someone killed him there."

"What? Wait." Shaking, she drew back. "No."

"Sit down, Pilar." Tyler was already leading them both to the curved love seat against the wall.

"No, no. This can't be right. I need to—"

"Sit," Tyler repeated and gently pushed both of them down. "Listen to me. Look at me." He waited while Pilar groped for Sophia's hand. "I know this is hard for both of you. Avano was in Sophia's apartment. We don't know why. It looked like he was meeting someone there."

Pilar blinked. Her mind seemed to be skipping, as if there was a tooth missing on a gear. "In Sophie's apartment? Why do you say that? What do you mean?"

"There was a bottle of wine on the table.

Two glasses." He'd memorized the scene. Quiet elegance, stark death. "It's likely whoever it was he met there killed him. The police have already questioned Sophia."

"Sophia." Her fingers gripped her daughter's like a clamp. "The police."

"And they're going to have more questions for her. For you. Maybe all of us. I know it's hard, hard to think straight, but you have to prepare yourself to deal with them. I think you should call a lawyer. Both of you."

"I don't want a lawyer. I don't need a lawyer. For God's sake, Ty, Tony's been murdered."

"That's right. In his daughter's apartment, only days after divorcing you and marrying someone else. Only days after Sophie went after him in public."

Guilt, ugly and fierce, bared its teeth inside Sophia. "Goddamn it, Ty, if either of us was going to kill him, we'd have done it years ago."

Tyler shifted his gaze to Sophia's. The energy was back, he noted, and it was furious. That, he decided, was a plus. "Is that what you're going to say to the cops? Is that what you're going to say to the reporters when they start calling? Publicity's your business, Sophie. Think."

Her breath was coming too fast. She couldn't stop it. Something inside her wanted to explode, to burst out of the fragile skin of control and scream. Then she felt her mother's hand tremble in hers, and reeled it back in. "All right. But not yet. Not now. We're entitled to mourn first." She drew her mother closer. "We're entitled to be human first."

She got to her feet, walked to the door on legs that felt stiff and brittle. "Would you go down, talk to *Nonna* and Eli? Tell them what they need to be told. I want to be alone with my mother."

"Okay. Pilar." He bent down, touched her knee. "I'm sorry." He met Sophia's eyes as he walked out. The great, dark depth of them was all he saw as she closed the door between them.

CHAPTER TEN

Ty was right, but Sophia would stew about that later. It might help to have something petty to brood about. The reporters started to call less than ten minutes after she'd told her mother, and before she'd been able to go downstairs and speak with her grandmother.

She knew the line they would take. Unity. And she was prepared to go head-to-head with the police to soften the blow for her mother.

There would be no comment to the press until she was able to write the appropriate release. There would be no interviews. She was perfectly aware her father's murder would generate a media circus, but the Giambellis would not step into the center ring and perform.

Which meant she had a great many phone calls to make to family members and key employees. But the first—damn Tyler—was to Helen Moore.

They needed legal advice.

"I've called Aunt Helen," she told Tereza.

"Good." Tereza sat in the front parlor, her back ruler-straight, her face composed. "Your mother?"

"She wanted a few minutes alone."

With a nod, Tereza lifted her hand, took Sophia's. It was a connection, and it was enough. "Who do you trust most on your staff to write a statement for the press and filter the calls?"

"Me. I want to do it myself, *Nonna.*"

"Good." Tereza gave her hand a squeeze, released it. "I'm sorry for your grief, *cara.* Tyler's told us everything he knows. I don't like that you were questioned before you were able to speak with Helen or James."

"I have nothing to hide. I know nothing. My father was shot while he sat in my chair in my apartment. How could I not tell them anything that might help them find who killed him?"

"If you know nothing, you could tell them nothing that would help." She dismissed the police with one impatient gesture. "Tyler, get Sophia some wine." When the phone rang again, she slapped a hand on the arm of her chair.

"I'll take care of it," Tyler began.

"No, we don't want a family member talking to the press today." Sophia rubbed her forehead, ordered herself to think. "You should get David. Ask him to come. If you could explain things to him, I'll get started on a statement. For now, it's simply, the family is in seclusion and has no comment."

"I'll get him here." Tyler crossed to her, lifted her face with a hand on her chin. "You don't need wine. You need an aspirin."

"I don't need either." She stepped back. "Give me a half hour," she said to her grandmother.

"Sophie." Eli left Tereza's side to put his arms around Sophia. "Take a breath."

"Can't."

"All right, do what's best for you. I'll start making the calls."

"I can do that."

"You can, but I will. And take the aspirin."

"All right, for you."

. . .

It helped. The aspirin and the work. Within an hour she was steadier, had the official statement drafted and had briefed David.

"I'll take care of the press, Sophia. You take care of yourself, and your mother."

"We'll get through. You need to be aware that some enterprising reporter is bound to try to get close to the villa, and to MacMillan's. You have children, and that connection to the family will also be made."

"I'll talk to my kids. They're not going to sell a story to the tabloids, Sophia."

"I'm sorry. I don't mean to imply that. But they're still children. They could be harassed and they could be caught off guard."

"I'll talk to them," he repeated. "I know this is rough for you. I can't imagine how rough for you. And your mother." He got to his feet. "Anything I can do, just tell me what it is."

"I appreciate that." She hesitated, measuring him as she did so. Petty resentments, company policies had to be put aside. "My grandparents trust you, or you wouldn't be here. So I'm going to trust you. I'm going to set you up here in the house so you can handle the phones. I'd give you my space, but I may need it."

She started for the door, then just stopped in the middle of the room. She looked, he thought, blank. As if some internal mechanism had shut down.

"Why don't you rest a little."

"I can't. As long as I keep moving, I can handle it. I know what people thought of him. I know what'll be said about him, in whispers over cocktails, in gleeful articles in the press."

What *I* thought of him. What *I* said to him. Oh God, don't think of it now.

"It can't hurt him. But it can and will hurt my mother. So I can't stop."

She hurried out. "I think the library would be best," she began. "You'll have privacy there, and It's convenient if you need anything we haven't thought of."

She was halfway down the steps when Maria opened the front door to the police. Claremont looked over the housekeeper's head and saw Sophia.

"Ms. Giambelli."

"Detective. It's all right, Maria. I'll take care of this. Do you have any more information for me?" she asked him as she continued down the steps.

"Not at this time. We'd like to speak to you again, and to your mother."

"My mother is resting. David, this is Detective . . ."

"Claremont," he finished. "And my partner, Detective Maguire."

"David Cutter, Detectives Claremont and Maguire. Mr. Cutter is chief operating officer of Giambelli-MacMillan. I'll show you into the parlor and be with you in just a moment."

"Is your mother at home, Ms. Giambelli?"

"I said my mother is resting. She's not up to speaking with you at this time."

"Sophia." Pilar came down the steps, one hand holding the banister, with Helen just behind her. "It's all right. I want to do what I can."

"Ms. Avano," Helen began, careful to use Pilar's married name, "is willing to answer your questions. I'm sure you'll take her emotional state into consideration. Judge Moore," she added with a cool nod. "I'm an old family friend."

Claremont knew of her. And had been under ruthless cross-examination by her husband. Lawyers at the ready, he mused.

"Are you representing Ms. Avano, Judge Moore?"

"I'm here to offer my friend my support and my advice, should that be necessary."

"Why don't we go sit down?" Pilar said. "Sophia, would you ask Maria to arrange for some coffee?"

"Of course."

Slick and civilized, Claremont thought. He saw where the daughter got her class. But classy women killed, just like all the other kinds.

Especially when they'd been tossed over for a younger model.

Still, she answered questions directly.

Hadn't seen or spoken with the deceased since the famous party. Hadn't been to her daughter's apartment in more than a month. Didn't have a key. Didn't own a gun, though she admitted before the judge could cut her off that there were guns in the house.

"You were upset when your husband finalized your divorce to marry Rene Foxx."

"Yes," Pilar agreed, even as Helen opened her mouth. "It's foolish to deny it, Helen. Naturally I was upset. I don't find the end of a marriage a reason to celebrate. Even when the marriage had become no more than a legality. He was my daughter's father."

"You argued?"

"No." Her lips curved, and put Claremont in mind of an elegantly sorrowful Madonna. "It was difficult to argue with Tony. He slipped around most arguments. I gave him what he wanted. There was really nothing else to do, was there?"

"I handled the divorce for Mrs. Avano," Helen put in. "It was amicable on both sides. Legally as simple as such matters can be."

"But you were upset nonetheless," Maguire stated. "Upset enough to phone your ex-husband's residence last week in the middle of the night and make certain threats and accusations."

"I did no such thing." For the first time a battle light came into her eyes. "I never called Tony's apartment, never spoke to Rene at all. She assumed I did."

"Mrs. Avano, we can easily check phone records."

"Then please do so." Her spine stiffened, and so did her voice. "However displeased I was with the choices Tony made, they were his choices. I'm not in the habit of calling anyone in the middle of the night to make threats or accusations."

"The current Mrs. Avano claims other-wise."

"Then she's mistaken, or she's lying. She called me, in the middle of the night, and accused me of this, was abusive and upset-ting. You'll find that call on your phone records, Detective, but you won't find one on mine."

"Why would she lie?"

"I don't know." On a sigh, Pilar rubbed her temple. "Perhaps she wasn't. I'm sure someone did call her, and she assumed it was me. She was angry. She disliked me on principle."

"Do you know what time Mr. Avano left the premises here the night of the party?"

"No. Frankly, I avoided both him and Rene as much as possible that evening. It was awkward and it was uncomfortable for me."

"Do you know why he went to your daughter's apartment at . . ." The cab com-pany had come through. Claremont looked at his pad as if refreshing his memory. "Three o'clock that morning?"

"No."

"Where were you at that time?"

"In bed. Most of the guests were gone by one. I went to my room sometime before two. Alone," she added, anticipating the question. "I said good night to Sophia, then I went straight to bed because I was tired. It had been a long day."

"Could we have a moment?" Helen asked, and gestured to indicate the detectives should step out of the room.

"You can get from here to San Francisco in an hour," Maguire speculated in the hallway. "She's got no alibi for the time in question. She's got a decent motive."

"Why meet the ex in your daughter's apartment?"

"All in the family."

"Maybe," Claremont responded, and stepped back in when the judge called.

"Detectives, Mrs. Avano is reluctant to bring up certain information. Anthony Avano was her husband for a number of years, and they share a daughter. She's distressed to say anything that damages his reputation. However, as I've advised her, it's more constructive to pass on this information, as it may be useful to your investigation. And moreover . . . Moreover, Pilar," she said quietly, "they're going to get the picture soon enough from other sources."

"All right." She got to her feet, roamed the room. "All right. You asked if I had any idea why he might have gone to Sophia's. I can't be sure, but . . . Tony had a weakness for women. Some people drink, some gamble, some have affairs. Tony had affairs. He may have arranged to meet someone there, to break off an affair or to . . ."

"Do you know who he might have been involved with?"

"No, I stopped looking a long time ago. But there was someone. He knew who'd called Rene that night, I'm sure of it. And he seemed edgy at the party. That was un-usual for Tony. He was rarely ruffled. He was a bit rude to David Cutter, and not as sociable as was his habit. I think, looking back, he was in some sort of trouble. I don't know. I didn't want to know so I didn't do anything about it. If I had . . . I can't know if it would have made a difference. That's painful."

Claremont rose. "We appreciate your co-operation, Mrs. Avano. We'd like to speak with the other members of the family now,

Mr. Cutter and any members of the staff who were here during the party."

He specifically wanted to question Sophia again. He took her alone, while his partner took David Cutter. "You didn't mention that you and your father had a heated argument on the night he was killed."

"No, I didn't, because you didn't ask. Now that you do, I'd have to qualify. An argument is between two people over a point of disagreement. There was no argument."

"Then how would you qualify it?"

"Hard words. Hard words that were a long time coming. It's difficult for me, Detective, to know they're the last words I'll ever say to him. Even though they were true, even though I meant them, it's difficult. I was angry. He'd been married hours after the divorce from my mother was final. He hadn't bothered to tell me of his plans, hadn't bothered to give my mother the courtesy of informing her, and he came to a family event with his new wife on his arm. It was careless and insensitive, and just like him. I told him so."

"My information is you threatened him."

"Did I? I might have. I was furious, hurt, embarrassed. Rene had cornered my mother and attacked her—verbally. There was no call for it; she had what she wanted. He let it happen. My father was brilliant at letting things happen and remaining somehow oblivious to the damage done."

Word spread. Across the country, and across the Atlantic. Donato sat in the office on the first floor of his home, drank brandy and considered. The house was finally quiet, though he expected the baby would be up squalling for its breast before long.

Gina was sleeping, and if it wasn't for that habitual middle-of-the-night circus, he could have slipped out and spent a relaxing hour with his mistress.

Best not to risk it.

Tony Avano was dead.

The meeting scheduled with Margaret Bowers the next morning would and should be postponed. That would buy him time. He'd preferred keeping his business dealings with Tony. He'd known just where he stood with Tony Avano.

Now Tony was dead, and there would be a great upheaval. There would be talk, gossip, delays, snags. He could use that to his advantage.

He must go back to California, of course. He would have to offer his support and his sympathies to Pilar and Sophia. And assure *La Signora* that he would do whatever she required him to do in order to maintain Giambelli's production.

Since it was only two days before Christmas, he would convince Gina that she must remain at home and not upset the children. Yes, that was good. And he could take his pretty lady along for company.

No one would know the difference.

Yes, this would give him time to figure out what had to be done, and how to do it.

Poor Tony, he thought, and lifted his brandy. Rest in peace.

Jeremy DeMorney turned down the volume on the evening news and removed his dinner jacket. He was glad he'd made it an early night. It was better to be home, alone, when the news hit, than out in public.

Tony Avano, the worthless bastard, was dead.

Almost a pity in a way. The current climate

had made Avano ripe for picking. And Jerry had waited a good long time for it.

Leaving behind a sorrowful ex-wife, he imagined, a merry widow and a grieving daughter. All more than he'd deserved.

As he undressed, Jerry considered flying back out to California to attend whatever memorial service the Giambellis planned. Then dismissed the idea.

It was a bit too well known that the late, unlamented Avano had slept with Jeremy's wife.

Oh, they'd handled it like civilized people, of course. Not counting the split lip Jerry had given his adulterous wife as a parting gift. Divorce, financial settlement and a pretense of manners in public.

Well, Jerry thought, they'd all excelled at pretenses.

He'd send a personal message to the family expressing his sympathy and regrets. Best, all around, he decided, to keep his distance from the family for the time being.

He'd make his move there when he was ready.

For the moment, he'd have a little wake of his own. Damned if he wasn't going to open a bottle of champagne and celebrate murder.

Sophia spent nearly a week handling her father's murder like a business assignment. With emotions on hold, she made calls, made arrangements, asked questions, answered them and watched her mother like a hawk.

When she ran into a wall, and she ran into plenty, she did what she could to scale over or tunnel under. The police gave her nothing but the same repetitive line. The investigation was ongoing. All leads were being actively pursued.

They treated her resentfully, she thought, no differently than they did a reporter. Or a suspect.

Rene refused to take her calls, and she grew weary of leaving dozens of messages on the machine. Sympathetic messages, concerned messages, polite ones, angry ones, bitter ones.

Her father *would* have a memorial service. With or without his widow's input or cooperation.

She made excuses to her mother, citing a

few problems at her San Francisco office that needed her attention, and prepared to drive to the city.

Tyler was pulling up in the drive as she stepped out of the house.

"Where're you going?"

"I have business."

"Where?"

She tried to move by him toward the garage, only to have him step into her path. "Look, I'm in a hurry. Go prune a vine."

"Where?"

Nerves wanted to snap, and that couldn't be allowed. "I need to run into the city. I have some work."

"Fine. We'll take my car."

"I don't need you today."

"Teamwork, remember?" He knew a woman who was teetering on a thin wire, and he wasn't letting her drive.

"I can handle this, MacMillan." Why the hell hadn't she said she was going shopping?

"Yeah, you can handle anything." He put one hand on her arm, opened the car door with the other. "Get in."

"Did it ever occur to you I'd rather be alone?"

"Did it ever occur to you I don't care?" To solve the problem he simply picked her up and plopped her on the seat. "Strap in," he ordered, and slammed the door.

She considered kicking the door open, then kicking him. But she was afraid she'd never stop. There was such a rage inside her, such a burning, raging grief. And she reminded herself, as she'd promised she would, that he had been there for her at the worst moment.

He slid behind the wheel. Maybe it was because he'd known her more than half his life. Maybe it was because he'd paid more attention to her over the past few weeks than he had over the last twenty years. Either way, Ty thought, he knew that face almost too well. And the composure on it was no real mask, at least not at the moment.

"So." He turned the car on, glanced toward her. "Where are you really going?"

"To see the police. I can't get any answers on the phone."

"Okay." He shifted into first and headed down the drive.

"I don't need a guard dog, Ty, or a big, broad shoulder or an emotional pillow."

"Okay." He just kept driving. "For the

record, I'd just as soon you didn't need a punching bag, either."

As an answer, she folded her arms, stared straight ahead. The mountains were shrouded with mist, laced with snow, like a soft-focused photograph. The staggering view did nothing to cheer her. In her mind all she could see was the torn-out sheet from an industry magazine that had come in her mail the day before.

The photograph of her, her grandmother, her mother that had been published months before had been defiled, as the Giambelli angels had been. Red pen had been used this time, slashing bloody ink over their faces, branding them murdering bitches this time.

Was it the answer to her repeated calls to Rene? Sophia wondered. Did the woman think such a childish trick would frighten her? She wouldn't let it frighten her. And as she'd burned it in the flames of the fireplace, Sophia had felt disgust, anger, but not fear.

Yet still, a day later, she couldn't get it out of her mind.

"Did Eli ask you to baby-sit me?" she demanded of Tyler.

"No."

"My grandmother?"

"No."

"Then who?"

"Here's the deal, Sophia. I take orders in business when I have to. I don't take them in my personal life. This is personal. Clear?"

"No." She looked away from the mountains now, studied his equally compelling profile. "You didn't even like my father, and you're not that crazy about me."

"I didn't like your father." He said it simply, without apology and without pleasure. And for that reason alone it didn't sting. "Jury's still out on you. But I do like your mother, and I really don't like Rene, or the fact that she tried to sic the cops on Pilar, and maybe on you, over this."

"Then you'll be thrilled to know my second stop today is Rene. I need to go a round or two with her about a memorial service."

"Boy, won't that be fun? Do you think there'll be hair pulling and biting involved?"

"You men really get off on that kind of thing, don't you? It's just sick."

"Yeah." He sighed, heavy and wistful, and

made her laugh, the first easy, genuine laugh in days.

It occurred to Sophia that she'd never been in an actual police station. Her idea of one had been fictionally generated so that she'd expected dark, dank corridors with worn linoleum; noisy, cramped offices; surly-eyed, snarling characters and the stench of bad coffee served in paper cups.

Secretly, she'd been looking forward to the experience.

Instead she found an office atmosphere with clean floors and wide hallways that smelled faintly of Lysol. She wouldn't have said it was quiet as a tomb, but when she walked toward the detectives' division with Ty, she could hear her heels click on the floor.

The detectives' area was scattered with desks, utilitarian, but not scarred and dented as had been her hope. There was the scent of coffee, but it smelled fresh and rich. She did see guns, so that was something. Strapped to belts or harnessed over shoulders. It seemed odd to see them in the well-lit room where the major sound was the clicking of computer keys.

As she scanned, she connected with Claremont. He glanced toward a door on the side of the room, then rose and walked toward them.

"Ms. Giambelli."

"I need to talk to you about my father. About arrangements, and your investigation."

"When I spoke to you on the phone—"

"I know what you told me on the phone, Detective. Basically nothing. I think I'm entitled to more information, and I'm certainly entitled to know when my father's body will be released. I'm going to tell you my next step will go over your head. I'll start using every connection I have. And believe me, my family has many connections."

"I'm aware of that. Why don't we use the lieutenant's office." He gestured, then cursed under his breath when the side door opened and his partner walked out with Rene.

She was magnificent in black. Pale of cheek, with her hair shining like the sun and coiled at the nape, she was the perfect picture of the society widow. Sophia imagined she'd studied the results carefully before stepping out and she hadn't been able to resist relieving the black with a delicate diamond starburst brooch.

Sophia stared at the pin for a long moment, then snapped her attention to Rene.

"What's she doing here?" Rene demanded. "I told you she's been harassing me. Calling me constantly, threatening me." She clenched a handkerchief in her hand. "I want to file a restraining order on her. On all of them. They murdered my poor Tony."

"Have you been practicing that act long, Rene?" Sophia asked icily. "It still needs a little work."

"I want police protection. They had Tony killed because of me. They're Italian. They have connections to the Mafia."

Sophia started to laugh, a little bubble of sound at first that built and built until she couldn't stop. She staggered back and sat on the low bench along the wall. "Oh that's it, that's right. There's a hotbed of organized crime in my grandmother's house. It just took an ex-model, a social-climbing bimbo gold digger to ferret it out."

She wasn't aware her laughter had turned to weeping, that tears were streaming down her cheeks. "I want to bury my father, Rene. Let me do that. Let me have some part in doing that, then we'll never have to see or speak to each other again."

Rene tucked her handkerchief back in her purse. She crossed the room, a room that had gone very quiet. And waited until Sophia got to her feet again. "He belongs to me. And you'll have part of nothing."

"Rene." Sophia reached out, sucked in a breath when her hand was slapped sharply away.

"Mrs. Avano." Claremont's tone was a warning even as he took her arm.

"I won't have her touch me. If you or anyone in your *family* calls me again, you'll deal with my lawyers." Rene threw her chin up and strolled out of the room.

"For spite," Sophia murmured. "Just for spite."

"Ms. Giambelli." Maguire touched her arm. "Why don't you come sit down, let me get you some coffee."

"I don't want any coffee. Will you tell me if there's any progress in your investigation?"

"We have nothing new to tell you. I'm sorry."

"When will my father's body be released?"

"Your father's remains are being released this morning, to his next of kin."

"I see. I've wasted my time, and yours. Excuse me." She walked out and was already yanking her phone from her purse. She tried Helen Moore first, only to be told the judge was on the bench and unavailable.

"You think she can stop Rene?"

"I don't know. I have to try." She called James Moore's office next, frustrated to be told he was in a meeting. As a last ditch, she asked for Linc.

"Linc? It's Sophia. I need help."

Pilar sat on a stone bench in the garden. It was cold, but God, she needed the air. She felt trapped in the house in a way she never had before. Trapped by the walls and the windows, guarded by the people who loved her best.

Watched, she thought, as carefully as an invalid who might pass at any moment.

They thought she was grieving, and she let them think it. Was that the bigger of her sins? she wondered. To allow everyone to believe she was devastated by grief.

When she felt nothing. Could feel nothing.

Unless it was, horribly, the slightest twinge of relief.

There had been shock and sorrow and grief, but it had all passed so quickly. And her lack of feeling shamed her, so much so, she'd avoided her family as much as possible. So much so, she'd spent nearly the whole of Christmas in her rooms, unable to comfort her child for fear the child would see her mother's falseness.

How could a woman go from loving to not loving to callousness so quickly? Pilar wondered. Had the lack of passion and compassion been in her all along? And had that lack been what had sent Tony away from her? Or had what he'd done so carelessly throughout their marriage killed whatever capacity she'd had to feel?

It hardly mattered. He was dead, and she was empty.

She got to her feet, turned toward the house, then stopped when she saw David on the path.

"I didn't want to disturb you."

"That's all right."

"I've been trying to keep out of your way."

"That wasn't necessary."

"I thought it was. You look tired, Pilar." And lonely, he thought.

"I suppose we all are. I know you've pulled a lot of extra duty these past few days. I hope you know how much it's appreciated." She nearly stepped back when he walked toward her, but made herself hold still. "How was your Christmas?"

"It was busy. Let's just say I'll be glad when January rolls around and the kids start school. Is there anything I can do for you?"

"No, nothing, really." She intended to excuse herself, escape to her rooms. Again. But there was something about him. And looking at him, she heard words pouring out of her mouth. "I'm so useless here, David. I can't help Sophia. I know she's trying to take her mind off everything with work, and spending so much time trying to train me in the office here. I just bungle everything."

"That's a foolish thing to say."

"It's not. I do. I never really worked in an office, and the short time I did was over twenty-five years ago. Everything's changed. I can't make the damn computer work, and I don't know the language, even the purpose half the time. Instead of rapping my knuckles over my mistakes as she should, she's patting my head because she doesn't want to upset me. And she's the one who's upset, and I can't help her."

She pressed her fingers to her temple. "So I run away. I'm so goddamn good at running away. I'm out here right now so that I don't have to face her. She's making herself sick over Tony, trying to stop Rene from claiming his body. She can't grieve, won't let herself. There's no closure, and won't be any until the police . . . But she needs this rite, this ritual, and Rene won't have it."

"She needs to deal with it in her own way. You know that. Just as you need to deal with it in yours."

"I don't know what mine is. I should go in. I have to find the right words."

Unwilling to leave her alone, David walked with her toward the house. "Pilar, do you think Sophia doesn't know what she means to you?"

"She knows. Just as she knows what she didn't mean to her father. It's difficult for a child to live with that."

"I know it. But they do."

She stopped on the side terrace, turned

to him. "Are you ever afraid you're not enough for them?"

"Every day."

She let out a half-laugh. "It's terrible of me, but it's a relief to hear you say that." She opened the side door to see Sophia on the sofa, her face stark white, with Linc Moore beside her, gripping her hand.

"What is it?" Pilar rushed across the room, crouched in front of her daughter. "Oh baby, what is it?"

"We were too late. Linc tried. He even got a temporary restraining order, but it was too late. She's had him cremated, Mama. She'd already arranged for it before . . ."

"I'm sorry." Still holding Sophia's hand, Linc reached out to Pilar. "She had him taken straight to the crematorium. It was already begun before we had the temporary restraining order."

"He's gone, Mama."

CHAPTER ELEVEN

Over the long winter, the vines slept. The fields stretched, acre upon acre, drinking the rains, hardening under frosts, softening again with the quick and teasing warm snaps.

For a farmer, for a crop, the year was a circle to be repeated over and over, with the variations and surprises, the pleasures and the tragedies absorbed into the whole.

Life was a continuing spiral running round.

Toward February, heavy rains delayed the pruning cycle and brought both frustration and that wet winter promise of a good harvest. The fields and mountains smoked with mists.

February was for waiting. For some, it seemed the waiting had already lasted forever.

On the third floor of Villa Giambelli, Tereza kept her office. She preferred the third floor, away from the hive of the house. And she loved her lofty view from the windows of all that was hers.

Every day she climbed the steps, a good discipline for the body, and worked there for three hours. Never less, and rarely these days, more. The room was comfortable. She believed comfortable surroundings increased productivity. She also believed in indulging herself where it mattered to her.

The desk had been her father's. It was old, the oak dark and the drawers deep. That was tradition. On it sat a two-line phone and a high-powered computer. That was progress.

Beneath it, old Sally snored quietly. That was home.

She believed, absolutely, in all three.

Because she did, her office was now occupied by her husband and his grandson, her daughter and granddaughter and David Cutter and Paulo Borelli.

The old and the new, she thought.

She waited while coffee was served and the rain beat like soft fists on the roof and windows.

"Thank you, Maria." That signaled the end of the social interlude and the beginning of business. Tereza folded her hands as the housekeeper slipped out, shutting the door.

"I'm sorry," she began, "we've been unable to meet in total before this. The loss of Sophia's father, and the circumstances of his death, postponed certain areas of business. And Eli's recent illness prevented holding this meeting."

She glanced toward him now. He still looked a bit frail to her. The cold had turned so quickly into fever and chills, she'd been frightened.

"I'm fine," he said, more to reassure her than the rest. "A little shaky on my pins yet, but coming 'round. A man doesn't have any choice but to come around when he's got so many nurses pecking at him."

She smiled, because he wanted her to, but she heard the faint wheeze in his chest. "While Eli was recuperating, I've kept him as current as possible on the movements of business. Sophia, I have your report, and your projections regarding the centennial campaign. While we'll also discuss this individually, I'd like you to bring everyone up to date."

"Of course." Sophia got to her feet, opened a portfolio that contained mock-ups of the ads, along with full target reports on message, consumer statistics and the venues selected.

"Phase one of the campaign will begin in June with advertising placed as indicated in your packets," she began as she passed the packets around. "We've created a three-pronged campaign, targeting our high-end consumer, our middle line and the most elusive, the young, casual wine drinker on a limited budget."

While she spoke, Tyler tuned her out. He'd heard the pitch before. Had, God help him, been in on various stages of its development. The exposure had taught him the value of what she did, but he couldn't drum up any real interest in it.

Long-range weather reports forecasted a warming trend. Too much, too soon would tease some of the grape varieties out of dormancy. He needed to keep a keen eye out for that, for the telltale signs of that slight movement in the buds, for the soft bleeding at the pruning cuts.

An early break meant the danger of frost damage.

He was prepared to deal with that, when the time came, but . . .

"I see we're keeping Tyler awake," Sophia said sweetly, and snapped him back.

"No, you're not. But since you interrupted my nap, the second phase deals with public participation. Wine tastings, vineyard tours, social events, auctions, galas—both here and in Italy—which generate publicity."

He rose to get more coffee from the cart. "Sophia knows what she's doing. I don't think anyone here's going to argue that."

"And in the fields?" Tereza asked. "Does Sophia know what she's doing?"

He took his time, sipped his coffee. "She's all right, for an apprentice field hand."

"Please, Ty, you'll embarrass me with all those fulsome compliments."

"Very well," Tereza murmured. "David? Comments on the campaign?"

"Clever, classy, thorough. My only concern, as a father of teenagers, is that the ads targeting the twenty-one to thirty market make wine look like a hell of a good time."

"Which it is," Sophia pointed out.

"And which we want to project it to be," he agreed. "But I'm wary about making the ads so slick and appealing to a young audience that those still too young will be influenced. That's the father talking," he admitted. "But I was also a boy who if and when I wanted to drink myself sick, did so without any marketing influence whatsoever."

Pilar made a little sound, then subsided. But as David sat beside her, had made certain he sat beside her, he heard it. "Pilar? Thoughts?"

"No, I was just . . . well, actually, I think the campaign's wonderful, and I know how hard Sophie's worked on it—and Ty, of course, and her team. But I think David has a valid point about this, well, third prong. It's difficult to market something that appeals to the young market group without luring the inappropriate ages in. If we could do some sort of disclaimer . . ."

"Disclaimers are boring and dilute the message," Sophia began, but she pursed her lips as she sat again. "Unless we make it fun, witty, responsible and something that blends with the message. Let me think about it."

"Good. Now, Paulie."

Now it was Sophia who tuned out while

the foreman spoke of the vines, of various vintages being tested in the casks and tanks.

Age, she thought. Age. Vintage. Ripeness. Perfection. She needed the hook. Patience. Good wine takes patience to make. Rewards. Age, rewards, patience. She'd find it.

Her fingers itched to get out her pen and scribble. She worked better if she set words down, saw them on paper. She got up for more coffee and, with her back to the room, scrawled quickly on a napkin.

Paulie was excused and David called up. Instead of the marketing projections, the cost analyses, the forecasts and numbers Sophia had expected, her grandmother set his written report aside.

"We'll deal with this later. At the moment I'd like your evaluation of our key people here."

"You have my written reports on that as well, *La Signora.*"

"I do," she agreed, and simply lifted her eyebrows.

"All right. Tyler doesn't need me in the vineyards, and he knows it. The fact that it's my job to oversee them and I'm another competent pair of hands hasn't yet taken the edge off his resistance. A resistance I can't blame him for, but that does get in the way of efficiency. Other than that, the MacMillan vineyards are as well run as any I've ever been associated with. As are Giambelli's. Adjustments are still being made, but his work on merging the operations, coordinating crews is excellent.

"Sophia does well enough in the vineyard, though it's not her strength. Just as the marketing and promotion isn't Tyler's. The fact that she carries the weight there, as he does in the field, results in a reasonably good and surprisingly interesting blend. However, there are some difficulties in the offices in San Francisco."

"I'm aware of the difficulties," Sophia said. "I'm handling them."

"Her," David corrected. "Sophia, you have a difficult, angry, uncooperative employee who's been trying for several weeks to undermine your authority."

"I have a meeting set up with her tomorrow afternoon. I know my people, David. I know how to deal with this."

"Are you interested in how I know just how difficult, angry and uncooperative

Kristin Drake's been?" He waited a beat. "She's been talking to other companies. Her résumé's landed on half a dozen desks in the last two weeks. One of my sources at La Coeur tells me she's making a number of claims and accusations, with you her favorite target, when she thinks she has the right ear."

Sophia absorbed the betrayal, the disappointment, and nodded. "I'll deal with her."

"See that you do," Tereza advised. "If an employee can't be loyal, at least she must be dignified. We won't tolerate a staff member using gossip or innuendo as a bargaining chip for a position with another company. And Pilar?"

"She's learning," David said. "Business isn't her strong suit. I think you misuse her, *La Signora.*"

"I beg your pardon?"

"In my opinion, your daughter would be more suited as a spokesperson, a liaison for the company where her charm and her elegance wouldn't be wasted as they are working at a keyboard. I wonder that you don't ask Pilar to help with the tours and the tastings, where visitors could be treated to her company and have the extra benefit of personal contact with a member of the family. She's an excellent hostess, *La Signora*. She is not an excellent clerk."

"You're saying I've made a mistake expecting my daughter to learn the business of the company?"

"Yes," David said easily and made Eli fall into a fit of coughing.

"Sorry, sorry." He waved a hand as Tyler leaped up to pour him a glass of water. "Tried to suck down that laugh. Shouldn't. Christ, Tereza, he's right and you know it." He took the glass from Tyler, sipped carefully until the pressure in his chest eased. "Hates to be wrong, and hardly ever is. Sophia? How's your mama working out as your assistant here?"

"She's hardly had time to . . . She's terrible," Sophia admitted and burst out laughing. "Oh, Mama, I'm so sorry, but you're just the worst office assistant ever created. I couldn't send you into the city to work with my team in a million years. You have ideas," she added, concerned when her mother said nothing. "Just like today, about the disclaimer. But you won't mention them unless you're pinned, and even then you don't know how to implement. More than all of that, you hate every minute you're stuck in my office."

"I'm trying. And obviously failing," she said as she got to her feet.

"Mama—"

"No, that's all right. I'd rather you be honest than patronize me. Let me make this easier on everyone involved. I quit. Now if you'll excuse me, I'll go find something to do that I'm good at. Like, sit somewhere looking elegant and charming."

"I'll go talk to her," Sophia began.

"You won't." Tereza lifted a hand. "She's a grown woman, not a child to be placated. Sit. We'll finish the meeting."

It was, Tereza thought as she lifted her coffee, encouraging to see her daughter show a snap of temper and a hint of spine.

Finally.

He didn't have time to smooth ruffled feathers, but since he felt he'd had some part in the ruffling, David sought Pilar out. Over the past weeks, Maria had become one of his conduits of news and family dynamics. With her help, he tracked Pilar down in the greenhouse.

He found her there wearing gardening gloves and an apron, repotting seedlings she'd started from cuttings.

"Got a minute?"

"I have all the time in the world," she said without sparing him a glance or an ounce of warmth. "I don't do anything."

"You don't do anything in an office that satisfies you or accomplishes a goal. That's different. I'm sorry my evaluation hurt your feelings, but—"

"But it's business." She looked at him now, dead on.

"Yeah. It's business. You want to type and file, Pilar? To sit in on meetings about publicity campaigns and marketing strategies?"

"I want to feel useful." She tossed down her little spade. Did they think she was like the flowers she tended here? she wondered. Did she? Something that required a controlled climate and careful handling to do nothing but look attractive in a nice setting?

"I'm tired. Sick and tired of being made to feel as if I have nothing to offer. No skills, no talents, no brains."

"Then you weren't listening."

"Oh, I heard you." She yanked off her

gloves, tossed them down as well. "I'm to be charming and elegant. Like some well-tailored doll that can be plunked down at the right time and the right place, and tucked away in the closet the rest of the time. Well, no thanks. I've been tucked away quite long enough."

She started to push by him, yanked her arm when he closed his hand over it. Then stared in shock as he simply took her other arm and held her in place.

No one handled her. It simply wasn't done.

"Just hold on."

"Take your hands off me."

"In a minute. First, charm is a talent. Elegance is a skill. And it takes brains to know the right thing to say at the right time, and to make people feel welcome. You're good at those things, so why not use them? Second, if you think handling tourists and accounts at tastings and tours is fluff work, you'll find out different if you work up the guts to try it."

"I don't need you to tell me—"

"Apparently you do."

She nearly gaped when he cut her off. It was something else rarely done. And she remembered just how he'd dealt with Tony the night of the party. He was using that same cold, clean slice with her now.

"I'll remind you, I don't work for you."

"I'll remind you," he countered, "essentially you do. Unless you're going to stalk off like a spoiled child, you'll continue to work for me."

"*Va' al diavolo.*"

"I don't have time for a trip to hell just now," he said equably. "I'm suggesting you put your talents in the proper arena. You need to know the business to handle the winery tours, have the patience to answer questions you'll hear over and over again. To push the product without appearing to push it. To be gracious, informative and entertaining. And before you start, you have to take a good, hard look at yourself and stop seeing the discarded wife of a man who didn't value anything as much as himself."

Her mouth fell open and her lips trembled before she could form words. "What a hideous thing to say."

"Maybe. But it's time somebody said it. Waste bothers me. You've let yourself be wasted, and it's starting to piss me off."

"You have no right to say these things to

me. Your position with Giambelli doesn't give you a license to be cruel."

"My position with the company doesn't give me the right to speak the truth as I see it. It doesn't give me the right for this, either," he added and jerked her against him. "But this time it's personal."

She was too shocked to stop him, to manage even the slightest protest. And when his mouth was on hers, hard and angry, she could do nothing but feel.

A man's mouth—hot, firm. A man's hands—demanding and strong. The jolt of having her body pressed up to his, to feel that heat, those lines. The sexual threat.

The blood rushed into her head, one long tidal wave of power. And her body, her heart, starved, leaped into the flood of pleasure.

On a low moan, she threw her arms around him. They bumped her worktable, sent pots tumbling. Clay cracked against clay with a sound like swords clashing. Nerves, needs, so long deadened, snapped into life to sizzle through her system. Everything seemed to waken at once, threatening overload as her knees went weak and her mouth went wild under his.

"What?" She was breathless, managed only a gasp as he lifted her off her feet and plunked her down on the bench. "What are we doing?"

"We'll think about it later."

He had to touch her, had to feel her flesh under his hands. Already he was tugging at her sweater, fueled by a sexual rush that made him feel like a teenager in the back of a Chevy.

Rain slapped against the glass walls, and the air was warm and moist, fragrant with flowers, with soil, with the scent of her. She was quaking against him, quick, hard trembles. Delicious little sounds were humming in her throat.

He wanted to gulp her down, swallow her whole and worry about the fine points later. He couldn't remember when he'd last had this ferocious urge to mate plunging inside of him.

"Pilar. Let me . . ." He fought with the button of her slacks.

If he hadn't said her name, she would have forgotten it. Forgotten everything and simply surrendered to the demands of her own body. But the sound of it jolted her back. And brought the first flutter of panic.

"Wait. This is—we can't."

She pushed against him, even as her head fell back and her system shivered at the scrape of his teeth on her throat. "David. No. Wait. Stop."

"Pilar." He couldn't catch his breath, find his balance. "I want you."

How many years had it been since she'd heard those words? How many years had it been since she'd seen them in a man's eyes? So many, Pilar thought, that she couldn't trust herself to think or act rationally when she did.

"David. I'm not ready for this."

He still had his hands on her, cupped at her waist just under her sweater where her skin was warm and still quivering. "Could've fooled me."

"I wasn't expecting . . ." He had such strong hands, she thought. Strong and hard at the palm. So unlike . . . "Please, could you step back?"

He stayed exactly where he was. "I wanted you the first minute I saw you. The minute you opened the front door."

Pleasure sprinted into her, chased by panic, and puzzlement. "I'm—"

"Don't." He spoke curtly. "Don't say you're flattered."

"Of course I am. You're very attractive, and—" And she couldn't *think* straight when he was touching her. "Please. Would you step back?"

"All right." But it cost him. "You know what happened here doesn't happen every time, with everyone."

"I think we took each other by surprise," she began and cautiously slid down from the bench.

"Pilar, we're not children."

"No, we're not." It flustered her to have to straighten her sweater, to remember how it had felt to have his hands under it. On her. "Which is one of the points. I'm forty-eight years old, David, and you're . . . well, you're not."

He hadn't thought anything in the situation would make him laugh. But that did. "You're not going to use a handful of years as an excuse."

"It's not an excuse. It's a fact. Another is that we've only known each other for a short time."

"Eight weeks and two days. And that's how long I've imagined getting my hands on you." He trailed his fingers over her hair while she stared at him. "I didn't plan on jumping you in your greenhouse and tearing off your clothes in the middle of your peat pots. But it worked for me at the time. You want something more conventional? I'll pick you up at seven for dinner."

"David. My husband's been dead only a few weeks."

"Ex-husband," he said icily. "Don't put him between us, Pilar. I won't tolerate that."

"Nearly thirty years can't be dismissed overnight, no matter what the circumstances."

He took her by the shoulders, lifted her up to her toes before she realized just how angry he was. "Tony Avano stopped being your safety zone, Pilar. Deal with it. And deal with me."

He kissed her again, hard and long, then let her go. "Seven o'clock," he said, and stalked out into the rain.

Worthless son of a bitch was *not* going to complicate his life, or Pilar's, from the grave, David determined. His strides were long, his shoulders hunched, and the fury bubbled just under his skin.

He wasn't going to allow it. There was going to be some straight talk, with all the secrets and shadows shoved into the light. Very soon.

Because he was scowling at his feet, and Sophia was looking down as she jogged through the rain, they ran hard into each other on the path.

"Oops," she managed, and slapped a hand on the hat she'd tossed on to protect her from the worst of the wet. "I thought you'd gone home."

"I had something to do first. I just tried to seduce your mother in the greenhouse. Do you have a problem with that?"

Sophia's hand fell to her side. "Excuse me?"

"You heard me. I'm attracted to your mother, and I just acted on it. I fully intend to act on it again as soon as possible. Is that a problem for you?"

"Ah . . ."

"No quick spin? No clever comeback?"

Even through the daze of shock, she could recognize a furious and frustrated male. "No, sorry. Processing."

"Well, when you've finished, send me a goddamn memo."

As he stormed off, Sophia could almost

see steam rising off him. Torn between shock and concern, she slapped a hand to the hat again and sprinted to the green-house.

When she burst in, Pilar was standing, staring at her workbench. Pots were scattered, tipped over, and several seedlings were crushed beyond redemption.

It gave Sophia a very good idea just what had gone on, and where. "Mama?"

Pilar jumped, then quickly grabbed her gardening gloves. "Yes?"

Slowly now, Sophia walked forward. Her mother's cheeks were flushed, her hair mussed the way a woman's hair was when a man's hands had run through it.

"I just saw David."

Pilar dropped the gloves from fingers that had gone numb, hastily bent to retrieve them. "Oh?"

"He said he tried to seduce you."

"He what?" It wasn't panic now but full-blown horror that snapped into Pilar's throat.

"And from the look of you, he got a good start on it."

"It was just a . . ." Unnerved, Pilar snatched up her apron, but couldn't quite

remember how to put it on. "We had a disagreement, and he was annoyed. It's really
not worth talking about."

"Mama." Gently, Sophia took the gloves,
then the apron, set them down. "Do you
have feelings for David?"

"Really, Sophia, what a question."

One you're not answering, she thought.
"Let's try this. Are you attracted to him?"

"He's an attractive man."

"Agreed."

"We're not—that is, I'm not . . ." At wits'
end, Pilar braced her hands on the bench.
"I'm too old for this."

"Don't be ridiculous. You're a beautiful
woman in the prime of her life. Why
shouldn't you have a romance?"

"I'm not looking for romance."

"Sex, then."

"Sophie!"

"Mama!" Sophia said in the same horrified
tone, then threw her arms around her
mother. "I started out here afraid I'd hurt
your feelings and that you'd be upset. Instead I find you flushed and rumpled after
what I assume was a delightful bit of man-
handling by our new and very sexy COO.
It's wonderful."

"It's not wonderful, and it's not going to happen again. Sophia, I was married for nearly three decades. I can hardly just pick myself up and jump into another man's arms at this point in my life."

"Dad's gone, Mama." Sophia kept her arms tight around Pilar, but her voice softened. "It's hard for me to accept that, to live with how it happened, and to adjust to being denied even the chance to say goodbye. It's hard, even knowing he really didn't love me."

"Oh, Sophie, he did."

"No." She drew back now. "Not the way I wanted, or needed or looked for. You did, always. He wasn't there for me. And he wasn't there for you. It wasn't in him to be. Now you have a chance to enjoy someone who'll pay attention to you."

"Oh, baby." Pilar reached out to stroke her daughter's cheek.

"I want that for you. And I'd be so sad, so angry if I thought you'd push that chance away because of something that never really existed. I love you. I want you happy."

"I know." Pilar kissed both of Sophia's cheeks. "I know. It takes time to adjust. And oh, *cara,* it's not just your father and what happened to us, what happened to him that's an issue. It's me. I don't know how to be with someone else, or if I want to be with anyone."

"How will you know if you don't try?" Sophia started to boost herself onto the bench, than thought better of it. Under the circumstances. "You like him, don't you?"

"Well, of course I do." Like? she thought. A woman didn't nearly roll naked in potting soil with a man she liked. "He's a very nice man," she managed. "A good father."

"And you're attracted to him. He's got a terrific ass."

"Sophia."

"If you tell me you haven't noticed, I'm going to have to break a commandment and call my mother a liar. Then there's that smile. That fast grin."

"He has kind eyes," Pilar murmured, forgetting herself and making her daughter sigh.

"Yes, he does. Are you going out with him?"

Pilar got busy tidying pots. "I don't know."

"Go. Explore a little. See what it feels like. And take one of the condoms in my nightstand."

"Oh, for heaven's sake."

"On second thought, don't take one." Sophia wrapped an arm around Pilar's waist and giggled. "Take two."

CHAPTER TWELVE

Maddy eyed her father shrewdly as he knotted his tie. It was his First Date tie, the gray with the navy blue stripes. She knew he'd *said* he and Ms. Giambelli were just going out to dinner so she and Theo would think it was a business kind of thing. But the tie was a dead giveaway.

She had to think about how she felt about it.

But at the moment, she was entertaining herself by pushing his parent buttons.

"It's a symbol of self-expression."

"It's unsanitary."

"It's an ancient tradition."

"It's not a Cutter family ancient tradition. You're not getting your nose pierced, Madeline. That's it."

She sighed and put on a good sulk. Actually, she had no desire to get her nose pierced but she did want a third piercing in her left earlobe. Working down to it, or over to it, from the nose was good strategy. The kind, she thought, her father would appreciate if he knew about it.

"It's my body."

"Not until you're eighteen, it's not. Until that happy day, it's mine. Go nag your brother."

"I can't. I'm not speaking to him."

She rolled onto her back on her father's bed, lifted her legs to the ceiling. They were clad in her usual black, but she was starting to get sort of tired of it. "Can I get a tattoo instead?"

"Oh sure. We'll all go get one this weekend." He turned. "How do I look?"

Maddy cocked her head, considered. "Better than average."

"You're such a comfort to me, Maddy."

"If I get an A on my science report, can I get my nose pierced?"

"If Theo gets an A on anything, I might consider letting him get his nose pierced."

Since both ends of the statement were equally far-fetched, she laughed. "Come on, Dad."

"Gotta go." He scooped her off the bed, carting her from the room with his arm around her waist and her feet dangling off the floor.

The habit, as old as she could remember, never failed to bring a bubble of happiness to her chest. "If I can't do the nose, could I just do another in my left ear? For a little stud?"

"If you're bound and determined to put more holes in yourself, I'll think about it." He paused by Theo's door, knocked with his free hand.

"Get lost, creep."

David looked down at Maddy. "I assume he means you." He pushed open the door to see his son stretched out on the bed, the phone at his ear, rather than sitting at his desk with his homework.

David felt twin pulls. Annoyance that the assignments were certainly not done, and pleased relief that Theo had already made new friends at school to interfere with his studies.

"Call you back," Theo muttered and hung up. "I was just taking a break."

"Yeah, for the entire month," Maddy commented.

"There's plenty of stuff you can nuke for dinner. I left the number of the restaurant on the pad by the phone, and you've got my cell number. Don't call unless you have to. No fighting, no naked strangers in the house, no touching the alcoholic beverages. Finish your homework, no phone or TV until it's done, and don't set fire to the house. Did I leave anything out?"

"No blood on the carpet," Maddy put in.

"Right. If you have to bleed, bleed on the tiles."

He kissed the top of Maddy's head, then dropped her to her feet. "I should be home by midnight."

"Dad, I need a car."

"Uh-huh. And I need a villa in the south of France. Go figure. Lights out at eleven," he added as he turned away.

"I've *got* to have wheels," Theo called after him, and swore under his breath as he heard his father walk down the stairs. "You might as well be dead out here without wheels." He flopped back on the bed to brood up at the ceiling.

Maddy just shook her head. "You're such a moron, Theo."

"You're so ugly, Maddy."

"You're never going to get a car if you nag him. If I help you get a car, you have to drive me to the mall twelve times, without being mean about it."

"How are you going to help me get a car, you little geek?" But he was already considering. She almost always got what she wanted.

She sauntered into the room, made herself at home. "First the deal. Then we discuss."

Tereza was not of the opinion that a parent stepped back at a certain point in a child's life and watched the proceedings in silence. After all, would a mother stand on shore and watch a child, whatever her age, bob helplessly in the sea without diving in?

Motherhood didn't end when a child reached her majority. In Tereza's opinion, it never ended. Whether the child liked it or not.

The fact that Pilar was a grown woman with a grown daughter of her own didn't stop Tereza from going to her room. And it certainly didn't stop her from speaking her mind as she watched Pilar dress for her evening out.

Her evening out with David Cutter.

"People will talk."

Pilar fumbled with her earrings. Every stage of the basic act of dressing had taken on enormous proportions.

"It's only dinner." With a man. An attractive man who'd made it perfectly clear he wanted to sleep with her. *Dio.*

"People find fuel for gossip in a thought. They'll run their engines for some time over you and David socializing together."

Pilar picked up her pearls. Were pearls too formal? Too old-fashioned? "Does that trouble you, Mama?"

"Does it trouble you?"

"Why should it? I haven't done anything to interest anyone." With fingers that seemed to have grown outsized and clumsy, she fought with the clasp.

"You're Giambelli." Tereza crossed the room, took the strand from Pilar's hand and hooked the clasp. "That alone is enough. Do you think because you chose to make a home and raise a daughter you've done nothing of interest?"

"You made a home, raised a daughter and

ran an empire. Comparatively, I fall very short. That was made clear today."

"You're being foolish."

"Am I, Mama?" She turned. "Just over two months ago you tossed me into the business, and it's taken me no time at all to prove I have no talent for it."

"I shouldn't have waited so long to do so. If I hadn't tossed you in, you'd have proven nothing. Years ago, I came here with specific goals in mind. I would run Giambelli and see it was the best in the world. I would marry and raise children, watch them grow happy and healthy."

Automatically she began to rearrange the bottles and pots on Pilar's vanity. "One day I would pass what I'd helped build into their hands. The many children I dreamed of weren't to be. I'm sorry for that, but not that you're my child. You may be sorry that your goals of marriage and children didn't come to be. But are you sorry, Pilar, that Sophia is yours?"

"Of course not."

"You think I'm disappointed in you." Her eyes met Pilar's in the mirror, and were level, clear. "And I was. I was disappointed that you allowed a man to rule your life, that you allowed him to make you feel less than you were. And because you did nothing to change it."

"I loved him for a long time. That may have been my mistake, but you can't dictate to your own heart."

"You think not?" Tereza asked. "In any case, nothing I said to you could sway you. And, in looking back, my mistake was in making it too easy for you to stay adrift the way you did. That's over now, and you're too young not to make new goals. I want you to take part in your heritage, to be part of what was passed to me. I insist on it."

"Even you can't make me a business-woman."

"Then make yourself something else," Tereza said impatiently as she turned to face Pilar directly. "Stop thinking of yourself as a reflection of what a man saw in you, and *be*. I asked you if it bothered you that people will talk. I wish you'd said the hell with people. Let them talk. It's time you gave them something to talk about."

Surprised, Pilar shook her head. "You sound like Sophie."

"Then listen. If you want David Cutter,

even for the moment, take. A woman who sits and waits to be given usually ends up empty-handed."

"It's only dinner," Pilar began, then broke off as Maria came to the door.

"Mr. Cutter is downstairs."

"Thank you, Maria. Tell him Miss Pilar will be right down." Tereza turned back to her daughter, recognized, even approved of, the slight panic she saw in Pilar's eyes. "You had that same look on your face when you were sixteen and a young man waited for you in the parlor. It's good to see it again." She leaned forward, brushed her lips over Pilar's cheek. "Enjoy your evening."

Alone, Pilar took a moment to settle. She wasn't sixteen, and it was only dinner, she reminded herself as she started out. It would be simple, it would be civilized and it would most probably be quite pleasant. That was all.

Nervous, she opened her bag at the top of the stairs to make certain she'd remembered everything. She blinked in shock as she dipped her fingers in and closed them over two packs of Trojans.

Sophia, she thought as she hastily shut

the bag again. For God's sake! The laugh that tickled her throat was young and foolish. When she let it come she felt ridiculously relieved.

She went downstairs to see what happened next.

It was a date. There was no other word for it, Pilar admitted. Nothing else brought this rosy glow to an evening or put this giddiness in the belly. It might have been decades since she'd had a date, but it was coming back to her, loud and clear.

She might have forgotten what it was like to sit across a candlelit table from a man and talk. Just talk. More, to have that man listen, to have *attention* paid. To watch his lips curve at something she said. But remembering it, experiencing it again, was like being offered a cool sip of water before you'd realized how desperately thirsty you'd become.

Not that she intended to let anything come of it but, well, friendship. Every time she let herself think of what her own daughter had slipped into her purse, Pilar's palms went damp.

But a friendship with an attractive, interesting man would be lovely.

"Pilar! How wonderful to see you."

Pilar recognized the cloud of scent and
the cheerful bite of the voice before she
looked up. "Susan." She was already fixing
on her social smile. "Don't you look wonderful. Susan Manley, David Cutter."

"No, don't get up, don't get up." Susan,
glowingly blond and just out of recovery
from her latest face-lift, fluttered a hand at
David. "I was just on my way back to my
table from powdering my nose, and saw
you here. Charlie and I are here with some
out-of-town clients of his. Dead bores, too,"
she said with a wink. "I was just saying to
Laura the other day how we should get together. It's been so long. I'm glad to see you
out, and looking so well, honey. I know what
a horrible time this has been for you. Such a
shock to everyone."

"Yes." Pilar felt the quick sting of the
prick, and the slow deflate of the pleasure
of the evening. "I appreciated your note."

"I only wish I could have done more. Well,
we don't want to talk about sad things, do
we." She gave Pilar's arm a little squeeze,

even as she sized up her dinner companion. "I hope your mother's well."

"Very, thank you."

"I have to get along. Can't leave poor Charlie floundering with those two. So nice to meet you, Mr. Cutter. Pilar, I'm going to call you next week. We'll have lunch."

"I'll count on it," Pilar replied, then picked up her wine as Susan glided off. "I'm sorry. The Valley's not much more than a small town in some ways. It's hard to go anywhere without running into people you know."

"Then why apologize for it?"

"It's awkward." She set down her wine again, left her fingers on the stem to run up and down. "And as my mother predicted, people will talk."

"Really?" He took her hand from the glass. "Then let's give them something to talk about." He brought her hand to his lips, nibbled lightly on the knuckles. "I like Susan," David said as Pilar stared at him. "She gave me the opening to do this. What," he wondered aloud, "do you suppose she'll say to Laura tomorrow when she calls her?"

"I can only imagine. David." There were thrills rocketing up her arm. Even when she slid her hand from his they shivered along the skin. "I'm not looking for . . . anything."

"That's funny, neither was I. Until I saw you." He leaned forward, intimately. "Let's do something sinful."

The blood rushed to her head. "What?"

"Let's"—his voice dropped into a seductive whisper—"order dessert."

The breath that had clogged in her lungs came out in a laughing whoosh. "Perfect."

And it was perfect, the drive home in the night under chilly stars and a cold white moon. Music playing softly on the radio as they debated, with some heat, a book they'd both recently read. Later, she'd think how odd it was to have felt so relaxed and so stimulated all at once.

She nearly sighed as she saw the lights of the villa. Nearly home, she thought. She'd started out the evening almost swallowed by her own nerves, and was ending it with regret that it couldn't have lasted longer.

"Kids are still up," David commented, noting the guest house was lit up like a Vegas casino. "I'll have to kill them."

"Yes, I've noticed what a terrifying and brutal father you are. And how your children fear you."

He slanted her a look. "I wouldn't mind seeing the occasional tremble out of them."

"I think it's way too late for that. You've gone and raised two happy, well-adjusted kids."

"Still working on it." He drummed his fingers on the steering wheel. "Theo got into some trouble back in New York. Shoplifting, sneaking out of the apartment. His grades, never stellar, plummeted."

"I'm sorry, David. The teenage years can be hard on everyone. Harder still when you're a single parent. I could tell you some hair-raising stories about Sophia at that age. Your son is a nice young man. I imagine that sort of behavior was just normal acting out."

"Gave me the jolt I suppose I needed. I was letting him run just a little too free because it was easier. Not enough hours in the day, not enough energy left at the end of it. It was harder on Maddy than Theo when their mother left, so I compensated more with her than him."

"Second guesses," she said. "I know all about them."

"I was into third guesses with Theo and Maddy. Anyway, that's one of the reasons I opted to buy the van and drive cross-country instead of dumping us all in a plane. It gave us some time. Nothing like a three-thousand-mile drive in an enclosed vehicle to cement a family unit—if you live through it."

"It was very brave of you."

"You want to talk courage?" He drove easily up the lane to the villa. "I've been chief taste-tester on this wine experiment Maddy's conducting. It's brutal."

She chuckled. "Be sure to let us know if we've got a competitor in the making." She started to reach for the door handle, but his hand came to her shoulder, stopped her.

"I'll come around. Let's finish the evening off right."

Nerves rolled back. Just exactly what did he mean by that? she wondered as he walked around the van. Was she supposed to ask him in so they could neck in the parlor? Surely not. It was out of the question.

He'd just walk her to the door. They could say good night, perhaps exchange a casual—very casual—kiss. Between friends, she reminded herself and geared back up as he opened her door.

"Thanks. It was a lovely dinner, a lovely evening."

"For me, too." He took her hand, not surprised to find it chilled. He'd seen the wariness come back into her eyes when he'd opened the door. And didn't mind it, not a bit. He wasn't above getting an ego boost from knowing he unnerved a woman.

"I want to see you again, Pilar."

"Oh. Well, of course. We're—"

"Not in company," he said, turning her toward him when they stood on the veranda. "Not for business. Alone." He drew her closer. "And for very personal reasons."

"David—"

But his mouth was on hers again. Gently, this time. Persuasively. Not with that abrupt and shocking flash of heat that had rudely slapped all those sleeping urges awake, but with a slow and simmering warmth that patiently unknotted every snag of tension inside her. Loosened her until her bones felt like wax melting.

When he drew back, his hands were on her face, fingers skimming over her cheekbones, then down, trailing lightly over her throat. "I'll call you."

She nodded, reached blindly behind her for the door. "Good night, David."

She stepped inside, closed the door. No matter how foolish she told herself she was, she knew she floated all the way upstairs.

The caves always made Sophia think of a smuggler's paradise. All those big, echoing spaces filled with huge casks of aging wine. She'd always enjoyed spending time there, and even when she was a child one of the winemakers would let her sit at a little table and sample a small glass from one of the casks.

She'd learned, very young, to tell the difference, through sight, through scent, through palate, between a premium vintage and an ordinary one. To understand the subtleties that lifted one wine over another.

If it had spoiled her for the ordinary, what was the harm in that? She looked for, recognized and demanded quality because she'd been taught to tolerate nothing less.

It wasn't wine she was thinking of now, though the wines had been drawn from the aging vats, and glasses were set out for sampling. It was men she had on her mind.

She'd made a study of them as well, she liked to think. She knew an inferior blend, recognized one who was likely to leave a bitter aftertaste and one who would prove himself over time.

That was why, she believed, she'd had no long-term, no serious relationship with a man herself. None of the ones she'd sampled had the right flavor, the proper bouquet, as it were, to convince her she'd be content with only one variety.

Though she was perfectly confident in her ability to make the right choices for herself, and to be able to enjoy without consequences the tasting flights, she wasn't so confident about her mother's skill in the same area.

"It's their third date in two weeks."

"Mmm." Ty held a glass of claret to an open fire to check its color. He, like his grandfather, like *La Signora,* stuck firm with the old and traditional methods. He rated it a two for both color and clarity, and noted down the superior marks on his chart.

"My mother and David." To get his attention, Sophia punched him lightly on the arm.

"What about them?"

"They're going out again tonight. Third time in two weeks."

"And that's my business because?"

She heaved out a breath. "She's vulnerable. I can't say I don't like him, because I do. And I didn't particularly want to. I even encouraged her initially when he showed some interest in her, but I thought it was just a little fling coming around."

"Sophia, it may surprise you, but I'm working here, and I really don't want to talk about your mother's personal business."

He swirled the wine gently, stuck his nose in the glass and inhaled. His concentration was completely focused.

"They haven't had sex."

He winced visibly and lost the wine's bouquet. "Damn it, Sophie."

"If they'd had sex by now, I wouldn't have to worry. That would mean it was just a nice little physical attraction instead of a thing. I think it's becoming a thing. And how much do we know about David really? Other than from a professional standpoint. He's divorced and we don't know why. He might be a womanizer, or an opportunist. When you think about it, he started after my mother right after my father . . ."

Tyler nosed the wine again, noted down his numbers. "Which sounds like you're saying your mother wouldn't appeal to him on her own."

"I certainly am not." Insulted, Sophia snatched up a glass of Merlot, scowled through it into the light. "She's beautiful, intelligent, charming and everything a man could want in a woman."

But not what her father had wanted, she remembered. In disgust, for herself, she marked the sample down for cloudiness. "I wouldn't worry about it if she'd talk to me. But all she'll say is she and David enjoy each other's company."

"Gee, you think?"

"Oh, shut up!" She nosed her wine, noted down her opinion, then sipping, letting the wine rest inside her lower gum, touched it with the tip of her tongue to register the sweetness first before moving it to the sides, to the rear of her mouth to judge its acidity and tannic content.

She swished it around, allowing the various taste elements to blend, then spat it out.

"It's immature yet."

Tyler tested it himself and found he

agreed with her. "We'll let it age a bit. A lot of things become what they're meant to if you leave them alone awhile."

"Is that philosophy I hear?"

"You want an opinion, or just somebody to agree with you?"

"I guess wanting both was expecting too much."

"There you go." He picked up the next glass, held it to the light. But he was looking at Sophia. It was hard not to, he admitted. Not to look, not to wonder. Here they were in a cool, damp cave, a fire snapping, the smells of smoke and wood and earth surrounding them, shadows dipping, dancing.

Some people would have said it was romantic. He was doing his best not to be one of them. Just as he'd been doing his best for some time not to think of her as a person, much less as a woman. She was, he reminded himself, a partner at best. And one he could have done without.

And right now his partner was worried. Maybe he thought she was borrowing trouble, or sticking her pretty nose where it didn't belong, but if he knew absolutely one thing about Sophia, it was that she loved her mother unreservedly.

"His ex-wife dumped him and the kids."

Sophia's gaze lifted from the wine she held, met his. "Dumped?"

"Yeah, decided there was a big old world out there, and she was entitled to it. Couldn't explore it or herself with a couple of kids and a husband hanging on. So she left."

"How do you know this?"

"Maddy talks to me." And he felt guilty for repeating things he'd been told. The kid didn't say much about her home life, but enough to give him a clear view. "She doesn't blab about it or anything, just lets stuff drop now and again. From what I gather, the mother doesn't contact them often, and Cutter's been running the show since she took off. Theo got in a little trouble, and Cutter took the position out here to get him out of the city."

"So he's a good father." She knew all too well what it was to be dumped by a parent. "That doesn't mean he's good for my mother."

"That's for her to decide, isn't it? You look for flaws in every man you see and you're going to find them."

"That's not what I do."

"It's exactly what you do."

"I don't have to look very deep with you." She offered in a sugary voice, "They're all so obvious."

"Lucky for both of us."

"Which is a step up from your pattern. You barely look at all. Easier to keep yourself wrapped up in the vines than risk getting wrapped up in a human being."

"Are we talking about my sex life? I must've missed a step."

"You don't have one."

"Not compared to yours." He set down the glass to make his notes. "Then again, who does? You go through men like a knife through cheese. A long, slow slice, a nibble, discard. You're making a mistake thinking you can set those standards for Pilar."

"I see." Hurt rippled through her. He'd made her sound cheap again. Like her father. Needing to punish him for it, she moved closer. "I haven't gone through you yet, have I, Ty? Haven't even managed the first cut. Is it because you're afraid to try on a woman who's able to think about sex the way a man does?"

"I don't want to try on a woman who

thinks about anything the way a man does. I'm narrow-minded that way."

"Why don't you expand your horizons?" She tipped her face up, invited. "Dare you," she teased.

"I'm not interested."

Still testing, she wound her arms around his neck, tightening them when he lifted his arms to pull them away. "Which one of us is bluffing?"

Her eyes were dark, fiery. The scent of her slid around him, into him. She brushed her lips over his, one seductive stroke.

"Why don't you sample me?" she asked softly.

It was a mistake, but it wouldn't be his first. He gripped her hips and ran his hands up her sides.

The scent of her was both ripe and elusive. A deliberate and effective torment for a man.

"Look at me," he ordered, and took the mouth she offered.

Took what and how he wanted. Long, slow, deep. And he let the taste of her slide over his tongue, as he would with a fine wine, then slip almost lazily, certainly pleasurably, into his system.

His lips rubbed over hers, turning her inside out. Somehow he'd flipped it all around on her, and the tempted had become the tempter. Knowing it, she couldn't resist.

There was so much more here than she'd imagined. More than she'd ever been offered, or had accepted.

He watched her, intensely. Even as he toyed with her mouth, sent her head spinning and her body churning, he watched her with all the patience of a cat. That alone was a fresh and shocking thrill.

He ran his hands down her sides again, those wide hands just brushing her breasts. And drew her away.

"You push my buttons, Sophia. I don't like it."

He turned away to take a pull from the bottle of water used to cleanse the palate.

"A vintner's also a scientist." The air felt thick as she drew in a breath. "You've heard of chemical reactions."

He turned, held the bottle out to her. "Yeah. And a good vintner always takes his time, because some chemical reactions leave nothing but a mess."

The little stab disappointed as much as it stung. "Can't you just say you want me?"

"Yeah, I can say it. I want you, enough that it sometimes hurts to breathe when you're too close."

Like now, he thought, when the taste of her was alive inside him.

"But when I get you into bed, you're going to look at me the way you looked at me just now. It's not going to be just another time, just another man. It's going to be me, and you're going to know it."

There was a ripple along her skin. She had to force herself not to rub her hands over her arms to chase it away again. "Why do you make that sound like a threat?"

"Because it is." Moving away from her, he picked up the next glass of wine and went back to work.

CHAPTER THIRTEEN

Claremont studied the Avano file. He spent a great deal of what he could eke out as spare time studying the data, the evidence, the crime scene and medical examiner reports. He could nearly recite the statements and interviews by rote.

After nearly eight weeks it was considered by most to be a dead end. No viable suspects, no tangible leads, no easy answers.

It stuck in his craw.

He didn't believe in perfect crimes but in missed opportunities.

What was he missing?

"Alex." Maguire stopped by his desk, sat on the corner. She already wore her coat against the misery that was February in San Francisco. Her youngest had a history project due the next day, her husband was fighting off a cold and they were having left-over meat loaf for dinner.

Nobody was going to be happy at her house, but she needed to be there.

"Go home," she told him.

"There's always a loose end," he complained.

"Yeah, but you're not always able to tie it off. Avano stays open, and it looks like it's going to stay that way unless we get lucky and something falls in our laps."

"I don't like luck."

"Yeah, well, I live for it."

"He uses the daughter's apartment for a meet," Claremont began and ignored his partner's long-suffering sigh. "Nobody sees him go in, nobody hears the gunshots, nobody sees anyone else go in or out."

"Because it was in the neighborhood of three in the morning. The neighbors were asleep and, used to city noises, didn't hear the pop of a twenty-five-caliber."

"Pissant gun. Woman's gun."

"Excuse me." She patted her own police-issue nine-millimeter.

"Civilian woman's gun," he corrected with what was nearly a smile. "Wine and cheese, late-night meet in an empty apartment.

Sneaking out on the wife, apparently. Victim's a guy who liked to cheat on the wife. Smells like a woman. And maybe that's the angle. Maybe it was set to smell like a woman."

"We looked at men, too."

"Maybe we need to look again. The ex–Mrs. Avano, as opposed to the widow Avano, has been seen socializing in the company of one David Cutter."

"That tells me her taste in men has improved."

"She stays legally married to a philandering son of a bitch for nearly thirty years. Why?"

"Look, my husband doesn't run around and I love him like crazy. But sometimes I wonder why I stay legally married to him. She's Catholic," Maguire finished with another sigh, knowing she wasn't getting home anytime soon. "Italian Catholic and practicing. Divorce wouldn't come easy."

"She gave him one when he asked."

"She didn't stand in his way. Different thing."

"Yeah, and as a divorced Catholic she wouldn't be able to remarry, would she? Or snuggle up with another man with the approval of the Church."

"So she kills him to clear the way? Reaching, Alex. On the Catholic sin-o-meter, murder edges out divorce."

"Or somebody does it for her. Cutter's brought in to the company, *over* Avano. Got to cause some friction. Cutter likes the look of Avano's estranged and soon-to-be-divorced wife."

"We ran Cutter up, down and sideways. He's squeaky."

"Maybe, or maybe he didn't have a good reason to get his hands dirty before. Look, we found out Avano was in financial trouble. Unless the widow's an Oscar-caliber actress, I'd say that came as a big, unpleasant surprise to her. So, going with the theory that Avano was keeping his money problems to himself, and wasn't the type to do without his beluga for long, where would he go for a fix? Not one of his society friends," Claremont continued. "Wouldn't be able to show his face at the next charity ball. He goes to Giambelli, where he's been bailed out periodically for years. To the ex-wife, maybe."

"And following your line, if she agreed,

Cutter got steamed over it. If she didn't, and Avano got nasty, Cutter got steamed over it. It's a long way from steamed to putting three bullets in a man."

Still, she considered. It was something to chew on, and there'd been precious little so far. "I guess we're chatting with David Cutter tomorrow."

David juggled the hours of his workday between the San Francisco offices, his home office, the vineyards and the winery. With two teenagers to raise and a demanding job, he often put in fourteen-hour days.

He'd never been happier in his life.

With La Coeur he'd spent most of his time behind a desk. Had occasionally traveled to sit on the other side of someone else's desk. He'd worked in an area that interested him and had earned him respect and a good salary.

And he'd been bored brainless.

The hands-on approach he was not only allowed but expected to use with Giambelli-MacMillan made each day a little adventure. He was dipping his fingers into areas of the wine business that had been only theory or paperwork before.

Distribution, bottling, shipping, marketing. And above all, the grape itself. From vine to table.

And what vines. To be able to see them, stretching, stretching, wrapped in the fogs and mists of the valley. The linear and the insubstantial that mingled light and shadow. And when the frost shimmered on them at dawn, or the cold moonlight drizzled down at midnight, there was magic there.

When he walked through the rows, breathing in the mystery of that damp air, and the wispy arms of the vines surrounded him, it was like living in a painting. One he could, and would, mark with his own brush strokes.

There was a romance in that romance he'd forgotten locked behind steel and glass in New York.

His home life still had bumps. Theo pushed and shoved against the rules on a daily basis. It seemed to David the boy was grounded as often as not.

Like father like son, he often thought. But it wasn't much of a comfort when he was in the middle of the combat zone. He began to wonder why his own father, faced with such a surly, hardheaded, argumentative off-spring, hadn't simply locked him in the attic until he'd turned twenty-one.

Maddy wasn't any easier. She appeared to have given up on the nose ring. Now she was campaigning to have her hair streaked. It baffled him constantly how a sensible girl could forever be pining to do weird things to her body.

He had no idea how to get inside the mind of a fourteen-year-old girl. And wasn't entirely sure he wanted to.

But they were settling in. They were making friends. They were finding a rhythm.

He found it odd neither of them had commented on his relationship with Pilar. Normally they teased him mercilessly about his dates. He thought perhaps they assumed it was business. Which was just as well.

He caught himself daydreaming, as he often did when his mind drifted to Pilar. He shook his head, shifted in his chair. This wasn't the time to indulge himself. He had a meeting with department heads in twenty minutes and needed to review his notes.

Because time was short, he wasn't pleased to be interrupted by the police.

"Detectives. What can I do for you?"

"A few minutes of your time," Claremont told him, while Maguire scanned the office and got the lay of the land.

"A few minutes is exactly what I can spare. Have a seat."

Big, cushy leather seats, Maguire noted. In a big, cushy corner office with a kick-ass view of San Francisco through the wide windows. A thoroughbred of offices for a desk jockey, and totally masculine with its biscuit-and-burgundy color scheme and glossy mahogany desk.

She wondered if the office was tailored to suit the man, or vice versa.

"I assume this has to do with Anthony Avano," David began. "Is there any progress in the investigation?"

"The case is still open, Mr. Cutter. How would you describe your relationship with Mr. Avano?"

"We didn't have one, Detective Clare-mont," David replied matter-of-factly.

"You were both executives for the same company, both worked primarily out of this building."

"Very briefly. I'd been with Giambelli less than two weeks before Avano was killed."

"In a couple of weeks, you'd have formed an impression," Maguire put in. "Had meetings, discussed business."

"You'd think, wouldn't you? But I'd yet to have a meeting with him, and we had only one discussion, which took place at the party the evening before his murder. It was the only time I met him face-to-face, and there really wasn't time to talk much business."

Didn't mention his impression, Claremont noted. But they'd get to that. "Why hadn't you met with him?"

"Scheduling conflicts." The tone was bland.

"Yours or his?"

David sat back. He didn't care for the direction of the questioning, or the implication. "His, apparently. Several attempts to reach him proved unsuccessful. In the time between my arrival and his death, Avano didn't come to the office, at least not when I was here, nor did he return my calls."

"Must've annoyed you."

"It did." David nodded at Maguire. "Which I dealt with during our brief conversation at the winery. I made it clear that I expected him to make time to meet with me during business hours. Obviously, that never happened."

"Did you meet with him outside of business hours?"

"No. Detectives, I didn't know the man. Had no real reason to like or dislike him or think about him particularly."

David kept his voice even, edging toward dismissive, as he would when winding up a tedious business meeting. "While I understand you have to explore every avenue in your investigation, I'd think you're scraping bottom if you're looking at me as a murder suspect."

"You're dating his ex-wife."

David felt the jolt in the belly, but his face stayed passive as he leaned forward again. Slowly. "That's right. His ex-wife, who was already his ex when he was murdered, already his ex when we began seeing each other socially. I don't believe that crosses any legal or moral line."

"Our information is that the ex–Mrs. Avano wasn't in the habit of seeing men socially, until very recently."

"That," David said to Maguire, "might be

because she hadn't met a man she cared to see socially, until very recently. I find that flattering, but not a reason to murder."

"Being dumped for a younger woman often is," Maguire said easily and watched cool eyes flare. Not just seeing her socially, she concluded. Seriously hung up.

"Which is it?" David demanded. "Pilar killed him because he wanted another woman, or she's heartless because she's interested in another man so soon after her ex-husband is murdered? How do you bend that premise both ways?"

Furious, Maguire thought, but controlled. Just the sort of makeup that could calmly sip wine and put bullets in a man.

"We're not accusing anyone," she continued. "We're just trying to get a clear picture."

"Let me help you out. Avano lived his own life his own way for twenty years. Pilar Giambelli lived hers, a great deal more admirably. Whatever business Avano might have had that night was his own, and nothing to do with her. My socializing with Ms. Giambelli, at this point, is completely our business."

"You assume Avano had business that night. Why?"

"I assume nothing." David inclined his head toward Claremont as he got to his feet. "I leave that to you. I have a meeting."

Claremont stayed where he was. "Were you aware Mr. Avano was having financial difficulties?"

"Avano's finances weren't my problem, or my concern."

"They would have been, if they connected to Giambelli. Weren't you curious as to why Mr. Avano was dodging you?"

"I'd been brought in from the outside. Some resentment was expected."

"He resented you."

"He may have. We never got around to discussing it."

"Now who's dodging?" Claremont got to his feet. "Do you own a handgun, Mr. Cutter?"

"No, I don't. I have two teenage children. There are no guns of any kind in my house, and never have been. On the night Avano was murdered, I was at home with my children."

"They can verify that."

David's hands curled into fists. "They'd know if I'd left the house." He wasn't having his kids interrogated by the police. Not over a worthless excuse of humanity like Avano. "That's all we're going to discuss until I consult an attorney."

"That's your right." Maguire rose and played what she banked was her trump card. "Thanks for your time, Mr. Cutter. We'll question Ms. Giambelli about her ex-husband's finances."

"I'd think his widow would know more."

Maguire continued. "Pilar Giambelli was married to him a lot longer, and part of the business for which he worked."

David slipped his hands into his pockets. "She knows less about the business than either of you." And thinking of her, David made his choice. "Avano had been, for the last three years, systematically embezzling money from Giambelli. Padded expense accounts, inflated sales figures, travel vouchers for trips not taken or taken but for personal reasons. Never a great deal at a time, and he picked various pockets so that it went unnoticed. In his position, professionally and personally, no one would

have, and no one did, question his figures."

Claremont nodded. "But you did."

"I did. I caught some of it the day of the
party and, in double-checking it, began to
see the pattern. It was clear to me he'd
been dipping for some time under his
name, under Pilar's and under his daughter's. He didn't trouble to forge their signatures on the vouchers, just signed them. To
a total of just over six hundred thousand in
the last three years."

"And when you confronted him . . ."
Maguire prompted.

"I never did. I intended to, and believe I
made that intention clear during our conversation at the party. My impression was he
understood I knew something. It was business, Detective, and would have been handled through the business. I reported the
problem to Tereza Giambelli and Eli MacMillan the day after the party. The conclusion
was that I would handle it, do what could be
done to arrange for Avano to pay the
money back. He would resign from the
company. If he refused any of the stipulations outlined, the Giambellis would take legal action."

"Why was this information withheld?"

"It was the wish of the senior Ms. Giambelli that her granddaughter not be humiliated by her father's behavior becoming public. I was asked to say nothing, unless directly asked by the police. At this point, *La Signora,* Eli MacMillan and myself are the only people who know. Avano's dead, and it seemed unnecessary to add to the scandal by painting him as a thief as well as a philanderer."

"Mr. Cutter," Claremont said. "When it's murder, nothing's unnecessary."

David had barely closed the door at the cops' back and taken a breath to steady himself when it opened again. Sophia didn't knock, didn't think to.

"What did they want?"

He had to adjust quickly and folded his concern and anger together, tucked them away. "We're both running late for the meeting." He scooped up his notes, slid them with the reports, the graphs, the memos into his briefcase.

"David." Sophia simply stayed with her back to the door. "I could've gone after the cops and tried to get answers I haven't been able to get from them. I hoped that you'd be more understanding."

"They had questions, Sophia. Follow-ups, I suppose you call them."

"Why you and not me or several other people in this building? You barely knew my father, had never worked with him or as far as I'm aware spent any time with him. What could you tell the police about him, or his murder, that they haven't already been told?"

"Little to nothing. I'm sorry, Sophia, but we'll need to table this, at least for now. People are waiting."

"David. Give me some credit. They came directly to your office, and stayed in here long enough for there to have been something. Word travels," she finished. "I have a right to know."

He said nothing for a moment, but studied her face. Yes, she had a right to know, he decided. And he had no right to take that away from her.

He picked up his phone. "Ms. Giambelli and I will be a few minutes late for the meeting," he told his assistant. He nodded to a chair as he hung up. "Sit down."

"I'll stand. You may have noticed, I'm not delicate."

"I've noticed you handle yourself. The police had some questions that sprang, at least in part, from the fact that I'm seeing your mother."

"I see. Do they have some theory that you and Mama have been engaged in some long, secret affair? That could have been put to rest easily enough by the fact that until a couple of months ago you lived a country apart. Added to the fact that my father had been living openly with another woman for several years, a few dinner dates is very small potatoes."

"I'm sure they're covering all angles."

"Do they suspect you or Mama?"

"I'd say they suspect everyone. It's part of their job description. You've been careful not to comment, to me in any case, on how you feel about my relationship with your mother."

"I haven't decided how I feel about it, precisely. When I do, I'll let you know."

"Fair enough," he said equably. "I know how I feel about it, so I'll tell you. I care very much about Pilar. I don't intend to cause her trouble or upset. I'd be sorry to cause you any, either, first because she loves you and second because I like you. But I was just in the position of choosing between causing you both some upset or having my kids interrogated and doing nothing to stop the investigation from wandering down a dead end."

She wanted to sit down now. Something told her she'd need to. Because of it, pride kept her on her feet. "What did you tell the police that's going to upset me?"

Truth, he thought, like medicine, was better given in one fast dose. "Your father had been embezzling from the company for several years. The amounts were spread out, and relatively moderate, which is one reason they went undetected as long as they did."

The color drained out of her face, but she didn't flinch. Didn't flinch even as the fist of betrayal slammed hard into her heart. "There's no mistake?" she began, then waved him off before he could answer. "No, of course there isn't. You wouldn't make one." There was a light lick of bitterness in the statement. She couldn't stop it. "How long have you known?"

"I confirmed it the day of the party. I intended to meet with your father within the next couple of days to discuss—"

"To fire him," she corrected.

"To ask for his resignation. As per your grandparents' instructions. I reported the embezzlement to them the day after the party. He would have been given the opportunity to pay back the funds and resign. They did that for you—for your mother, too, for the company, but mostly for you. I'm sorry."

She nodded, turning away as she rubbed her hands over her arms. "Yes, of course. I appreciate your being honest with me now."

"Sophia—"

"Please, don't." She closed in as he stepped forward. "Don't apologize again. I'm not going to fall apart. I already knew he was a thief. I saw one of my mother's heirloom brooches on Rene's lapel. It was to come to me, so I know my mother didn't give it to him. I knew when I saw her wearing it, on her widow's black, that he'd stolen it. Not that he'd have thought of it that way. Any more than he'd have thought of the money he siphoned from the company as stealing. Pilar, he'd think, has so many trinkets. She wouldn't mind. The company, he'd tell himself, can afford to lend me a bit more capital. Yes, he was a champ at rationalizing his pathetic behavior."

"If you'd rather go home than attend the meeting, I can make your excuses."

"I have no intention of missing the meeting." She turned back. "Isn't it odd? I knew what he did to Mama all those years—I saw it for myself. But I managed to forgive him, or to tell myself it was just what he was, and make it, if not all right, somehow marginally acceptable. Now he's stolen money and jewelry, so much less important than stealing a person's dignity and self-respect as he did with my mother. But it took this for me to face fully that he was worthless as a human being. It took this for me to stop bleeding for him. I wonder why that is? Well, I'll see you at the meeting."

"Take a few minutes."

"No. He's already had more of my time than he was entitled to."

Yes, he thought as she walked out of his office. Very much like her grandmother.

Since it was Sophia's turn to drive, Tyler rode back from the city in silence. Unless, he thought, you counted the blast of the radio. He'd turned it down twice, only to have her snap the volume back up again. Departmental meetings gave him a headache and so did the opera currently screaming out of the speakers, but he decided to let it go. It certainly prevented any pretext of conversation.

She didn't look to be in the mood for conversation. He wasn't sure just what she looked in the mood for, but it sure as hell wasn't talk.

She drove too fast, but he'd gotten used to that. And even with whatever storm was brewing inside her, she wasn't careless as she swung around the curves and slopes of the road.

Still, he nearly sighed when he spotted the rooftops of home. He was about to get there, in one piece, where he could shrug out of his city clothes and fall into blessed silence and solitude.

Even with her mouth so firmly shut, he thought, the woman just wore him out.

But when she stopped at the end of the drive, she turned off the engine and was out of the car before he was.

"What're you doing?"

"Coming in," she called over her shoulder, adding a brief, glittering look to her words.

"Why?"

"Because I don't feel like going home."

He jangled his keys in his hand. "It's been a long day."

"Hasn't it just?"

"I've got things to do."

"That's handy. I'm looking for things to do. Be a pal, MacMillan. Buy me a drink."

Resigned, he jabbed his key in the lock. "Buy your own drink. You know where everything is."

"Gracious to the last. That's what I like about you." She strolled in and headed straight to the great room and the wine rack. "With you, Ty, there are no pretenses, no games. You are what you are. Surly, rude, predictable."

She chose a bottle at random. Variety and vintage didn't matter at the moment. While she uncorked it, she looked around the room. Stone and wood—hard materials, expertly and cleanly worked into a dignified setting for big, simple furnishings and plain colors.

No flowers, she thought, no soft edges, no polish. "Take this place, for example. No frills, no fuss. A manly man lives here, it says, who doesn't have time for appearances. Don't give a flying fuck about appearances, do you, Ty?"

"Not particularly."

"That's so damn stalwart of you. You're a stalwart individual." She poured out two glasses. "Some people live and die by appearances, you know. They're what matter most. Me, I'm more of a happy-medium type. You can't trust someone who has appearances as his religion, and the ones who don't give that flying fuck, you end up trusting too much."

"If you're going to drink my wine and take up my space, you might as well tell me what's put you in this mood and get it over with."

"Oh, I have many moods." She drank the wine, too quickly for pleasure, and poured a second glass for herself. "I'm a multifaceted woman, Tyler. You haven't seen the half of me."

She crossed to him, slowly. A kind of sexual gunfighter's swagger. "Would you like to see more?"

"No."

"Oh now, don't disappoint me and lie. No games, no pretenses, remember." She trailed a fingertip up his shirt. "You really want to get your hands on me, and conveniently, I really want to be handled."

"You want to get drunk and get laid? Sorry, doesn't suit my plans for the evening." He plucked the glass out of her hand.

"What's the matter? Want me to buy you dinner first?"

He set the glass down. "I think more of myself than that. And surprise, more of you."

"Fine. I'll just find someone who isn't so picky." She took three strides toward the door when he grabbed her arm. "Let go. You had your chance."

"I'm taking you home."

"I'm not going home."

"You're going where I take you."

"I said let go!" She whirled. She was prepared to scratch and claw and slap, could already feel the release of it gush through her. And was more surprised than he when she grabbed on hard and collapsed into tears.

"Shit. Okay." He did the only thing that came to mind. He picked her up, carried her to a chair and sat with her on his lap. "Get it all out, and we'll both feel better."

While she wept, the phone rang from somewhere under the sofa cushion where he'd lost it the last time. And the old mantel clock began to bong the hour.

She wasn't ashamed of tears. They were, after all, just another form of passion. But she preferred other methods of release. When she'd cried herself dry, she stayed where she was, curled warm against him and comforted more than she'd imagined.

He didn't pat and stroke, didn't rock or murmur all those foolish and reassuring words people tended to use to sop up tears. He simply let her hold on and purge herself.

As a result, she was more grateful than she'd imagined as well.

"Sorry."

"Yeah, that makes two of us."

The response made her relax. She drew a long breath, breathing in the scent of him, holding it in, as she held on to him. Then letting go.

"If you'd taken me up on the jungle sex, I wouldn't have blubbered all over you."

"Well, if I'd known my choices at the time . . ."

She laughed, and let her head rest on his shoulder just a moment before she climbed out of his lap. "We're probably better off this way. My father stole from the company."

Before he could decide how to respond, she took a step toward him. "You knew."

"No."

"But you're not surprised."

He got to his feet, sincerely hoping this wasn't the start of another battle. "No, I'm not surprised."

"I see." She looked away from him, stared hard into the hearth where last night's fire had burned to ashes. Apt, she thought. She felt just like that—cold and empty. "All right. Well." She stiffened her spine, wiped away the last traces of tears. "I pay my debts. I'll fix you dinner."

He started to protest. Then weighed the options of solitude against a hot meal. The woman could cook, he recalled. "You know where the kitchen is."

"Yes, I do." She stepped closer, rose on her toes and kissed his cheek. "Down payment," she told him, and shrugged out of her jacket as she left the room.

CHAPTER FOURTEEN

"You didn't call me back."

Margaret tracked Tyler down in the MacMillan winery. She'd had several satisfying and successful meetings since her return from Venice. Her career was advancing well, she was certain she looked her best after two carefully outlined shopping forays before her return to California. She was developing the polish she'd always believed international travel sheened on a woman.

There was one last goal she intended to achieve while she was stateside. Bagging Tyler MacMillan.

"Sorry. I've been swamped." February was a slow month in winemaking, but that didn't mean there wasn't work. Sophia had scheduled a wine-tasting party that evening on his turf. While he wasn't particularly pleased about it, he understood the value. And knew the importance of making certain everything was in place.

"I can imagine. I looked over the plans for the centennial campaign. You've done a terrific job."

"Sophia has."

Margaret wandered with him as he moved into the tasting room. "You don't give yourself enough credit, Ty. When are you coming over to take a look at the operation in Italy? I think you'd be impressed and pleased."

"There're noises about it. I don't have time now."

"When you do, I'll show you the area. Buy you some pasta at this terrific little trattoria I found. They're serving our wine there now, and I'm negotiating with some of the top hotels to spotlight our label this summer."

"Sounds like you've been busy, too."

"I love it. There's still a little resistance with some of the accounts that were used to Tony Avano and his style of business. But I'm bringing them around. Do the police have any more on what happened to him?"

"Not that I've heard." How soon, Tyler

wondered, would word of the embezzlement leak?

"It's terrible. He was a very popular guy
with the accounts. And they loved him in
Italy. They're not as open to sitting around
drinking grappa and smoking cigars with
me."

He stopped, smiled at her. "That's a picture."

"I know how to play with the boys. I have
to head back end of the week, make several
stops here in the States on my way. I was
hoping we could get together. I'll fix you
dinner."

What was with women offering to cook for
him? Did he look hungry? "That's—" He
broke off as he saw Maddy come in. The
kid always lifted his spirits. "Hey. It's the
mad scientist."

Secretly delighted, Maddy sneered at him.
"I've got my secret formula." She held up
two peanut butter jars filled with dark liquid.

"Looks pretty scary." Ty took it, tipped the
one she held out to him side to side and
watched it swish.

"Maybe you could try it at your tasting
tonight. See what people say."

"Hmmm." He could only imagine the

comments of the wine snobs after a sip of Maddy's kitchen wine. And because he could, he began to grin. "It's a thought."

"Aren't you going to introduce me to your friend?" It wasn't that Margaret didn't like children, mostly at a safe distance. But she was trying to make some time here.

"Oh, sorry. Margaret Bowers, Maddy Cutter."

"Oh, you must be David's little girl. Your father and I had some meetings today."

"No kidding." Resentment at being called a little girl simmered. "Me, too. Can I stay for some of the tasting?" She turned to Ty, ignoring Margaret. "I'm going to do this whole report on the wine, so I want to, like, observe and stuff."

"Sure." He opened the jar, nosed it. Amusement gleamed in his eyes. "I'd like to observe this one myself."

"Ty? How about tomorrow night?"

"Tomorrow?"

"Dinner." Margaret kept her voice casual. "There's a lot regarding the Italian operation I'd like to discuss with you. I'm hoping you can educate me a bit, pump up my weak areas. There are some aspects I'm cloudy on, and I think talking to an expert vintner who has English as his primary language would really help."

"Sure." He was much more interested in Maddy's wine at the moment, and moved behind the bar to get a glass.

"Seven? I've got a lovely Merlot I brought back with me."

"Great." The liquid Ty poured into the glass would never be a lovely anything.

"See you then. Nice to have met you, Maddy."

"Okay." She gave a quick snort when Margaret went out. "You're such a dork."

"Excuse me?"

"She was hitting on you and you're, like, oblivious."

"She wasn't hitting on me and you're not supposed to talk that way."

"Was too." Maddy slid onto a stool at the bar. "Women know these things."

"Maybe, but you don't qualify as a woman."

"I've had my period."

He'd started to drink, had to set the glass back down as he winced. "Please."

"It's a biological function. And when a female is physically able to conceive, she is, physically, a woman."

"Fine. Great." It wasn't a debate he wanted to enter into. "Shut up." He let the wine, such as it was, lie on his tongue. It was unsophisticated to say the least, highly acidic and oversweet thanks to the sugar she must have added.

Still, she'd succeeded in making wine in a kitchen bowl. Bad wine, but that wasn't the point.

"Did you drink any of this?"

"Maybe." She set the second jar on the counter. "Here's the miracle wine. No additives. I read about how sometimes they add ox blood for color and body. I didn't know where to get any. Besides, it sounds disgusting."

"We don't approve of that kind of practice. A little calcium carbonate would deacidify it some, but we'll just let it stand on its own. Altogether, it's not a complete failure as a jug wine. You pulled it off, kid. Nice going."

A brave man, he poured a swallow of the miracle wine, examined, nosed, sipped. "Interesting. Cloudy, immature and biting, but it's wine."

"Will you read my report and check my charts when I'm done?"

"Sure."

"Good." She fluttered her lashes. "I'll fix you dinner."

God, she tickled him. "Smart-ass."

"At last," David said as he came in. "Someone who agrees with me." He walked over, hooked an arm around his daughter's neck. "Five minutes, remember?"

"We got distracted. Ty said I could come to the tasting."

"Maddy—"

"Please. He's going to put my wine in."

David glanced over. "You're a brave man, MacMillan."

"You never spent an evening chugging any Run, Walk and Fall Down?"

With a grin, David covered Maddy's ears. "Once or twice, and fortunately I lived to regret it. Your wine club might object to the addition."

"Yeah." The thought of that tickled Ty, too. "It'll broaden their outlook."

"Or poison them."

"Please, Dad. It's for science."

"That's what you said about the rotten eggs you kept in your bedroom. We didn't really leave New York for professional reasons," he said to Ty. "The new tenants are probably still fumigating. Okay, but you turn into a pumpkin at ten. Let's go. Theo's in the van. He's driving us back."

"We'll all die," Maddy said solemnly.

"Scram. I'll be right out."

He plucked her off the stool, gave her a light whack on the butt to send her along.

"I just wanted to say I appreciate your letting her hang around."

"She doesn't get in the way."

"Sure she does."

Tyler set the glasses in the sink under the bar. "Okay, she does. But I don't mind."

"If I thought you did, I'd've herded her off. I also realize you're more comfortable with her than you are with me. I get in your way, and you do mind."

"I don't need a supervisor."

"No, you don't. But the company needed, and needs, fresh blood. An outsider. Someone who can look at the big picture from all angles and suggest a different way when it's viable."

"You got suggestions for me, Cutter?"

"The first might be taking the chip from your shoulder and the stick from your ass, then we can build a campfire with them and have a couple of beers."

Tyler said nothing for a moment as he tried to judge if he was amused or annoyed. "Add yours and we could have a hell of a blaze."

"There's an idea. I'll bring Maddy back around later. I'll come back at ten to pick her up."

"I can drop her home, save you a trip."

"Appreciate it." David headed toward the door, paused. "Listen, would you let me know if she gets . . . if she starts to get a crush on you. It's probably normal, but I'd like to head it off if it veers that way."

"It's not like that. I think I'm more big brother, maybe uncle material. But your boy's got a champion crush on Sophie."

David stared. Blinked. Then rubbed his hands over his face. "Missed that one. I thought it came and went the first week. Hell."

"She can handle it. Nothing she does better than handle the male of the species. She won't bruise him."

"He manages to bruise himself." He thought of Pilar, and winced.

"Hard to fault his taste, huh? Under the circumstances?"

David shot back a bland look. "Another smart-ass," he muttered and walked out.

Pilar chose a simple cocktail suit, thinking the sage green with satin lapels was midway between professional and celebratory. Perfect, she hoped, for hosting the wine tasting.

She'd taken on the role to prove herself—to her family, to David and even to herself. She'd spent a week assisting with tours, being trained—delicately, she thought now. Staff members treated family members with kid gloves.

It had jarred her to realize just how little she knew about the winery, about the vineyards, about the process and about the public areas and retail venue. It would take more than a week and some subtle education to learn how to handle any of those areas on her own. But by God, she could handle a group at a wine tasting.

And was determined to prove it.

She was going to learn how to handle a great many things, including her own life. Part of that life included sex. So, good for her.

And on that thought, she lowered to the edge of her bed. The idea of moving toward an intimate relationship with David terrified her. The fact that it did, irritated her. And terrified and irritated, she had made herself, she admitted, a nervous wreck.

The knock on her door had her springing to her feet again, grabbing her brush and fixing what she hoped was a confident and casual expression on her face. "Yes? Come in."

She sighed hugely and gave up the pretense when she saw Helen. "Thank God it's you. I'm so tired of pretending to be a twenty-first-century woman."

"You look like one. Fabulous dress."

"Under it, I'm quaking. I'm glad you and James are here for the tasting."

"We dragged Linc along. His current honey is working tonight."

"Still the intern?"

"Yeah." Helen sat on the curvy velvet chaise, made herself at home. "I'm starting to think he's getting serious about her."

"And?"

"I don't know. She's a nice girl, raised well. Focused, which he could use, and independent, which I appreciate."

"But he's your baby."

"But he's my baby," Helen agreed. "I miss the little boy sometimes, with the scabbed knees and loose shoelaces. Still see him in that tall, gorgeous lawyer in the three-piece suit that strolls in and out of my life now. And Jesus," she said with a sigh. "I'm old. How's your baby holding up?"

Pilar set down her brush. "You already know about what Tony did."

"Your mother thought it best that I know, so that I can cover any legalities that might come up. I'm sorry, Pilar."

"So am I. It was so unnecessary." She turned. "And so like him. That's what you're thinking."

"It doesn't matter what I think. Unless I see you start blaming yourself."

"No, not this time. And I hope never again. But it's rough, very rough on Sophia."

"She'll get through it. Our babies turned into strong, capable adults while we weren't looking, Pilar."

"I know. When did we blink? And still, we can't help worrying about them, can we?"

"The job never ends. Sophia was just heading over to MacMillan's as we came in. Drafted Linc to go with her in case there was any heavy lifting involved in the setup. He'll keep her mind occupied."

"It's always good to see them together, almost like brother and sister."

"Mmm. Now, sit down." Helen patted the chaise. "Catch your breath and tell me all about your romance with David Cutter. With nearly thirty years of marriage under my belt, I have to live vicariously."

"It's not really . . . we're enjoying each other's company."

"No sex yet, huh?"

"Helen." Giving up, Pilar dropped onto the chaise. "How can I have sex with him?"

"If you've forgotten how it works, there are a number of very good books on the subject. Videos. Internet sites." Behind her lenses, her eyes danced. "I'll give you a list."

"I'm serious."

"Me too. Some very hot stuff in there."

"Stop it." But she laughed. "David's been very patient, but I'm not stupid. He wants sex, and he's not going to keep settling for necking on the porch or—"

"Necking? Come on, Pilar. Details, all the details."

"Let's just say he has a very creative

mouth, and when he uses it, I remember what it's like to be twenty."

"Oh." Helen fanned a hand in front of her face. "Yes."

"But I'm *not* twenty. And my body sure as hell isn't twenty. How can I possibly let him see me naked, Helen? My breasts are heading to Mexico."

"Honey, mine landed in Argentina three years ago. James doesn't seem to mind."

"But that's the point. You've been together for nearly thirty years. You've gone through the changes together. Worse, David's younger than I am."

"Worse? I can think of a lot worse than that."

"Try to be on my side here. He's a forty-three-year-old man. I'm a forty-eight-year-old woman. There's a huge difference there. A man his age most usually dates younger women. Often much younger women with tight bodies that don't sag."

"Often paired with empty heads that don't think," Helen finished. "Pilar, the fact is, he's dating you. And if you're so self-conscious about your body, though that irritates me when I think of what's become of mine in comparison, make sure it's dark the first time you jump him."

"You're a big help."

"Yes, I am, because if he's put off by breasts that aren't twenty-two years old and perky, then he's not worth your time. Better to find out than to speculate and project. Do you want to sleep with him? Just yes or no," Helen added before Pilar could respond. "Gut instinct, primal urge. No qualifiers."

"Yes."

"Then buy yourself some incredible underwear and go for it."

Pilar bit her lip. "I already bought the underwear."

"Hot damn. Let's see."

Nearly twenty-four hours after the tasting, and Tyler could still form a picture in his mind that made him laugh. Two dozen snooty, slick-faced club members had gotten the shock of their narrow lives with a sample of what he was calling Vin de Madeline.

"'Unsophisticated,'" he said, cracking

himself up again, "'but nubile.' Jesus, where do they get that stuff? Nubile."

"Try to contain your hilarity." Sophia sat behind the desk in her office in the villa and continued to study the models Kris had chosen for the ads. "And I'd appreciate it if you'd warn me the next time you decide to add a mystery vintage to the selection."

"Last-minute candidate. And it was in the name of science."

"The tastings are in the name of tradition, reputation and promotion." She glanced up briefly, gave up when he just grinned at her. "Okay, it was funny, and we'll be able to turn it into an interesting, lighthearted article for the newsletter. Maybe even get a little human-interest and anecdotal press out of it."

"Does your blood run on publicity?"

"You betcha. Which is fortunate for all involved, as some members would've been very offended if I hadn't been there to spin it."

"Some members are pompous, tight-assed idiots."

"Yes, and those pompous, tight-assed idiots buy a great deal of our wine and talk it up at social events. As the winemaker is as unsophisticated and nubile as her wine, we can play it to our advantage." She made another note, weighed it down with the silly green glass frog Ty had given her for Christmas. "Next time you want to experiment, give me some warning."

He stretched out his legs. "Loosen up, Giambelli."

"That, from the king of the party animals." She picked up an eight-by-ten glossy, held it out to him. "What do you think of her?"

He took the picture, studied the sloe-eyed blonde. "Does this come with her phone number?"

"That's what I thought. She's too sexy. I told Kris I wanted wholesome." Sophia scowled into middle distance. "I have to fire her. She's not even trying to adjust to the changes. Worse, she's ignoring direct orders, giving the rest of the team grief." She sighed. "My spies tell me she had a meeting with Jerry DeMorney from La Coeur just the other day."

"If she's causing trouble, why are you worried about axing her? Don't give me the line about not being able to replace her during the campaign or the reorganization."

"All right. I hesitate because she's good,

and I hate to lose her. And she has intimate knowledge of the campaign, of my long-range plans, and could very well lure some other members of the staff away with her. I hesitate, on a personal level, because I think she was involved with my father, and firing her might push her to make that public. Whatever I do, it's going to cause trouble. But it can't be put off any longer. I'll take care of it tomorrow."

"I could do it."

Sophia closed the file folder. "That's actually very nice of you. But it should come from me. I should warn you that cutting her loose is going to mean more work for the rest of us. Especially since my mother isn't going to be doing, or trying to do, any of the grunt work."

"That sure cheers me up."

"I was thinking about asking Theo if he wanted a part-time job. We could use a gofer a couple afternoons a week."

"Great. Then he can hang around here mooning over you on a regular basis."

"The more he's around me, the quicker he'll get over it. Daily contact'll take the edge off his hormones."

"You think?" Ty murmured.

"Why, Tyler, was that a twisted sort of compliment, or just your cranky way of saying I make you edgy?"

"Neither." He studied the glossy again. "I go for sleepy-eyed blondes with full, pouty lips."

"Peroxide and collagen."

"So?"

"God, I love men." She got up from the desk, walked to him, cupped his face in her hands and gave him a smacking kiss on the mouth. "You're just so cute."

One hard tug on her hand had her tumbling into his lap. An instant later her quick laugh was cut off, and her heart pounding.

He hadn't kissed her this way before, with impatience and heat and hunger all mixed together in a near brutal assault. He hadn't kissed her as if he couldn't get enough. Would never get enough. Her body quivered once—in surprise, in defense, in response. Then her fingers raked through his hair, fisted there.

More, she thought. She wanted more of this edge, this recklessness, even the reluctant need.

When he would have drawn away, she

went with him, sliding up against the hard lines of him even as he broke the kiss.

She scraped her bottom lip with her teeth, slowly. Deliberately. And watched his gaze lower to follow the movement. "What was that for?"

"I felt like it."

"Good enough. Do it again."

He hadn't meant to do it the first time. But now his appetite for her was stirred, and not quite sated. "Why the hell not?"

Her lips curved as he took them. Not quite as desperate now, not quite as rough. He could imagine, too well, what it would be like to slide into her. Into all that soft heat. But he wasn't sure how a man could get free again, or walk away whole.

Even as he thought it, he was flipping open the buttons of her shirt. Even as he thought it, she was pulling him to the floor.

"Hurry." Breathless, she arched when his hands closed over her.

Fast. He could imagine it fast, and hard and furious. A mindless coupling, all heat and no light. It was what she wanted. What they both wanted. He dragged her up, clamped his mouth over hers again. His belly tightened, desire and anticipation, as she tugged at his belt.

The office door swung open. "Ty, I need to—" Eli stopped in mid-stride as he stared at his grandson, at the girl he thought of as his granddaughter, tangled together on the floor. Color flooded his cheeks as he stumbled back.

"Excuse me."

When the door slammed, Tyler was already rocking back on his heels. Mind swimming, body churning, he rubbed his hands over his face. "Oh perfect. Just perfect."

"Oops."

At Sophia's response, Tyler spread his fingers and stared at her through them. "Oops?"

"My brain's a little impaired. It's the best I can do. Oh, God." She sat up, pulled her shirt together. "Not your typical family moment." Giving up, she dropped her head to her knees. "Jesus. How do we handle this?"

"I don't know. I guess I have to talk to him."

She lifted her head slightly. "I could do it."

"You fire unsatisfactory staff members; I talk to shocked grandfathers."

"Fair enough." She lowered her knees, stared down as she buttoned her shirt again. "Ty, I'm really sorry. I'd never do anything to upset Eli, or to cause trouble between the two of you."

"I know." He pushed to his feet and after a brief hesitation held out his hand to help her up.

"I want to make love with you."

His already jangled system suffered. "I think what we both want's pretty clear. I just don't know what we're going to do about it. I have to go after him."

"Yes."

When he hurried out, she walked to the windows, crossed her arms. And very much wished she had something equally vital and specific to do. All that was left for her was to think.

Tyler found his grandfather walking toward the vineyards, Sally faithfully at his heels. He didn't speak, hadn't worked out what he would say once he did. He merely fell into step beside Eli and began to walk through the rows.

"Going to have to keep a frost watch," Eli commented. "Warm snap's teased the vines."

"Yeah, I'm on it. Ah . . . it's nearly disking time."

"Hope the rain doesn't slow that down." Like his grandson, Eli studied the canes and racked his brain for the right words. "I . . . should've knocked."

"No, I shouldn't have . . ." Stalling, Ty leaned down, ruffled Sally's fur. "It just happened."

"Well." Eli cleared his throat. He didn't have to talk to Tyler about the ways and means of sex. Thank Christ. He'd done that deed years before. His grandson was a grown man, who knew about the birds and bees, and about responsibility. But . . .

"Holy hell, Ty. You and Sophie."

"It just happened," he said again. "I guess it shouldn't have, and I guess I should tell you it won't happen again."

"Not my business. It's just the two of you—hell, Ty, you were almost raised together. I know you've got no blood tie, and there's nothing stopping either of you from such a thing. Just a shock, is all."

"All around," Tyler agreed.

Eli walked a little farther. "Do you love her?"

Inside his gut, Tyler felt the slippery knots of guilt tighten. "Grandpa, it's not always about love."

Now Eli stopped, turned and faced Tyler. "My equipment may be older than yours, boy, but it works the same way. I know it's not always about love. I was just asking."

"We've got this heat going on, that's all. If it's all the same to you, I'd rather not go into that end of things."

"Oh, it's all the same to me. You're both adults and you got two working brains between you. Both of you were raised right, so what you do is your own business. Next time, though, lock the damn door first."

It was nearly six when Tyler got home. He was worn out, worked up and irritated with himself. He thought a cold beer and a hot shower might help smooth him back out. Reaching for the refrigerator handle, he saw the note he'd stuck there the night before as a reminder.

Dinner at M's—7.

"Shit." He lowered his forehead to the appliance. He could just make it, he supposed, if he busted his ass. But he just didn't have it in him. He wasn't in any mood to discuss business, even if it included a decent meal and good company.

He'd never make good company himself that night.

He reached for the phone, only to find he'd misplaced it again. Swearing, he yanked open the fridge, intending to pop the top on the beer before starting to search. And there was the phone, tucked between a bottle of Corona and a carton of milk.

He'd make it up to Margaret, he thought, as he looked up her phone number. Take her out to dinner, or lunch. Whatever, before she left the city.

She didn't hear the phone ring. Her head was under the shower and she was singing.

She'd looked forward to the evening all day, shuffling meetings, writing reports, making calls. And finally stopping on the way home for a man-sized steak and a couple of enormous Idaho potatoes. She'd bought an apple pie at the bakery and fully intended to pass it off as her own.

A man didn't have to know everything.

It was, she knew, just the sort of meal Ty would appreciate.

She'd already set the table, arranged candles, chosen music, had the outfit she'd selected lying on her bed. And the bed itself was plumped with pillows and made with fresh sheets.

They'd had two or three dates before. Not that she fooled herself into believing Ty had thought of them as dates. But she hoped to change that after tonight.

She stepped out of the shower and began to prepare herself.

It was always exciting to groom yourself for a man. Part of the anticipation. Margaret's feminist beliefs didn't deny her the pleasure of that sort of ritual, but helped her celebrate the female rite of it.

She creamed, scented, slid into silk and

imagined seducing Tyler MacMillan over apple pie.

She'd always had a yen for him, she supposed as she checked the apartment to see that everything was in place. The promotion, the travel, the excitement of her new responsibilities had, in a very real way, she decided, given her the confidence to make him fully aware of that yen.

She took out the wine she'd earmarked for the evening. And noticed the message light blinking on her kitchen machine.

"Margaret. It's Ty. Listen, I'm going to have to take a rain check on dinner. I should have called sooner but . . . something came up at the office. Sorry. I'll call you tomorrow. If you don't have plans, I'll take you out and we can go over business. Really sorry I didn't get back to you sooner."

She stared at the machine, imagined herself ripping it out of the wall and heaving it. Of course that wouldn't change anything, and she was too practical a woman to indulge in useless tantrums.

Too practical, she thought, struggling against tears of disappointment, to let food and wine go to waste because some idiot, inconsiderate *man* stood her up.

The hell with him. There were plenty more where he came from. Plenty, she reminded herself as she yanked her broiler open and prepared to cook the steak. She'd had a number of interesting offers in Italy. When she got back, she might just take one of them and see where it led.

But for now, she was opening the god-damn wine and getting good and drunk.

CHAPTER FIFTEEN

Pilar approached the guest house by the back door. It was a friendly habit. She felt she had become friends with Theo. He was an interesting, and interested, young man once you chipped through the surface. A boy, she thought, who needed the softening influence of a mother.

She was touched that he seemed to enjoy rather than resent her company when he came by the villa to use the pool. She'd managed to lure him up to the music room and have him play—or at least play around with—the piano. It had been an easy step from there to open up a dialogue, and a debate, over music.

She hoped he was as entertained by them as she was.

Maddy was a different matter. The girl was

polite but consistently cool. And watched, Pilar thought, everything and everyone. It wasn't resentment so much as a measuring. A measuring, Pilar knew, that was directly connected to her relationship with Maddy's father.

That aspect appeared to have gone straight over Theo's head. But Pilar recognized the female-to-female judgment in Maddy's eyes. So far, she hadn't come up to snuff.

Pilar wondered if David was as unaware as his son that Maddy was guarding her territory.

She hitched her shoulder bag as she started up the back walk. The contents weren't bribes, she assured herself. Just tokens. And she wouldn't stay any longer than was comfortable for all of them. Though part of her hoped they'd want her to stay awhile. Fix them lunch, listen to their chatter.

She so missed having someone to mother.

If fate had dealt her another hand, she'd have had a houseful of children, a big messy dog, ripped seams to sew, spats to referee.

Instead she'd produced one bright and beautiful daughter who'd needed so little tending. And at forty-eight was reduced to nurturing flowers instead of the children she'd longed for.

And self-pity, Pilar reminded herself, was unattractive. She knocked briskly on the kitchen door and had her smile ready.

It wobbled a bit when David answered. He wore a work shirt and jeans, and held a cup of coffee. "Now this is handy." He took her hand to draw her inside. "I was just thinking about you."

"I didn't expect you to be home."

"Working out of here today." Because he wanted to, and because he knew it would fluster her, he kept her hand firm in his as he leaned down to kiss her.

"Oh, well. When I didn't see the van—"

"Theo and Maddy ganged up on me. Professional day, no school. Every parent's nightmare. We solved it by letting them nag me into giving Theo the keys and driving off to the mall and the movies for the day. Which is why your visit's perfectly timed."

"Really?" She tugged her hand free, fiddled with the strap of her bag. "It is?"

"Keeps me from sitting here imagining all

the trouble they could get into. Want some coffee?"

"No, I really should . . . I just stopped by to drop off a couple of things for the kids." It flustered her to be in the house alone with him. In all the time he'd been there, she'd managed to avoid that single event. "Maddy's so interested in the whole wine-making process, I thought she'd like to read about the history of Giambelli, California."

Pilar tugged the book she'd picked up at the winery gift shop out of the bag.

"Right up her alley. She'll appreciate it and pound Ty and me with brand-new questions."

"She has an active mind."

"Tell me about it."

"I brought this sheet music along for Theo. He's so into the techno-rock business, but I thought he might get a kick out of trying some of the classics."

"Sergeant Pepper." David studied the sheet. "Where'd you dig this up?"

"I used to play it and drive my mother crazy. It was my job."

"Did you wear love beads and bell-bottoms?" he teased.

"Naturally. I made a terrific pair out of paisley when I was Maddy's age."

"Made? So many hidden talents." He maneuvered her—it was simply a matter of shifting closer—until her back was to the kitchen counter. "You didn't bring me a present."

"I didn't know you'd be here."

"And now that I am?" He edged closer, laying his palms on the counter on either side of her. "Got anything in your bag for me?"

"Sorry." She tried to laugh, to keep it light, but it was hard when she was strangling. "Next time. I really should get back to the winery. I'm helping with a tour this afternoon."

"What time?"

"Four-thirty."

"Mmm." He glanced at the kitchen clock. "An hour and a half. I wonder what we could do with ninety minutes?"

"I could fix you lunch."

"I've got a better idea." And with his hands at her waist, he circled her slowly toward the inside door.

"David."

"Nobody home but you and me," he said,

nibbling at her jaw, her throat, her mouth as he guided her out of the kitchen. "You know what I was thinking the other day?"

"No." How could she? She didn't know what she was thinking right now.

"That it's a complex business. My girlfriend lives with her mother."

She did laugh now, at the idea of being called anyone's girlfriend.

"And I live with my kids. No place to go to do all the things I've imagined doing with you. Do you know the things I've imagined doing with you?"

"I'm getting the picture. David, it's the middle of the day."

"The middle of the day." He paused at the base of the steps. "And an opportunity. I hate wasted opportunities, don't you?"

She was walking up the steps with him, which seemed a miraculous feat to her, since her knees were knocking and her heart laboring as if she'd already scaled a mountain. "I wasn't expecting . . ." Her words kept becoming muffled against his mouth. "I'm not prepared."

"Sweetheart, I'll take care of that."

Take care of it? How could he arrange for her to be wearing sexy underwear, or turn the merciless daylight into the soft, flattering shadows of night? How could he . . .

Then it struck her that he meant protection and made her feel giddy and foolish.

"No, I didn't mean . . . David, I'm not young."

"Neither am I." He eased back slightly at his bedroom door. Sweeping her inside wasn't the right way. She needed words, and maybe, he realized, so did he. "Pilar, I have a lot of complicated feelings for you. One that isn't complicated, for me, is that it's you I want. All there is of you."

Nerves were swimming now, in a stream of heat. "David, you need to know. Tony was my first. And he was my last. It's been a very long time. And I'm . . . God. I'm so out of practice."

"Knowing there hasn't been anyone else flatters me, Pilar." He brushed his lips over hers. "It humbles me." And again. "It excites me." His mouth came back to hers a third time in a kiss that trembled on the edge between seduction and demand.

"Come to my bed." He guided her toward it, fascinated by the way their hearts hammered together. "Let me touch you. Touch me."

"I can't get my breath." She struggled to gulp in air as he slipped her jacket off. "I know I'm tense, I'm sorry. I can't seem to relax."

"I don't want you relaxed." He kept his eyes on hers as he unbuttoned her blouse, while his fingers whispered along exposed flesh. "Not this time. Put your hands on my shoulders, Pilar. Step out of your shoes."

She was trembling, and so was he. Like the first time, he thought. For her. For him. And just as terrifying and tremendous.

The late winter sun was a white wash of light through the windows. In the silence of the house he could hear every catch of her breath. When he skimmed his fingers lightly over her, she was all soft skin and quivers.

"Smooth. Warm. Beautiful."

He was making her believe his words. And if her fingers shook as she unbuttoned his shirt, he didn't seem to mind. If she jerked stupidly when his knuckles brushed her midriff, when he unhooked her trousers, he didn't sneer impatiently.

And best of all, he didn't stop.

His hands stroked her, slow and firm. It made her want to weep to be touched again. To feel again that gathering of heat in the belly, the long, liquid pulls that followed it. It seemed natural to lie back on the bed, to have his body, the hard weight of it, press down on hers.

It seemed natural, and glorious, to finally give herself again.

She forgot about the sunlight, and all the flaws it would reveal. And she reveled in the sensation of taking a mate.

He didn't want to rush. But her hesitation had become eagerness. She moved under him, hips arching, hands touching with quick little bites and scrapes of her nails that aroused him beyond belief.

He forgot about patience, and all the doubts he wanted to assuage. And feasted.

Their fingers linked as they rolled over the bed, then broke apart to find new secrets to explore. His mouth closed over her breast, thrilling both of them. As the wave of pleasure swamped her, she crooned out his name, then moaned when his teeth tugged at her.

The whip of power slashed through her, locked her on that glorious edge between excitement and release where the blood rages and the body yearns. She shuddered there, helplessly, and let the glory of every ache, every burn batter her.

When his hand stroked down to find her, she was already hot, already wet.

She exploded under him, too stunned to be embarrassed by the quick-trigger response, too shocked to resist the wild plunging of her own body. Her world went bright, blindingly, and she surrendered herself to the sudden urgency of his hands and mouth.

Mine. The soft, damp skin that smelled of spring, the subtle curves, the eager and open response. He wanted to take all that was his now. To give all that he had. She moved with him, as if they'd come together, just this way, a thousand times. Reached for him as if her arms had always held him warm and close.

There was more, so much more he wanted to show her, to take from her in this first exploration. But the need pumped madly through both of them and pounded at control.

She watched him as he ranged himself over her again.

Once more, her arms lifted, opened. And holding, she took him in.

Arched to him, in welcome, closed around him in acceptance.

They moved together in the sunlight, a pace that quickened, a need that pulsed, then plunged.

She cried out, muffling the sound against the side of his throat. Tasted him there as her heart took the final leap.

The sun was shining in San Francisco, too, but it only added dimension to Sophia's headache. She faced Kris across her desk. The worst of it was, in Sophia's opinion, the woman hadn't seen the termination coming. How she could have missed it, with all the warnings and directives, only added fuel to the fire that had brought them to this point.

"You don't want to be here, Kris. You've made that clear."

"I've done better work in this office than anyone else in the company. You know it, I know it. And you don't like it."

"On the contrary, I've always respected your work."

"That's bullshit."

Sophia took a steadying breath, ordered herself to remain calm, to stay professional.

"You have a great deal of talent, which I admire. What I don't admire, and what can no longer be tolerated or overlooked, is your deliberate rejection of company policy and your attitude toward authority."

"You mean my attitude toward you."

"Here's a bulletin for you. I am authority."

"Because your name's Giambelli."

"Whether or not that's the case isn't the issue, or any of your concern."

"If Tony was still alive, you wouldn't be sitting behind that desk. I would."

Sophia swallowed the bitterness that rose in her throat. "Is that how he got you into bed?" she said with a twist of amusement in her tone. "Promising you my job? That was clever of him, foolish of you. My father didn't run this company and had no weight here."

"You saw to that. All three Giambelli women."

"No, he saw to it. But that's beside the point. The fact is I'm head of this department, and you no longer work for me. You'll be given the standard termination package, including the full two weeks' salary. I want your office cleared of your personal property by the end of business today."

They both got to their feet. Sophia had the impression that without the desk between them, Kris would have taken more than a verbal shot. It only showed how far their relationship had deteriorated that Sophia was sorry they couldn't go a couple of rounds.

"That's fine. I have other offers. Everyone in the business knows who's the real power here, the creative power."

"I hope you get just what you deserve at La Coeur," Sophia replied and watched Kris's jaw drop in surprise. "There are no secrets. But I'll warn you to remember the confidentiality clause you signed when you joined this firm. If you pass information about Giambelli to a competitor, you open yourself up for a lawsuit."

"I don't need to pass anything on. Your upcoming campaign's ill-conceived and trite. It's an embarrassment."

"Isn't it lucky, then, that you won't have to be associated with it anymore?" Sophia came around the desk now, passing close to Kris, almost hoping she'd strike out. When Sophia reached the door, she opened it. "I think we've said all we have to say to each other."

"This department's going to sink because

when I go, others will go with me. Let's see how far you and the farmer go on your own." Kris sauntered toward the door, paused for one smirk. "Tony and I had a good laugh over the two of you."

"I'm shocked you took the time for humor or conversation."

"He respected me," Kris shot back. "He knew who really ran this department. We had some interesting conversations about you. Bitch number three."

Sophia's hand clamped down on Kris's arm. "So it was you. Petty vandalism, anonymous letters. You're lucky I don't have you arrested as well as fired."

"Call a cop . . . then try to prove it. That'll give me one last laugh." She yanked her arm free, strolled away.

Leaving her door open, Sophia went straight back to her desk and called security. She wanted Kris escorted from the building. Now that the first slap of temper had passed, she wasn't surprised that it had been Kris who'd defaced the heirlooms and sent the photograph.

But it disgusted.

Nothing she could do about it. Just as she couldn't do anything about files Kris might have already copied and taken out, but she could make certain there wasn't a last-minute foray.

Far from satisfied, she sent for both P.J. and Trace.

While she waited, she paced. While she paced, Tyler walked in.

"I saw Kris steam down the hall," he commented, and dropped comfortably into a chair. "She called me a brain-dead, pussy-whipped farmer. I assume you're the pussy with the whip."

"Shows what she knows. Your brain's alive and well, and so far you've been pretty damn resistant to the whip. God! I'm so pissed."

"I figured it didn't go so well when I saw the tongues of fire shooting out of her ears."

"I kept hoping she'd take a punch at me so I could flatten her. I'd feel a lot better right now if she had. She called me bitch number three. I'd like to show her what a genuine Italian bitch can do when pushed. Smearing nail polish on our angels, sending me anonymous mail."

"Whoa, back up. What mail?"

"Nothing." She waved a hand in the air, kept pacing.

He snagged her hand, tugged it down. "What mail?"

"Just a photo from a few months back— my mother, grandmother and me. She used a red pen this time, but the sentiment was the same as on the Giambelli angels."

"Why didn't you tell me?"

"Because the envelope was addressed to me, because it pissed me off and because I wasn't giving the person who sent it the satisfaction of discussing it."

"You get another, I want to know about it. Clear?"

"Fine, great, you're first in line." Too angry to stay put, she pulled away. "She said my father was going to help her land my job. I imagine he promised her that, had no qualms about promising her what was mine any more than he had qualms about taking my mother's jewelry for Rene."

And it stung, he thought, watching her face. Even now Avano managed to prick through the shell of defense and nick her heart. "I'm sorry."

"You're thinking they deserved each other. So am I. Gotta calm down, gotta calm down," she repeated like a mantra. "It's over and done, and stewing over it won't help. We have to go forward. I have to talk to P.J. and Trace to start, and I have to be calm. I have to be composed."

"You want me to take off?"

"No. This would be better as a team." She dragged her top drawer open, rooted out her aspirin. "I should have fired her weeks ago. You were right about that. I was wrong."

"I need to write this down. Can I borrow a pencil?"

"Shut up." Grateful that his easy calm steadied her, she heaved a breath, then twisted open a bottle of water. "Tell me straight out, Ty, what you think of the centennial campaign."

"How many times do I have to tell you, this isn't my area."

"As a consumer, damn it." She tossed three extra-strength Tylenol back and took a long pull from the water bottle. "You have a goddamn opinion on everything else in the world, don't you?"

"That's calm and composed," he commented. "I think it's smart. What else do you want?"

"That's enough." Drained, she sat on the corner of her desk. "She got to me. I hate knowing that." She glanced at her watch. "I need to get this dealt with, then we have a meeting with Margaret."

The little tug of guilt had him shifting in his chair. "I was supposed to meet with her myself last night; had to postpone. I haven't been able to get in touch with her today."

"She should be up on six."

"Oh well." Hell. "Mind if I use your phone?"

Sophia gestured and stepped out to ask her assistant to get some coffee.

"She's not there," Ty said when Sophia came back in. "Missed two morning meetings."

"That's not like Margaret. Let's try her at home again," she began, then switched gears as P.J. and Trace came to her door.

"Come on in. Sit." She gestured, then quietly closed the door. "I need you to know," she said as she crossed back to her desk, "that I've had to let Kris go."

P.J. and Trace exchanged quick, sidelong looks.

"Which I see comes as no surprise to either of you." When there was no response, Sophia decided to lay her cards on the table. "I'm going to say I hope both of you know how much I value you, hope you know how important you are to this department and to the company and to me personally. I understand there may be some continued dissatisfaction over the changes made late last year, and if either of you has specific problems or comments, I'm open to discussion."

"How about a question?" Trace said.

"Questions, then."

"Who's taking over for Kris?"

"No one."

"You don't intend to bring in someone to fill her position?"

"I'd prefer if the two of you share her work, her title and her authority."

"Dibs on her office," P.J. announced.

"Damn it." Trace hissed out a breath.

"Okay, let's backtrack." Sophia moved to the door, opening it at her assistant's knock so the coffee could be passed around. "Not only not surprised by the recent turn of events, but unless I miss my mark, not particularly upset or disappointed."

"It's rude to speak of the recently terminated." P.J. studied her coffee, then gazed at Sophia. "But . . . you're not in the office every day. Never have been because that's not how you work. You do a lot of the travel, the outside meetings. And since December, you work at home at least three days a week. We're here."

"And?"

"What P.J. is trying to say without risking a trip to hell for bitchiness is that Kris is hard to work with. Harder to work for," Trace added. "Which is how she saw things when you weren't around. She figured she was in charge and we, along with everybody else in the department, were her minions. I was getting pretty sick of being a minion. I've been looking around for another job."

"You could have talked to me. Damn it, Trace."

"I was going to. Before I made any decision. Now, well, problem solved. Except I think P.J. and I should flip for Kris's office."

"I called dibs. Snooze, lose. Sophia, she's been trying to work people up around here. Kind of a corporate mutiny or whatever. She might have gotten some supporters. You may lose some good people when she goes."

"All right. I'll set up a full staff meeting this afternoon. Do damage control. I'm sorry I haven't been on top of this. When it all shakes down, I'd like recommendations. People you think should be considered for promotion or reassignment. As of now, you're co-managers. I'll put through the paperwork."

"Cool." P.J. leaped up. "I'm going to go draw up how I'll rearrange my new office." She turned to Ty. "I'd just like to say that being the strong, silent type doesn't make you pussy-whipped. It makes you interesting. Kris was really steamed that you didn't try to muscle your way in and end up falling on your ass. Instead you don't say anything unless you've got something to say. And when you do, it makes sense."

"Suck up," Trace said under his breath.

"I don't have to suck up, I've got the big office." With a flutter of her lashes, she walked out.

"I like working here. I like working with you. I'd've been bummed if things had worked out differently." With that said he walked out whistling.

"Feel better?" Tyler asked.

"Considerably. A little angry with myself for letting things go this far and this long, but otherwise considerably better."

"Good. Why don't you go set up that staff meeting deal, and I'll try to track down Margaret. You up for a dinner meeting thing if she wants to?"

"Sure, but that's not going to make her happy. She has the hots for you."

"Get out."

"Buy a clue," Sophia said lightly, and stepped out again to arrange for the meeting with her assistant.

Women, Tyler thought as he hunted up Margaret's home number in Sophia's Rolodex. And they said men always had sex on the brain. Just because he and Margaret got along, had gone out once or twice, didn't mean—

He shifted his thoughts when a man answered on the third ring. "I'm trying to reach Margaret Bowers."

"Who's calling?"

"Tyler MacMillan."

"Mr. MacMillan." There was the briefest pause. "This is Detective Claremont."

"Claremont? Sorry, I must've dialed the wrong number."

"No, you didn't. I'm in Ms. Bowers's apartment. She's dead."

PART THREE

The Blooming

Flowers are lovely; love is flower-like;
Friendship is a sheltering tree.

—SAMUEL TAYLOR COLERIDGE

CHAPTER SIXTEEN

March roared across the valley on a raw and galloping wind. It hardened the ground and rattled the naked fingers of the vines. The dawn mists had a bite that chewed through the bones. There would be worries about damage and loss until the true warmth of spring arrived.

There would be worries about many things.

Sophia stopped at the vineyards first, and was disappointed that Tyler wasn't stalking down the rows examining the canes for early growth. She knew the disking phase was about to begin, weather permitting. Men with disk harrows would pulverize and aerate the soil, breaking up the crusted earth, turning the mustard plants and their nitrogen into the ground.

For the vintner, the quiet of February blew into the busy and critical month of March.

Winter, a fickle white witch, held the valley. And gave those who lived there too much time to think.

He'd be brooding, of course. Sitting up in his office, she imagined as she changed directions for the house. Going over his charts and logs and records. Making some notes in his vintner's journal. But brooding all the same.

Time to put a stop to it.

She started to knock on the door. No, she decided, when you knocked it was too easy to be told to go away. Instead she opened the door, pulling off her jacket as she stepped inside.

"Ty?" She tossed the jacket over the newel post and, following instinct, headed for his office.

"I've got work to do here." He didn't bother to look up.

Until moments before he'd been at the window. He'd seen her walking through the rows, changing her angle to aim for the house. He'd even thought about going down and locking the door. But it had seemed both petty and useless.

He'd known her too long to believe a lock would keep her out.

She sat across from his desk, leaned back and waited until the silence irked him enough to speak. "What?"

"You look like hell."

"Thanks."

"No word from the police yet?"

"You're just as likely to hear as I am."

True enough, she mused. And the wait was making her edgy. It had been nearly a week since Margaret's body had been found. On the floor by a table set for two, with an untouched steak on the platter, candles guttered out and an empty bottle of Merlot.

It was that, she knew, that continued to prey on Tyler's mind. The other place had been set for him.

"I spoke with her parents today. They're going to take her back to Columbus for the funeral. It's hard for them. For you."

"If I hadn't canceled—"

"You don't know if it would have made any difference or not." She got up to go to him. Standing behind him, she began to rub his shoulders. "If she had a heart condition no one knew about, she could have become ill anytime."

"If I'd been there—"

"If. Maybe." Feeling for him, she brushed a kiss on the top of his head. "Take it from me, those two words will make you crazy."

"She was too young for a goddamn heart attack. And don't give me the line of statistics. The cops are looking into it, and not passing on information. That means something."

"All it means right now is that it was an unattended death, and that she was connected, through Giambelli, to my father. It's just routine, Ty. Until we know differently, it's just routine."

"You said she had feelings for me."

If she could go back, Sophia decided, she'd bite off her tongue before uttering that single, careless remark. "I was just razzing you."

"No, you weren't." Giving up, he closed his vintner's log. "You know what they say about hindsight. I didn't see it. She didn't interest me that way, so I didn't want to see it."

"That's not your fault, and picking at that isn't helping anything. I'm sorry this happened. I liked her." Without thinking, she hooked her arms around his shoulders, rested her cheek on his head.

"So did I."

"Come downstairs. I'll fix soup."

"Why?"

"Because it'll give us both something to do besides think. And wait." She swiveled his chair around until he faced her. "Besides, I have gossip, and no one to share it with."

"I don't like gossip."

"Too bad." She pulled at his hand, pleased when he let her tug him to his feet. "My mother slept with David."

"Ah, damn it, Sophie. Why do you tell me things like that?"

She smiled a little, hooking her arm through his. "Because you can't spread gossip like that outside of the family, and I don't think it's an appropriate subject for *Nonna* and I to discuss over breakfast."

"But it's appropriate to discuss with me over soup." He just couldn't understand the female mind. "How do you know, anyway?"

"Really, Ty," she exclaimed as they started downstairs. "In the first place, I know Mama, and one look at her was enough. In the second, I saw the two of them together yesterday, and it showed."

He didn't ask how it showed. She was too likely to tell him, and he wouldn't understand anyway. "How do you feel about it?"

"I don't know. Part of me is delighted. Good for you, Mama! Another is standing back with her jaw on the ground thinking my mother isn't supposed to have sex. That's the immature part. I'm working on it."

He stopped at the base of the steps, turned her. "You're a good daughter." With a casual tap of his finger, he tipped up her chin. "And not a half-bad person, as people go."

"Oh, I can be bad. If he hurts her, David's going to find out just how bad I can be."

"I'll hold him down, you skin him."

"That's a deal." Her eyes changed as he continued to look into them. And her blood began to move. "Ty." She lifted a hand to his face as he leaned toward her.

And the knock on the door had her cursing. "For God's sake! What is wrong with our timing? I want you to remember where we were. I really want you to remember it."

"I think I've got it bookmarked." No less irritated by the interruption than she, he stalked to the door, yanked it open. And felt a clench in his gut.

"Mr. MacMillan." Claremont stood beside Maguire in the chilly air. "Can we come in?"

They moved into the living room where the atmosphere was masculine and messy. He hadn't thought to light a fire that morning, so the hearth was cold. A newspaper, several days old, was still piled on the coffee table. A paperback book peeked up from under it. Maguire couldn't quite make out the title.

He didn't bother to pick up, as a lot of people did, she noted. And he didn't look as if he particularly wanted to sit down. But when he dropped into a chair, Sophia edged onto the arm of it beside him. And made them a unit.

Claremont took out his notepad and set the rhythm. "You said you and Margaret Bowers dated."

"No, I didn't. I said we went out a couple of times."

"That's generally interpreted as dating."

"I didn't interpret it that way. I interpreted it as we went out a couple of times."

"You were supposed to have dinner with her on the night she died."

"Yeah." There'd been no expression and no condemnation in Claremont's voice. But it still stung. "As I told you before, I got hung up here, called her somewhere around six. I got her machine and left a message that I couldn't make it."

"Didn't give her much notice," Maguire put in.

"No, I didn't."

"Just what hung you up?"

"Work."

"At the villa?"

"That's what I said the last time you asked. It still goes. Basically, I lost track of time and forgot about dinner until I got home."

"You called her at six, so you still had an hour. You could've made it." Maguire tilted her head. "Or called and told her you'd be a bit late."

"I could've. I didn't. I didn't feel like driving into the city. Is that a problem?"

"Ms. Bowers died with the table still set for two. That's a problem."

"Detective Claremont?" Sophia interrupted, her tone pleasant. "Ty isn't being specific because, I imagine, he feels it might embarrass me. We had a moment in the office in the villa that evening."

"Sophia."

"Ty," she said equably, "I believe the detectives will understand that you might not have been in the mood to drive down to San Francisco and have dinner with one woman when you'd very shortly before been rolling around on the office floor with another. We had a moment," she continued. "Unplanned and impromptu and very likely inappropriate, and were interrupted when Tyler's grandfather stepped into the room."

To emphasize her point, she ran her fingers through Ty's hair. "Mr. MacMillan senior can verify that if you feel it necessary to ask him if we were indeed groping each other during working hours. Under those circumstances, I think it's understandable that Ty might have been a bit frazzled and not in the mood to drive to the city for a business dinner with Margaret. But the main point is, unless I'm just stupid, that he didn't go in the first place and so is unconnected to what happened to her."

Claremont listened patiently, nodded, then looked back at Tyler. It was, he supposed, a step to have his impression of the two of them verified. And another to note that MacMillan looked uncomfortable, and the Giambelli woman amused.

"Have you ever had dinner in Ms. Bowers's apartment before?"

"No. I've been there. Picked her up once for a business deal at the Four Seasons. We went together. That was about a year ago."

"Why don't you just ask if he's ever slept with her?" Sophia suggested. "Ty, did you and Margaret ever—"

"No." Torn between irritation and embarrassment, he shot her a fulminating look. "Jesus, Sophie."

Before he could gather his composure, she patted his shoulder and took over. "She was attracted to him, and he was oblivious. Men often are, and Ty's a bit more dense about that sort of thing than most. I've been trying to get him in bed for—"

"Will you stop it?" He had to struggle not to simply lower his head into his hands. "Listen, I'm sorry about what happened to Margaret. She was a nice woman. I liked her. And maybe if I hadn't canceled I could've called nine-one-one when she had the heart attack. But I don't see what these questions have to do with anything."

"Did you ever give Ms. Bowers a bottle of wine?"

Tyler dragged his hand through his hair. "I don't know. Probably. I give a lot of people, and business associates, bottles of wine. Kind of goes with the territory."

"Wine carrying the Giambelli label, the Italian label?"

"No, I use my own. Why?"

"Ms. Bowers consumed nearly an entire bottle of Castello di Giambelli Merlot on the evening you were to dine with her. The bottle contained digitalis."

"I don't get it." Even as Tyler reared up in his seat, Sophia was clamping a hand on his shoulder.

"She was murdered?" Sophia demanded. "Poisoned? Margaret was . . . If you'd been there. If you'd had the wine . . ."

"It's possible that if more than one person had shared the bottle, the dosage wouldn't have been lethal," Claremont stated. "But Ms. Bowers consumed nearly the entire bottle, in what was certainly one sitting. Do you have any idea how digitalis found its way into a bottle of Italian Merlot, and into Ms. Bowers's apartment?"

"I have to call my grandmother." Sophia

sprang to her feet. "If there's been product tampering, we have to deal with it quickly. I need all the information on that bottle. The vintage. I have to have a copy of the label to run it down."

"Your grandmother's been informed," Maguire told her. "As have the proper Italian authorities. Product tampering is a possibility, but at this point we have no idea when Ms. Bowers obtained the bottle, or if it was given to her. We can't confirm she didn't add the dose to the wine herself."

"Kill herself? That's ridiculous." Ty got to his feet. "She wasn't suicidal. She was doing great when I talked to her, happy with her job, excited about the new responsibilities, the travel."

"Do you have any enemies, Mr. MacMillan? Someone who might have known your plans with Ms. Bowers that evening?"

"No. And I'm not a target. In the first place, if the wine was tampered with, I'd have known it. I'd have nosed it or tasted it. It's what I do."

"Exactly," Maguire concurred.

Sophia felt her hackles rise. "Ty, you've answered enough questions. We're going to call a lawyer."

"I don't need a goddamn lawyer."

"We're calling Uncle James. Now."

"That's your right." Claremont got to his feet. "A question for you, Ms. Giambelli. Do you know anything about the relationship between Ms. Bowers and your father?"

Her blood iced over. "As far as I know, they didn't have one outside of business."

"I see. Well, thank you for your time."

"My father and Margaret."

"It's just as likely he was pulling your chain."

But Sophia worried on the nugget—chewing it, measuring its texture. "If there was something between them, and their deaths are connected—"

"Don't rush it, Sophie." He put a hand over hers briefly, then downshifted to turn into the villa. He knew how shaken she was. She hadn't voiced the slightest objection when he'd gotten behind the wheel of her car to drive them.

"If there's been tampering. If there's a chance, the slightest chance there are other bottles—"

"Don't rush it," he said again. He stopped

the car, shifted to her. He took her hand now, held it. "We'll have to check it out. Every step, every detail. We can't panic. Because if there has been tampering, Sophie, that's just what whoever did it wants. Panic, chaos, scandal."

"I know. The scandal's my job. I can handle it. I'll think of something to turn the publicity. But . . . my father and Margaret, Ty. If there was something there—" She tightened her grip on his hand when he started to shake his head. "I *have* to think of it. If there was, did he know about the tampering? How many times a year did he travel to Italy? Eight, ten, twelve?"

"Don't go there, Sophia."

"Why? You have. You think I can't see it? You have, others will. So I have to get there first. I don't want to believe this of him. I have to accept all the rest, but I don't want to believe this."

"You're making too big a leap, too fast. Slow down. Facts, Soph. Let's start with facts."

"The facts are two people are dead." Because her hand wanted to tremble, she drew it from his and pushed out of the car. "Margaret took over most of my father's accounts and responsibilities. Whether or not there was a personal relationship between them, that's a connection."

"Okay." He wanted to offer her something, but it seemed all she wanted was cold logic. "We'll look at that connection and see where it takes us. First we deal with the wine," he said as they started up the stairs. "Then with the fallout."

The family was in the front parlor, with David standing by the window talking on the phone. Tereza sat, soldier-straight, sipping coffee. She nodded when Ty and Sophia came in, and merely gestured to chairs.

"James is on his way." Eli paced back and forth in front of the fire. The strain seemed to have weight, and caused his face to sag. "David's talking to Italy now, getting damage control started."

"Let me get you some coffee," Pilar began.

"Mama. Sit."

"I need to do something."

"Mama." Sophia rose and walked to the coffee cart to stand beside Pilar. "Dad and Margaret?"

"I don't know." Her hands were steady on

the pot, even as her insides shivered. "I just don't. I would've thought— It was my impression Rene kept him on a short leash."

"Not short enough." Sophia kept her voice quiet. "He was involved with a woman at my office."

"Oh." It was a kind of sigh. "I wish I could tell you, Sophie. But I just don't know. I'm sorry."

"Understand this." Sophia turned at her grandmother's voice. Waited. "If there was something between Tony Avano and Margaret Bowers, the police will speculate that any of us, any of us who are connected to them, might have had a part in their deaths. We're family here. We'll stand by each other, and for each other until this is done."

She glanced toward David when he lowered the phone. "So?"

"We're tracking it," he began. "We'll recall all bottles of Merlot of that vintage. We should, very shortly, be able to determine which cask the bottle was drawn from. I'll leave in the morning."

"No. Eli and I will leave in the morning." Tereza lifted a hand, closed her fingers around Eli's when he gripped it. "This is for me. I leave it to you to see that the California operation is secure. That there's no breach. You and Tyler must make certain of it."

"Paulie and I can start with the wineries," Tyler suggested. "David can look at the bottling."

David nodded. "We'll go over the personnel files, one by one. You know the crews better than I do. It's most likely the problem's contained in Italy, but we'll make certain California's secure."

Sophia already had her memo pad in her lap. "I'll have press releases, both English and Italian, ready in an hour. I'll need all the details on the recall. We'll want a story on how exacting the winemaking process is for Giambelli-MacMillan. How safe, how secure. We'll certainly take some hits in Italy, but we may be able to keep it below crisis point here. We'll need to allow camera crews in the vineyards, and the wineries both here and overseas. *Nonna,* with you and Eli going over, we'll be able to show that Giambelli is family-run, and that *La Signora* continues to take a personal interest."

"It is family-run," Tereza said flatly. "And I take a very personal interest."

"I know that." Sophia lowered her book.

"It's important to make sure the press and the consumer know it. Believe it. Are impressed by it. We'll need to use Mama here—Mama, Ty, me. We'll show the roots, the family involvement and concern. A hundred years of tradition, excellence *and* responsibility. I know how to do this."

"She's right." No one was more surprised than Sophia when Tyler spoke. "Mostly I don't give a damn about publicity or perception, which," he added, "is why the two of you dumped me into it. And I'd as soon have a plague of locusts in my winery as reporters. I still mostly don't give a damn, but I know a little more about it. Enough to be sure Sophia will find a way to spin this around to damp down the worst of the damage, and probably find one to turn it around to benefit the company. She'll find the way because she cares more than anybody."

"Agreed. So, we each do what we do best." Tereza looked at Eli, and something passed between them in that beat of silence. "But we do nothing else until we meet with James Moore. It's not only the reputation of the company that must be protected, but the company itself. Sophia, draft your release. David will help you with the details. Then we'll let the lawyers look at it. And everything else."

It was a blow to the pride. That, Tereza thought as she stood at her office window, was the hardest to accept. What was hers had been violated, threatened. The work of a lifetime besmirched by one tainted bottle of wine.

Now, in so many ways, she had to trust others to save her legacy.

"We'll handle this, Tereza."

"Yes." She lifted a hand to cover the one Eli laid on her shoulder. "I was remembering when I was a young girl and my grandfather walked with me down the rows back home. He said to me that it wasn't enough to plant. That what was planted must be tended, protected, cherished and disciplined. The vines were his children. They became mine."

"You've raised them well."

"And paid the price. I was less of a wife to the man I married here so long ago than I might have been, less of a mother to the daughter I birthed. I had the responsibility passed to me, and the ambition, Eli. Such ambition."

It lived in her still, and she didn't regret it.

"Would there have been more children if I hadn't wished so desperately for my vines to be fertile? Would my child have made the choices she made if I had been more her mother?"

"Things happen as they're meant to happen."

"That's the practical Scot. We Italians, we tend to believe more in chance. And retribution."

"What's happened isn't retribution, Tereza. It's either a terrible accident or a criminal act. You're not responsible either way."

"I took responsibility the day I took Giambelli." Her eyes scanned the vines, the sleeping promise of them. "Aren't I responsible for pushing Sophia and Tyler together? Thinking of the company, never imagining what might happen between them on another level."

"Tereza." He turned her to face him. "Realigning so that they work together doesn't trickle down and make you the trigger for shooting those two very healthy young people onto the office floor."

She sighed. "No, but it proves I didn't take their health into account. We're passing our heritage into their hands. I expected them to fight. We both did. But sex can make enemies of people. And that I didn't anticipate. God, that makes me feel old."

"Tereza." He pressed his lips to her forehead. "We *are* old."

He said it to make her laugh, and she obliged him. "Well. We didn't become enemies. We can hope each of them took something from us."

"I love you, Tereza."

"I know. I didn't marry you for love, Eli."

"I know, my dear."

"For business," she said, stepping back from him. "A merger. A wise business move. I respected you. I liked you a great deal and enjoyed your company. Instead of being punished for such calculation, I was rewarded. I love you very much. I hope you know that, too."

"I do. We'll weather this, Tereza."

"I don't need you by my side. But I want you there. Very much want you there. That, I think, says more. Means more."

He took the hand she held out to him. "We'll go down. James should be here soon."

James looked over Sophia's proposed release, nodded. "Good." He slipped off his reading glasses. "Clear, calm, with a personal touch. I wouldn't change a thing, from a legal standpoint."

"Then I'll go up, finalize it, alert the troops and get it out."

"Take Linc with you." James winked at her. "He's a good general dogsbody."

He waited until they'd left the room. "Tereza, Eli, I'll be consulting with your lawyers in Italy. At this point you're handling the problem quickly and decisively. This should cut down on any potential legal actions against the company. You may be looking at some suits here. You need to be prepared for that. I'll get what I can from the police. Unless it's substantiated that the chemical was in the wine prior to it being opened, you've nothing to worry about other than damaging publicity. If Giambelli is found liable through negligence, we'll deal with it."

"Negligence isn't my concern, James. If the wine was tainted before it was opened, it wasn't negligence but murder."

"Right now that's speculation. From the questions the police asked you, and you, Tyler, they're speculating as well. They don't know when the digitalis was added to the wine. From a legal standpoint, this keeps Giambelli one very vital step back from the problem."

"The problem," Tyler said, "is a woman's dead."

"That's a problem for the police. And while you may not like it, I'm going to advise you not to answer any more questions from them without counsel present. It's their job to build a case. It's not yours to help them."

"I knew her."

"That's right. And she had prepared a cozy and romantic dinner for two on the night she died. A dinner you didn't attend. Right now the police wonder just how well you knew her. Let them wonder. And while they're wondering, we'll look into Margaret Bowers. Who she was, who she knew, what she wanted."

· · ·

"Hell of a mess, huh?"

Sophia glanced up at Linc. "I have a feeling we're going to be sweeping it up for a long time."

"Plenty of brooms. You've got Dad, so you've got the best. And no way Mom'll stay out of it. Then you've got me."

She managed a smile. "A triple threat."

"Damn right. Moore, Moore and Moore. Who could ask for anything—"

"Stop. I'll have to hit you." She finished proofing the release on her screen, then faxed it to P.J. "Better if this comes out of the San Francisco office than here. I want it personal, but I don't want it to look like a family cover-up. I've started these follow-ups and story pitches. Why don't you take a look, put your legal mind to them and see if I've covered my ass."

"Sure. Always liked your ass."

"Ha ha." She got up to let him take her place at the desk. "How's the doctor?"

"Cruising right along. You ought to snag a date and meet us some night. We could hit some hot spots, have a few laughs. You look like you could use a few laughs."

"More than a few. My social life doesn't

exist these days, and that looks to be the pattern for the foreseeable future."

"This from the party queen?"

"The party queen's lost her crown." Since he was using her computer, she grabbed the phone to check in with P.J.

"You ask me, you could use a little break, Sophie. You're edgy. Were edgy," he added when she shot him a look, "before this last flurry of crap hit. All work and no play and yadda-yadda."

"I don't have time to play," she snapped. "I don't have time to think past the next move, or take a breath without worrying what's going to jump in my face next. I've been putting in twelve-hour days, minimum, for nearly three months. I have calluses on my damn hands, had to fire a top staff member, and I haven't had sex for six god-damn months."

"Whoa. Ouch. And I didn't mean the calluses. I'd offer to help you out there, but the doctor's liable to object."

She blew out a breath. "I think I'm going to take up yoga." She dragged open her desk drawer, pulled out her aspirin as P.J. came on the line. "Fax come through?" She listened, nodded as she worked off the top of the bottle. "Get it out on the wire ASAP, then . . . What? Christ, when? All right, all right. Get the release out. Get me the information, word for word. I'll work up a response. Don't give any comments, just use the release. See that all department heads, all key personnel have a copy of it. That's the company line until further notice. Keep me updated."

She hung up, stared over at Linc. "It's out. It's already leaked."

CHAPTER SEVENTEEN

GIAMBELLI-MACMILLAN, THE GIANT OF THE WINE INDUSTRY, HAS SUFFERED ANOTHER CRISIS. IT HAS BEEN CONFIRMED THAT A TAINTED BOTTLE OF WINE WAS RESPONSIBLE FOR THE DEATH OF MARGARET BOWERS, AN EXECUTIVE WITH THE COMPANY. POLICE ARE INVESTIGATING. THE POSSIBILITY OF PRODUCT TAMPERING IS BEING CONSIDERED, AND GIAMBELLI-MACMILLAN IS RECALLING BOTTLES OF CASTELLO DI GIAMBELLI MERLOT, 1992. SINCE THE MERGER OF THE GIAMBELLI-MACMILLAN WINERIES LAST DECEMBER . . .

Perfect, Jerry thought as he watched the evening newscast. Absolutely perfect. They'd scramble, of course. Already were scrambling. But what would the public hear?

Giambelli. Death. Wine.

Bottles would be poured down the sink. More would sit unsold on the shelf. It would sting quite a bit and for quite some time. It would cut into profits, short- and long-term. Profits La Coeur would reap.

That alone was a great satisfaction. Professionally and personally. Very personally.

It was true a couple of people had died. But that wasn't his fault. He had nothing to do with it—directly. And when the police caught the one who did, the damage to Giambelli would only be compounded.

He'd wait awhile. Bide his time. Watch the show. Then, if it seemed advantageous, there could be another anonymous call.

Not to the media this time. But to the police.

"Digitalis comes from foxglove." Maddy knew. She'd looked it up.

"What?" Distracted, David looked over briefly. He had a mountain of paperwork on his desk. In Italian. He was much better at speaking it than reading it.

"Would they have grown foxglove near the vines?" Maddy demanded. "Like they grow mustard plants between the rows here? For nitrogen. I don't think they would because they'd know foxglove had digitalis. But maybe they made a mistake. Could it infect the grapes if the plants were grown there, and turned into the soil?"

"I don't know. Maddy, this isn't for you to worry about."

"Why? You're worried."

"It's my job to worry."

"I could help."

"Honey, if you want to help, you could give me a little space here. Do your homework."

Her lips began to pout. A sure sign of personal insult, but David was too distracted to notice.

"I've done my homework."

"Well, help Theo with his. Or something."

"But if the digitalis—"

"Maddy." At his wits' end, he snapped at her. "This isn't a story or a project. It's a very real problem, and I have to deal with it. Go find something to do."

"Fine." She shut the door of his office and let the resentment burn as she stomped away. He never wanted her to help when it was something important.

Do your homework, talk to Theo, clean up your room. He always fell back on those crappy deals when she wanted to do something that mattered.

She bet he wouldn't have told Pilar Giambelli to find something to do. And she didn't know squat about science. Music and art and looking pretty, that's all *she* knew. Girl things. Not important things.

She stalked to Theo's room. He was sprawled on the bed, his music blaring, his guitar lying on his belly, and the phone at his ear. From the dopey look on his face it was a girl on the other end.

Men were so lame.

"Dad wants you to do your homework."

"Beat it." He crossed his ankles. "Nah. It's nothing. Just my idiot sister."

The phone knocked hard against his jaw when Maddy launched herself at him. In seconds Theo was dealing with the shock of pain, the squeals in his ear and the pummels and kicks of a furious Maddy.

"Ow! Wait! Damn it, Maddy. Call you back." He managed to drop the phone, and in the nick of time protect his privates from a knee jab. "What the hell?"

After a long, sweaty minute, he managed

to flip her—she didn't fight like a girl, but he still outweighed her—and pin her down. "Cut it out, you crazy little bitch. What's your problem?"

"I'm not *nothing!*" She spat it at him and made a valiant attempt with her knee again.

"No, you're just nutszoid." He licked the corner of his mouth, cursed at the unmistakable taste. "I'm bleeding. When I tell Dad—"

"You can't tell him anything. He doesn't listen to anybody except her."

"Her, who?"

"You know who. Get off me, you big, fat jerk. You're just as bad as he is, making gooey noises to some girl, and not listening to anybody."

"I was having a conversation," he said with great dignity to counter the gooey snipe. "And if you hit me again, I'm hitting you back. Even if Dad grounds me for it. Now what's your problem?"

"I don't have a problem. It's the men in this house making asses of themselves over the women in the villa that's the problem. It's disgusting. It's embarrassing."

Watching her, Theo wiped the blood from his mouth. He had a very creative fantasy life going where Sophia was concerned. And his baby sister wasn't going to spoil it for him.

He shook back his mop of curly hair. Yawned. "You're just jealous."

"I am not."

"Sure you are. 'Cause you're skinny and flat-chested."

"I'd rather have brains than breasts."

"Good thing. I don't know why you're having a snit-fit because Dad's hanging with Pilar. He's hung with women before."

"You're so stupid." Every dreg of disgust gathered in her voice. "He's not hanging out with her, putz-face. He's in love with her."

"Get out. What do you know?" But his stomach did a funny little jump as he dragged a bag of chips off his dresser. "Man."

"It's going to change everything. That's the way it works." There was a terrible pressure in her chest, but she got to her feet. "Nothing's ever going to be the same again, and that sucks out loud."

"Nothing's been the same. Not since Mom took off."

"It got *better.*" The tears wanted to escape, but rather than let them fall in front of him, she stormed out of the room.

"Yeah," Theo muttered. "But it didn't stay the same."

Sophia hoped air, cold and clear, would blow some of the clouds from her mind. She had to think, and think precisely. She was spinning as quickly as she could, but the newscast had caused some damage. Too often the first impression was all people ever remembered.

Now her job was to shift that impression. To show the public that while Giambelli had been violated, the company had done nothing to violate the public. That took more than words, she knew, more even than placement and delivery. It took tangible action.

If her grandparents weren't even now packed for Italy, she would have urged them to do so. To be visible at the source of the problem. Not to fall back on the safety of "no comment" but to comment often and to comment specifically. Use the company name again and again, she thought, making mental notes. Make it personal, make the company breathe.

But . . . they had to tread carefully around Margaret Bowers. Sympathy, of course, but not so much it implied responsibility.

To do that, to help them do that, Sophia had to stop thinking of Margaret as a person.

If that was cold, she would be cold. And deal with her conscience later.

She stood at the edge of the vineyard. It was guarded, she thought, against pests, disease, the vagaries of weather. Whatever threatened to invade or damage it was fought against. This was no different. She'd fight the war, and on her terms. She wouldn't regret any act that won it.

She caught a shadow of movement. "Who's there?" Her mind leaped toward trespasser, saboteur. Murderer. Without hesitation she charged, and found her arms full of struggling young girl.

"Let go! I can be here. I'm allowed."

"Sorry. I'm sorry." Sophia stepped back. "You scared me."

She hadn't looked scared, Maddy thought. But she had looked scary. "I'm not doing anything wrong."

"I didn't say you were. I said you scared

me. I guess we're all a little jumpy right now. Look . . ."

She caught the glimmer of tears on the girl's cheeks. As she didn't like having her own crying jags brought into issue, she gave Maddy the same consideration.

"I just came out to clear my head. Too much going on in there right now." Sophia glanced back at the house.

"My father's working."

There was just enough defense in the statement to have Sophia speculating. "There's a lot of pressure on him right now. On everybody. My grandparents are leaving for Italy first thing in the morning. I worry about them. They're not young anymore."

After her father's rebuff, Sophia's casual confidence soothed. Still cautious, Maddy fell into step beside her. "They don't act old. Not, like, decrepit or anything."

"No, they don't, do they? But still. I wish I could go instead, but they need me here right now."

Maddy's lips trembled as she looked toward the lights of the guest house. Nobody, it seemed, needed her. Anywhere. "At least you've got something to do."

"Yeah. Now if I could just figure out what to do next. So much going on."

She slanted Maddy a look. The kid was wound up and sulking about something. Sophia remembered very well what it was like to be fourteen, wound up and sulking.

Life was full of immediacy and intense moments at fourteen, she thought, that made professional crises seem like paper cuts.

"I guess, on some level, we're in the same boat. My mother," she said when Maddy remained silent. "Your father. It's a little weird."

Maddy shrugged, then hunched her shoulders. "I gotta go."

"All right, but I'd like to tell you something. Woman to woman, daughter to daughter, whatever. My mother's gone a long time without someone, without a good man, to care about her. I don't know what it's been like for you, or your brother or your father. But for me, after the general strangeness of it, it's nice to see her have a good man who makes her happy. I hope you'll give her a chance."

"It doesn't matter what I do. Or think. Or say."

Defiant misery, Sophia mused. Yes, she remembered that, too. "Yes, it matters. When someone loves us, what we think and what we do matters." She looked over at the sound of running feet. "From the looks of it, somebody loves you."

"Maddy!" Breathless, David plucked his daughter off her feet. He managed to embrace and shake her at the same time. "What are you doing? You can't go wandering off like that after dark."

"I just took a walk."

"And cost me a year of my life. You want to fight with your brother, be my guest, but you're not to leave the house again without permission. Clear?"

"Yes, sir." Though secretly pleased, she grimaced. "I didn't think you'd notice."

"Think again." He hooked his arm around her neck, a casual habit of affection Sophia had noticed. And envied. Her father had never touched her like that.

"Partly my fault," Sophia told him. "I kept her longer than I should have. She's a terrific sounding board. My mind was going off in too many directions."

"You should give it a rest. You're going to

need all circuits up and working tomorrow. Is your mother free?"

He didn't notice the way Maddy stiffened, but Sophia did. "I imagine. Why?"

"I'm slogging through reports and memos, in Italian. It'd go faster with someone who reads it better than I do."

"I'll tell her." Sophia looked at Maddy now. "She'll want to help."

"Appreciate it. Now I'll just drag this baggage home and pound it awhile. See you at the briefing. Eight o'clock."

"I'll be ready. 'Night, Maddy." She watched them walk through the fields toward the guest house, their shadows close enough to merge into one form in the moonlight.

Hard to blame the kid for wanting to keep it that way. Hard to make room for changes. For people, when your life seemed just fine as it was.

But changes happened. It was smarter to be a part of them. Better yet, she decided, to initiate them.

Tyler kept the radio and the TV off. He ignored the phone. One thing he could control was his own reaction to the press, and the best way to control it was to ignore the press altogether. At least for a few hours.

He was working his way through his own files, his logs, every record he had available. He could, and would, ascertain that the MacMillan area of the company was secure.

What he couldn't seem to control were his own questions about Margaret. An accident, suicide or murder? None of the options was appealing. He eliminated suicide. She hadn't been the type, and he sure as hell didn't have the towering ego that suggested she'd killed herself in despair because he'd broken a dinner date.

Maybe she had been interested in him, and maybe he'd ignored the signals because he hadn't felt the same way. And hadn't wanted the complications. Life was complicated enough without tangling up business and personal relationships.

Plus, she just hadn't been his type.

He didn't go for the fast-track career woman with attitude and an agenda. That kind of woman just took too much energy.

Take Sophia.

Christ, he was beginning to think he'd explode if he didn't take Sophia. And wasn't that the point? he reminded himself as he roamed restlessly downstairs again. Thinking about her that way muddled up the mind, strained the body and complicated an already complex business association.

Now more than ever it was essential he keep his mind on his job. The current crisis was going to pull his time and energy away from the vineyards when he could least afford it. Long-range forecasts warned him that frost vigils would be necessary. Several casks of wine were on the point of being ready for bottling. Disking had already started.

He didn't have time to worry about police investigations, potential lawsuits. Or a woman. And of all of them, he was finding the woman the hardest to shove out of his mind.

Because she'd invaded his system, he thought. And she'd be stuck there, irritating him, until he got her out again. So why didn't he just march over to the villa, storm up her terrace steps and deal with it. Finish it.

He knew exactly how pathetic and self-serving that was as rationalization. And decided he didn't give a damn.

He grabbed a jacket, strode to the front door and yanked it open.

And there she was, stalking up his steps.

"I don't like irritable, macho men," she told him as she slammed the door at her back.

"I don't like bossy, aggressive women."

They dove at each other. Even as their mouths began a mutual assault she boosted herself up, wrapped her legs around his hips. "I want a bed this time." Her breath already tattered, she tugged at his shirt. "We'll try out the floor later."

"I want you naked." He nipped his teeth into her throat and began to stagger up the steps. "I don't care where."

"God, you have this incredible taste." She raced her lips over his face, his neck. "It's so basic." Her breath caught when he rapped her back against the wall at the top of the steps. Her fingers fisted in his hair. "This is just sex, right?"

"Yeah, right, whatever." His mouth crushed down on hers. Using the wall to brace her, he began dragging her sweater over her head. "God. You're so built." He tossed her sweater aside, took his mouth over the soft swell of breast that rose above her bra. "We're not going to make the bed."

Her heart hammered as he used his teeth on her. "Okay. Next time."

Her feet hit the floor. At least she thought they did. It was hard to know where she was, who she was with as the geyser of greed erupted inside her. Hands were pulling at clothes; something ripped. Mouths ran hot over flesh. Everything blurred. Over the wild beat of blood she could hear her own whimpers, pleas, demands, a kind of mad chant that merged with his.

She was already wet, already aching when his fingers found her. The violent glory of the orgasm ripped through her, molten gold release, so strong, so welcome she might have melted bonelessly to the floor.

"Uh-uh. No you don't." He pressed her back against the wall and, riding on her thrill, continued to drive her. "I want you screaming. Go up again."

She couldn't have stopped herself. Welcoming the burn, craving it, she let him take, empty her out until her mind was filled with the dark and the feral.

And filled, she tore at him, whipped him past reason. She watched his eyes go opaque and knew it was she who blinded him. Heard his breath heave and tear, and thrilled that she could weaken him.

"Now." Once more she anchored her hands in his hair and shuddered, shuddered as she poised on the next thin edge. "Now, now, now."

When he plunged into her, she came again. Brutally. Her nails dug into the sweat-slicked slope of his shoulders as her hips pistoned. Lightning-fast. With his mouth fused to hers, he swallowed the small, greedy sounds she made. Fed on them as he hitched her up to give more. Take more.

Pleasure careened through him, left him shattered, stupefied.

He managed to hold on to her as both of them slid to the floor.

Sprawled over him, her heart still racing, Sophia began to laugh. *"Dio. Grazie a Dio.* Decanted at last. No real finesse, but a fine body and excellent staying power."

"We'll work on finesse when I'm not ready to howl at the moon."

"Wasn't complaining." To prove it, she brushed her lips lightly over his chest. "I feel fabulous. At least I think I do."

"I can verify that. You feel incredible." He blew out a breath. "I'm winded."

"That makes two of us." She lifted her head, studied his face. "Are you finished?"

"Not hardly."

"Oh, good, because neither am I." She shifted, straddled him. "Ty?"

"Mmmm." His hands were already stroking up her torso. She was so smooth, he thought. Smooth, dusky, exotic.

"We probably need to set guidelines."

"Yeah." She had a pretty little mole on the curve of her left hip. A kind of sexual punctuation.

"You want to get into that now?"

"No."

"Good. Me either." She braced her hands on either side of his head, leaned down. She brushed her lips at the corners of his mouth, teasing little sips. "Bed?" she whispered.

He reared up, wrapped his arms around her. "Next time."

Sometime around midnight, she found herself facedown on his bed. The sheets were tangled and hot, and her bones were limp as water.

Even after so long a sexual drought it was hard for her to believe the human body could recharge as often, and at such intense power.

"Water," she croaked, afraid now that she'd satisfied one craving, thirst would kill her. "I need water. I'll give you anything— wild, sexual favors—if you'll just give me a bottle of water."

"You've already paid out the wild, sexual favors."

"Oh, right." She groped over, patted his shoulder blindly. "Be a pal, MacMillan."

"Okay, but where are we?"

"On the bed." She sighed gustily. "We finally made it."

"Right. Be right back." He staggered up, and since he'd been crossways on the bed, misjudged direction and rapped smartly into a chair.

Listening to his muttered curses, Sophia smiled into the sheet. God, he was cute. Funny. Smarter than she'd given him credit for. And incredible in bed. On the floor. Against the wall. She couldn't remember any man appealing to her on so many levels. Especially when you considered he was the type who had to be held at gunpoint to put on a suit and tie.

Which was, she supposed, why he always looked so sexy in them. The caveman temporarily civilized.

Lost for the moment in that thought, she yelped when Ty held the iced water to her bare shoulder. "Ha ha," she muttered, but was grateful enough to roll over, sit up and gulp down half the glass.

"Hey. I figured you'd share."

"I didn't say anything about sharing."

"Then I want more sexual favors."

"You couldn't possibly," she chuckled.

"You know how much I like proving you wrong."

She sighed as his hand snuck up her thigh. "That's true." Still she handed him the rest of the water. "I might have a few sexual favors left in me. But then I really have to go home. Early briefing tomorrow."

He drained the glass, set it aside. "We're not thinking about that now." He hooked an arm around her waist, then rolled until she was under him. "Let me tell you just what I have in mind."

. . .

It had been, Sophia mused, a very long time since she'd snuck into the house at two in the morning. Still, it was one of those skills, like riding a bike or, well, sex, that came back to you. She dimmed her headlights before they flashed against the windows of the villa and eased the car gently, slowly around the bend and into the garage.

She crept out into the chilly night and stood just a moment under the brilliant wheel of stars. She felt outrageously tired, wonderfully used, and alive.

Tyler MacMillan, she decided, was a man just full of surprises, of secret pockets and marvelous, marvelous energy. She'd learned a great deal about him in the past few months. Aspects and angles she hadn't bothered to explore. And she was looking forward to continuing that exploration.

But for now, she'd better get in the house and get some sleep or she'd be useless the next day.

Odd, she thought as she walked quietly around the back, she'd wanted to stay with him. Sleep with him. All curled up against that long, warm body. Safe, cozy, secure.

She'd trained herself over the years to click off emotionally after sex. A man's way, she liked to think. Sleeping, and waking, in the same bed after the fun and games were over could be awkward. It could be intimate. Avoiding that, making certain she didn't need that, kept things from getting messy.

But she'd had to order herself to leave Tyler's bed. Because she was tired, she assured herself. Because it had been a difficult day. He wasn't really any different from anyone else she'd been with.

Perhaps she liked him more, she considered as she navigated through the shrubbery. And was more attracted to him than she'd expected to be. That didn't make him different. Just . . . new. After a while the polish would wear off the shiny excitement, and that would be that.

That, she thought, was always that.

If you looked for love and lifetimes, you were doomed to disappoint, or be disappointed. Better, much better, to seize the moment, wring it dry, then move on.

Because thinking was dulling her mood, she blocked out the questions. And rounding the last bend in the gardens, came face-to-face with her mother.

They stared at each other, the surprised

breath each puffed out frosting into little clouds.

"Um. Nice night," Sophia commented.

"Yes. Very. I was just, ah . . . David . . ." Stumped, Pilar gestured vaguely toward the guest house. "He needed help with some translating."

"I see." A wild giggle tried to claw its way out of Sophia's throat. "Is that what your generation calls it?" A small choking sound escaped. "If we're going to sneak the rest of the way in, let's do it. We could freeze out here trying to come up with reasonable excuses."

"I *was* translating." Pilar hurried to the door, fumbled with the knob. "There was a lot of—"

"Oh, Mama." The laughter won. Sophia clutched her belly and stumbled inside. "Stop bragging."

"I was merely . . ." Floundering, Pilar pushed at her hair. She had a very good idea how she looked—tumbled and flushed. Like a woman who'd just slid out of bed. Or in this case, off the living room sofa. Taking the offensive seemed to be the safest course. "You're out late."

"Yeah. I was translating. With Ty."

"With . . . Oh. Oh."

"I'm starving, how about you?" Enjoying herself, Sophia pulled open the refrigerator. "I never got around to dinner." She spoke casually, with her head in the fridge. "Do you have a problem with me and Ty?"

"No—yes. No," Pilar stuttered. "I don't know. I absolutely don't know how I'm supposed to handle this."

"Let's have pie."

"Pie."

Sophia pulled out what was left of a deep-dish apple. "You look wonderful, Mama."

Pilar brushed at her hair again. "I couldn't possibly."

"Wonderful." Sophia set the dish on the counter and reached up for plates. "I had a few emotional bumps about you and David. I wasn't used to seeing you as—to seeing you, I suppose. But when I run into you sneaking into the house in the middle of the night, looking wonderful, I can't help but see you."

"I don't have to sneak into my own house."

"Oh." Wielding a pie cutter, Sophia asked, "Then why were you?"

"I was just . . . Let's have pie."

"Good call." Sophia cut two huge hunks, then smiled when Pilar stroked her hair. She leaned in, and for a moment the two of them stood in the bright kitchen light in silence. "It was a long, lousy day. It's nice to end it well."

"Yes. Though you gave me a hell of a shock outside."

"Me? Imagine my surprise, reliving my teenage years, then running into my mother."

"Reliving? Really?" Sophia carried the plates to the kitchen table while Pilar got forks.

"Oh well, why dwell on the past?" Grinning wickedly, Sophia licked pie from her thumb. "David's very hot."

"Sophie."

"Very hot. Great shoulders, that charmingly boyish face, that intelligent brain. Quite a package you've bagged there, Mama."

"He's not a trophy. And I certainly hope you don't think of Ty as one."

"He's got a terrific butt."

"I know."

"I meant Ty."

"I know," Pilar repeated. "What, am I

blind?" With an unladylike snort, she plopped into a chair. "This is ridiculous, it's rude and it's—"

"Fun," Sophia finished and sat down to scoop up some pie. "We share an interest in fashion, and more recently in the business. Why shouldn't we share an interest in . . . *Nonna*."

"Well, of course we share an interest in . . ." Pilar dropped her fork with a clatter as she followed the direction of Sophia's blank stare. "Mama. What are you doing up?"

"You think I don't know when people come and go in my house?" Somehow elegant in a thick chenille robe and slippers, Tereza swept into the room. "What, no wine?"

"We were just . . . hungry," Sophia managed.

"Ha. No wonder. Sex is a laborious business if done properly. I'm hungry myself."

Sophia slapped a hand to her mouth, but it was too late. The burst of laughter erupted. "Go, Eli."

Tereza merely took the last piece of pie as her daughter stared down at her plate, shoulders shaking. "We'll have wine. I believe the occasion calls for it. I think this is surely the first time all three generations of Giambelli women have sat together in the kitchen after making love. You needn't look so stunned, Pilar. Sex is a natural function, after all. And since you've chosen a worthy partner this time, we'll have wine."

She chose a bottle of sauvignon blanc from the kitchen rack and uncorked it. "These are trying times. There have been others, and there will be more." She poured three glasses. "It's essential that we live while we move through them. I approve of David Cutter, if my approval matters."

"Thank you. It does, of course."

Sophia was biting her lip to hide a grin when Tereza turned toward her. "If you hurt Tyler, I'll be both angry and disappointed in you. I love him very much."

"Well, I like that." Deflated, Sophia set her fork down. "Why would I?"

"Remember what I said. Tomorrow, we'll fight for what we are, what we have. Tonight." She lifted her glass. "Tonight, we celebrate it. *Salute.*"

CHAPTER EIGHTEEN

It was a war, waged on several fronts. Sophia fought her battles on the airwaves, in print and on the telephone. She spent hours updating press releases, giving interviews, reassuring accounts.

And every day she started over, beating back rumor, innuendo and speculation. Until the crisis passed, her time in the vineyards was over. That was Tyler's battlefield. She found herself resenting not being able to soldier there as well. To take part in the disking, the frost vigils, in the careful guarding of the emerging buds.

She worried about her grandparents, forging their front on the Italian line. Every day the reports came in. The recall was being implemented. And soon, bottle by bottle, the wine would be tested.

She couldn't think about the cost, short- or long-term. That, she left in David's hands.

When she needed to step back from the hype and spin, she stood at her office window and watched men with harrows work the earth. It would be a year of rare vintage, she promised herself.

They only had to survive it.

She jumped at the next ring of her phone, and buried the very real need to ignore it.

"Sophia Giambelli."

Ten minutes later she hung up, then released pent-up rage with a vicious stream of Italian curses.

"Does that help?" Pilar asked as she stood by the doorway.

"Not enough." Sophia pressed her fingers to her temples and wondered how best to handle this next stage of combat. "I'm glad you're here. Can you come in, sit down a minute."

"Fifteen, actually. I've just finished up another tour." Pilar settled into a chair. "They're coming in droves. Curiosity seekers for the most part now. Some reporters, though that's down to a trickle since your press conference."

"It's likely to build again. I just got off the phone with a producer of *The Larry Mann Show.*"

"Larry Mann." Pilar wrinkled her nose. "Trash television, at its worst. You aren't going to give them anything."

"They've already got something. They've got Rene." Unable to sit still, Sophia shoved away from her desk. "She's going to tape a show tomorrow revealing family secrets, supposedly, telling the true story of Dad's death. We're invited to participate. They want either you or me, or both of us, on the show to give our side of it."

"It won't do, Sophie. As satisfying as it might be to slap her back in public, it isn't the way. And that isn't the forum."

"Why do you think I was cursing?" She snatched up her frog paperweight, passed it restlessly from hand to hand. "We'll take the high road and ignore her. But God, how I'd love to wrestle in the mud with that bitch. She's been giving interviews right and left, and she's good enough at them to do considerable damage. I've talked to both Aunt Helen and Uncle James about legal action."

"Don't."

"She can't be allowed to use the family, to slander." Sophia scowled down at the frog. His cheerfully silly face usually lightened her mood. "I can't get down and dirty with her, which is a crying shame. But I can slap her back legally."

"Listen to me first," Pilar said, leaning forward. "I'm not being soft. I'm not being manipulated. Taking legal action, at least right now when we've so many other battles to fight, only gives some credence to her and what she's saying. I know your instincts are to fight, and mine are generally to retreat, but maybe, this time, we do neither. We just stand in place."

"I've thought of that. I've thought of it from both angles. But when it comes down to it, you fight fire with fire."

"Not always, honey. Sometimes you just drown it. We'll just drown her out, with good Giambelli wine."

Sophia inhaled, exhaled slowly as she sat back. She set the paperweight down again, turning it around and around while she considered. Behind her, the fax beeped and whined, but she ignored it while she figured the angles.

"That's good." Nodding, she looked at her

mother again. "That's very good. Drown the flames with one good flood. We're going to have a party. Spring ball, black tie. How much time do you need to put it together?"

To her credit Pilar only blinked. "Three weeks."

"Good. Work up the guest list. Once we've got invitations out, I'll plant some items with reporters. Rene opts for trash, we'll opt for elegance."

"A party?" Tyler raised his voice over the rumble of disking. "Ever hear of Nero and his fiddle?"

"Rome's not burning. That's my point." Impatient, Sophia dragged him farther from the work. "Giambelli takes their responsibilities seriously, are cooperating with the authorities here and in Italy. *Merda!*" She swore as her cell phone rang. "Wait."

She pulled the phone from her pocket. "Sophia Giambelli. *Si. Va bene.*" With an absent signal to Ty she paced a few feet away.

He stood, watched her move, issue what were undoubtedly orders in Italian.

Around them, the disking progressed. The

noisy, systematic turning of earth and cover crop. Warmth teased the vines to bud, even as the breeze that shivered down from the mountains promised a night of chills.

In the middle of it all, in the center of the ageless cycle, was Sophia. The dynamo with the future at her fingertips.

The center of it, he thought again. Maybe she'd been there, always.

She strode down the row, up again, then down, her voice rising, a kind of fascinating foreign music.

He didn't bother to curse, didn't even bother to question when he felt that last lock snick open inside him.

He'd been expecting that.

He was crazy about her, he admitted. Gone. Over the line. And sooner or later, he'd have to figure out what to do about it.

She jammed the phone back in her pocket, blew at her bangs. "Italian publicity branch," she said to Ty. "A few snags that needed picking loose. Sorry for the interruption. Now where . . ."

She trailed off, staring up at him. "What are you grinning at?" she demanded.

"Am I? Maybe it's because you're not so hard to look at, even in fast-forward."

"Fast-forward's the only speed that works right now. Anyway, the party. We need to make a statement, and continue with the plans for the centennial. The first gala's midsummer. We do this more intimate gathering to show unity, responsibility and confidence."

She began ticking points off with her fingers. "The recall was initiated voluntarily, and at considerable expense, before it was a legal issue. *La Signora* and Mr. MacMillan have traveled to Italy personally to offer any assistance in the investigation. However," she continued, "and we need to get to the however soon, Giambelli is confident the problem is under control. The family, and that's what we have to emphasize, remains gracious, hospitable and involved with the community. We show our polish, while Rene digs in the muck."

"Polish." He studied the vines. He reminded himself to check the overhead sprinklers, again, should they be needed for frost protection overnight. "If we're going to be polished, how come I have to fool around with a TV crew and walk around in the mud?"

"To illustrate the dedication and hard work

that goes into every bottle of wine produced. Don't be cranky, MacMillan. The last few days have been vicious."

"I'd be less cranky if outsiders would stay out of the way."

"Does that include me?"

He shifted his attention from the vines, looked at her beautiful face. "Doesn't seem to."

"Then why haven't you come sneaking through my terrace doors in the night?"

His lips quirked. "Thought about it."

"Think harder." When she leaned into him, and he stepped back, she asked, "What? Got a headache?"

"No, an audience. I'd as soon not advertise I'm sleeping with my co-operator."

"Sleeping with me has nothing to do with business." Her voice chilled several degrees, just the kind of cold snap that wrought damage. "But if you're ashamed of it—" She shrugged, turned and walked away.

He had to deal with the sting first, then the innate reluctance for public scenes. He caught up with her in five strides, grabbed her arm. "I'm not ashamed of anything. Just because I like keeping my personal life private—" Her sulky jerk back irritated him enough to tighten his grip and curl his fingers around her other arm. "There's enough gossip around here without adding to it. If I can't keep my mind on my work, I can't expect my men to. Ah, the hell with it."

He lifted her to her toes, pressed his mouth hard to hers.

There was a thrill in that, she thought. In that quick whip of strength and temper.

"Okay?" he demanded and dropped her flat on her feet again.

"Almost." She ran her hands up his chest, felt him tremble. A thrill, she thought, in knowing you were physically outmatched but still had power. She laid her lips on his, teasing until his hand took a fistful of the back of her sweater, until her hands were locked possessively around his neck and her own stomach muscles went loose.

"That," she murmured, "was just fine."

"Leave your terrace doors unlocked."

"They have been."

"I have to get back to work."

"Me too."

But they stayed as they were, mouths a breath apart. Something was happening inside her. A quivering, but not that lustful shiver in the belly. This was around her heart, and more ache than pleasure. Fascinated, she started to give in to it. And the phone in her pocket began to ring again.

"Well," she said a little unsteadily as she eased away. "Round two. I'll see you later."

She dragged her phone out as she hurried away. She'd think about Ty later. Think about a lot of things later. "Sophia Giambelli. *Nonna,* I'm glad you caught me. I tried to reach you earlier, but . . ."

She trailed off, alerted by her grandmother's tone. She stopped walking, stood at the edge of the vineyard. Despite the wash of sunlight, her skin chilled.

She was already running back as she broke the connection. "Ty!"

Alarmed, he whirled back, caught her on the fly. "What is it? What happened?"

"They found more. Two more bottles that were tainted."

"Damn it. Well, we were expecting it. We knew there had to be tampering."

"There's more. It could be worse. *Nonna*—she and Eli—" She had to stop, organize her thoughts. "There was an old man, he worked for *Nonna*'s grandfather. Started in the vineyard when he was just a boy. He retired, technically, over a year ago. And late last year he died. He had a bad heart."

He was already following her, already feeling the dread. "Go on."

"His granddaughter, the one who found him, says he'd been drinking our Merlot. She came to my grandmother after the news of the recall broke. They're having his body exhumed."

"His name was Bernardo Baptista." Sophia had all the details in neatly typed notes, but she didn't need them. She had every word in her head. "He was seventy-three. He died in December from an apparent heart attack while sitting in front of his own fire after a simple meal and several glasses of Castello di Giambelli Merlot, '92."

As Margaret Bowers had, David thought grimly. "You said Baptista had a weak heart."

"He'd had some minor heart problems and was suffering from a lingering head cold at the time of his death. The cold adds another layer. Baptista was known for his nose. He'd worked wine for over sixty years. But as he was ill, it was unlikely he'd have detected any problem with the wine. His granddaughter swears he hadn't opened it before that night. She'd seen it that afternoon when she'd visited him. He kept it, and a few other gifts from the company, on display. He was very proud of his association with Giambelli."

"The wine had been a gift."

"According to his granddaughter, yes."

"From?"

"She doesn't know. He was given a retirement party, and as is customary, Giambelli presents an employee with parting gifts. I've checked, and that particular wine was not on the gift list. He'd have been presented with a Cabernet, a white and a sparkling. First label. However, it's not uncommon for an employee to be allowed to choose another selection, or to be given wine by other members of the company."

"How soon will they know if the wine caused his death?" Pilar moved to the desk where Sophia sat, rubbed a hand over her daughter's shoulder.

"A matter of days."

"We do what we can to track the wine," David decided. "Meanwhile, we continue as we have been. I'm going to suggest to *La Signora* and Eli that we hire an outside investigator."

"I'll work on a statement. It's best if we announce the new finds, and Giambelli's part in implementing the recall and the testing. I don't want to have to chase the release again."

"Let me know what I can do to help," Pilar told her.

"Get that guest list together."

"Honey, you can't possibly want to hold a party now."

"On the contrary." The worry, the sadness over an old man she remembered with affection hardened into determination. "We'll just twist the angle. We hold a gala here, for charity. We've done it before, and a great deal more for good causes. I want people to remember that. A thousand a plate. All food, wine and entertainment donated by Giambelli-MacMillan, with proceeds going to the homeless."

She scribbled notes as she spoke, already drafting invitations, releases, responses in her head. "Our family wants to help yours be safe and secure. There are a lot of people who owe *La Signora* more than a grand for a fancy meal. If they need to be reminded of that, I'll see to it."

She cocked her head, waiting for David's reaction.

"You're the expert there," he said after a moment. "It's a shaky line to walk, but in my opinion, you have superior balance."

"Thanks. Meanwhile, we have to pretend a cool disinterest in the press Rene is generating. There'll be fallout from that, and it'll be personal. What's personal to Giambelli will, naturally, touch on business."

Pilar slid into a discreet chair at a quiet table in the bar at the Four Seasons. She was sure if she'd mentioned her intentions to anyone, she'd have been told she was making a mistake.

She probably was.

But this was something she had to do, something she should have done long ago. She ordered a mineral water and prepared to wait. She had no doubt Rene would be late. Just as she'd had no doubt Rene would meet her. She wouldn't have been able to resist making an entrance or having a confrontation with an enemy she perceived as weaker.

Pilar nursed her drink and sat patiently. She had a lot of experience with waiting.

Rene didn't disappoint. She swept in. She was, Pilar supposed, the kind of woman who liked to sweep into a room, trailing furs though the weather was too warm for them.

She looked well—fit, rested, glowing. Too often in the past, Pilar admitted, she'd studied this stunning and *younger* woman and felt inadequate in comparison.

A natural response, she imagined. But that didn't stop it from being foolish and useless.

It was easy to see why Tony had been attracted. Easier to understand why he'd been caught. Rene was no empty-headed Barbie, but a tough-minded female who would have known just how to get what she wanted, and to keep it.

"Pilar."

"Rene. Thanks for meeting me."

"Oh, how could I resist?" Rene dumped her fur and slid into her chair. "You're looking a little strained. Champagne cocktail," she told the waitress without glancing up.

Pilar's stomach didn't clench as it once

would have. "You're not. You had a few weeks in Europe early this year. It must have agreed with you."

"Tony and I had planned on an extended vacation. He wouldn't have wanted me to sit home and brood." Rene angled herself, crossed long, silky legs. "That was always your job."

"Rene, I was never the other woman, and neither were you. I was out of the picture long before you and Tony met."

"You were never out of the picture. You and your family kept your hooks in Tony, and you made sure he never got what he deserved from Giambelli. Now he's dead, and you'll pay me what you should have paid him." She picked up her drink the minute it was served. "Did you think I'd let you drag his name, and mine by association, through the dirt?"

"Odd, I was going to ask you the same thing." Pilar folded her hands on the table. A small, tidy move that gave her a moment to gather herself. "Whatever else, Rene, he was my daughter's father. I never wanted to see his name sullied. I want, more than I can tell you, to know who killed him, and why."

"You did, one way or the other. By cutting him out of the company. He wasn't meeting another woman that night. He wouldn't have dared. And I was enough for him, the way you never were."

Pilar thought about mentioning Kris, but knew it wasn't worth the effort. "No, I was never enough for him. I don't know who he was meeting that night, or why, but—"

"I'll tell you what I think," Rene interrupted. "He had something on you, you, your family. And you had him killed. Maybe you even used that little twit Margaret to do it, and that's why she's dead now."

Weariness replaced pity. "That's ridiculous, even for you. If this is the kind of thing you're saying to reporters, that you intend to say on television, you're opening yourself up to serious legal action."

"Please." Rene sipped again. "Do you think I haven't consulted an attorney to see what I can say and how I can say it? You saw to it that Tony was about to be cut off, and that I came away with next to nothing. I intend to get what's coming to me."

"Really? And since we're so cold-blooded, aren't you afraid of retribution?"

Rene glanced toward a nearby table. Two

men sat, sipping water. "Bodyguards. Round the clock. Don't even bother threatening me."

"You've created quite a fantasy world, and appear to be enjoying it. I'm sorry about you and Tony, sincerely, as you were perfect for each other. I came here to ask you to be reasonable, to show some decency toward my family and to think of Tony's child before you speak to the press. But that's a waste of time for both of us. I thought you might have loved him, but that was foolish of me. So we'll try this."

She leaned in, surprising Rene with the sudden and very cold gleam in her eye. "Do what you want, say what you want. In the end, you'll only look ridiculous. And though it's small of me, I'll enjoy that. More, I think, than you will saying it or doing it. Keep being the strident trophy wife, Rene, it suits you," Pilar said as she reached in her purse for money. "Just as those rather gaudy earrings suit you—a great deal more than they did me when Tony gave them to me for our fifth wedding anniversary."

She tossed a twenty on the table between them. "I'd consider them and anything else of mine he helped himself to over the years full payment. You'll never get anything else out of me, or Giambelli."

She didn't sweep out. She'd leave the drama for Rene. Instead she sauntered, and felt good about it. Just as she felt good about dropping another bill on the table where Rene's bodyguards sat watch.

"This round's on me," she told them and walked out laughing.

"*I put on* a pretty good show." Steaming now, Pilar paced back and forth over the Aubusson in Helen Moore's living room. "And, by God, I think I came out on top. But I was so angry. This woman is gunning for my family and she's wearing my damn earrings while she's taking aim."

"You've got documentation on the jewelry, insurance records and so on. We could take issue."

"I hated those stupid earrings." Pilar gave a bad-natured shrug. "Tony gave them to me as a peace offering after one of his affairs. I got the bill, too, of course. Damn it, it's hard swallowing how often I was a fool."

"Then spit it out. Sure you don't want a drink?"

"No, I'm driving, and should be heading back already." Pilar hissed out a breath, sucked in another. "I had to blow off steam first or I might have given in to road rage and ended up in jail."

"Good thing you have a friend on the bench. Listen to me. I think you did exactly right by facing off with her. A lot of people would disagree, but they don't know you like I do."

Helen poured herself a couple of fingers of vodka over ice. "You had things to say, and you've waited too long to say them."

"It won't change anything."

"With her? Maybe, maybe not." Helen sat, stretched out. "But the point is, it changed something for you. You took charge. And personally, I'd have paid good money to see you tell her off. She'll go on her little rant on her trashy talk show and very likely end up getting hammered by various audience members who take offense at her designer suit and ten pounds of jewelry. Wives," she continued, "who've been cheated on, left holding the bag for women like her. God, Pilar, they'll rip her to tattered shreds before it's done, and you

NORA ROBERTS · 506

can bet Larry Mann and his producers are counting on just that."

Pilar stopped pacing. "I never thought of that."

"Honey, Rene Foxx is just one of God's many custard pies. She hit you in the face, sure, but so what? Time to wipe her off."

"You're right. I worry about the family, about Sophie. Even though it's tabloid press, it's press, and it's going to embarrass her. I wish I knew how to shut her up."

"You could get a temporary restraining order. I'm a judge, I know these things," Helen said dryly. "You could file suit—libel, defamation. And you might win. Probably would. But as your lawyer, and your friend, my advice is to let her have her rope. She'll hang herself with it sooner or later."

"The sooner the better. We're in an awful mess, Helen."

"I know. I'm sorry."

"If she says things that hint we may have arranged for Tony to be killed, that Margaret was involved . . . The police have already questioned us about a relationship between Margaret and Tony. It worries me."

"Margaret was the unlucky victim of some maniac's lunacy. Product tampering doesn't even have a target, that's why it's lunacy. Tony was deliberate. One has nothing to do with the other, and you shouldn't start linking them in your mind."

"The press is linking them."

"The press would link a monkey with an elephant if it upped the ratings and sold papers."

"You're right there, too. I'll tell you something, Helen, over the anger, under the worry I felt when I talked to Rene, I realized something. I confronted her on this point because it mattered, because it was important, because I needed to take a stand."

Sipping her drink, Helen nodded. "And?"

"And it made me realize that I never, not once, confronted her or any of the others, the countless other women in and out of Tony's life. Because it stopped, he stopped being important. I had no stand to take. That's very sad," she said quietly. "And not all his fault. No, it wasn't," she went on before Helen could do more than spit out an oath. "It takes two to make a marriage, and I never pushed him to be one of those two in ours."

"He started chipping at your self-esteem right from the beginning."

"That's true." Pilar held out a hand, took Helen's glass for a small and absent sip. "But a great deal that happened, and didn't happen, between us was as much my doing as his. I'm not looking back with regret. I'm looking back, Helen, because I'm never, never going to make those mistakes again."

"Okay, fine." Helen took the vodka back, toasted with it. "To the new Giambelli woman. Since you're forging a new path, come sit down and tell me all about your sex life now that you have one."

On a low sound of pleasure, Pilar stretched her arms to the ceiling. "Since you ask . . . I'm having an incredible, exciting, illicit affair with a younger man."

"I hate you."

"You're going to loathe me when I tell you he has this wonderful, hard, tireless body."

"Bitch."

Laughing, she dropped onto the arm of the sofa. "I had no idea, really, how a woman could get through life without having a clue what it's like to be pressed down under a body like that. Tony was slim and rather delicate."

"Not much of a yardstick."

"You're telling me." She winced. "Oh, that's terrible. That's sick."

"No, that's great. James has . . . a comfortable body. Sweet old bear," Helen said fondly. "But you won't mind if I enjoy a few thrills through your sexual adventure?"

"Of course not. What are friends for?"

Sophia was ready for a little sexual adventure of her own. God knew she needed one. She'd worked herself to near exhaustion, then worried herself over the line.

A swim after she'd shut down for the day had helped, then a turn in the whirlpool to loosen muscles tensed from that work and worry. She'd added one more phase to the water therapy with a long, sumptuous bath full of oil and scent.

She'd lit candles throughout the room, fragrant with lemongrass and vanilla and jasmine. In their shifting light she chose a nightgown of black silk with a low, lacy bodice and thin straps. Why be subtle?

She'd selected the wine from the private cellar. A young, frisky Chardonnay. She set it on ice to keep it cool, curled into a chair to wait for Ty. And fell dead asleep.

It felt odd sneaking into a house where he'd always been welcome. Odd and exciting.

He'd had moments, off and on during his life, where he'd imagined slipping into Sophia's bedroom in the dark. Hell, what man wouldn't?

But actually doing it, knowing she'd be waiting for him, was a lot better than any midnight fantasy.

He knew when he opened those doors they'd fall on each other like animals.

He could already taste her.

He could see the candlelight beating against the glass. Exotic, sensual. The turn of the knob in his hand barely made a click and rang like a trumpet in his head.

He braced for her, closing the door at his back. Then he saw her, curled in a ball of fatigue in the chair.

"Ah, hell, Sophie. Look at you."

He crossed the room quietly, crouched down and did what he rarely had the opportunity to do. He studied her without her knowing it.

Soft skin that hinted of rose and gold. Thick, inky lashes and a full, lush mouth perfectly shaped to meet a man's.

"You're one gorgeous piece of work," he

murmured. "And you wore yourself out, didn't you?"

He glanced around the room, noting the wine, the candles, the bed already turned down and heaped with pillows. "The thought's just going to have to count for tonight. Come on, baby," he whispered as he slid his arms under her. "Let's put you to bed."

She stirred, shifted, snuggled. He decided there had to be a medal for a man who would tuck in a woman who looked, smelled, felt like this one and not crawl in eagerly after her.

"Hmmm. Ty."

"Good guess. Here you go," he said, laying her down. "Go back to sleep."

Her eyes fluttered open as he pulled the duvet up. "What? Where are you going?"

"For a long, lonely walk in the cold, dark night." Amused at both of them now, he leaned down to brush a chaste kiss on her forehead. "Followed by the requisite cold shower."

"Why?" She took his hand, tucked it under her cheek. "It's nice and warm in here."

"Baby, you're beat. I'll take a rain check."

"Don't go. Please, I don't want you to go."

"I'll be back." He leaned down again, intending to kiss her good night. But her lips were soft and tasted of lazy invitation. He sank into them, and into her as she reached for him.

"Don't go," she said again. "Make love with me. It'll be like a dream."

It was dreamlike. Scents and shadows and sighs. Slow, and tender where neither had expected it, where neither would have asked. He slid into bed with her, floated with her on the easy stroke of her hands, the gentle rise of her body.

And the sweetness of it drifted through him like starlight.

He found her mouth again, and everything he'd ever wanted.

Her breathing thickened as sensations began to layer. His hands were rough from work, and smoothed over her like velvet. His body was hard, and covered hers like silk. His mouth was firm, and took from her with endless and devastating patience.

No wildness here, no greed. No brilliant flashes of urgency. Tonight was to savor and soothe. To offer and welcome.

The first crest was like being lifted onto clouds.

She moaned under him, one long, low sound as her body bowed fluidly to his. Satisfaction and surrender. She skimmed her fingers in his hair, saw the shades of it shift in the light and shadow. He did that, she thought as she lost herself in him. Shifted and changed. There were so many facets to him.

And here, gently, he was showing her yet another. Her fingers curled, drawing him down until mouth met mouth, and she could answer.

In the dark, he could see the glint of the candlelight in her eyes, gold dust splashed over rich pools. The air was scented sweet. She watched him, and he watched her as he slipped inside her.

"This is different," he told her, and touched his mouth to hers as she shook her head. "This is different. Yesterday I wanted you. Tonight, I need you."

Her vision blurred with tears. Her lips trembled with words she didn't know how to say. And then she was so full of him, she could only sob out his name, and give.

CHAPTER NINETEEN

What did a seventy-three-year-old wine-maker from Italy have in common with a thirty-six-year-old sales executive from California? Giambelli, David thought. It was the only link he could find between them.

Except the manner of their deaths.

Tests on the exhumed body of Bernardo Baptista had confirmed he'd ingested a dangerous dosage of digitalis, along with his Merlot. It couldn't be construed as a co-incidence. Police on both sides of the Atlantic were calling it homicide and the Giambelli wine the murder weapon.

But why? What motive linked Margaret Bowers and Baptista?

He left his children tucked in their beds, and after checking on the Giambelli vine-yards, drove toward MacMillan. As the temperature had dropped, he and Paulie had turned on the sprinklers, had walked the rows as water coated the vines and the thin skin of ice formed a protective shield against the threatening hard frost. He knew Paulie would stand watch through the night, making certain there was a constant and steady flow of water. Pre-dawn temperatures were forecast to hover near the critical twenty-nine-degree mark.

In an instant, vines could be murdered as efficiently and as ruthlessly as people.

This, at least, he could control. He could understand the brutality of nature, and fight it. How could a rational person understand cold-blooded and seemingly random murder?

He could see the fine mist of water swirling over the MacMillan vines, the tiny drops going to glimmer in the cold light of the moon. He pulled on his gloves, grabbed his thermos of coffee and left the car to walk in the freezing damp.

He found Tyler sitting on an overturned crate, sipping from his own thermos. "Thought you might be by." In invitation, Ty banged the toe of his boot on another crate. "Pull up a chair."

"Where's your foreman?"

"Sent him home just a bit ago. No point in both of us losing a night's sleep." The truth was Ty liked sitting alone in the vineyard, thinking his thoughts while the sprinklers hissed.

"We're doing all we can do." Ty shrugged, scanning the rows that turned to a fairyland of sparkle under the lights. "System's running smooth."

David settled down, uncapped his thermos. Like Ty he wore a ski cap pulled over his head and a thick jacket that repelled both cold and damp. "Paulie took the watch at Giambelli. Frost alarms went off just after midnight. We were already prepped for it."

"This one's usual for the end of March. It's the ones that sneak in on you at the end of April, into May. I got it covered here, if you want to get some sleep."

"Nobody's getting much of that lately. Did you know Baptista?"

"Not really. My grandfather did. *La Signora*'s taking it hard. Not that she'll let it show," he said. "Not outside the family, and not much inside, for that matter. But she's knocked back by it. They all are—the Giambelli women."

"Product tampering—"

"It's not just that. That's the business end. This is personal. They went over for the funeral when he died. I guess Sophia thought of him as a kind of mascot. Said he used to sneak her candy. Poor old bastard."

David hunched forward, holding the thermos cup of coffee between his knees. "I've been thinking on it, trying to find the real connection. Probably a waste of time since I'm a corporate suit, not a detective."

Tyler studied him over his coffee. "From what I've seen so far you're not much of a time-waster. And you're not so bad, for a suit."

With a half-laugh, David lifted his own coffee. Steam from it rose and merged with the mist. "Coming from you, that's a hell of a kudo."

"Damn right."

"Well. From what I can tell, Margaret never even met Baptista. He was dead before she took over Avano's accounts and started the travel to Italy."

"Doesn't matter if they were random victims."

David shook his head. "It matters if they're not."

"Yeah, I've been thinking that, too." Tyler got up to stretch his legs, and they began to walk the rows together.

Somewhere along the way, he realized, he'd lost his resentment of David. Just as well, he thought. It took so much damn energy to hold a grudge. And it was a waste of that energy and valuable time when both of them were on the same page in any case.

"They both worked for Giambelli, both knew the family." Ty paused. "Both knew Avano."

"He was dead before Margaret uncorked the bottle. Still, we don't know how long she had it. He'd have had plenty of reason to want her out of the way."

"Avano was an asshole," Tyler said flatly. "He was a prick on top of it. But I can't see him as a killer. Too much thought, too much effort and not enough guts."

"Did anybody like him?"

"Sophie." Tyler shrugged and wished he could keep her out of his mind for more than ten minutes at a time. "At least she tried to. And yeah, actually, plenty did, and not just women."

It was the first time David had been offered a straight and uncensored picture of Anthony Avano. "Because?"

"He had a good line, put on a good show. Slick. I'd've said grease through a goose slick, but he got away with it." As his own father did, Ty mused. "Some people, they just slither through life, knocking over by-standers with, you know, impunity. He was one of them."

"*La Signora* kept him on."

"For Pilar, for Sophia. That's the family end. On the business front, well, he knew how to keep the accounts happy."

"Yeah, his expense account shows just how much he put into that effort. So with Margaret leapfrogging over him, he was los-ing his opportunities to wine and dine on Giambelli's tab. Had to piss him off. At the company, at the family, at her."

"His style would've been to try to fuck her, not kill her."

Tyler stopped, his breath streaming out as he looked over the rows, scanned them line after line. It was colder now. His internal farmer's gauge told him it was edging down toward thirty degrees.

"I'm not a corporate suit, but I've got to figure all this trouble is costing the company plenty in profit and in appearances, which can translate to the same thing. If somebody wanted to cause the family trouble, they found an inventive and nasty way to do it."

"Between the recall, immediate public panic and long-term consumer distrust in the label, it's going to cost millions. It's going to affect profit across the board, and that includes what's yours."

"Yeah." He'd already faced the grim reality of that. "I figure Sophia's smart enough to take the edge off that long-term distrust."

"She's going to have to be more than smart. She'll have to be brilliant."

"She is. That's what makes her a pain in the ass."

"Stuck on her, are you?" David waved the comment away. "Sorry. Too personal."

"I was wondering if you were asking as a corporate suit, an associate or as the guy who's dating her mother."

"I was aiming toward friend."

Tyler thought about it a moment, then nodded. "Okay, that works for me. I guess you could say I've been stuck on her on and off since I was twenty. Sophie at sixteen," he remembered. "Christ. She was like a lightning bolt. And she knew it. Irritated the hell out of me."

For a moment, while the misting water sizzled and froze, David was silent. "There was a girl when I was in college." He was pleasantly surprised when Tyler tugged a flask from his pocket and offered it. "Marcella Roux. French. Legs up to her ears, and this sexy little overbite."

"An overbite." Ty settled into the image. "That's a good one."

"Oh yeah." David drank, letting the brandy punch into his system. "God, Marcella Roux. She scared the hell out of me."

"A woman who looks like that, who *is* like that, just wears you out." Tyler took the flask, drank. "Me, I figured if you had to be stuck on a woman, which is an annoyance itself, you might as well get stuck on one who's easy to be around and doesn't make you jumpy half the time. I put considerable effort into that theory the last ten years. Didn't do me a damn bit of good."

"I can beat that," David said after a moment. "Yeah, I can beat it. I had a wife, and we had a couple kids—good kids—and I figured we were chasing the American dream. Well, that went into the toilet. But I had the kids. Maybe I screwed up there a few times, but that's part of the job. And my focus was on the goal. Give them a decent life, be a good father. Women, well, being a good father doesn't mean being a monk. But you keep that area down on the list of priorities. No serious relationships, not again. No sir, who needs it. Then Pilar opens the door, and she's holding flowers. There are all kinds of lightning bolts."

"Maybe. They still fry your brain."

They walked the rows in the coldest hour before dawn, while the sprinklers hissed and the vines glittered, iced silver, and safe.

Two hundred and fifty guests, a seven-course dinner, each with appropriate wines, followed by a concert in the ballroom and ending with dancing.

It had been a feat to pull off, and Sophia gave her mother full marks for helping to perfect each detail. She added a pat on the back for herself for carefully salting the guests with recognizable names and faces from all over the globe.

The UN, she thought as she sat with every appearance of serenity through the aria by the Italian soprano, had nothing on the Giambellis.

The quarter million raised for charity would not only do good work, it was damn good PR. Particularly good since all members of the family were in attendance, including her great-uncle the priest, who'd agreed to make the trip after a personal, and insistent, call from his sister.

Unity, solidarity, responsibility and tradition. Those were the key words she was pounding into the media. And with words went images. The gracious villa opening its doors for the sake of charity. The family, four generations, bound together by blood and wine, and one man's vision.

Oh yes, she was using Cezare Giambelli, the simple farmer who'd built an empire on sweat and dreams. It was irresistible. And while she didn't expect it to turn the tide of adversity, it had stemmed it.

The only irritant in the evening was Kris Drake.

Missed a step there, Sophia decided. She'd issued an invitation to Jeremy De-Morney quite purposefully. Inviting a handful of important competitors illustrated Giambelli's openness, and again a sense of community. It hadn't occurred to her Jerry would bring a former Giambelli employee as his date.

Should have, she reminded herself. It was clever, sneaky and slyly amusing on his part. And just like him. On top of that she had to give Kris credit for sheer balls. Brass ones.

Scored off me this round, she admitted. But felt she'd got back her own by being flawlessly gracious to both of them.

"You're not paying attention." Tyler gave her a quick elbow jab. "If I have to, you have to."

She leaned toward him slightly. "I hear every note. And I can write mental copy at the same time. Two different parts of the brain."

"Your brain has too many parts. How long does this last?"

The pure, rich notes throbbed on the air. "She's magnificent. And nearly finished. She's singing of tragedy, of heartbreak."

"I thought it was supposed to be about love."

"Same thing."

He glanced toward her, saw the sheen of tears, the single drop that spilled from those dark, deep eyes and clung perfectly to her lashes. "Are those real, or for the crowd?"

"You're such a peasant. Quiet." She linked her fingers with his, allowed herself to think of nothing, to feel nothing but the music for the final moments.

When the last note shimmered into silence, she rose, along with the others, into thunderous applause.

"Can we get out of here for five minutes now?" Ty whispered in her ear.

"Worse than a peasant, a barbarian. *Brava!*" she called out. "You go ahead," she added under her breath. "I need to play hostess. You should grab Uncle James, who looks as miserable as you do. Go out and have a drink and a cigar and be men."

"If you don't think it took a man to sit here, and stay awake, during nearly an hour of opera, baby, you better think again."

She watched him escape, then moved forward, hands extended to the diva. *"Signora, bellissima!"*

Pilar did her duty as well, but her mind wasn't full of music or publicity copy. It was reeling with details and timing. The chairs had to be removed, quickly and smoothly, to clear the ballroom for dancing. The terrace doors would be flung open at precisely the right minute and the orchestra set up there would begin to play. But not before the diva had been allowed her moment of adulation. She waited while Tereza and Eli presented the singer with roses, then signaled David, Helen and a few hand-chosen friends to add their congratulations and praise.

As others followed suit, she nodded at the waiting staff. Then frowned when she saw her aunt Francesca still sitting, and obviously sound asleep. Sedated herself again, Pilar thought, winding her way through guests.

"Don." She squeezed her cousin's arm, smiling an apology to the couple he'd been speaking with. "Your mother isn't well," she said quietly. "Could you help me take her to her room?"

"Sure. I'm sorry, Pilar," he continued as they moved aside. "I should've kept a closer eye on her." He scanned the crowd, looking for his wife. "I thought Gina was with her."

"It's all right. *Zia* Francesca?" Pilar leaned

down, spoke quietly, soothingly in Italian as she and Don helped the woman to her feet.

"Ma che vuoi?" She seemed dazed as she slapped at Pilar's hand. *"Lasciame in pace."*

"We're just going to take you to bed, Mama." Don took a firmer grip. "You're tired."

"Sì, sì." She stopped struggling. *"Vorrei del vino."*

"You've already had enough wine," Don told her, but Pilar shook her head at him.

"I'll bring you some, once you're in your room."

"You're a good girl, Pilar." Docile as a lamb, Francesca shuffled out of the ballroom. "So much sweeter of nature than Gina. Don should have married you."

"We're cousins, *Zia* Francesca," Pilar reminded her.

"You are? Oh, of course. My mind is muddled. Traveling is very stressful."

"I know. You'll feel better when you're in your nightgown and in bed."

Mindful of the time, Pilar rang for a maid as soon as they'd carted Francesca to her room. Though she was sorry for it, she dumped the matter on Don and rushed back to take her place in the ballroom.

"Problem?" Sophia asked her.

"Aunt Francesca."

"Ah, that's always fun. Well, having a priest in the family should help cancel out the odd drunk. Are we ready?"

"We are." Pilar dimmed the lights. At the signal, the terrace doors were opened and music poured in. As Tereza and Eli led the first dance, Sophia slid an arm around her mother's waist.

"Perfect. Wonderful job."

"God bless us, every one." She blew out a breath. "I could use a drink myself."

"When this is over, we'll kill a bottle of champagne apiece. Right now"—she gave Pilar a little nudge—"dance."

It looked like socializing, but it was work. Putting on the confident front, answering questions, some subtle, some not, on the situation from interested guests and the invited press. Expressing sorrow and outrage, both sincerely felt, while getting the intended message across.

Giambelli-MacMillan was alive and well and making wine.

"Sophia! Lovely, lovely event."

"Thank you, Mrs. Elliot. I'm so glad you could attend."

"Wouldn't have missed it. You know Blake and I are very active on behalf of the homeless. Our restaurant contributes generously to the shelters."

And your restaurant, Sophia thought as she made appropriate noises, canceled its standing order on all Giambelli and MacMillan labels at the first sign of trouble. "Perhaps at some point your business and ours could work together on a fund-raiser. Food and wine, after all, the perfect marriage."

"Mmm. Well."

"You've known my family since before I was born." To establish intimacy, Pilar took the woman's arm, walked with her away from the music. "I hope you know how much we value that association, and that friendship."

"Blake and I have nothing but the greatest respect for your grandmother, and for Eli. We couldn't be more sorry about your recent troubles."

"When friends have troubles, they look to other friends for support."

"On a personal level, you have it. But business is business, Sophia. We have to protect our clientele."

"As do we. Giambelli stands by its product. Any of us at any time can be the victim of tampering and sabotage. If we, and those who do business with us, allow the perpetrators of that to win, it only opens others up to the same risk."

"Be that as it may, Sophia, until we're assured the Giambelli label is clean, we can't and won't serve it. I'm sorry for it, and I'm impressed with the way you're handling your difficulties. Blake and I wouldn't be here tonight if we didn't support you and your family on a personal level. Our patrons expect fine food well served when they come to us, not to gamble on a glass of wine that may be tainted."

"Four bottles out of how many thousands," Sophia began.

"One is too many. I'm sorry, dear, but that's the reality. Excuse me."

Sophia marched directly to a waiter, took a glass of red and, after turning a slow circle in case anyone was watching, drank deeply.

"You look a little stressed." Kris sidled up beside her, chose a glass of champagne. "Must come from actually having to work for a living."

"You're mistaken." Her voice might have

frosted the air between them. "I don't work for a living, but for love."

"Spoken like a princess." Pleased with herself, Kris sipped her wine. As far as she was concerned, she had one function to fulfill that evening: to dig under Sophia's skin. "Isn't that what Tony used to call you? His princess."

"Yes." Sophia braced for the rush of grief, but it never came. That, itself, was a sorrow. "He never understood me. Apparently neither do you."

"Oh, I understand you. And your family. You're in trouble. With Tony gone and you and farm boy in charge, your company's lost the edge. Now you're flaunting yourself in your evening gowns and your heirloom pearls to try to drum up business and cover up mistakes. Really, you're no different from the guy on the corner panhandling. At least he's honest about it."

Carefully, deliberately, Sophia set her wine aside and edged forward. Before she could speak, Jerry strode over, laid a hand on Kris's arm.

"Kris." There was warning in his tone. "This is inappropriate. Sophia, I'm sorry."

"I don't need anyone to apologize for me."

Kris tossed back her hair. "I'm not on company time here, but my own."

"I'm not interested in apologies. From either of you. You're a guest in my home, and as long as you behave as such, you'll be treated as a guest. If you insult me here, or any of my family, I'll have you removed. Just as I had you removed from my offices. Don't delude yourself into thinking I'll hesitate to cause a scene."

Kris pursed her lips in a kind of kiss. "Wouldn't that play nicely in the press?"

"Dare me," Sophia spat back. "Then we'll see which one of us spins it best tomorrow. Either way, Kris, you'll be out on your ass and your new boss might not care for that, right, Jerry?"

"Sophia! How lovely you look." Helen hugged an arm around Sophia's shoulders, squeezing hard. "Excuse us, won't you?" She said it brightly while she pulled Sophia away. "You want to turn down the kill lights in your eyes, honey? You're scaring the guests."

"I'd like to fry Kris with them, and Jerry with her."

"Not worth it, sweetie."

"I know it, I know it. She wouldn't have

gotten to me if I hadn't already been steaming over Anne Elliot."

"Let's just take a little walk to the powder room while you calm down. Remind yourself you've put on a terrific show here. You've made an impression."

"Too little, for too much."

"Sophie, you're trembling."

"I'm just angry. Just angry." She held it in as they walked down to the family level. "And scared," she admitted when she slipped into a powder room with Helen. "Aunt Helen, I poured money into this event. Money, given the situation, I should have been more careful with. The Elliots aren't going to budge. Then Kris drops down like a crow smelling fresh kill."

"She's just one more of Tony's castoffs, and not worth your energy or your time."

"She knows the way I think." There wasn't room to pace off the heat, so Sophia simply stood and simmered in it. "The way I work. I should've found a way to keep her in the company, a way to control her."

"Stop it. You can't take on the blame for her. Anyone can see she's viciously jealous of you. I know things are shaky now, but I talked with a number of people tonight who're solidly behind you, who are appalled by what happened."

"Yes, and some of them may even be swayed to put their money where their sentiments are. But there are more, too many more, who won't. I had reports from the wait staff that a number of guests are avoiding the wine or watching others drink it, and live, first. It's horrible. And such a strain on *Nonna*. I'm starting to see it, and that worries me."

"Sophie, when a company's been in business a hundred years, it has crises. This is just one of them."

"We've never had anything like this. We're losing accounts, Aunt Helen. You know it. There are jokes, you've heard them. Having trouble with your wife? Don't see a lawyer, give her a bottle of Giambelli."

"Honey, I'm a lawyer, we've been jokes for centuries." But she stroked Sophia's hair. She hadn't realized how much the child worried, hadn't realized it went so deep. "You're taking too much of this on yourself."

"It's my job to maintain the image, not only as the next generation but as an executive. If I can't swing this . . . I know I put a lot of eggs in tonight's basket, and I hate seeing some of them broken."

"Some," Helen reminded her. "Far from all."

"But I'm not getting the message out. We're the victims here, why can't people see that? We were attacked. We're *still* being attacked—financially, emotionally, legally. The police . . . For God's sake, there are rumors drifting around that Margaret and my father were in some sort of conspiracy together, and Mama knew."

"Just Rene's blathering."

"Yes, but if the police start taking it seriously, start questioning her as a suspect, I don't know what we'll do."

"That's not going to happen."

"Oh, Aunt Helen, it could. With Rene streaming around from talk show to tabloid fanning the flames, and no sign of those responsible being caught, Mama's top of the list. Right along with me."

She'd thought of it, hadn't been able to help it. But hearing it said so bluntly brought a chill to Helen's skin. "Now you listen. No one is going to accuse you or your mother of anything. The police may look, but only to eliminate. If they step closer than that, they'll have to go through James, through me, even Linc."

She drew Sophia into a hug. "Don't you worry about that."

She patted Sophia's back and stared at her own face in the mirror. The encouraging smile was gone, and concern had taken its place. She was grateful attorney-client privilege with Tereza prevented her from adding to the girl's fears.

Only that morning, all financial records of the company had been subpoenaed.

Sophia freshened her lipstick, powdered her nose and squared her shoulders. No one would have seen the fear or despair now. She glittered, and glowed, her laugh warm and careless as she joined the guests.

She flirted, she danced and continued to campaign. Her spirits lifted considerably when she charmed and cajoled another major account into lifting its ban on the Giambelli label.

Pleased with herself, she took a short break to harass Linc. "Are you still hanging around this loser?" she asked Andrea.

"Well, he cries every time I try to dump him."

"I do not. I just look really forlorn. I was about to come looking for you," he told Sophia. "We're going to take off."

"So early?"

"The string quartet isn't really my scene. I'm just here because Mom bribed me with pound cake. But I wanted to see you before we headed out, to ask how you're holding up."

"Oh, fine."

He tapped her nose. "It's okay. Andrea knows the score."

"It's rough," she admitted. "*Nonna's* having a hard time accepting what happened to *Signore* Baptista. He meant a lot to her. I guess we're all feeling squeezed between the various investigations. In fact, I whined all over your mom a little bit ago."

"She's used to it. You know you can call me and whine anytime."

"I know." She kissed Linc's cheek. "You're not really so bad. And you have good taste in doctors. Go. Escape." She stepped aside. "Come back," she added to Andrea, and began another circuit of the room.

"There you are." Tyler caught her, pulled

her toward a corner. "I can't take much more of this. I'm deserting the field."

"Now, buck up." She measured the crowd. Beginning to thin, she judged, but not by much. That was a good sign. "Hold out another hour and I'll make it worth your while."

"My while's worth quite a bit."

"I'll bear that in mind. Go charm Betina Renaldi. She's old, influential and very susceptible to rugged young men with tight butts."

"Boy, are you going to owe me."

"Just ask her to dance and tell her how much we value her patronage."

"If she pinches my tight butt, I'm taking it out on you."

"Mmm. I look forward to it." She circled just in time to spot an argument brewing between Don and Gina. Quickly, she cut across the ballroom.

"Let's not do this here." In what would be taken as an affectionate gesture, she stepped between them and linked arms. "We don't need to add to the gossip mill."

"You think you can tell me how to behave?" Gina would have wrenched her arm free if Sophia hadn't borne down. "You, whose father was a gigolo, whose family has no honor."

"Careful, Gina, careful. That family keeps you in diapers. Let's go outside."

"You go to hell." She rammed Sophia hard against Don. "You, and all of you." Her voice spiked, causing several heads to turn. Sophia managed to drag her to the doorway of the ballroom before she broke free.

"If you cause a scene here," Sophia said, "it'll cost you as much as the rest of us. Your children are Giambelli. Remember it."

Gina's lip quivered, but she lowered her voice. "You remember it. You both remember it, and that what I do, I do for them."

"Don. Damn it. Go after her, calm her down."

"I can't. She won't listen." He moved behind the doors, took out a handkerchief to wipe his sweaty brow. "She's pregnant again."

"Oh." Torn between relief and annoyance, Sophia patted his arm. "Congratulations."

"I didn't want another child. She knew. We fought about it. Then she tells me tonight, as we're dressing and the children are screaming and my head's bursting. She expects me to be thrilled, and when I'm not, she rips at me."

He shoved the cloth back in his pocket.

"I'm sorry. Really. Very sorry, but impressions tonight are vital. Whether or not you're happy about this, you have to fix it. She's pregnant, vulnerable and her hormones are raging. Added to that, she didn't get in that condition by herself. You need to go to her."

"I can't," he said again. "She won't speak to me now. I was upset. All during the evening she sulked or reminded me it was God's will, a blessing. I needed to get away from her. Five precious minutes away from that nagging. So I slipped out to make a phone call. I called— There's another woman."

"Oh, perfect." She didn't bother to curse. "Isn't that just perfect."

"I didn't know Gina followed me. Didn't know she'd overheard. She waited until I was back inside to confront me, to accuse, to claw. No, she won't speak to me now."

"Well, you both picked your moment."

"Please, I know what I have to do, and I will. Promise me you won't tell *Zia* Tereza of this."

"Do you think I'd go running to *Nonna* like a tattletale?"

"Sophie. I didn't mean it that way." Relieved at her angry claim not to be a gossip, he took her hands. "I'll fix it. I will. If you could just go after Gina now, convince her to behave, to be patient. Not to do anything rash. Already with the investigation I'm under such pressure."

"This isn't about you, Donato." She pulled her hands away. "You're just one more man who couldn't keep his dick in his pants. But it is about Giambelli. So I'll do what I can with Gina. For once, she actually has my sympathy. And you will fix it. You'll break it off with the other woman and deal with your marriage and your children."

"I love her. Sophie, you understand what it is to be in love."

"I understand you have three children and another on the way. You'll be responsible to your family, Donato. You'll be a man, or I'll personally see you pay for it. *Capisce?*"

"You said you wouldn't go to *La Signora*. I trusted you."

"*La Signora* isn't the only Giambelli woman who knows how to deal with cheats and liars. Or cowards. *Cacasotto.*"

He went white. "You're too hard."

"Try me, and you'll see just how hard. Now, be smart. Go back in and smile. Announce to your aunt that you're about to bring another Giambelli into the world. And stay away from me until I can stand the sight of you again."

She left him there, quivering with rage. Hard, she thought. Maybe. And maybe part of her rage had been directed at her father, another cheat, another liar, another father who ignored his responsibilities.

Marriage, she thought, meant nothing to some. No more than a game whose rules were broken for the thrill of it. She hurried through the family wing, but found no sign of Gina.

Idiot woman, she decided, and was unsure who she disliked more at the moment, Gina or Donato.

She called out quietly, peeked into the nursery where the children and the young woman hired to tend them for the evening slept.

Thinking Gina might have taken her rage outside, she stepped out on the terrace. Music from the quartet drifted out into the night.

She wished she could drift herself, just leave it all to work itself out. Enraged wives, straying husbands. Cops and lawyers and faceless enemies. She was tired of it, all of it.

She wanted Ty. She wanted to dance with him with her head on his shoulder and all her worries in someone else's brain for a few hours.

Instead she ordered herself to go back and do what needed to be done.

She heard a faint sound from the room behind her and started to turn. "Gina?"

A vicious shove sent her flying back. Her heels skidded, lost purchase on the terrace floor. She caught a blur of movement as she fell. And when her head hit the stone of the rail, she saw nothing but an explosion of light.

CHAPTER TWENTY

Tyler decided to finish off his evening by dancing with Tereza. She felt small but reassuringly sturdy in her beaded gown. Her hand was dry and cool in his.

"Why aren't you exhausted?" he asked her.

"I will be, when the last guest leaves."

Over her head, he scanned the room. Too many people still left, he thought, and it was already after midnight. "We could start booting them out."

"Unfailingly gracious. I like that about you." When he grinned down at her, she studied him carefully. "None of this means anything to you."

"Of course it does. The vineyards—"

"Not the vineyards, Tyler." She gestured toward the terrace doors, the lights, the music. "This, the fancy clothes, the inane chatter, the wash of gilt."

"Not a damn thing."

"But you come, for your grandfather."

"For my grandfather, and for you, *La Signora.* For . . . the family. If it didn't matter, I'd have taken a hike last year when you reorganized my life."

"You haven't quite forgiven me for that," she chuckled.

"Not quite." But he shifted her hand and, in a rare gallant gesture, kissed her knuckles.

"If you'd walked away, I'd have found a way to bring you back. I'd have made you sorry, but I'd have brought you back. You're needed here. I'm going to tell you something, because your grandfather won't."

"Is he sick?" Tyler missed a step as he turned his head to seek out Eli in the crowd.

"Look at me. At me," she said with quiet intensity. "I'd rather he didn't know what we're speaking of."

"Has he seen a doctor? What's wrong with him?"

"He is sick—but in his heart. Your father called him."

"What does he want? Money?"

"No, he knows he'll get no more money." She would have kept it to herself. She detested passing burdens. But the boy, she'd decided after much thought, had a right to know. A right to defend his own, even against his own. "He's outraged. The recent problems, the scandals are interfering with his social calendar and causing him, he claims, considerable embarrassment. Apparently the police have asked questions about him in the course of their investigation. He blames Eli."

"He won't call again. I'll take care of it."

"I know you will. You're a good boy, Tyler."

He looked down at her again, forced a smile. "Am I?"

"Yes, good enough. I wouldn't shift this burden to you, but Eli has a soft heart. This has bruised it."

"I don't . . . have the soft heart."

"Soft enough." She lifted her hand from his shoulder to his cheek. "I depend on you." When his face registered surprise she continued. "Does hearing that surprise you or frighten you?"

"Maybe both."

"Adjust." It was an order, smoothly given, as she stepped back from him. "Now, you're dismissed. Go find Sophia and lure her away."

"She's not easily lured."

"I imagine you can handle her. There aren't many who can. I haven't seen her for some time now. Go find her, take her mind off work for a few hours."

And that, Tyler mused, was akin to a blessing. He wasn't sure that he wanted it. Didn't know what he planned to do with it. For the moment, he was going to tuck it away and follow the spirit of Tereza's order. Find Sophia, and escape.

She wasn't in the ballroom or on the terrace. He avoided asking people if they'd seen her as that smacked too close to an eager idiot trying to find his date. Which he supposed was pretty much the case.

Regardless, he prowled the wing, poking into a reception room where some of the guests had gathered to sit and chat. He found the Moores there, with James puffing on a cigar and Helen sipping tea while he discoursed on some ancient, landmark case. Linc and his date, who he thought had left an hour before, were either held hostage or enthralled on the sofa.

"Ty, come on in. Have a cigar."

"No, thanks. I'm just . . . *La Signora* asked me to find Sophia."

"Haven't seen her for a while. Wow, look at the time." Linc surged to his feet, dragging Andrea to hers. "We've really got to go."

"She might've gone downstairs, Ty," Helen offered. "To freshen up or catch her breath."

"Yeah, right. I'll check."

He started down, and ran into Pilar on the steps. "Your mother's wondering where Sophia is."

"Isn't she upstairs?" Distracted, Pilar shook back her hair. She wanted nothing more than ten minutes of fresh air and a tall glass of water. "I haven't seen her for, oh, half an hour at least. I was just down trying to talk to Gina through the door of her room. She's locked herself in. Fighting with Don, apparently. She's throwing things around, weeping hysterically, and of course she's woken the children. They're shrieking."

"Thanks for the tip. I'll make sure to avoid that part of the house."

"Why don't you check her room? I got enough out of Gina to know Sophia tried to referee. She might be in there cooling off. Is David in the ballroom?"

"Didn't see him," Ty said as he walked by. "He's probably around somewhere."

He turned toward Sophia's room. If he found her, he thought it might be a fine idea to lock the doors and take her mind off work, as ordered. He'd been wondering all night just what she had on under that red dress.

He knocked lightly, eased the door open. The room was dark and cold. With a shake of his head, he started across to close the terrace doors.

"You're going to freeze your excellent ass off in here, Sophie," he muttered, and heard a quiet moan.

Puzzled, he stepped out and saw her in the sprinkle of light that dripped down from the ballroom. She was sprawled on the terrace, braced on one elbow as she tried to shift. He leaped forward, dropped down on his knees beside her.

"Easy, baby. What'd you do? Take a spill?"

"I don't know . . . I . . . Ty?"

"Yeah. Jesus, you're freezing. Come on, let's get you inside."

"I'm okay. Just a little jumbled. Let me get my head clear."

"Inside. You took a knock, Soph. You're bleeding."

"I'm . . ." She touched her fingers to the pump of pain on her forehead, then stared dully at the red smear she took away. "Bleeding," she managed as her lids closed again.

"Oh no, no, you don't." He shifted his grip. "No passing out." His heart staggered in his chest as he lifted her. Her face was sheet-white, her eyes glazed, and the scrape on her forehead was oozing blood. "That's what you get for wearing those skinny heels. I don't know how women walk on them without breaking their ankles."

He kept talking, to calm them both, as he laid her on the bed and turned back to shut the terrace doors. "Let's warm you up some, and we'll take a look at the damage."

"Ty." She gripped his hand as he pulled a throw over her. Despite the pain, her mind was clearing now. "I didn't fall. Somebody pushed me."

"Pushed you? I'm going to turn on this light so I can see where you're hurt."

She turned her head away from the glare. "I think I'm hurt everywhere."

"Quiet now. Just lie still." His hands were gentle, even as his temper raged. The head wound was nasty, a vicious scrape already swelling and full of grit. Her arm was scraped as well, just below the shoulder.

"I'm going to get you out of this dress."

"Sorry, handsome. I have a headache."

Appreciating her attempt at humor, he eased her forward, searching for a zipper, buttons, hooks. Something. "Honey, how the hell does this thing work?"

"Under the left arm." Every inch of her was beginning to ache. "Little zipper, then you sort of peel it off the rest of the way."

"I've been wondering what you had on under here," he babbled as he undressed her. He imagined there was a name for the strapless deal that cinched at her waist and curved up high at the hips. He'd have just called it stupendous. Stockings came up to her thighs and were hooked by little garters shaped like roses. While he appreciated the architecture of the underwear, he was more relieved that there wasn't extensive damage to the woman in it.

Her right knee was a little scraped up, and the sheer, silky stocking was a ruin.

Someone, he promised himself, was going to pay and pay dearly for putting marks on her. But that would have to wait.

"Not so bad, see?" His voice was easy as he helped her sit up a little to see for herself. "Looks like you fell on your right side, a little bruise coming up on your hip there, scraped knee and shoulder. Your head took the worst of it, so that's lucky, considering."

"That's a really amusing way to tell me I have a hard head. Ty, I didn't fall. I was pushed."

"I know. We'll get to that after I clean you up some."

When he rose, she just lay back. "Get me a bottle of aspirin while you're in there."

"I don't think you should take anything before you get to the hospital."

"I'm not going to the hospital for a couple of scrapes and bumps." She heard water hitting the sink in the adjoining bath. "If you try to make me, I'll cry and go very female and make you feel horrible. Believe me, I'm ready to make someone feel horrible, and you're in the line of fire. Don't use my good washcloths. There're some everyday ones in the linen closet, and antiseptic and aspirin."

"Shut up, Sophie."

She tugged the blanket higher. "It's cold in here."

He came back in carrying her Murano glass bowl, one of her best guest towels, already wet slopping inside, and a glass of water.

"What did you do with the potpourri that was in that dish?"

"Don't worry about it. Come on, let's play doctor."

"Aspirin. I'm begging you."

He pulled a bottle out of his pocket, opened it and shook out two.

"Please, let's not be stingy. I want four."

He let her take them and began cleaning the head wound. It took effort to keep his hands steady, to draw breath smoothly. "Who pushed you?"

"I don't know. I'd come down looking for Gina. She and Don had a fight."

"Yeah, I heard about it."

"I couldn't find her, came in here. I wanted a minute to myself, and some air, so I went out on the terrace. I heard something behind me, started to turn around. The next thing I know I'm skidding—couldn't catch my balance. Then lights out. How bad's my face?"

"Nothing bad about your face. That's part of your problem. You're going to have a knot up here, right along the hairline. Cut's not deep, just a good-sized shallow scrape. You have any impression who pushed you? Man? Woman?"

"No. It was fast, and it was dark. I guess it might have been Gina, or Don for that matter. They were both furious with me. That's what happens when you get in the middle."

"If it was either of them, they're going to look a whole lot worse than you before I'm finished."

The quick little leap of her heart made her feel foolish. And went a long way to cooling her own bubbling temper. "My hero. But I don't know if it was either of them. Could just as easily have been someone who'd come in to poke around in my room, then gave me a shove so I wouldn't catch them."

"We'll take a look around, see if anything's missing or messed with. Hold your breath."

"What?"

"Hold your breath," he repeated, then watched her face contort in pain as he used the peroxide he'd had in his other pocket.

"Festa di cazzo! Coglioni! Mostro!"

"A minute ago I was a hero." Sympathetically, he blew on the sting. "Better in a minute. Let's deal with the rest."

"Va via."

"Would you mind cursing at me in English?"

"I said go away. Don't touch me."

"Come on, be a big, brave girl. I'll give you a lollipop after." He yanked the blanket aside, dealt quickly, ruthlessly with the other scrapes.

"I'm going to put this gunk on them." He pulled out a tube of antiseptic cream. "Bandage them up. How's your vision?"

Her breath was puffing from the exertion of trying to fight him off, and he wasn't even winded. It killed her. "I can see you well enough, you sadist. You're enjoying this."

"It does have certain side benefits. Name the first five presidents of the United States."

"Sneezy, Dopey, Moe, Larry and Curly."

Christ, was it any wonder he'd fallen for her? "Close enough. Probably don't have a concussion. There you go, baby." He kissed her sulking lips gently. "All done."

"I want my lollipop."

"You bet." But he just leaned down, held on. "Scared me," he murmured against her cheek. "Scared hell out of me, Sophie."

Hearing that, knowing that, had her heart making that same little leap. "It's okay now. You're not really a bastard."

"Still hurting?"

"No."

"How do you say 'liar' in Italian?"

"Never mind. It feels better when you're holding me. Thanks."

"No charge. Where do you keep your glittery things?"

"Jewelry? Costume is in the jewelry armoire, the real things are in my safe. You think I surprised a thief?"

"Easy enough to find out." He sat up, then rose to turn on the rest of the lights.

They saw it at the same time. Despite the lingering pain, Sophia shot straight out of bed. There was as much anger as terror in her belly as she read the message, scrawled in red, on her mirror.

BITCH #3

"Kris. Damn it, that's her style. If she thinks I'm going to let her get away with . . ." She trailed off as terror overwhelmed every other feeling. "Number three. Mama. *Nonna.*"

"Put something on," Tyler ordered. "And lock the doors. I'll check it out."

"No, you won't." She was already marching to her closet. "We'll check it out. Nobody pushes me around," she said as she dragged on a sweater and pants. "Nobody."

They found similar messages on the bureau mirrors in Pilar's and Tereza's rooms. But they didn't find Kris Drake.

"There must be something else we can do."

Sophia wiped furiously at the letters smearing her mirror. The local police had responded, taken statements, examined the vandalism. And had told her nothing she hadn't concluded for herself. Someone had entered each bedroom, left an ugly little message written in red lipstick on the glass. And had knocked her down.

"There's nothing else we can do tonight." Tyler took her wrist, drew her hand down. "I'll take care of that."

"It was addressed to me." But she threw the rag down in disgust.

"The cops are going to question her, Sophie."

"And I'm sure she'll tell them she waltzed in here, scrawled this love note and knocked me down." She let out a sound of frustration, then clamped her teeth down on it. "Doesn't matter. The police may not be able to prove she did this, but I know she did. And sooner or later, I'll make her pay for it."

"And I'll hold your coat. In the meantime, go to bed."

"I can't sleep now."

He took her hand, led her to the bed. She was still in her clothes, and he wore his shirt and tuxedo pants. He eased onto the bed with her, pulled up the blanket.

"Try."

She lay still a moment, amazed when he made no move to touch her, to seduce, to take. He reached over, turned out the light.

"Ty?"

"Hmmm."

"It doesn't hurt as much when you hold me."

"Good. Go to sleep."

And settling her head on his shoulder, she was able to do as he asked.

Claremont stretched back in his chair as Maguire read the incident report. "So, what do you think?"

"The youngest Ms. Giambelli gets knocked down, banged up a little. All three of them receive an unpleasant message that smudges up their mirrors. On the surface?" she said, tossing the paperwork back on his desk. "Looks like a prank. A female one."

"And under the surface?"

"Sophia G wasn't hurt badly, but if it had been her grandmother who walked in at the wrong time, it could have been a lot more serious. Old bones break easier. And from the timeline the locals were able to put together, she was lying out there in the night chill for at least fifteen, twenty minutes. Very unpleasant. Might've been longer if our young hunk hadn't gone hunting for her. So we have a mean prank, and somebody who's doing whatever's handy to needle them."

"And from the youngest Giambelli's statement, Kristin Drake fits the bill."

"She's denied it, vehemently," Maguire
countered, but they both knew she was
playing devil's advocate. "Nobody can
place her in that part of the house during
the evening. No handy fingerprints to tie her
in."

"Sophia G's lying about it? Mistaken?"

"I don't think so." Maguire pursed her lips.
"No point in lying about it, and she doesn't
strike me as a woman who does anything
without a point. Careful, too. She wouldn't
accuse unless she was sure. The Drake
woman took a slap at her. It may be as simple as that. Or it may be a lot more."

"It bothers me. If we have somebody
who's gone to the time, trouble, the risk, to
taint wine, somebody who was willing to
kill, why would that person bother with
something as petty as a message on a mirror?"

"We don't know it's the same person."

Links clicking onto links. That's the way
he saw it. "Hypothetically, using a vendetta
against the Giambellis to connect."

"To kick at them, then. Gonna throw a big

party, are you? Want to pretend everything's getting back to normal? Take this."

"Maybe. Drake's a connection. She worked for the company, she had an affair with Avano. If she's pissed enough to've caused the trouble at the party, she might've been pissed enough to put a couple bullets in a lover."

"Ex-lover, according to her statement." She frowned. "Frankly, partner, she was a dead end before, and I don't see this little sneak attack pinning her to the Avano homicide. Different styles."

"It's interesting though, isn't it? The Giambellis go for years, decades, without any substantial trouble. In the past few months, they've had nothing but. It's interesting."

Tyler paced outside with the phone. The house seemed too small when he was talking to his father. California seemed too small when he was talking to his father.

Not that he was doing any talking at the moment, just listening to the usual gripes and complaints.

He let them run through his head. The country club was rife with gossip and black humor involving him. His current wife—Ty had actually lost track of how many Mrs. MacMillans there'd been by this time—had been humiliated at the spa. Expected invitations for various social functions had not been forthcoming.

Something had to be done about it, and quickly. It was Eli's responsibility to keep the family name above reproach, which he had obviously ignored by marrying the Italian woman in the first place. But be that as it may, it was essential, it was imperative, that the MacMillan name, label and company be severed from Giambelli. He expected Tyler to use all his influence before it was too late. Eli was old, and obviously long past the time for retirement.

"Finished?" Tyler didn't wait for his father's assent or objection. "Because here's how it's going to be. You have any complaints or comments, you direct them to me. If you call and harass Granddad again, I'll do whatever I can, legally, to revoke that trust fund you've been living off of for the last thirty years."

"You have no right to—"

"No, *you* have no right. You never worked a day for this company, any more than you and my mother worked a day to be parents. Until he's ready to step aside, Eli MacMillan runs this show. And when he's ready to step aside, I'll run it. Believe me, I won't be as patient as he's been. You cause him one more moment's grief, and we'll have more than a phone conversation about it."

"Are you threatening me? Do you plan to send someone after me like Tony Avano?"

"No, I know how to hit you where it hurts. I'll see to it all your major credit cards are canceled. Remember, you're not dealing with an old man now. Don't fuck with me."

He jabbed the off button, considered heaving the phone, then spotted Sophia standing at the edge of the patio.

"I'm sorry. I didn't mean to eavesdrop." If he'd looked angry, she could have brushed it off, but he looked miserable. She knew, how well she knew, what it was like. So she went to him, cupped his face in her hands. "Sorry," she said again.

"No big deal. Just a conversation with dear old Dad." Disgusted, he tossed the phone onto the patio table. "What do you need?"

"I heard the weather report, so I know

there's a frost warning tonight. I wondered if you wanted any company out there."

"No, thanks. I can handle it." He lifted her bangs, studied the healing wound. "Very attractive."

"Those things always look worse a few days later. But I don't feel stiff when I wake up in the morning anymore. Ty . . . tell me what's wrong."

"Nothing. I handled it."

"Yes, yes, you can handle anything. Me too. We're so annoying." She gave his shoulders a squeeze. "I told you where it hurt. Now you tell me."

He started to shrug her off, then realized he didn't want to. "My father. He's sniping at my grandfather about all the bad press, all the police business. Interfering with his tennis lessons, or something. I told him to lay off."

"Will he?"

"If he doesn't, I'm going to talk to Helen about putting some leaks in his trust fund. That'll shut him up quick enough. The son of a bitch. The son of a bitch never did a day's work in his life—worse, never stirred himself up to show an ounce of gratitude for what he was given. Just takes and takes, then whines if he runs into a bump. No wonder he and your father got along so well."

He caught himself, cursed. "Goddamn it, Sophie. Sorry."

"No, don't be. You're right."

There was a bond here, she thought, that neither of them had acknowledged before. Perhaps this was the time.

"Ty, have you ever considered how lucky we are, you and I, that certain genes skipped a generation? Don't close off," she said before he could draw away. "You're so like Eli."

She combed her fingers through his hair. She'd come to love the way she could tease out the reds. "Tough guy," she said as she touched her lips to his cheek. "Solid as a rock. Don't let the weak space between you and Eli cut at you."

As his temper deflated, he laid his forehead lightly on hers. "I never needed him— my father." Not, he thought, the way you needed yours. "Never wanted him."

"And I needed, wanted too much from mine for too long. That's part of what made us what we are. I like who we are."

"I guess you're not half-bad, considering."

He gave her arms a casual caress. "Thanks." He leaned down, kissed the top of her head. "I wouldn't mind a little company on frost watch tonight."

"I'll bring the coffee."

CHAPTER TWENTY-ONE

Tiny flowering buds, bursting open as the lengthening days bathed them in sunlight, covered the vines. The earth was turned, opened to hold the promise of new plantings. Trees held their spring leaves in tight fists of stingy green, but here and there sprouts, brave and young, speared out of the ground. In the woods, nests were heavy with eggs, and mother ducks guarded their newly hatched babies while they swam in the stream.

April, Tereza thought, meant rebirth. And work. And hope that winter was over at last.

"The Canada geese are about to hatch," Eli told her as they took their morning walk in the cool and quiet mist.

She nodded. Her father had used that same natural barometer to judge the timing of the year's harvest. She had learned to watch the sky, the birds, the ground, as much as she watched the vines. "It'll be a good year. We had plenty of winter rain."

"Still a couple weeks yet to worry about frosts. But I think we've timed the new plantings well."

She looked over the rise of land to where the ground was well plowed. She'd given fifty acres for the new plantings, vines of European origin grafted to rootstock native to America. They'd chosen prime varieties—Cabernet Sauvignon, Merlot, Chenin Blanc. And, consulting with Tyler, had done much the same on MacMillan ground.

"In five years, perhaps four, we'll see them bear fruit." She had learned, too, to look from the moment to the future in one sweeping glance. Cycle would always spin into cycle.

"We'll have been together a quarter of a century, Eli, when what we plant now comes home to us."

"Tereza." He took her shoulders, turned her to face him, and she felt a shiver of alarm. "This is my last harvest."

"Eli—"

"I'm not going to die." To reassure, he ran

his hands down her arms. "I want to retire. I've been thinking of it, seriously thinking of it since you and I traveled to Italy. We've let ourselves become too rooted here and there," he said, gesturing toward MacMillan land, "and at the *castello.* Let's do this last planting, you and I, and let our children harvest. It's time."

"We talked of this. Five years or so we said before we stepped aside. A gradual process."

"I know. But these last months have reminded me how quickly a life, even a way of life, can end. There are places I want to see before my time's up. I want to see them with you. I'm tired, Tereza, of living my life to the demands of each season."

"My life, the whole of it, has been Giambelli." Tereza stepped away from him, touched a delicate white blossom. "How can I turn from it now, when it's wounded. Eli, how can we pass something to our children that's blighted?"

"Because we trust them. Because we believe in them. Because, Tereza, they've earned the chance."

"I don't know what to say to this."

"Think about it. There's plenty of time before the harvest. I've thought. I don't want to give Ty what he's earned, what he deserves, in my will. I want to give it to him while I'm alive. There's been enough death this year." He looked over the buds toward the new plantings. "It's time to let things grow."

So she turned from the vines toward him. A tall man weathered by time, by sun, by wind, with an old and faithful dog at his side. "I don't know if I can give you what you're asking me. But I'll promise to think about it."

"Effervescence is the essential ingredient in a sparkling wine." Pilar led a winery tour through a favorite phase. The creation of champagne. "But the first stage is to make the still wine. These"—she pointed at the racked bottles in the cellars—"are aged for several months, then blended. We call the blend *cuvée,* from the French, where it's believed the process has its origin. We're grateful to that very fortunate monk Dom Pérignon for making the discovery and being the first to, as he called it, drink stars."

"If it's just wine, what makes it bubble?"

"The second fermentation, which Dom Pérignon discovered in the seventeenth century."

Her answer was smooth and practiced. Questions tossed out by groups no longer spooked her or made her scramble for answers.

Dressed in a trim suit and low heels, she stepped to the side as she spoke so her group could take a closer look at the racked wine.

"It was initially thought to be a problem," she continued. "Wine bottled in fall popping their corks, or what was in those days cotton wadding, in the spring. Very troublesome, and in particular in the Champagne district of France. The Benedictine, the cellar master at the Abbey in Hautvillers, applied himself to this problem. He ordered thicker stoppers, but this caused the bottles themselves to break. Determined, he ordered stronger bottles. Both the stoppers and the bottles held, and the monk was able to sample the re-fermented wine. It was the first champagne toast."

She paused to give the group an opportunity to shuffle around the racks. Voices echoed in the cellars, so she waited until they subsided.

"Today . . ." A little flutter of anxiety rippled through her when David joined her group. "Today we create champagne quite purposely, though for the best we follow the traditional methods developed centuries ago in that French abbey. Using *méthode champenoise,* the winemaker bottles the young, blended wines. A small quantity of yeast and sugar is added to each bottle, then the bottle is capped, as you see here."

She took the sample bottle to pass among the tour. "The additive triggers the second fermentation, which we call, again in the French, *prise de mousse.* The bubbles result from the conversion of sugar into alcohol. Capped, the bubbles can't escape into the air. These bottles are then aged, from two to four years."

"There's gunk in here," someone commented.

"The sample bottle demonstrates sedimentation and particle separation. This is a natural process during this second aging and fermentation. The bottles are stored neck down on these inclined racks, and are lifted out and twisted every day for months."

"By hand?"

Pilar smiled at the woman who frowned at the wall of bottles. "Yes. As you've seen through the tour, Giambelli-MacMillan believes every bottle of wine offered to the consumer requires the art, the science and the labor necessary to earn the label. This turning process is called riddling, or in French, *remuage,* and accelerates the particle separation so that in a matter of months the wine is clear. When it is, the bottles are racked upside down to keep the particles in the neck."

"If they drink that stuff, it's no wonder it kills them."

It was said in a whisper, but it carried. Pilar tensed, felt her rhythm break, but kept going. "It's the winemaker's task to determine when the wine's reached its peak. At this point, the bottle is frozen at the neck in a solution of brine. In that way, the cap can be removed, no wine is lost and the frozen sediment slides out. *Dégorgement,* or disgorging. The bottle is topped off with more wine or a bit of *la dosage*—brandy or sugar to sweeten it—"

"Or a little digitalis."

Her rhythm faltered again, and a number of people shifted uneasily. Still she shook her head as David took a step forward. "Throughout the process, as with any wine bearing our label, there are safety checks and security measures. When the sparkling wine is judged ready, it's corked and shipped to market so that you can bring it to your table for your own celebration.

"There are cheaper and less cumbersome ways to create champagne, but Giambelli-MacMillan believes tradition, quality and attention to detail are essential to our wines."

She smiled as she took back the sample bottle. "At the end of the tour, you'll be able to judge for yourself in our tasting room."

Pilar let the guests mingle in the tasting room, enjoy their complimentary samples, and answered individual questions. It was, she'd discovered, very much like entertaining. That, she'd always had the knack for. Better, it made her feel not just part of the family, but part of the team.

"Nice job." David stepped up beside her.

"Thanks."

"Despite the heckler."

"He isn't my first. I think I've gotten the hang of it. At least my palms don't sweat anymore. I'm still studying. There are times I feel like I'm back in school cramming for exams, but it's satisfying. I still have to—"

She broke off as a man at the end of the bar began to gag. He clutched his throat, staggered back. Even as Pilar rushed forward, he began to laugh uproariously.

The same joker, David realized, who'd made the sarcastic cracks in the cellar. Before he could deal with the situation, Pilar was taking over.

"I'm sorry." Her voice was a coo of polite concern. "Isn't the wine to your taste?"

He gave another snort of laughter even as his wife jabbed her elbow viciously into his side. "Cut it out, Barry."

"Aw, come on. It's funny."

"Humor's often subjective, isn't it?" Pilar said pleasantly. "Of course, we at Giambelli-MacMillan have difficulty finding amusement in the tragic deaths of two of our own, but we appreciate your trying to lighten the mood. Perhaps you should try it again, with our Merlot." She signaled to the bartender. "It's more appropriate."

"No, thanks." He patted his belly. "I'm more of a beer man."

"Really? I'd never have guessed."

"You're such a jerk, Barry." His wife snatched her purse off the bar and steamed out the door.

"It was a *joke*! Jeez." Hitching up his belt, he hurried after her. "Can't anybody take a joke?"

"Well now." Pilar turned to her group. People were either goggling or pretending to look elsewhere. "Now that we've had our comic relief, I hope you've enjoyed your tour. I'm here to answer any questions you may have. Please feel free to visit our retail shop, where our wines, including those you've sampled, are available. We at Villa Giambelli hope you'll visit us again, and stop by our sister facility at the MacMillan Winery, only minutes away here in Napa. We wish you *buon viaggio,* wherever your travels take you."

David waited until people began to wander off before he took Pilar's arm and led her outside. "I was premature on the nice job. I should've said fabulous. Fabulous job. Though I'd've been more inclined to crack that idiot over the head with the bottle of Merlot than offer him one."

"Oh, I do. Mentally." She drew a deep breath, stepped away from the vine-covered stone of the old winery. "We get someone like Barry once or twice a week. Responding in an obnoxiously pleasant manner seems to work best. It helps that I'm family."

"I haven't come in before during your tours. Didn't want you to think I was checking up on you." He lifted her pearls, let them run through his fingers. "You, Ms. Giambelli, are a natural."

"You know what? You're right." She agreed, delighted with herself. "Just as you were right to push me into this. It gives me something tangible to do."

"I didn't push you. The fact that no one does is one of your secrets. You figured out a long time ago how to live your life the way that made sense to you at the time. Times changed. I opened a door, but you're the one who walked through it."

"That's very interesting." Amused at both of them, she cocked her head. "I'm not sure my family would agree with you. I'm not sure I do."

"It took spine to stay in a marriage that wasn't a marriage because you took your vows seriously. It would have been easier to walk away. I know all about that."

"You give me too much credit."

"I don't think so, but if you want to be grateful I gave you a nudge into this job, I'll take it. Especially," he added, sliding his hands up her arms, "if you think of a way to pay me back."

"I could think of something." She let her fingers link with his. Flirting, she thought, got easier with practice. She'd certainly been enjoying her lessons. "We could start with dinner."

"I've been scoping out this little inn."

"That's very nice." But dinner at the inn was a date—and formal, however much they enjoyed each other's company. She was, she realized, looking for something less. And something more.

"But I meant cooking you dinner. You and your children."

"Cooking? For all of us?"

"I'm a very good cook," she informed him. "And it's a rare thing for me to have a kitchen to myself. You have a nice kitchen. But if you think it'd be awkward, or your kids would be uncomfortable with the idea, the inn would be fine."

"Cooking," he said again. "Like at the stove. With pots." He lifted her off her feet for a kiss. "When do we eat?"

We're getting a home-cooked meal tonight. Pilar's cooking. I don't know what's on the menu, but you will like it. Be home by six. Until then, try to pretend you're human children and not the mutants I won in a poker game.

Love, Dad.

Maddy read the note stuck on the refrigerator, grimaced. Why did they have to have company? How come she didn't have a say in who got to come over? Did he really think she and Theo were so brain-damaged they'd believe a woman came over and fiddled around in a guy's kitchen just to cook?

Please.

Okay, she amended. Maybe Theo was brain-damaged enough, but she'd fix that.

Taking the note, she jogged upstairs. Theo was already in his room, already on the phone, already ruining his eardrums with the music up to scream. He didn't need to hit the kitchen for fuel after school, she thought with a sniff. He, in direct violation of house rules, kept enough junk food stockpiled in his room to feed a small country.

She had that information tucked into her get-back-at-Theo file.

"Ms. Giambelli's fixing dinner."

"What? Go away. I'm on the phone."

"You're not supposed to be on the phone until after you do your homework. Ms. Giambelli's coming over, so you'd better get off. She might tell Dad you're screwing off again."

"Sophia?"

"No, jerkweed."

"Listen, call you back. My sister's being a pest, so I have to kill her. Yeah. Later." He hung up, stuffed taco chips in his mouth. "Who's coming over, for what?"

"The woman Dad's sleeping with is coming over to fix dinner."

"Yeah." Theo's voice brightened. "Like, on the stove?"

"Don't you get it?" Disgusted, she waved the note. "It's a tactic. She's trying to squeeze in."

"Hey, anybody wants to squeeze into the

kitchen who can actually cook is fine with me. What's she making?"

"It doesn't *matter* what she's making. How can you be so slow? She's pushing it to the next level. Cooking for him, for us. Showing him what a big, happy family we can be."

"I don't care what she's doing, as long as I get to eat. Get off it, Maddy. I mean get—off—it. Dad's entitled to have a girlfriend."

"Moron. I don't care if he's got ten girlfriends. What are we going to do if he decides he wants a wife?"

Theo considered it, crunched on more chips. "I dunno."

"'I dunno,'" she mocked. "She'll start changing the rules, start taking over. That's what happens. She's not going to care about us. We're just add-ons."

"Ms. Giambelli's cool."

"Sure, now. She's sweet and nice. When she gets what she wants, she won't have to be sweet and nice and cool. She can start telling us what to do, and what not to do. It'll all have to be her way."

She turned her head as she heard the kitchen door open. "See, she's just walking right in. This is our house."

Maddy stomped to her room, slammed the door. She intended to stay there until her father got home.

She made it an hour. She could hear the music from downstairs, the laughter. It was infuriating to hear her brother's horsey laugh. The traitor. It was more infuriating that no one came up for her, or tried to talk her out of her sulks.

So she'd show them she didn't care, either way.

She wandered down, nose in the air. Something smelled really good, and that was just another strike against Pilar in Maddy's mind. She was just showing off, that was all. Making some big, fancy dinner.

When she walked into the kitchen, she had to grit her teeth. Theo was at the kitchen table, banging on his electric keyboard while Pilar stood stirring something at the stove.

"You need to add lyrics," Pilar said.

He liked playing his music for her. She listened. When he played her something that sucked, she said so. Well, in a nice way, Theo thought. That kind of thing told him she was paying attention, real attention.

Their mother never had. To much of any-thing.

"I'm not good with the word part. I just like doing the melody."

"Then you need a partner." She turned, set down her spoon. "Hi, Maddy. How's the essay going?"

"What essay?" She caught Theo's warn-ing hiss and shrugged, not sure whether she was furious or grateful that he'd cov-ered for her. "Oh. It's okay." She opened the refrigerator, took her time selecting a soft drink. "What's this gunk in here?"

"Depends. There's cheese gunk for the manicotti. The other's a marinade for the antipasto. Your father tells me you like Ital-ian food, so I figured I was safe."

"I'm not eating carbs today." She knew it was mean, and didn't need Theo's glare to tell her so. But when she made a face at him behind Pilar's back, he didn't respond in kind as he usually did. Instead he just looked away, like he was embarrassed or something.

And that stung.

"Anyway, I made plans to go to a friend's house for dinner."

"Oh, that's too bad." Casually Pilar got out

a bowl to begin mixing the filling for tiramisú. "Your father didn't mention it."

"He doesn't have to tell you everything."

It was the first directly rude comment the girl had made to her. Pilar calculated the barriers were down. "He certainly doesn't, and as you're nearly fifteen you're old enough to know what you like to eat, and where you like to eat it. Theo, would you excuse Maddy and me for a minute?"

"Sure." He grabbed his keyboard, sent Maddy a disgusted look. "Who's the moron?" he muttered as he walked by her.

"Why don't we sit down?"

Maddy's insides felt sticky, her throat hot. "I didn't come down to sit and talk. I just came to get a drink. I have to finish my essay."

"There isn't any essay. Sit down, Maddy."

She sat, sprawled, with a look of deliberate unconcern and boredom on her face. Pilar had no right lecturing her, and Maddy intended to make that very clear after the woman had blown off steam.

Pilar poured herself a demitasse of the espresso she'd brewed for the tiramisú. She sat across from Maddy at the table, sipped. "I should warn you I have an advantage here as I not only was a fourteen-year-old girl, but was once the mother of one."

"You're not my mother."

"No, I'm not. And it's hard, isn't it, to have a woman come into your home this way? I'm trying to think how I'd feel about it. Probably very much the way you do. Annoyed, nervous, resentful. It's easier for Theo. He's a boy and doesn't know the things we know."

Maddy opened her mouth, then shut it again when she realized she didn't know how to respond.

"You've been in charge a long time. Your men wouldn't agree, would likely be insulted by that statement," she added and was pleased to see the faint smirk curve Maddy's lips. "But the female force, a smart female force, usually pushes the buttons. You've done a good job keeping these guys in line, and I'm not here to take your control away."

"You're already changing things. Actions have reactions. It's scientific. I'm not stupid."

"No, you're smart." Scared little girl, Pilar thought, with a grown-up brain. "I always wanted to be smart, and never felt smart enough. I compensated, I think, by being good, being quiet, keeping peace. Those actions had reactions, too."

"If you keep quiet, nobody listens."

"You're absolutely right. Your father . . . he makes me feel smart enough and strong enough to say what I'm thinking, what I'm feeling. That's a powerful thing. You already know that."

Maddy frowned down at the table. "I guess."

"I admire him, Maddy—the man he is, the father he is. That's powerful, too. I don't expect you to throw out the welcome mat for me, but I'm hoping you won't lock the door in my face."

"Why do you care what I do?"

"Couple of reasons. I like you. Sorry, but it's true. I like your independence, and your mind, and your sense of family loyalty. I imagine if I wasn't involved with your father, we'd get along very well. But I am involved with him, and I'm taking some of his time and attention away from you. I'd say I was sorry about that, but we'd both know it wasn't true. I want some of his time and attention, too. Because, Maddy, another reason I care what you do is I'm in love with your father."

Pilar pushed her cup away and, pressing a hand to her stomach, rose. "I haven't said that out loud before. That habit of keeping quiet, I suppose. Boy. Feels strange."

Maddy shifted in her chair. She was sitting up now, ramrod straight. And her own stomach was jumping. "My mother loved him, too. Enough to marry him."

"I'm sure she did. She—"

"No! You're going to make all the excuses, all the reasons why. And they're all bullshit. All of them. When it wasn't just exactly the way she wanted, she left us. That's the truth. We didn't matter."

Her first instinct, always, was to comfort. Console. There were a dozen things she could say to soothe, but this little girl with wet, defiant eyes wouldn't hear them.

Why should she? Pilar decided.

"No, you're right. You didn't matter enough." Pilar sat again. She wanted to reach out, to draw this young girl close. But it wasn't the way, or the time. "I know what it's like not to matter enough. I do, Maddy," she said firmly, laying a hand over the girl's before she could jerk away. "How sad and angry it makes you feel, how the questions and doubts and wishes run through your head in the middle of the night."

"Adults can come and go whenever they want. Kids can't."

"That's right. Your father didn't leave. You mattered to him. You and Theo matter most to him. You know that nothing I could say or do or be will change that."

"Other things could change. And when one thing does, others do. It's cause and effect."

"Well, I can't promise you that things won't change. Things do. People do. But right now your father makes me happy. And I make him happy. I don't want to hurt you because of that, Maddy. I can promise to try very hard not to hurt you or Theo. To respect what you think and what you feel. I can promise that."

"He was my father first," Maddy said in a fierce whisper.

"And he'll be your father last. Always. If I wanted to change that, if I wanted for some reason to ruin that, I couldn't. Don't you know how much he loves you? You could make him choose. Look at me, Maddy. Look at me," she said quietly and waited for the girl's gaze to lift. "If it's what you want so much, you could make him choose between you and me. I wouldn't have a chance. I'm asking you to give me one. If you can't, just can't, I'll make an excuse, clean this stuff up and be out of here before he gets home."

Maddy wiped a tear off her cheek as she stared across the table. "Why?"

"Because I don't want to hurt him, either."

Maddy sniffled, frowned down at the table. "Can I taste that?"

Pilar lifted a brow at her cup of espresso, then silently slid it toward Maddy. The girl sniffed it first, wrinkled her nose, but lifted the cup and tasted.

"It's horrible. How can anybody drink that?"

"An acquired taste, I guess. You'd like it better in the tiramisu."

"Maybe." Maddy pushed the cup back across the table. "I guess I'll give it a chance."

One thing Pilar was sure of: No one had a problem with her cooking. It had been a long time since she'd personally prepared a family dinner. Long enough for her to be outrageously pleased at the requests for second helpings and the cheerful compliments between bites.

She'd used the dining room for the meal, hoping that thin layer of formality would be less threatening to Maddy. But the formality had broken down the minute Theo had the first bite of her manicotti and announced it "awesome grub."

Theo did most of the talking, with his sister watching, digesting, then occasionally skewering through with a pointed question. It made her laugh, then it warmed her heart when David used a sports metaphor to illustrate an opinion and Maddy and she shared female amusement over the male mind.

"Dad played baseball in college," Maddy told her.

"Really? Another hidden talent. Were you good?"

"I was great. First base."

"Yeah, and he was so worried about his batting average, he never got past first base with the girls." Theo snickered, and easily ducked David's swing.

"A lot you know. I was a home run . . ." He

trailed off. "Any way I play that, I'm in trouble. So instead I'll just say that was an amazing meal. On behalf of myself and my two gluttons, I thank you."

"You're welcome, but on behalf of your two gluttons, I'd like to point out you outate the table."

"I have a fast metabolism," he claimed as Pilar got to her feet.

"That's what they all say."

"Oh no." He laid a hand over hers before she could stack the dishes. "House rule. He who cooks, cleans not."

"I see. Well, that's a rule I can get behind." She lifted her plate, offered it to him. "Enjoy."

"Another house rule," he said over Theo's whoop of laughter. "Dad gets to delegate. Theo and Maddy will be delighted to do the dishes."

"Figures." Maddy heaved a sigh. "What do you get to do?"

"I get to work off some of this excellent meal by taking the chef for a walk." Testing the waters with his kids, he leaned in and kissed Pilar warmly. "That work for you?"

"Hard to complain."

She went with him, pleased to be out in

the spring night. "That's a lot of mess to leave two teenagers to handle."

"Builds character. Besides, it'll give them time to talk about how I lured you outside for a make-out session."

"Oh. Have I been lured?"

"Sure hope so." He turned her into his arms, drawing her closer when she lifted her mouth to his. A long, slow thrill rippled through him at the way she sighed against him. The way she fit. "Haven't had much time to be together lately."

"It's hard. So much going on." Content for now, she rested her head on his shoulder. "I know I've been hovering around Sophie. I can't help it. Thinking of her being attacked, right in our own home. Knowing someone walked in and out of her room, and mine, and my mother's . . . I've caught myself lying in bed at night listening for sounds the way I never have before."

"I look out my window some nights, across the fields, and see your light. I want to tell you not to worry, but until this is settled, you will. We all will."

"If it helps, I feel better when I look out my window and see the light in yours. It helps knowing you're so close."

"Pilar." He drew her away, then lowered his forehead to hers.

"What is it?"

"There're some problems in the Italian offices. Some discrepancies in the figures that have turned up during the audit. I might have to go over for a few days. I don't like leaving now." His gaze shifted past her, back to the house with the kitchen lights bright in the window.

"The kids can stay at the villa while you're gone. We'll take care of them, David. You don't have to worry about that."

"No." Tereza had already decreed that his children would be guests of the villa during his travel. Still, he would worry about them. About everyone. "I don't like leaving you, either. Come with me."

"Oh, David." There was a rush of excitement at the thought. The Italian spring, the balmy nights, a lover. How wonderful that her life had taken this turn, that such things were possible. "I'd love that, but it won't do. I wouldn't feel right about leaving my mother just now. And you'd do what you have to do faster and easier if you knew I was here with your children."

"Do you have to be practical?"

"I don't want to be," she said softly. "I'd love to say yes, to just run away." Feeling young, foolish, ridiculously happy, she turned in a circle. "To make love with you in one of those huge old beds in the *castello.* To sneak away for an evening to Venice and dance in the *piazza,* steal kisses in the shadows of the bridges. Ask me again." She spun back to him. "When all this is over, ask me again. I'll go."

Something was different. Something . . . more free about her, he realized. That made her only more alluring.

"Why don't I ask you now? Go with me to Venice when this is over."

"Yes." She threw out her hands, gripped his. "I love you, David."

He went very still. "What did you say?"

"I'm in love with you. I'm sorry, it's too much, too fast, but I can't stop it. I don't want to stop it."

"I didn't ask for qualifications, just for you to repeat yourself. This is handy. Very handy." He jerked her forward, and when she started to spill into his arms, he lifted her, spun her in a circle. "I had it figured wrong. By my astute calculations, it was going to take at least another two months before I could make you fall in love with me."

His lips raced over her face. "It was tough on me," he continued. "Because I was already in love with you. I should've known you wouldn't let me suffer for long."

She pressed her cheek to his. She could love. Her heart glowed with the joy of it. And be loved. "What did you say?"

"Let me paraphrase." He eased her back again. "I love you, Pilar. One look at you. One look, and I started to believe in second chances." He brought her close again, and this time his lips were tender. "You're mine."

CHAPTER TWENTY-TWO

Venice was a woman, *la bella donna,* elegant in her age, sensual in her watery curves, mysterious in her shadows. The first sight of her, rising over the Grand Canal with her colors tattered and faded like old ballgowns, called to the blood. The light, a white, washing sun, would sweep over her and lose itself like a wanderer in her sinuous veins, her secret turns.

Here was a city whose heart was sly and female, and whose pulse beat in deep, dark rivers.

Venice wasn't a city to be wasted on meetings with lawyers and accountants. It wasn't a city where a man could be content shut up in an office, hour by hour, while the sweet seductress of spring sang outside the stone and glass of his prison.

Reminding himself Venice had been built on commerce didn't help David's mood. Knowing the curvy streets and bridges were even now jammed with tourists burning up their Visa cards in the endless shops where tacky was often mistaken for art didn't stop him from wanting to be among them.

It didn't stop him from wishing he could stroll those ancient streets with Pilar, and buy her some ridiculous trinket they would laugh over for years. He'd have enjoyed that. Enjoyed watching Theo inhale a gelato like water, listening to Maddy interrogate some hapless gondolier over the history and architecture of the canals.

He missed his family. He missed his lover. And he hadn't been gone fully sixty-eight hours.

The accountant was droning on in Italian and in a whispery voice difficult enough to understand when full attention was paid. David reminded himself he hadn't been sent to Venice to daydream but to do a job.

"Scusi." He held up a hand, flipped over another page of a report fully an inch thick. "I wonder if we might go over this area again." He spoke slowly, deliberately stum-

bling a bit over the Italian. "I want to make sure I understand clearly."

As he'd hoped, his tactic hit its target with the Italian's manners. The new section of figures was explained, patiently.

"The numbers," the Italian said, switching out of compassion to English, "do not match."

"Yes, I see. They don't match in a number of departmental expenditures. Across the board. This perplexes me, *signore,* but I'm more perplexed by the activities attributed to the Cardianili account. Orders, shipments, breakage, salaries, expenses. All very clearly recorded."

"*Sì.* In that area there is no . . . what is it? Discrepancy. The figures are correct."

"Apparently they are. However, there is no Cardianili account. No Giambelli client or customer by that name. There's no Cardianili warehouse in Rome at the address recorded in the files. If there's no customer, no client, no warehouse, where do you suppose these orders, over the last three years, have been sent?"

The accountant blinked behind the lenses of wire-framed glasses. "I could not say. There is a mistake, of course."

"Of course. There's a mistake." And David believed he knew who'd made it.

He swiveled in his chair and addressed the lawyer. "*Signore,* have you had the opportunity to study the documents I gave you yesterday?"

"I have."

"And the name of the account executive in charge of this account?"

"Listed as Anthony Avano."

"And the invoices, the expense chits, the correspondence relating to the account were signed by Anthony Avano?"

"They were. Until December of last year his signature appears on much of the paperwork. After that time, Margaret Bowers's signature appears in the file."

"We'll need to have those signatures verified as genuine."

"I understand."

"And the signature who approved, and ordered, the shipments, the expenditures and signed off on the payments from the account. Donato Giambelli."

"*Signore* Cutter, I will have the signatures verified, will look into this matter from a legal point of view and advise you of your position and your recourse. I will do that," he added, "when I have the permission to do so from *Signora* Giambelli herself. This is a delicate matter."

"I realize that, which is why Donato Giambelli was not informed of this meeting. I trust your discretion, *signori.* The Giambellis won't wish more public scandal, as a company or as a family. If you would give me a moment, please, to contact *La Signora* in California and relate to her what we've just discussed?"

It was always tricky for an outsider to question the integrity, the honesty, of one of the core. David was neither Italian nor a Giambelli. Two strikes, he decided. The fact that he'd been brought into the organization barely four months before was the third.

He was going up against Donato Giambelli with one out already on his slate. There were two ways, in his opinion, to handle the situation. He could be aggressive and swing away. Or he could wait, with the bat on his shoulder, for the perfect pitch.

Back to sports metaphors, he thought as he stood at the window of his office, hands in his pockets, and watched the water traffic stream by. Apt enough. What was business but another game? Skill, strategy, luck were required.

Donato would assume he had home-field advantage. But the minute he walked into the office, he would be on David's turf. That David intended to make clear.

His interoffice phone buzzed.

"*Signore* Giambelli is here to see you, *Signore* Cutter."

"Thank you. Tell him I'll be right with him."

Let him sweat just a little, David decided. If the grapevine here climbed as quickly as it did in most companies, Don already knew a meeting had been held. Accountants, lawyers, questions, files. And he would wonder, he would worry.

He would, if he was smart, have some reasonable explanation in hand. Answers lined up, fall guy in place. Smartest move would be fury, outrage. And he would be counting heavily on family loyalty, on the stream of blood to carry him through the crisis.

David walked to the door himself, opened it and watched Donato pace the outer office. "Don, thanks for coming in. Sorry to keep you waiting."

"You made it sound important, so I made time." He stepped into the office, scanned the room quickly. Relaxed a little when he found it empty. "If I'd been informed before you made your travel arrangements, I would have cleared my calendar so that I could have shown you Venice."

"The arrangements were made quickly, but I've seen Venice before. I'm looking forward to seeing the *castello,* though, and the vineyards. Have a seat."

"If you let me know when you plan to go, I'll arrange to escort you. I go there myself, regularly, to make certain all is as it should be." He sat, folded his hands. "Now, what can I do for you?"

Swing away, David decided, and took his place behind his desk. "You could explain the Cardianili account."

Don's face went blank. As his eyes darted from side to side, he worked up a puzzled smile. "I don't understand."

"Neither do I," David said pleasantly. "That's why I'm asking you to explain it."

"Ah, well, David. You give my memory too much credit. I can't remember every account, or details of it. If you'll give me time to pull files and information—"

"Oh, I already have them." David tapped a finger on the file on his desk. Not so smart, he decided, surprised. And not prepared. "Your signature appears on a number of expense chits, correspondence and other paperwork pertaining to this account."

"My signature appears on many such account papers." Don was beginning to sweat—lightly, visibly. "I can hardly remember all of them."

"This one should stick out. As it doesn't exist. There is no Cardianili account, Donato. There's considerable paperwork generated for it, a great deal of money involved. Invoices and expenses, but no account. No man by the name of"—he paused, flipped open the file and drew out a sheet of Giambelli letterhead—"Giorgio Cardianili, with whom you appear to have corresponded several times over the last few years. He doesn't exist, nor does the warehouse with an address in Rome to which several shipments of wine are listed to have been shipped. This warehouse, where you, on company expense, traveled to on business twice in the last eight months, isn't there. How would you explain that?"

"I don't understand." Donato sprang to

his feet. But he didn't look outraged. He looked terrified. "What are you accusing me of?"

"At the moment, nothing. I'm asking you to explain this file."

"I have no explanation. I don't know of this file, this account."

"Then how is it your signature appears in it? How is it your expense account was charged more than ten million lire in connection to this account?"

"A mistake." Donato moistened his lips. He snatched the letterhead from the file. "A forgery. Someone uses me to steal money from *La Signora,* from my family. *Mia famiglia,*" he said, and his hand shook as he thumped it against his heart. "I'll look into this immediately."

No, not smart at all, David decided. Not nearly smart enough. "You have forty-eight hours."

"You would dare? You would dare give me such an ultimatum when someone steals from my family?"

"The ultimatum, as you call it, comes from *La Signora.* She requires your explanation within two days. In the meantime, all activity on this account is frozen. Two days from now, all paperwork generated from this matter is to be turned over to the police."

"The police?" Don went white. His composure in tatters, his hands began to tremble and his voice to hitch. "This is ridiculous. It's obviously an internal problem of some kind. We don't want an outside investigation, the publicity—"

"*La Signora* wants results. Whatever the cost."

Now he paused, struggled to think, to find a rope swinging over the pit he'd so suddenly found himself standing over. "With Tony Avano as account executive, it's easy to see the source of the problem."

"Indeed. But I didn't identify Avano as the account exec."

"Naturally I assumed . . ." Don wiped the back of his hand over his mouth. "A major account."

"I didn't qualify Cardianili as major. Take your two days," David said quietly. "And take my advice. Think of your wife and children. *La Signora* will be more likely to show compassion if you stand up for what's been done, and stand up for your family."

"Don't tell me what to do about my family. About my position. I've been with Giambelli all my life. I *am* Giambelli. And will be long after you're gone. I want that file."

"You're welcome to it." David ignored the imperious and outstretched hand, and closed the folder. "In forty-eight hours."

It puzzled David that Donato Giambelli was so unprepared, so *clueless.* Not innocent, he thought as he crossed St. Mark's Square. Donato had his hand in the muck up to his elbow. But he hadn't put the scam together. He hadn't run the show. Avano, possibly. Quite possibly, though the amount skimmed under his name was petty cash next to what Donato had raked in.

And Avano had been dead four months.

The detectives in charge of his homicide investigation would likely be interested in this new information. And how much of that dingy light would land on Pilar?

Swearing under his breath, he moved toward one of the tables spilling out on the walkway. He sat, and for a time simply watched the flood of tourists pour across the stones, in and out of the cathedral. And in and out of the shops that lined the square.

Avano had been milking the company, he thought. That was a given, and already known. But what David now carried in his briefcase took things to another level. Donato stepped it all up to fraud.

And Margaret? There was nothing to indicate she'd had knowledge of or participation in any skimming prior to her promotion. Had she turned so quickly? Or had she learned of the false account and that knowledge had led to her death?

Whatever the explanation, it didn't answer the thorniest of questions: Who was in charge now? Who was it Donato was surely calling in panic for instructions, for help?

Would whoever that was believe, as easily as Donato had believed, that *La Signora* intended to take the matter to the police? Or would they be cool-headed and call the bluff?

In any case, within two days Donato Giambelli was going to be out on his ass. Which added one more layer to David's headache. Don would have to be replaced, and quickly. The internal investigation would have to continue until all leaks were plugged.

His own time in Italy would likely be extended, and at a point in his life where he wanted and needed to be home.

He ordered a glass of wine, checked the time, then took out his cell phone. "Maria? This is David Cutter. Is Pilar available?"

"One moment, Mr. Cutter."

He tried to imagine where she was in the house, what she was doing.

The last night they'd been together, they'd made love in his van on the edge of the vineyard. Like a couple of giddy teenagers, he remembered. So eager for each other, so desperate to touch.

And remembering brought on a painful longing.

It was easier, he found, to imagine her sitting across from him, while the light dimming toward dusk struck the dome of the cathedral like an arrow, and the air filled with the flurry of pigeons on the wing.

When all this is over, he promised himself, he would have that moment with her.

"David?"

The fact that she was a little breathless made him smile. She'd hurried. "I was just sitting here, in St. Mark's Square." He picked up the glass of wine the waiter brought him, sipped. "Drinking an interesting little Chianti and thinking of you."

"Is there music?"

"A small orchestra across the plaza, playing American show tunes. Sort of spoils the moment."

"Not at all. Not for me."

"How are the kids?"

"They're fine. Actually, I think Maddy and I are cautiously approaching friendship. She came out to the greenhouse yesterday after school. I got a lesson on photosynthesis, most of which was over my head. Theo broke up with the girl he's been seeing."

"Julie?"

"Julie was last winter, David. Keep up. Carrie. He and Carrie broke up, and he moped for about ten minutes. He's sworn off girls and intends to dedicate his life to his music."

"Been there. That should last maybe a day."

"I'll let you know. How's everything there?"

"Better now, for talking to you. Will you tell the kids I'll call them tonight? I'll make it about six your time."

"All right. I guess you don't know when you might be coming home?"

"Not yet. There are some complications. I miss you, Pilar."

"I miss you, too. Do me a favor?"

"You've got it."

"Just sit there awhile. Drink your wine, listen to the music, watch the light change. I'll think of you there."

"I'll think of you here, too. Bye."

When he hung up, he lingered over the wine. It had been an experience to talk to a woman—to her—about his children that way. To someone who understood them, appreciated them. It connected them in a way that made them almost like family. And that, he realized, was what he wanted. He wanted a family again. All the links that made the circle.

On an unsteady breath, he set down his wine. He wanted a wife. He wanted Pilar to be his wife.

Too fast? he wondered. Too much?

No. No, it wasn't. Any way he looked at it, it was exactly right. They were grown-ups with half their lives behind them. Why should they waste the rest of it inching along in stages?

He got to his feet, tossed some lire on the table.

Why should he waste another minute? What better place to buy a ring for the woman he loved than Venice? When he turned, and the first window to catch his eye was a jeweler's, David considered it a sign.

It wasn't as easy as he assumed it would be. He didn't want a diamond. It occurred to him that Avano had probably given her one, and he discovered in himself a deep-seated aversion to giving Pilar anything Avano had.

He wanted something that spoke to the two of them, something that showed her he understood her as no one else had. Or could.

Competitive, he supposed as he wandered into yet another shop. And so what?

He climbed the stairs on the jammed Rialto bridge, where the stores were shoved cheek by jowl on that rise above the water. Eager shoppers elbowed and shoved their way through as if terrified the last souvenir would be snatched away before they could buy it.

He bumped his way past the stalls offering leather goods, T-shirts and trinkets and tried to focus on the shop windows. Each one ran like rivers with gold, gems. A dazzle that confused the eye. Discouraged, annoyed, tired from the long hike, he nearly called it a night. He could wait, ask his Venice assistant for a recommendation.

Then he turned, looked into one more window. And saw it.

The ring was set with five stones, all in delicate heart shapes that made a quiet stream of color. Like her flowers, he thought. Five stones, he thought, stepping closer. One for each of them and each of their children. He imagined the blue was sapphire, the red ruby, the green emerald. The purple and the gold stones he wasn't as sure of. What did it matter? It was perfect.

Thirty minutes later he walked out. He had the description of the ring—amethyst and citrine for the last two stones, he reminded himself—in his pocket. The ring was tucked in his pocket as well. He'd had it engraved with the date he'd bought it.

He wanted her to know, always, that he'd found it on the evening he'd sat in Campo San Marco while the light went soft, talking to her.

His steps were lighter than they had been as he left the bridge. He wandered the narrow streets now, giving himself the treat of an aimless walk. The crowds were thinning as night fell and turned the canals a glossy black. Now and then he could hear the echo of his own footsteps or the lap of water against a bridge.

He decided not to go back to his apartment, but ducked under the awning of a sidewalk trattoria. If he went back, he'd work and spoil the pleasure, the anticipation of the evening. He ordered the turbot, a half carafe of the house white.

He idled his way through the meal, smiling sentimentally at a couple obviously honeymooning, enjoying the little boy who escaped from his parents to charm the waiters. It was, he supposed, a typical reaction of a man in love that he'd find everyone and everything a simple delight.

He lingered over coffee and thought of what he would say, how he would say it, when he offered the ring to Pilar.

Most of the squares were empty as he headed back across the city. The shops were shut down and the sidewalk grifters had long since packed up their wares.

Now and then he saw the little beam of light from a gondola carrying tourists down a side canal or heard a voice rise and carry over the water, but for the most part, he was—at last—alone in the city.

Enjoying himself, he took his time, walked off the meal and let the stress of the day drain while he absorbed Venice after dark.

He crossed another bridge, walked through the shadows of another twisting street. He glanced up when light poured out of a window above him, and smiled as a young woman began to draw in the wash that fluttered faintly in the breeze. Her hair was dark and tumbled around her shoulders. Her arms were long and slim, with a flash of gold at her wrist. She was singing, and the cheerful bell of her voice rang into the empty street.

The moment etched itself on his brain.

The dark-haired woman who was late bringing in the day's wash but singing nonetheless, the scent of her supper that wafted down. She caught his eye, laughed, a sound full of fun and flirtation.

David stopped, turned, intending to call a greeting up to her. And doing so, likely saved his own life.

He felt the pain, a sudden, horrendous fire in the shoulder. Heard, dimly, a kind of muffled explosion even as the woman's face blurred.

Then he was falling, falling slowly and forever to the sounds of screams and running feet until he lay bleeding and unconscious on the cool cobbles of the Venetian street.

He wasn't out for long. There was a moment when his world seemed washed with red, and through that dull mist voices rose and fell. The Italian slipped incomprehensibly through his numb brain.

He felt heat more than pain, as if someone held him over the licking flames of a fire. And he thought, quite clearly: I've been shot.

Someone tugged at him, stirred his body so that pain woke and cut through the fire like a silver sword. He tried to speak, to protest, to defend himself, but managed little more than a moan as his vision grayed.

When it cleared again, he found himself staring up into the face of the young woman he'd watched pulling in her wash.

"You must've worked late tonight." The

words came clear in his head, slurred through his lips.

"Signore, per piacere. Sta zitto. Riposta. L'aiuto sta venendo."

He listened solemnly, translating the Italian as slowly, as painstakingly as a first-year student. She wanted him to be quiet, to rest. That was nice of her, he thought dimly. Help was coming. Help for what?

Oh, that's right. He'd been shot.

He told her so, first in English, then in Italian. "I need to call my children. I need to tell them I'm all right. Do you have a phone?"

And with his head cradled in her lap, he went back under.

"You're a very lucky man, Mr. Cutter."

David tried to focus on the man's face. Whatever drugs the doctors had pumped into him were high-test. He wasn't feeling any pain, but he was hard-pressed to feel anything. "It's hard to agree with you at the moment. I'm sorry, I've forgotten your name."

"DeMarco. I'm Lieutenant DeMarco. Your doctor says you need rest, of course. But I have just a few questions. Perhaps if you tell me what you remember?"

He remembered a pretty woman drawing in the wash, and the way the lights glimmered on the water, on the stones. "I was walking," he began, then struggled to sit up. "Pilar's ring. I'd just bought a ring."

"I have it. Calm yourself. I have the ring, your wallet, your watch. They'll be safe."

The police, David remembered. People called the police when someone got shot on the street. This one looked like a cop, not as slick as the detective back in San Francisco. DeMarco was a little dumpy, a little bald. He made up for both with a luxurious black moustache that flowed over his upper lip. His English was precise and correct.

"I was walking back to my apartment—wandering a little. I'd done some shopping—the ring—after work. Had some dinner. It was a nice evening and I'd been shut up in an office all day. I saw a woman in a window. She was pulling in her wash. She made a picture. She was singing. I stopped to look up. Then I hit the street. I felt . . ." Gingerly, he lifted an arm to his shoulder. "I knew I'd been shot."

"You've been shot before?"

"No." David grimaced. "It felt just like you think it would. I must've passed out. The woman was there with me when I came to. She ran down, I guess, when she saw what happened."

"And did you see who shot you?"

"I didn't see anything but the cobbles rushing up at me."

"Why do you think, Mr. Cutter, that someone would shoot you?"

"I don't know. Robbery, I guess."

"Yet your valuables were not taken. What is your business in Venice?"

"I'm chief operating officer for Giambelli-MacMillan. I had meetings."

"Ah. You work for *La Signora.*"

"I do."

"There is some trouble, yes, for *La Signora* in America?"

"There has been, but I don't see what it has to do with my getting mugged in Venice. I need to call my children."

"Yes, yes, this will be arranged. Do you know anyone in Venice who might wish you harm, Mr. Cutter?"

"No." As soon as he denied it, he thought of Donato. "No," he repeated. "I don't know anyone who'd shoot me down on the street. You said you had my valuables, Lieutenant. The ring I bought, my wallet, my watch. My briefcase."

"No briefcase was found." DeMarco sat back. The woman who'd witnessed the shooting had claimed the victim was carrying a briefcase. She had described him very well. "What were the contents of this briefcase?"

"Papers from the office," David said. "Just paperwork."

It was difficult, Tereza thought, to stand up under so many blows. Under such constant assault, the spirit began to wilt. She kept her spine straight as she walked with Eli into the family parlor. She knew the children were there, waiting for the call from their father.

Innocence, she mused as she looked in to see Maddy sprawled on the sofa with her nose in a book, Theo banging away on the piano. Why did innocence have to be stolen this way, and so quickly?

She gave Eli's arm a squeeze. To reassure him, to brace herself, then stepped inside.

Pilar glanced up from her needlework. One look at her mother and her heart froze. The embroidery hoop slid out of her hands as she got slowly to her feet. "Mama?"

"Please sit. Theo." She gestured to quiet him. "Maddy. First I must tell you, your father is all right."

"What happened?" Maddy rolled off the couch. "Something happened to him. That's why he hasn't called. He's never late calling."

"He was hurt, but he's all right. He's in the hospital."

"An accident?" Pilar stepped up, laid a hand on Maddy's shoulder. When previously the girl would have shrugged her off, she merely clung tighter.

"No, not an accident. He was shot."

"Shot?" Theo shoved away from the piano. Terror coated his throat like bile. "That's wrong, that's a mistake. Dad doesn't go around getting shot."

"He was taken right away to the hospital," Tereza continued. "I've spoken with the doctor who treated him. Your father's doing very well. He's already listed in good condition."

"Listen to me." Eli moved forward, took

Maddy's hand, then Theo's. "We wouldn't tell you he's all right if he wasn't. I know you're scared, and you're worried, and so are we. But the doctor was very clear. Your father's healthy and strong. He's going to make a full recovery."

"I want him to come home." Maddy's lip trembled. "I want him to come home now."

"He'll come home as soon as they release him from the hospital," Tereza told her. "I'm going to make the arrangements. Does your father love you, Madeline?"

"Sure he does."

"Do you know how worried he is about you right now? About you and your brother, and how this worry makes it harder for him to rest, to heal? He needs you to be strong for him."

When the phone rang, Maddy whirled away, leaped on it. "Hello? Hello? Daddy!" Tears gushed out of her eyes, shook her body down to the toes. Still, she slapped at Theo when he tried to grab the phone. "It's okay." Her voice broke, and she turned to Tereza. "It's okay," she repeated, swiping a hand under her nose, breathing deep. "So, hey. Do you get to keep the bullet?"

She listened to her father's voice, and watched *La Signora* nod at her.

"Yeah, Theo's right here, shoving at me. Can I hit him? Too late," she responded. "I already did. Yeah, here he is."

She passed the phone to her brother.

"You're a strong young woman," Tereza told her. "Your father should be very proud."

"Make him come home, okay? Just make him come home." She walked into Pilar's arms and felt better for crying there.

CHAPTER TWENTY-THREE

Her head throbbed like an open wound, but it was nothing compared to the ache in her heart. She ignored both and took her place behind her desk.

Over Eli's and Pilar's objections, Tereza allowed the children to attend this emergency meeting. She was still head of the Giambelli family, and they had a right to know why she believed their father had been hurt.

They had a right to know it fell to her blood.

"I've spoken with David," she began, and smiled at his children. "Before his doctor came in and forced him to rest."

"It's a good sign." Sophia ranged herself beside Theo. He looked so young, so defenseless. "Guys are such babies when they're hurt. They just can't stop talking about it."

"Get out. We're like, stoic." Theo was trying to be, but his stomach kept pitching on him.

"Be that as it may," Tereza continued. "With his doctor's approval, he'll fly home in just a few days. Meanwhile the police are investigating the incident. I've also talked to the man in charge of the investigation."

And had, in short and ruthless order, researched his record. DeMarco would do. Tereza folded her hands on the lieutenant's file. "There were a number of witnesses. They have a description, though not a particularly good one, of the assailant. I don't know that they'll find him, or that he particularly matters."

"How can you say that?" Maddy jerked up in her chair. "He shot my father."

Approving the reaction, Tereza spoke to her as she would to an equal. "Because I believe he was hired to do so, as one buys and uses any tool. To take away papers in your father's possession. A misguided and despicable act of self-protection. There have been . . . discrepancies in a number of accounts. The details of that can wait. It became clear earlier today, through David's work, that my nephew has been funneling money from the company into a dummy account."

"Donato." Sophia felt a sharp pinch in the heart. "Stealing from you?"

"From us." That Tereza had already accepted and absorbed. "He met with David, on my orders, this afternoon in Venice and would have realized his actions would soon be uncovered. This was his response. My family's caused your pain," she said to Theo and Maddy. "I'm head of the family and responsible for that pain."

"Dad works for you. He was doing his job." As his stomach continued to shudder, Theo clenched his teeth. "It's that bastard's fault, not yours. Is he in jail?"

"No. They've yet to find him. It appears he's run." Disdain edged her voice. "Left his wife, his children and has run. I promise you he will be found; he will be punished. I'll see to it."

"He'll need money. Resources," Ty put in.

"You'll need someone in Venice to clear this up." Sophia rose. "I'll leave tonight."

"I won't put another of mine in danger."

"*Nonna,* if Donato was using an account

to skim funds, he had help. My father. It's my blood," she continued in Italian, "as much as yours. My honor, as much as yours. You can't deny me my right to make amends." She took another breath, switched to English. "I'll leave tonight."

"Hell." Tyler scowled. "We'll leave tonight."

"I don't need a baby-sitter."

"Yeah, right." He lifted his gaze now, met hers with chilled steel. "We've got an equal stake in this, Giambelli. You go, I go. I'll check out the vineyards, the winery," he said to Tereza. "If anything's off there, I'll spot it. I'll leave the paper trail to the paper pusher."

So, Tereza thought as she looked at Eli across the room. The next step in the cycle. We pass the burdens to the young.

"Agreed." Tereza ignored Sophia's hissing breath. "Your mother will worry less if you're not alone."

"No, I'll just spread the worry out over two people. Mama, Gina and her children?"

"They'll be provided for. I don't believe in the sins of the father." Tereza shifted her gaze to Sophia's, held it. "I believe in the child."

· · ·

The first thing David did when he was released from the hospital, or more accurately, when he released himself from the hospital, was buy flowers.

When the first bouquet seemed inadequate, he bought another, then a third.

It wasn't easy carrying a huge load of flowers, one arm in a sling, through the crowded streets of Venice, but he managed it. Just as he managed to find the spot where he'd been shot.

He'd prepared himself for the jolt, but hadn't realized there'd be fury along with it. Someone had thought him dispensable, had pierced his flesh with steel, spilled his blood. And had come very close to making his children orphans.

Someone, David promised himself as he stood on the stains of his own blood with his good arm full of flowers, was going to pay for thinking it. Whatever, and however long, it took.

He glanced up. Though there was no wash hanging out today, the window was open. He shifted his flowers, turned away from the street and entered the building. It amazed him how exhausted he was after the climb. Limbs weak, skin slicked with sweat. It pissed him off to find himself gasping for air and leaning limply on the wall outside the apartment door.

How the hell was he supposed to get back to the Giambelli apartment, pack, book a flight when he could barely make it up these stairs? The fact that the doctor had said essentially that before David had signed himself out only annoyed him.

So much so that, still puffing, he straightened and knocked.

He didn't expect her to be home, intended to leave the flowers on her doorstep or hunt up a cooperative neighbor who'd take them for her. But the door opened, and there she was.

"*Signorina.*"

"*Sì?*" She stared at him blankly, then her pretty face lit up. "*Signore! Come sta? Oh, oh, che bellezza!*" She gathered the flowers and gestured him in. "I called the hospital this morning," she continued in rapid Italian. "They said you were resting. I've been so frightened. I couldn't believe such a thing could happen right outside . . . Oh." She tapped her head with her hand. "You're

American," she said in careful English. "*Scusami.* Sorry. I don't have good English."

"I speak Italian. I wanted to thank you."

"Me? I did nothing. Please come in, sit. You look so pale."

"You were there." He glanced around her apartment. Small, simple, with pretty little touches. "If you hadn't been, and if I hadn't looked up because you were late bringing in your wash and made such a lovely picture doing it, I might not be standing here now. *Signorina.*" He took her hand, lifted it to his lips. "*Mille grazie.*"

"*Prego.*" She angled her head. "A romantic story. Come, I'll make you coffee."

"You don't need to trouble."

"Please, if I've saved your life, I have to tend to it." She carried the flowers to the kitchen.

"Ah . . . one of the reasons I was walking by so late was that I'd done some shopping before dinner. I'd just bought a ring, an engagement ring for the woman I love."

"Oh." She sighed, laid the flowers on the counter. She took another long look at him. "Pity for me. Lucky for her. I'll still make you coffee."

"I could use some. *Signorina,* I don't know your name."

"Elana."

"Elana, I hope you'll take this as intended. I think you're the second most beautiful woman in the world."

She laughed and began to fill a vase with his flowers. "Yes, very lucky for her."

David was fed up with pain, fatigue, doctors and the pedestrian jumble that was Venice by the time he made it back to his rooms. He'd already come to the conclusion that he wouldn't be heading back home that evening. He'd be lucky to undress himself and get into bed, much less stay on his feet long enough to pack.

His shoulder was screaming, his legs unsteady, and he cursed as he fought to work the key into the lock left-handed. Still that left hand came up, fisted to fight, when the door jerked open.

"There you are!" Sophia jammed her hands on her hips. "Are you out of your mind? Checking yourself out of the hospital, wandering around Venice by yourself.

Look at you, pale as a sheet. Men are such morons."

"Thanks, thanks a lot. Mind if I come in? I think this is still my room."

"Ty's out hunting for you right now." She took his good arm as she spoke and helped him inside. "We've been worried to death since we went by the hospital and found out you'd left, over doctor's orders."

"Even in Italy they can't seem to make hospital food palatable." Giving in, he sank into a chair. "A man could starve to death in there. Besides, I wasn't expecting anyone this soon. What did you do, beam your-selves here?"

"We left last night. I've been traveling a very long time, on very little sleep, and have spent entirely too long pacing these rooms worried about you. So don't mess with me." She uncapped a bottle, handed him a pill.

"What is this?"

"Pain medication. You left the hospital without your prescription."

"Drugs. You brought me drugs. Will you marry me?"

"Morons," she repeated, and stalked to the mini-fridge for a bottle of water. "David, where have you *been*?"

"Taking a beautiful woman flowers." He sat back, reaching for the bottle, then sighing when Sophia jerked it out of reach. "Come on, don't tease a man about his pharmaceuticals."

"You've been with a woman?"

"Having coffee," he said, "with the woman who saved my life. I took her some flowers to thank her."

Considering, Sophia cocked her head. He looked exhausted, a little sweaty and very romantic with his arm in a sling and the shadows under those deep blue eyes.

"I suppose that's all right. Is she pretty?"

"I told her she was the second most beautiful woman in the world, but I'll happily bump her down to third place if you give me that damn water. Don't make me chew this pill, I'm begging you."

She handed over the bottle, then crouched in front of him. "David, I'm so sorry about this."

"Yeah, me too. The kids are okay, right?"

"They're fine. Worried about you, but reassured enough that Theo's starting to think it's pretty cool that you got shot. Not everybody's father . . ."

"Honey, don't do that to yourself."

"I won't. I'm not." She drew a deep breath. "Anyway, Maddy was kidding about the bullet last night. She said something to you about keeping it? But she's into it now, according to my mother. Wants to study it."

"That's my girl."

"They're great kids, David. Probably comes from having a father who'd think of buying flowers for a woman when he felt like something recently scraped off the sidewalk. Come on, let's get you into bed."

"That's what they all say." The slow, goofy grin he gave her told Sophia the medication was doing the job. "Your mother can't keep her hands off me."

"Good drugs, huh?"

"Really good. Maybe if I could lie down for a minute."

"Sure. Why don't you try it on a large flat surface?" She levered him up.

"Sophie? Pilar's not all twisted up about this, is she?"

"Of course she is. But she'll get untwisted when you get home where she can fuss over you."

"I'm okay, just a little fuzzy in the head now." He chuckled, leaning heavily on her as she led him to the bedroom. And would've sworn he was floating. "Better living through chemistry."

"You bet. Almost there."

"I wanna go home. How'm I gonna pack one-handed?"

"Don't you worry. I'll pack for you."

"You will? Really?" He turned his head to give her a kiss on the cheek and missed by three inches. "Thanks."

"No problem. Here we go. All the way down. Easy. I don't want to hurt— Oh! I'm sorry," she said when he yelped.

"No, it's not the arm. It's—in my pocket. The box. Rolled on it." He groped for it, swore and felt only mildly embarrassed when she reached in to retrieve it herself.

"Buying baubles, are we?" She flipped the box open, blinked. "Oh my."

"I guess I should tell you, I bought it for your mother. Gonna ask her to marry me." He pulled himself up a bit on the pillow and slid straight down again. "Got a problem with that?"

"I might, seeing as you proposed to me five minutes ago, you fickle bastard." A little teary-eyed, she sat on the side of the bed. "It's beautiful, David. She'll love it. She loves you."

"She's everything I've ever wanted. Beautiful, beautiful Pilar. Inside and out. Second chances all around. I'll be careful with her."

"I know you will. I know it. The year's not half over," she said quietly. "Everything's moving so fast. But some things," she added, "some things are moving in the right direction." She leaned over, kissed his cheek. "Close your eyes for a while. Papa."

When Tyler got back, she was making minestrone. It always knocked him back a step to see her working in the kitchen.

"He's here," she said without looking around. "Sleeping."

"I told you he could take care of himself."

"Yes, he did a wonderful job of that by getting shot, didn't he? Stay away from that soup," she added as he leaned over the pot. "It's for David."

"There's enough here for everybody."

"It's not done yet. You should drive up to the vineyard. You can stay at the *castello* tonight. I'm having files messengered over. I can work on the computer here."

"Well, you worked all that out, didn't you?"

"We're not here to sightsee." She walked out of the kitchen.

He took a moment to make sure his temper was on a leash, then followed her into the small office. "Why don't we just have this out?"

"Nothing to have out, Ty. I've got a lot on my mind."

"I know why you didn't want me to come."

"Really?" She booted up the computer. "Could it be that I have a great deal of work to do in a short amount of time?"

"It could be that you're pissed off, betrayed, hurt. Those things slice at you. And when you're hurt, you're vulnerable. Defenses go down. You're afraid I'll get too close. Don't want me too close, do you, Sophia?" He took her chin so that she had no choice but to look at him. "You never did."

"I'd say we've been as close as it gets. And it was my idea."

"Sex is easy. Stand up."

"I'm busy, Ty, and just not in the mood for a quick office fuck."

He hauled her up fast enough, violently enough, to upend her chair. "Don't try to boil everything down to that."

Moving too fast, she thought again. Too many things with too much speed. If she wasn't at the wheel, how could she maintain the right direction?

"I don't want any more than that. Anything else is too much trouble. I said I've got a lot on my mind. And you're hurting me."

"I've never hurt you." He eased his grip. "Maybe that's part of the problem. You ever ask yourself why you end up with the kind of guy you usually end up with?"

"No." She tossed her chin up.

"Older guys. Slick guys. The kind who slide right out the door when you give them the boot. I'm not slick, Sophie, and I won't slide."

"Then you'll just end up with rug burn on your ass."

"Like hell." His smile was lethal as he lifted her onto her toes. "I don't slide, Sophie. I stick. You better take some time and think about that." He let her go, strode to the door. "I'll be back."

Frowning after him, she rubbed her arms. Big son of a bitch had probably left bruises, she thought. "Don't rush on my account."

She started to drop back down in the chair, changed her mind and kicked the desk. The petty gesture made her feel marginally better.

Why didn't the man ever do what she expected him to do? She figured he'd make a show at the public relations deal, then slither away, bored brainless. But he'd stuck, and that thought made her kick the desk again.

They'd acted on some pure, healthy animal lust, she thought and picked up the chair. Had some stupendous sex. She'd expected him to cool off in that area, too. But no.

And what if it was true that she was a little worried because she didn't show any signs of cooling off, either? She was used to certain patterns in her life. Who wasn't? She'd never had any intention of developing serious feelings for Tyler MacMillan.

God, it was infuriating to know she had.

Worse, he'd been exactly and perfectly right in his rundown of her. She was pissed off, she did feel betrayed, she was feeling hurt and vulnerable and she wished Tyler was six thousand miles away in California. Because she wanted, so desperately, for him to be right here. Within easy leaning distance.

She wasn't going to lean. Her family was a mess. The company she'd been raised to run was in trouble. And the man who would very likely become her stepfather was lying in the next room with a bullet hole in his shoulder.

Wasn't that enough to worry about without thinking about her fear of commitment?

Not that she had a fear of commitment. Exactly. And if she did, Sophia decided and sat down again, she'd just have to think about it later.

He slept for two hours and woke feeling like a man who'd been shot, David supposed. But one who'd lived through it. Now that he was sitting up and being fed minestrone, he decided he could start thinking again.

"You've got your color back," Sophia told him.

"Most of my brain, too." Enough to realize she was playing with her soup rather than eating it. "Feel like filling me in?"

"I can tell you what's been done, or what I know. I don't imagine I can fill in all the gaps. They're looking for Donato, not only the police but a private investigator hired by my grandparents. They've interviewed Gina. I'm told she's hysterical and claims not to know anything. I believe her. If she did know something, and Don dumped her and the kids in the middle of this mess, she'd scramble to make trouble for him. They haven't been able to identify the woman he's been seeing. If he's in love with her, as he told me, I imagine Don took her along for company, so to speak."

"Rough on Gina."

"Yeah." She pushed away from the table, tired of pretending to eat. "Yeah. I was mildly fond of Don. Could barely tolerate Gina and felt even less warmly toward her progeny. Now she's deserted by her cheating, stealing, possibly murderous husband. And . . . damn it, I can't feel for her. I just can't."

"It's not impossible she pushed Don financially so he started to dip."

"Even if she did, he's responsible for his own choices, his own actions. Anyway, it's not that. I just can't stand her. Just can't. I'm a horrible person. But enough about me."

She waved that away, picked up a small hunk of bread to nibble and tear at while she paced. "It's assumed that Don had funds stashed, funds he bled from the company. Enough to run on for a while, I suppose, but to be frank with you, he's just not smart enough to stay underground."

"I agree with you. He had help in all of this."

"My father."

"To a point," David said, watching her. "And after he died, maybe Margaret. Their take in this, if they had one, was minimal. Not enough to convince me that either of them had a starring role."

She paused. "You think they were used, rather than users?"

"I think your father might have simply looked the other way. As for Margaret, she was just finding her rhythm."

"Then she was killed," Sophia said quietly. "My father was killed. It could all circle back to this. Somehow."

"Possibly. Still, Don isn't coolheaded enough, isn't long-thinking enough to have set up the kind of scam that slipped by the Giambelli accountants for several years. He was the inside man, with the connections. But somebody drew the blueprint. Maybe the mistress," he added with a shrug.

"Maybe. They'll find him. Either sunning himself by the surf on some tropical beach or floating facedown in it. While they look, we put the pieces back together."

She came back, sat. "Donato could have tampered with or hired someone to tamper with the wine."

"I know."

"I'm having trouble with the reason. Revenge? Why damage the reputation, and thereby the fiscal security, of the company that feeds you? And kill to do it?"

She paused, studied his bandaged arm. "Well, I guess he's shown he has no real problem with that area. He could have done it all." She pressed her fingers to her temples. "Killed my father. Rene's a high-maintenance woman, and Dad needed plenty of money. He knew he was being phased out of Giambelli. He'd burned his bridges with Mama, and I'd let him know he'd set the ones between us smoldering."

"He was responsible for his own choices, Sophia." David used her words. "His own actions."

"I'm resigned to that. Or very nearly. And I can imagine what those choices might have been. He could have pressured Don for more, a bigger cut, whatever. It wouldn't have been out of character for him to have threatened blackmail, in a civilized way, of course. He might have known about the tampering, about poor *Signore* Baptista. Then Margaret because she wanted more, or because he was afraid she'd find out about the embezzlement. You because he realized there was no way out."

"Why steal the paperwork?"

"I don't know, David. He couldn't have been thinking rationally. I suppose he thought you'd be dead, he'd have the files and that would be that. But you weren't dead, and it must have gotten through his head the files weren't going to hang him. He'd already hanged himself. Meanwhile, we have another public relations nightmare to get through. Ever think about ditching us and running back to La Coeur?"

"Nope. Sophia, why don't you try eating that bread instead of shredding it?"

"Yes, Daddy." She winced at the petulant sound in her own voice. "Sorry. Jet lag and general nastiness. Why don't I go deal with that packing for you? Since you insist on leaving rather than staying in my sparkling

company, you've got a very early flight tomorrow."

He was sweating like a pig. The terrace
doors were wide open, and the cool air rising off Lake Como swept into the room. It
didn't stop the sweat. Only turned it to ice.

He'd waited until his lover was asleep before he'd crept out of bed and into the adjoining parlor. He hadn't been able to
perform, but she'd pretended it hadn't mattered. How could a man maintain an erec-
tion at such a time?

Perhaps it didn't matter, really. She'd been
thrilled with the trip, with his sweeping her
away to the elegant resort on the lake,
something he'd promised dozens of times
in the past and had never fulfilled. He'd
made a game of it, given her a ridiculous
amount of cash so she could charge the
room to her card. He wasn't known there,
he told her. He wanted it to stay that way.
What would he do if someone mentioned
seeing him there with a woman other than
his wife?

He thought that had been clever. Very
clever. He had almost believed it a game

himself. Until he'd seen the news report. Seen his own face. He could only be grateful his mistress had been in the salon. He could easily keep her away from newspapers, from the television.

But they couldn't stay. Someone would see him, recognize him.

He needed help, and knew only one source.

His hands shook horribly as he dialed New York. "It's Donato."

"I expected it would be." Jerry glanced at his watch, calculated. Giambelli had the three A.M. sweats, he thought. "You've been a very busy boy, Don."

"They think I shot David Cutter."

"Yes, I know. What were you thinking?"

"I wasn't— I didn't." His English was failing him. "*Dio.* You told me to get out of Venice right away when I told you what Cutter said. I did. I never even went home to my family. I can prove it," he whispered desperately. "I can prove I wasn't in Venice when he was shot."

"Can you? I don't know what good that's going to do you, Don. The story I get is you hired a trigger."

"Hired a . . . what is this? They say I hired

someone to shoot him? For what reason? The damage was done. You said so yourself."

"Here's how I look at it." Oh, it was getting better, Jerry thought. Better, sweeter than he'd ever imagined. "You killed two people, probably three with Avano. David Cutter," he continued, amused by Donato's panicked sputter. "What's one more? You're royally fucked, pal."

"I need help. I have to get out of the country. I have money, but not enough. I need a—a—a passport. A new name, a change of my face."

"That all sounds very reasonable, Don, but why tell me?"

"You can get these things."

"You overestimate my reach and my interest in you. Let's consider this conversation a severing of our business association."

"You can't do this. If they take me, they take you."

"Oh, I don't think so. There's no way to connect me to you. I've made sure of that. In fact, when I hang up the phone, I intend to call the police and tell them you contacted me, that I tried to convince you to turn yourself in. It shouldn't take them too long to trace this call back to you. That's fair warning, given our previous relationship. I'd hit the road and hit it fast."

"None of this would've happened— It was your idea."

"I'm just full of ideas." Serenely, Jerry examined his manicure. "But you'll note, I never killed anyone. Be smart, Don, if you can manage it. Keep running."

He hung up, poured himself a glass of wine, lit a cigar for good measure. Then he picked up the phone and called the police.

CHAPTER TWENTY-FOUR

With a mixture of regret and relief, David watched Venice recede.

"There's no reason for you to haul yourself out of bed and tag along to the airport this way," he told Tyler as the water taxi plowed its way through early-morning traffic. "I don't need a baby-sitter."

"Yeah, I'm getting a lot of that lately." Tyler sipped his coffee and hunched his shoulders against the cool, damp air. "It's starting to piss me off."

"I know how to get on a plane."

"Here's the deal. I put you on at this end, they pick you up on the other end. Live with it."

David took a closer look. Tyler's face was unshaven, his expression foul. For some reason it perked David up. "Rough night?"

"I've had better."

"You going to be able to get back okay? Your Italian's pretty limited, isn't it?"

"Kiss ass."

David laughed, gently shifted his shoulder. "There, I feel better now. Sophia giving you a hard time?"

"She's been giving me a hard time for twenty years. It's stopped spoiling my day."

"If I offer you some advice, are you going to pitch me overboard? Remember, I'm wounded."

"I don't need any advice where Sophia's concerned." Despite himself, Tyler frowned over at David. "What is it?"

"Keep pushing. I don't think anyone's ever kept pushing her. Not the male of the species, anyway. If she doesn't kill you for it, she's yours."

"Thanks, but maybe I don't want her."

David settled back to enjoy the ride. "Oh yeah." He chuckled. "You do."

Yeah, Tyler admitted. He did. Which was why he was risking her considerable wrath. She didn't like anyone touching her things. Didn't like being told what to do, even—no, he corrected as he packed up her little portable office, *especially*—when it was what was best.

"What the hell are you doing?"

He glanced up, and there she was. Still damp from the shower and sending off sparks of temper. "Packing your saddlebags, partner. We're riding out."

"Get your hands off my stuff." She rushed in, snatched back her laptop, pressing it against her like a beloved child. "I'm not going anywhere. I just got here."

"I'm going back to the *castello.* Where I go, you go. Any reason you can't work there?"

"Yes. Several."

"And they are?"

She hugged the computer tighter. "I'll think of them."

"While you're thinking, pack the rest of your gear."

"I just unpacked."

"Then you should remember where everything goes." With this indisputable logic, he strolled out.

It irritated her. He'd caught her off guard and when her brain was still mushy from a sleepless night. It annoyed because she'd been planning on making the drive north and spending at least a day or two working out of the *castello.*

It irked as she recognized how petty it was for her to sulk in silence on the drive.

And it added one more layer of temper that he seemed so sublimely unconcerned.

"We're taking separate bedrooms," she announced. "It's time we put the brakes on that area of our relationship."

"Okay."

She'd already opened her mouth to skewer him and his carelessly agreeable response had it hanging slack. "Okay," she managed. "Fine."

"Okay, fine. You know, we're weeks ahead in the growing season back home. Looks like they're just finishing up the new plantings. Talked to the operator yesterday. He tells me the weather's been good, no frosts for weeks, and they're seeing the beginnings of new bloom. Keeps up warm through the bloom, we'll get a normal set. Oh, that's the conversion of flower to grape."

"I know what a normal set is," she said between her teeth.

"Just making conversation."

He turned off the highway and started the drive through the gentle hills. "It's pretty country. I guess it's been a few years since I made the trip over. Never seen it this early in the spring."

She had, but had nearly forgotten. The quiet green of the hills, the pretty contrast of colorful houses, the long, sleek rows riding the slopes. Fields of sunflowers waiting for summer, and the shadow of far-off mountains that were a faint smudge against a blue sky.

The crowds of Venice, the urbanity of Milan were more than highway miles from here. This was a little heart of Italy that pumped steadily, fed by the earth and rain.

The vineyards here were the root of her destiny, had ordained it when Cezare Giambelli planted his first row. A simple dream, she thought, to grand plan. A humble enterprise to international empire.

Now that it was threatened, was it any wonder she'd use whatever came to hand to defend it?

She saw the winery, the original stone structure and its various additions. Her great-great-grandfather had placed the first stones. Then his son had added more, then his son's daughter. One day, she thought, she might place her own.

On the rise, with the fields spreading out like skirts, the *castello* ruled. Gracious and grand with its colonnaded facade, its sweep of balconies, its high arching windows, it stood as a testament to one man's vision.

He would have fought, she thought. Not just for the ledgers, not only for the profit. For the land. For the name. It struck her here, more deeply than in the fields at home, more than within the walls of her offices and meeting rooms. Here, where one man changed his life, and by doing so forged hers.

Tyler stopped so the car faced the house, its entrance gardens in young bud. "Great place," he said simply and climbed out of the car.

She got out more slowly, breathing in the sight of it as much as she breathed in the lightly scented air. Vines spilled over decorative mosaic walls. An old pear tree bloomed wildly, already shedding some of its petals like snow. She remembered suddenly the taste of the fruit, sweet and simple, and how when she'd been a child the juice trickled down her throat as she walked down the rows with her mother.

"You wanted me to feel this," she stated, and with the hood of the car between them turned to him. "Did you think I didn't?" She pressed a closed fist to her heart. "Did you think I didn't feel it before?"

"Sophie." He leaned on the hood, a friendly, companionable stance. "I think you feel all sorts of things. But I know some of them can get lost in the worry and the, well, the now. Focus too hard on the now, you lose sight of the big picture."

"So you badgered me out of the penthouse in Venice so I'd see the big picture."

"That's part of it. It's blooming time, Sophie. Whatever else is going on, it's blooming time. You don't want to miss it."

He walked back to the trunk, popped it.

"Is that a metaphor?" she asked as she joined him, reaching by to grab her laptop herself.

"Me, I'm just a farmer. What do I know from metaphors?"

"Just a farmer, my ass." She hitched the strap of the laptop on her shoulder, plucked out her briefcase.

"Excuse me, but I'm no longer supposed to think about your ass." He pulled his suitcase out, then studied hers in disgust. "Why is your suitcase twice as big as mine, and three times as heavy? I'm bigger than you."

"Because." She fluttered her lashes. "I'm a girl. I suppose I should apologize for being snotty to you."

"Why?" He hauled her case out. "You wouldn't mean it."

"I'd sort of mean it. Here, let me give you a hand." She reached in, picked up the little tote that held her cosmetics, then slowly strolled away.

Pilar opened the door to the police. At least this time, she thought, she'd been expecting them. "Detective Claremont, Detective Maguire, thanks for coming."

She stepped back in welcome, gestured to the parlor.

"It's a beautiful day for a drive," she continued. "But I know you're both very busy, so I appreciate the time and trouble."

She'd already arranged for coffee and biscotti, and moved to serve the moment the cops were seated. Claremont and Maguire exchanged looks behind her back, then Maguire shrugged.

"What can we do for you, Ms. Giambelli?"

"Reassure me, I hope. Which, I know, isn't your job." She passed out the coffee, impressing Maguire by remembering how each of them took it.

"What reassurances are you looking for?" Claremont asked her.

"I realize you, your department, is in contact with the Italian authorities." Pilar took her seat but didn't touch her coffee. She was jumpy enough. "As you may already know, my mother has some influence over there. Lieutenant DeMarco has been as forthcoming as possible with information. I'm aware that my cousin contacted Jeremy DeMorney yesterday, and that Jerry informed the New York police of the phone call. Jerry was concerned enough to call my stepfather to tell him directly."

"If you're that well informed, I don't know what we can tell you."

"Detective Claremont, this is my family." Pilar let that statement hang. "I know that the authorities were eventually able to trace Don's call to the Lake Como area. I also know he was gone when they arrived to take him into custody. I'm asking you whether, in your opinion, my cousin killed my . . . killed Anthony Avano."

"Ms. Giambelli." Maguire set her coffee aside. "It isn't our function to speculate. We gather evidence."

"We've been connected, you and I, for months. You've looked into my life, into the personal details of it. While I understand that the nature of your business requires a certain professional distance, I'm asking for a little compassion. It's possible Donato is still in Italy. My daughter's in Italy, Detective Maguire. A man I care for, very much, was nearly killed. A man I was married to for half my life is dead. My only child is six thousand miles away. Please don't leave me helpless."

"Ms. Giambelli—"

"Alex," Maguire began before he could finish. "I'm sorry, Pilar, I can't tell you what you want to hear. I just don't have the answer. You know your cousin better than I do. Tell me."

"I've thought of it, of little else, for days," Pilar began. "I wish I could say we were close, that I understood his heart and his mind. But I don't. A week ago I would have said, oh, Donato. He can be foolish, but he has a good nature. Now there's no doubt he was a thief, that he and the man I was married to were in league together stealing from the woman who allowed them to make a living."

She picked up her coffee cup to fill her hands. "Stealing from me. From my daughter. But even then, even knowing this, when I try to picture him sitting in my daughter's living room, facing a man he'd known all those years and killing him. I can't do it. I can't put the gun in Don's hand. I don't know if that's because it doesn't belong there, or because I can't bear to believe it."

"You're worried he'll go after your daughter. There's no reason for him to do that."

"If he's done all these things, isn't the fact that she exists reason enough?"

In her office, behind closed doors, Kris Drake raged. The Giambellis, headed by that little bitch Sophia, were still trying to ruin her. Sicced the cops on her, she thought as she pounded a fist into her palm. It wouldn't do them a damn bit of good. They thought they could weasel it all around, pin her with Tony's murder. Even tie her to the product tampering, to big-shot Cutter's little accident in Venice.

Shaking with fury, she thumbed open a pill bottle, dry-swallowed a tranquilizer.

They couldn't prove she'd been the one to give Sophia that helpful shove on the terrace. They couldn't prove anything. So what if she'd slept with Tony? It wasn't a crime. He'd been good to her, appreciated her, understood her and what she wanted to accomplish.

He'd made her promises. Promises the Giambelli bitches had seen to he couldn't keep. The lousy cheat, she thought with affection. They'd have made a good team if he'd just listened to her. If he hadn't let that whore talk him into marriage.

But it all lay down on the Giambellis, she reminded herself. They'd made certain that slut Rene Foxx knew about her, too. Now her name was being tossed around in the press, and she was getting smirking looks from coworkers.

Just as she had at Giambelli.

She'd come too far, worked too hard to let

those Italian divas ruin her career. Without Jerry's support, she might already be out on her ear. Thank God he was standing up for her, that he understood she was a victim, a target.

She *owed* him the inside information she was passing on. Let Giambelli try to sue her over it. La Coeur would fight for her. Jerry had made that clear from the beginning. She was valued here.

La Coeur was going to give her everything she'd always wanted. Prestige, power, status, money. By the time she was forty, she'd be listed as one of the top one hundred women in business. She'd be the fucking female executive of the year.

And not because someone had handed it to her in the cradle. Because she'd earned it.

But it wasn't enough. Not enough payback for the interrogations by the police, for the smears in the press, for the slights given her when she'd been at Giambelli.

Giambelli was going down, she thought. But there were ways to make the family tremble as it fell.

· · ·

It was a long flight across an ocean, across a continent. He slept through most of it, and when he'd revived himself with coffee, called in for an update. Though he reached Eli and got filled in on what happened in Italy since he'd left, he was disappointed to have missed his kids and Pilar.

He wanted home. And by the time he landed at the Napa airfield, he resented even the short drive that separated him from it.

Then he crossed the tarmac to where he'd been told his driver would be waiting, and found it.

"Dad!"

Theo and Maddy sprang from opposite doors of the limo. The rush of emotion had him dropping his briefcase as he lunged toward them. He grabbed Maddy with his good arm, then had a line of pain spurting through his shoulder as he tried to hug Theo.

"Sorry, bad wing."

When Theo kissed him, surprise and pleasure flustered him. He couldn't remember the last time this boy, this young man, had done so. "God, I'm glad to see you."

He pressed his lips to his daughter's hair, leaned into his son. "So glad to see you."

"Don't ever do that again." Maddy kept her face pressed against his chest. She could smell him, feel his heart beat. "Not ever again."

"That's a deal. Don't cry, baby. Everything's okay now."

Afraid he was going to blubber as well, Theo pulled himself back, cleared his throat. "So, did you bring us something?"

"You've heard of Ferraris?"

"Holy shit, Dad! I mean . . . wow." Theo looked toward the plane as if he expected to see a sleek Italian sports car unloaded.

"Just wondering if you'd heard of them. But I did manage to pick up a couple things that actually fit in my suitcases, which are right over there." David jerked his head.

"Man."

"And if you haul them for me like a good slave, we'll go car shopping this weekend."

Theo's jaw dropped. "No joke?"

"No Ferrari, but no joke."

"Cool! Hey, why'd you wait so long to get shot?"

"Smart-ass. It's good to be home. Let's

get out of here and . . ." He trailed off as he looked back toward the car.

Pilar stood beside it, her hair blowing in the wind. As their eyes met, she began walking toward him. Then she was running.

Maddy watched her, and took her first shaky step toward adulthood by moving aside.

"What's she crying for now?" Theo wanted to know as Pilar clung to his father and sobbed.

"Women wait until it's over before they cry, especially when it's important." Maddy studied the way her father turned his face into Pilar's hair. "This is important."

An hour later, he was on the living room sofa being plied with tea. Maddy sat at his feet, her head resting on his knee while she toyed with the necklace he'd brought her from Venice. Not a little-girl's trinket—she had a good eye for such things—but a real piece of jewelry.

Theo was still wearing the designer sunglasses, and occasionally checked himself out in the mirror to admire his European cool.

"Well, now that you're settled, I've got to get going." Pilar leaned over the back of the sofa, brushed her lips over David's hair. "Welcome home."

He might have been handicapped, but his good arm was quick enough. He reached back, grabbed her hand. "What's your hurry?"

"You've had a long day. We're going to miss you guys over at the main house," she said to Theo and Maddy. "I hope you'll keep coming around."

Maddy rubbed her cheek on David's knee, but her eyes were on Pilar's face. "Dad, didn't you bring Ms. Giambelli a present from Venice?"

"As a matter of fact."

"Well, that's a relief." Pilar gave his uninjured shoulder a squeeze. "You can give it to me tomorrow. You need to rest now."

"I rested for six thousand miles. I can't handle any more tea. Would you mind taking that into the kitchen, give me a minute here with the kids?"

"Sure. I'll give you a call tomorrow, see how you're feeling."

"Don't run off," he said as she began to clear the tray. "Just wait."

He shifted on the couch, tried to put the words he wanted to use together in his mind as she took the tray out. "Listen . . . Theo, you want to sit down a minute."

Obligingly, visions of sports cars dancing in his head, Theo plopped down on the couch. "Can we look at convertibles? It'd be so cool to tool around with the top down. Chicks really dig on that."

"Jeez, Theo." Maddy turned herself around until she was kneeling, her hands resting on David's knees. "You don't score a convertible by telling him you're going to use it to pick up girls. Anyway, shut up so Dad can tell us how he wants to ask Ms. Giambelli to marry him."

David's grin at the first half of her statement faded. "How the hell do you do that?" he demanded. "It's spooky."

"It's just following logic. That's what you wanted to tell us, right?"

"I wanted to talk to you about it. Any point in doing that now?"

"Dad." Theo gave him a manly pat. "It's cool."

"Thank you, Theo. Maddy?"

"When you have a family, you're supposed to stay with them. Sometimes people don't—"

"Maddy—"

"Uh-uh." She shook her head. "She'll stay because she wants to. Maybe sometimes that's better."

A few minutes later, he was walking Pilar home, across the edge of the vineyard. The moon was beginning its slow rise.

"Really, David, I know the way home, and you shouldn't be out in the evening air."

"I need the air and the exercise and a little time with you."

"Maddy and Theo are going to need a lot of reassurance."

"And how about you?"

She laced her fingers with his. "I'm feeling considerably steadier. I didn't mean to fall apart at the airport. I swore I wouldn't."

"You want the truth? I liked it. It's good for the ego for a man to have a woman cry over him."

He brought their joined hands to his lips, kissed her knuckles as they stepped onto the garden path. "Remember that first night? I ran into you out here. Christ, you were gorgeous. And furious. Talking to yourself."

"Sneaking a temper cigarette," she remembered. "And very embarrassed to have been caught at it by the new COO."

"The new, fatally attractive COO."

"Oh yes, that, too."

He stopped, pulled her gently into an embrace. "I wanted to touch you that night. Now I can." He skimmed his fingers down her cheek. "I love you, Pilar."

"David. I love you, too."

"I called you from St. Mark's, talked to you while the music played and the light faded. Remember that?"

"Of course I do. It was the night you were—"

"Ssh." He laid a finger over her lips. "I hung up, and sat there thinking of you. And I knew." He took the box out of his pocket.

She stepped back. Pressure dropped onto her chest, leaden weights of panic. "Oh, David. Wait."

"Don't put me off. Don't be rational, don't be reasonable. Just marry me." He struggled a moment, then let out a frustrated laugh. "Can't open the damn box. Give me a hand, will you?"

Starlight glittered on his hair, bright silver on deep gold. His eyes were dark, direct and full of love and amusement. As her breath jerked, she could smell a hint of night jasmine and early roses. All so perfect, she thought. So perfect it terrified her.

"David, we've both been here before, both know it doesn't always work. You have young children who've already been hurt."

"We haven't been here together, and we both know it takes two people who want to make it work. You won't hurt my kids, because as my odd and wonderful daughter just told me, you won't stay because you're supposed to, but because you want to. And that's better."

Some of the weight lifted. "She said that?"

"Yes. Theo, being a man of few words, just told me it was cool."

Her eyes wanted to blur, but she blinked tears away. It was a time for clear sight. "You're going to buy him a car. He'd tell you anything you want to hear."

"See why I love you? You've got him nailed."

"David, I'm nearly fifty."

He only smiled. "And?"

"And I . . ." Suddenly it felt foolish. "I suppose I just had to say it one more time."

"Okay, you're old. Got it."

"Not that much older than—" She broke off this time, blowing out a breath when he laughed. "I can't think straight."

"Good. Pilar, let me put it this way. Whatever your birth certificate says, whatever you've done or haven't done up to this moment, I love you. I want to spend the rest of my life with you, to share my family with you, and to share yours. So help me open this damn box."

"I'll do it." She expected her fingers to tremble, but they didn't. The pressure in her chest was gone, and a lightness took its place. "It's beautiful." She counted the stones, understood the symbol. "It's perfect."

He took it out of the box, slid it onto her finger. "That's what I thought."

When Pilar went into the house, Eli was brewing tea in the kitchen. "How's David doing?"

"Well, I think. Better than I'd imagined." She ran her thumb over the ring that felt so new, and so right, on her finger. "He just needs to rest."

"Don't we all?" He sighed. "Your mother went up to her office. I'm worried about her, Pilar. She's barely eaten today."

"I'll go up, take her some tea." She rubbed a hand over his back. "We'll all get through this, Eli."

"I know it. I believe it, but I'm starting to wonder at the cost. She's a proud woman. This is damaging that part of her."

Eli's worry wormed its way into Pilar as she carried the tray to her mother's office. It occurred to her that it was the second time in one evening she'd brought tea to someone who probably didn't want it.

Still, it was a gesture meant to soothe, and she would do her best.

The door was open, and Tereza was at her desk. A logbook was open on it.

"Mama." Pilar sailed in. "I wish you wouldn't work so hard. You put the rest of us to shame."

"I'm not in the mood for tea, Pilar, or company."

"Well, I am." She set the tray on the table and began to pour. "David's looking remarkably well. You'll see for yourself tomorrow."

"It shames me, one of my own would do such a thing."

"And of course, you're responsible. As always."

"Who else?"

"The man who shot him. I used to think, used to let myself think, that I was responsible for the shameful things Tony did."

"You weren't blood."

"No, I chose him, and that's worse. But I wasn't responsible for what he did. He was. If there was responsibility on my part, it was for allowing him to do what he did *to* me, and to Sophia." She brought the tea to the desk, set the cup down. "Giambelli is more than wine."

"Hah. You think I need to be told that?"

"I think you need to be told it now. I think you need to be reminded of all it's done, all the good. The millions of dollars to charity the family has dispersed over the years. The countless families who've made their livings through the company. Field workers, winemakers, bottlers, distributors, factory workers, clerks. Every one of them depends on us, and what do we do, Mama."

She sat on the side of the desk, saw with satisfaction that she had her mother's full attention. "We work, worry, and we gamble every season on the weather. We do our best, and we hold faith. That hasn't changed. It never will."

"Was I unfair to him, Pilar. To Donato?"

"You'd question yourself? Now I see why Eli's worried. If I tell you the truth, will you believe me?"

Tired, Tereza got up from the desk, walked to the window. She couldn't see the vineyards in the dark. But she saw them in her mind. "You don't lie. Why wouldn't I believe you?"

"You can be hard. It's frightening sometimes. When I was little, I'd see you striding out along the rows and I'd think you were like a general out of one of my history books. Straight and stern. Then you might stop, study the vine, speak with one of the workers. You always knew their names."

"A good general knows her troops."

"No, Mama, most don't. They're faceless, nameless pawns. Have to be for the general to so ruthlessly send them to battle. You always knew their names, because it always mattered to you who they were. Sophia knows, too. That was your gift to her."

"God, you comfort me."

"I hope I do. You've never been unfair. Not to Donato. Not to anyone. And you aren't responsible for the acts of greed or cruelty or selfishness of those who only see faceless pawns."

"Pilar." Tereza laid her forehead on the window glass, such a rare gesture of fatigue that Pilar rose quickly to go to her. "*Signore* Baptista. He haunts me."

"Mama. He'd never blame you. He'd never blame *La Signora.* And I think he'd be disappointed in you if you blamed yourself."

"I hope you're right. Maybe I will have tea." She turned, touched Pilar's cheek. "You have a good, strong heart. I always knew that. But you have clearer vision than I once gave you credit for."

"Broader, I think. It took me a long time to work up the courage to take the blinders off. It's changed my life."

"For the good. I'll think about what you said."

She started to sit, then saw the flash of

stones on Pilar's finger. Tereza's hand whipped out, snake-fast, and grabbed.

"So, what is this?"

"It's a ring."

"I see it's a ring," Tereza said dryly. "But not, I think, another you've bought to re-place what you once wore there."

"No, I didn't buy it. And it's not a replace-ment. Your tea's getting cold."

"You weren't wearing such a ring when you left to pick up David, to take him home."

"Nothing wrong with your eyesight, even when you're brooding. All right. I just wanted to call Sophia first, to . . . Mama, David asked me to marry him. I said yes."

"I see."

"That's it? That's all you have to say?"

"I'm not finished." Tereza tugged Pilar's hand under the desk light, examined the ring, the stones. She, too, recognized sym-bols. And valued such things.

"He gave you a family to wear on your hand."

"Yes. His and mine. Ours."

"Difficult for a woman with your heart to refuse such a gesture." Her fingers curled tight into Pilar's. "You told me what you thought about something in my heart. Now I'll tell you. Once a man asked you to marry him. You said yes. Ah!" She lifted a finger before Pilar could speak. "You were a girl then. You're a woman now, and you've chosen a better man. *Cara.*" Tereza framed Pilar's face, kissed both her cheeks. "I'm happy for you. Now I have a question."

"All right."

"Why did you send him home, then bring me tea? Why didn't you bring him in to ask my blessing, and Eli's and drink champagne, as is proper? Never mind." She waved it away. "Call him now. Tell them all to come."

"Mama. He's tired, not well."

"Not so tired, and well enough to have mussed your hair and kissed the lipstick off your mouth. Call," she ordered in a tone that cut off any argument. "This needs to be done properly, with family. We'll go down, open our best vintage and call Sophia at the *castello*. I approve of his children," she added, turning to the desk to close her logbook and return it to its place. "The girl will have my mother's seed pearls, and the boy my father's silver cuff links."

"Thank you, Mama."

"You've given me—all of us—something to celebrate. Tell them to hurry up," she ordered, and strode out, straight and slim, calling for Maria to bring the wine.

PART FOUR

The Fruit

Who buys a minute's mirth to wail a week?
Or sells eternity to get a toy?
For one sweet grape who will the vine destroy?

—WILLIAM SHAKESPEARE

CHAPTER TWENTY-FIVE

Tyler was filthy, his back carried a nagging ache dead center, and he had a nasty scrape, poorly bandaged, across the knuckles of his left hand.

He was in heaven.

The mountains here weren't so different from the jagged outcroppings of his own Vacas. Where his soil was gravelly, this was rocky, but still high in the pH that would produce a soft wine.

He could understand why Cezare Giambelli had put the roots of his dream here, had fought his plow through this rocky soil. There was a rough beauty in the shadow of these hills that called to certain men, that challenged them. It wasn't a matter of taming it, Ty reflected, but of accepting it for what it was, and all it could be.

If he had to spend time away from his own vineyards, this was the place to do it. The weather was perfect, the days long and sweet and the *castello* operator more than willing to use the time and skill of another vintner.

And the muscle of one, Tyler thought as he strolled back through the rows toward the great house. He'd spent a good part of his days helping the crew install new pipelines from the reservoir to the young plantings. It was a good system, well planned, and the hours he'd spent with the crew had given him a chance to have a hand in this arm of the company.

And to casually question the men about Donato.

The language barrier wasn't as much of a problem as he'd anticipated. Those who didn't speak English were still willing to talk. With hand signals, facial expressions and the generous assistance of various inter-preters, Tyler got a clear enough picture.

There wasn't a man in the fields who con-sidered Donato Giambelli more than a joke.

Now, with the shadows lengthening toward evening, Tyler considered that opin-ion. He moved from field to garden where hydrangeas bloomed big as basketballs and rivers of pale pink impatiens wound a trail up a slope toward a grotto. Water spewed there in a fountain guarded by Poseidon.

The Italians, he thought, were big on their gods, and their fountains and flowers. Cezare Giambelli had certainly used them all here in this pretty palace tucked in the hills.

A very rich little palace, Tyler mused, setting his hands on his hips as he turned a slow circle. The kind of place an ambitious man with a demanding wife would covet.

Personally, he thought it was a nice place to visit, but how could anyone live there, with all those rooms, all those servants. The grounds alone, with the gardens, the lawns, the trees, the pools and statuary, would require a small army to maintain.

Then again, some men liked to have little armies at their disposal.

He passed between the mosaic walls with their bas-relief figures of well-endowed nymphs, walked down the steps circling yet another pool swimming with lily pads. From there he couldn't see the fields, the heart of the realm. More accurately, he decided, those who worked the fields couldn't see whoever lingered here. He supposed Cezare had wanted some privacy in certain corners of his empire.

What could be seen, beyond the flowers, the sprawl of terraces, was the swimming pool. And rising out of it, like Venus, was Sophia.

She wore a simple black suit that sleeked over her body like the water that streamed from it. Her hair was slicked back, and he could see the glint of something, probably diamonds, fire at her ears. Who but Sophia would swim wearing diamonds?

Watching her, he felt an uncomfortable combination of lust and longing.

She was perfect—elegant, lusty and clever. He wondered, as his belly tightened at the sight of her, if there was anything more unsettling to a man than perfection in a woman.

One thing, he decided, as he started toward her. Loving that woman to the point of stupidity.

"Water must be cold."

She went still, the towel she'd picked up concealing her face for another instant. "It was. I wanted it cold." Casually, she laid the towel aside and took her time slipping into a terry-cloth robe.

She knew he looked at her, studied her in that thorough and patient way of his. She wanted him to. Every time she'd passed a window that day, she looked toward the fields, picked him out among the men.

She'd studied him.

"You're filthy."

"Yeah."

"And pleased to be so," she decided. Filthy, she thought, sweaty. And gorgeous in a primitive way that shouldn't be so damned appealing. "What did you do to your hand?"

"Scraped several layers of skin off, that's all." He turned it over, glancing at it. "I could use a drink."

"Honey, you could use a shower."

"Both. Why don't I clean up? I'll meet you in the center courtyard in an hour."

"Why?"

"We'll open a bottle of wine and tell each other all about our day. Couple things I want to run by you."

"All right, that suits me. I have a few things of my own. Some of us can dig without ending up covered with dirt."

"Wear something pretty," he called after her and grinned when she glanced back over her shoulder. "Just because I'm not touching doesn't mean I don't like to look."

He picked up the damp towel when she went into the house, breathed in the scent of her. Beauty, he thought, was rough on a man. No, he didn't want to tame her any more than he wanted to tame the land. But by God, it was time for acceptance, on both sides.

She was going to give him plenty to look at. Plenty to wish for. She was, after all, an expert at packaging. She wore blue, the color of a lightning strike. The bodice dipped low, to frame the rising swell of her breasts; the skirt rose high to showcase the long, slim length of her thighs. She added a thin chain of diamonds with a single sapphire drop that lay cozily at her cleavage.

She slipped into ice-pick heels, dabbed scent in all the right places and considered herself ready.

And looked at herself in the mirror.

Why was she so unhappy? The turmoil around her was upsetting, it was challenging, but it wasn't the cause of this gut-deep unhappiness. She was all right when she was working, when she was focused on what had to be done and how best to do it. But the minute she stopped, the minute her mind drifted from the immediate task at hand, there it was. This dragging sadness, the flattening of spirit.

And with it, she admitted, an anger she couldn't identify. She didn't even know whom she was angry with anymore. Don, her father, herself. Ty.

What did it matter? She would do what needed to be done and worry about the rest later.

For now she'd have some wine and conversation, fill Tyler in on what she'd learned that day. And have the side benefit of putting him in a sexual spin. All in all, a fine way to spend the evening.

"God. I hate myself," she said aloud. "And I don't know why."

She kept him waiting, but he'd expected that. The fact was it gave him time to put everything in place. The tiled courtyard was shadowy with evening. Candlelight speared up from the table, from torchères lanced in the circling garden, from luminaries tucked among the flowerpots.

He'd chosen the wine, a soft, young white, and had begged some canapés from the kitchen staff. The staff, he'd noted, who were devoted to Sophia and appreciated the flavor of romance.

A good thing, he decided, as they'd been the ones to scurry around setting up the candles, adding little bottles of spring flowers he'd never have thought of, even putting music on low through the outdoor speakers.

He could only hope he lived up to their expectations.

He heard the sound of her heels on the tiles but didn't get up. Sophia, he thought, was too used to men springing to attention in her presence. Or falling at her feet.

"What's all this?"

"The staff got into it." He gestured to the chair beside him. "Ask for a little wine and cheese around here, you get the royal treatment." He looked at her while he took the wine from the bucket. "Look what happens when I ask you to wear something pretty. Comes from being in a castle."

"Not your style, but you seem to be coping."

"Digging a few ditches today put me in a good mood." He handed her a glass, tapped his to it. *"Salute."*

"As I said, I did some digging of my own. The domestic staff's been very informative. I've learned Don made regular visits here, unreported visits. While he never stayed here alone, he rarely came with Gina."

"Ah, the love nest."

"Apparently. The mistress's name is *Signorina* Chezzo. She's young, blonde, silly and likes breakfast in bed. She's been a frequent guest for the last few years. Don insulted the staff by bribing them to keep her visits secret, but since no one here has any love for Gina, they took his money and complied. They'd have been discreet without the money, of course."

"Of course. They tell you about his other visitors?"

"Yes. My father, but we'd already deduced that, and the woman my father came with once, who wasn't Rene. Kris."

Tyler frowned into his wine. "I didn't get that from the vineyard."

"Easier for me to nudge it out of the domestic staff. Anyway, it's hardly fresh news. It's fairly obvious he'd used my apartment for assignations when it suited him. Why not the *castello.*"

"You don't want me to say I'm sorry, but I am."

"No, I don't mind you saying it. I'm sorry, too. It makes it that much more lovely that Mama's found someone who'll make her happy. Someone she can trust. Someone we can all trust. I say that knowing he once worked for Jerry DeMorney at La Coeur, and that Jerry's also been a guest here."

This time Tyler nodded. "I thought so. The crew could only give me a description, and that wasn't clear. They tend to pay more attention to women than men in suits. Ties it together, doesn't it?"

"Does it?" Restless, she rose, sipping her wine as she paced. "Jerry hated my father. A civilized sort of loathing, I'd always assumed."

"Why?"

"You really stay out of the loop, don't you?" she replied. "A few years back my father had a blistering affair with Jerry's wife. They kept it quiet, but it was still fairly common knowledge in the inner circle. She left Jerry, or he kicked her out. That piece of the pie gets served up differently depending on who's cutting it. Jerry and my father had been reasonably friendly before that, and after things chilled. But there was some heat under the chill, which I discovered two years ago when Jerry hit on me."

"He came on to you?"

"Clear and strong. I wasn't interested. He was annoyed and had a number of uncomplimentary things to say about my father, me, my family."

"Damn it, Sophie, why didn't you mention this before?"

"Because he made a point of coming to see me the very next day, full of apologies. He said he'd been more upset about the divorce than he'd realized, felt terrible, and ashamed, at taking it out on me, and that he'd come to terms with the fact that his marriage had been over before all of that happened. And so on and so forth. It was reasonable, understandable. He said all the right things, and I didn't think of it again."

"What do you think of it now?"

"I see a crafty little triangle. My father, Kris, Jerry. Who was using whom, I can't say, but I think Jerry's involved, or at least knows about the embezzlement, maybe even the tampering. It would be profitable for La Coeur, has been, for Giambelli to be fighting consumer unease, public scandal, internal discord. Add Kris in and you have my plans, my campaign, my work tossed in their lap before I have a chance to implement them. Corporate sabotage, spies, that's common enough in business."

"Murder isn't."

"No, that's what makes it personal. He could've killed my father. I can more easily see him with a gun in his hand than I can Donato. I don't know if that's wishful thinking. It's a long way from corporate espionage to cold-blooded murder. But . . ."

"But?"

"Hindsight," she said with a shrug. "Thinking back on the things he said to me when he lost control, and more, how he said them. He was a man on the edge, and one ready to dive off. Within twelve hours, he's apologetic, sheepish, controlled and bringing me dozens of roses. And still, in a mildly civilized way, hitting on me. I should've seen the first incident was truth, and the rest facade. But I didn't. Because I'm used to men hitting on me."

The unhappiness, the dissatisfaction struggled toward the surface again before she tamped it down. "And I use it, when it suits me, to get what I want."

"Why shouldn't you? You're smart enough to use the tools at hand. If a guy lets you, it's his problem. Not yours."

"Well." She laughed a little, sipped her wine. "That's unexpected, coming from a man I've used them on."

"Didn't hurt me any." He stretched out his legs, crossed his ankles and knew she was trying to puzzle him out. Fine and good, Ty thought. Let her do the wondering for a change. "Anyway, the guy fitting DeMorney's description spent time in the winery," Tyler told her. "Had access to the bottling plant. With Donato."

"Ah." How sad, she thought. "So the triangle re-forms into a four-sided box. Jerry links to Don, Don links to my father. Both Jerry and Dad link to Kris. Tidy."

"What do you want to do about it?"

"Tell the police, here and at home. And I want to talk to David. He'll know more about Jerry's work at La Coeur." She plucked a strawberry from a dish, bit into it slowly. "Tomorrow I'm going into Venice.

I've agreed to give some interviews, during which I'll hang Don up by the balls. Disgrace to the family, a betrayal to the loyal employees and customers of Giambelli. Our shock, sorrow and regret, and our unhesitating cooperation with the authorities in the hopes that he will be brought to justice quickly, and spare his innocent and pregnant wife, his young children, his grieving mother any more pain."

She reached for the bottle to fill her glass again. "You think that's cold and hard and just a little nasty."

"No. I think it's hard on you. Hard to be the one saying those things, keeping your head up when you do. You've got your grandmother's spine, Sophie."

"Again, unexpected, but *grazie.* I'm going to have to deal with Gina and my aunt, as well. If they want family support, emotional and the all-important financial, they'll cooperate with the line we're taking publicly."

"What time are we leaving?"

"I don't need you for this."

"Don't be stupid, it doesn't suit you. MacMillan is just as involved, just as vulnerable. It'll play better in the press if we do this as a team. Family, company, partnership. Solidarity."

"We leave at seven, sharp." She sat again. "I'll type up a statement, some responses for you. You can go over them on the way in, so they'll be fresh in your mind should you be questioned."

"Fine. But let's try to keep that the only area where you put words in my mouth."

"It's hard to resist with you taciturn types, but I'll try."

He spread some pâté on a cracker, handed it to her. "So, let's change channels awhile. What do you think about your mother and David?"

"I think it's great."

"Do you?"

"Yes, don't you?"

"As a matter of fact. But it seemed to me you've been a little off since they called with the big announcement."

"I think, under the circumstances, I'm allowed to be a little off. But that's one turn of events I can be pleased about. It feels right. I'm happy for her. For them. He'll be good to her, and for her. And the kids . . . She always wanted more children, now she'll have them. Even if they come half-grown."

"I was half-grown, and she managed to be more of a mother to me than my own."

Her shoulders, tensed when he'd tossed the question at her, relaxed again. "She's too young to be your mother."

"That's what I used to tell her. And she'd say it's not the age, it's the seniority."

"She loves you. A lot."

"Feeling's mutual. What're you smiling at?"

"I don't know. I suppose I've been a little down today, with one thing or another. And I didn't expect to end the day sitting out here with you, actually relaxing. Feels better to have said all that ugly business out loud. Cleanse the palate," she added with another sip of wine. "Then move on to something pleasant we can actually agree on."

"We've got more common ground than either of us might have thought a year ago."

"I suppose we do. And I'm impressed that instead of having this discussion inside, with your boots propped up on a coffee table, we're sitting out here. Wine, candlelight, even music." She leaned back, looked up at the sky. "Stars. It's nice to know you can appreciate an attractive venue, even for a discussion that's primarily business and distressful."

"There's that. But mostly I wanted to set this up out here so we'd have a pretty setting when I seduce you."

She choked on her wine, managed to laugh it off. "Seduce me? Where's that on your agenda?"

"Coming right up." He grazed a fingertip over her thigh, just below the hem of her skirt. "I like your dress."

"Thank you. I put it on to torment you."

"Figured that." His gaze met hers. "Bull's-eye."

She leaned over for the bottle again, filled his glass. When it came to sexual skirmishes, she considered herself a veteran. "We agreed that part of our relationship was over."

"No, you were having a snit about something, and I let you."

"A snit." She dipped a fingertip in her wine, tapped it gently on her tongue. "I don't have snits."

"Yeah, you do. All the time. You've always been a brat. A really sexy brat. And for the last while, you've had some pretty rough times."

The spine he'd just complimented her on stiffened. "I'm not looking for your sympathy, MacMillan, or your tolerance."

"See." His grin, a calculated insult, flashed. "You're working up toward a snit."

Temper snuck up her backbone, added heat to rigidity. "Let me tell you something; if this is your idea of a seduction, it's a wonder you've ever scored with a woman."

"Here's a difference between me and most of the men you know." His legs were stretched out, his voice lazy. "I don't keep score. I don't think about you like a notch on the bedpost, or a trophy."

"Oh yes, Tyler MacMillan. High-minded, moralistic, *reasonable.*"

Again he grinned at her, but this time it was full of fun. "You think that insults me? You're just using temper as a defense. It's your mechanism. Mostly I don't mind much giving it right back to you, but I'm not in the mood for a fight. I want to make love with you, starting out here, slow, and working our way in, upstairs into that great, big bed in your room."

"When I want you in my bed, you'll know it."

"Exactly." Taking his time, he rose, pulled

her to her feet. "You're really stuck on me, aren't you?"

"Stuck?" Her mouth would have fallen open if she hadn't been so busy sneering. "Please. You'll embarrass yourself."

"Crazy about me." He slipped his arms around her, chuckling when she pushed against his chest and arched away. "I saw you today, more than once, standing at the window looking at me."

"I don't know what you're talking about. I might have looked out the window."

"Looking at me," he continued, slowly drawing her against him. "The way I was looking at you. Wanting me." He nuzzled gently at her neck. "The way I was wanting you. And more." His lips brushed her cheek as she turned her head away. "There's more than the wanting between us."

"There's nothing—" She gasped when his hand squeezed the back of her neck, then moaned when his mouth crushed down on hers.

"If it was just this, just the heat, you wouldn't be so scared."

"I'm not afraid of anything."

He eased back. "You don't need to be. I'm not going to hurt you."

She shook her head, but his lips came back to hers again. Gentle now, and unbearably kind. No, she thought as she softened against him. He wouldn't hurt her. But she was bound to hurt him.

"Ty." She started to push at him again, and ended by gripping his shirt. She'd missed this, the warmth he brought into her. Those twisted sensations of risk and safety. "This is a mistake."

"It doesn't feel like one. You know what I think?" He lifted her into his arms. "I think it's stupid to argue, especially when we both know I'm right."

"Stop it. You're not carrying me into the house. The staff will gossip about it for weeks."

"I figure they've already laid bets on how this was going to turn out." He elbowed open a door. "And if you don't want servants talking about what you do, you shouldn't have servants. When we get home, I figure you should move in with me. Then it'll be nobody's business what we do."

"Move—move *in* with you? Have you lost your mind? Put me down, Ty. I'm not going to be carried up the steps like a heroine in a romance novel."

"You don't like it? Okay, we'll do it this way." He shifted, hauling her up and over his shoulder. "Better?"

"This isn't funny."

"Baby." He patted her butt. "It is from where I'm standing. Anyway, there's plenty of room for your stuff at my place. Got three extra bedrooms with empty closets. That ought to be enough for your clothes."

"I'm not moving in with you."

"Yes, you are." He walked into her bedroom, kicked the door shut behind him. He had to give the staff credit. He hadn't seen one of them on the trip upstairs. Hadn't heard a peep. He gave Sophia full marks, too. She wasn't kicking and screaming. Too much class, he supposed as, still carrying her, he lit the candles scattered through the room.

"Tyler, I can recommend a good therapist. There's absolutely no shame in seeking help for mental instability."

"I'll keep it in mind. God knows I haven't been clear in the head since I got tangled up with you. We can make an appointment together, after you move in."

"I'm not moving in with you."

"Yes, you are." He let her slide down until she was back on her feet and facing him. "Because it's what I want."

"If you think I give a single damn about what you want right now—"

"Because," he continued, skimming his fingers over her cheek, "I'm as crazy about you as you are about me. That shut you up, didn't it? It's time, Sophia, we started dealing with it instead of dancing around it."

"I'm sorry." Her voice shook. "I don't want this."

"I'm sorry you don't want it, too. Because it's the way it is. Look at me." He framed her face with his hands. "I wasn't looking for this, either. But it's been there, for a long time. Let's see where it takes us."

He lowered his mouth to hers. "Just us."

Just him, she thought. She wanted to believe it, wanted to trust all these soft and liquid feelings that were flowing into her. To love someone and have it be strong and true. To be capable of that. Worthy of it.

She wanted to believe it.

To be loved by an honest man, one who would make promises and keep them. Who would care for her, even when she didn't deserve it.

That was a miracle.

She wanted to believe in miracles.

His mouth was warm and firm on hers, patiently stirring desire. The steady, irresistible rise of passion was a relief. This she could understand, this she could trust. And this, she thought as she wrapped her arms around him, she could give.

She went with him willingly when he lowered her to the bed.

He kept the heat banked. This time there would be no mistaking what happened between them was an act of love. Generous, selfless and sweet. He linked his fingers with hers as he deepened the kiss, as he tasted the beginning of surrender on her lips.

It was meant to be there, in the old bed in the *castello* where it had all begun a century before. There, another beginning, another promise. Another dream. As he looked down at her, he knew it.

"Blooming time," he said quietly. "Ours."

"Always the farmer," she said with a smile as she unbuttoned his shirt. But her hand trembled, went limp when he took it in his, pressed it to his lips.

"Ours," he repeated.

He undressed her slowly, watched the candlelight shimmer over her skin, listened to the way her breath caught, released, caught again when he touched her. Did she know the barriers between them were crumbling? He did; he felt them fall when she quivered. And knew the precise moment her body yielded to her heart.

They seemed to sink into the bed like lovers in a pool. She gave herself to the sensations of those hard palms sliding over her, that persuasive mouth roaming where it pleased.

She reached for him, rose to him. And answered. The quiet beauty of knowing he would be there, that he would hold on even as she did, poured through her like wine in the blood.

When he pressed his lips to her heart, she wanted to weep.

No one else, he thought as he lost himself in her. No one else had ever unlocked him this way. He felt her rise under him, an arch of welcome. He heard her broken moan merge with his as she crested. And knew when he looked down at her that she was steeped in what they gave each other.

A blend, rare and perfect, finally shared.

Once again he linked his hands with hers, holding tight now. "Take me in, Sophie." His body shook, control ruthlessly held, as he slipped inside her. "Take me. I love you."

Her breath caught again as sensation swarmed into her, tore at her heart. Fear and joy bursting. "Ty. Don't."

He laid his lips on hers, the kiss gentle. Devastating. "I love you. Take me." He kept his eyes open and on hers, watched tears swim and shimmer. "Tell me."

"Ty." Her heart quaked, seemed to spill over. Then her fingers curled strong to his. "Ty," she said again. *"Ti amo."*

She met his mouth with hers now, clung, and let him sweep her away.

"Say it again." Drifting, Ty ran a fingertip up and down her spine. "In Italian like that."

She shook her head, her only sign that she heard the request, and kept her cheek pressed against his heart.

"I like the way it sounds. I want to hear it again."

"Ty—"

"There's no point trying to take it back."

He continued his lazy stroke, and his voice was clear and calm. "You won't get away with it."

"People say all kinds of things in the heat of passion." She scooted away, and nearly made it off the bed.

"Heat of passion? You start using clichés like that, I know you're fumbling." In one easy move, he flipped her back on the bed. "Say it again. It's not as hard the second time. Believe me."

"I want you to listen to me." She pushed herself up, dragged at the bedcovers. For the first time she could remember, her own nudity left her feeling uneasy and exposed. "Whatever I might be feeling at the moment doesn't mean . . . God! I hate when you look at me like that. Amused patience. It's infuriating. It's insulting."

"And you're trying to change the subject. I'm not going to fight with you, Sophia. Not about this. Just tell me again."

"Don't you understand?" She bunched her hands into fists. "I know what I'm capable of. I know my strengths and my weaknesses. I'll just screw this up."

"No, you won't. I won't let you."

She raked a hand through her hair. "You underestimate me, MacMillan."

"No. You underestimate yourself."

It was that, she realized as she slowly lowered her hand again. That simple and quiet faith in her, more than she had in herself, that left her helpless. "No one else would ever say that to me. You're the only one who'd say that to me. Maybe that's why I'm . . ."

His nerves were starting to stretch, but he gave her ankle an easy pat. "Keep going. Almost there."

"That's something else. You push. Nobody else ever pushed."

"None of the others loved you. You're stalling, Sophie. Chicken."

She narrowed her eyes. His were that calm lake blue, she thought. Just a little amused, just a little . . . No, she realized with a hard jolt. Not smug and amused. There was strain behind them, and nerves. And still he waited for her to give him what he needed.

"You're not the first man I've been with," she burst out.

"Stop the presses." He leaned forward, caught her chin in his hand. The patience on his face was beginning to shift toward temper. It delighted her. "But here's a flash for you. I'm damn well going to be the last."

And that, she decided, was exactly right. "Okay, Ty, here it is. I've never said it to another man. Never had to be careful not to because it was never an issue. I'm probably not doing you any favors by saying it to you, but you'll have to deal with it now. I love you."

"There, that wasn't so hard." He ran his hands over her shoulders as relief pumped into him. "But you didn't say it in Italian. It sounds really great in Italian."

"You idiot. *Ti amo.*" She laughed, launching herself at him.

CHAPTER TWENTY-SIX

Lieutenant DeMarco smoothed a fingertip along his moustache. "I appreciate your coming in, *signorina.* The information you and *Signore* MacMillan bring me is interesting. It will be looked into."

"What exactly does that mean? Looked into. I'm telling you my cousin used the *castello* for assignations with his mistress, for clandestine meetings with a competitor and with an employee I personally terminated."

"None of which is illegal." DeMarco spread his hands. "Interesting, even suspicious, which is why I will look into it. However, the meetings were hardly clandestine, as many employees at the *castello* and at the vineyards were aware of them."

"They weren't aware of Jeremy DeMorney's identity, or his connection with La Coeur." Tyler put a hand over Sophia's as he spoke. If he wasn't mistaken she was about to shoot off her chair and directly through the roof. "What this implies is that DeMorney was involved in the sabotage that's resulted in several deaths. Possibly others at La Coeur are involved, or at least aware."

Since she couldn't shove away Ty's hand, Sophia fisted her own. "Jerry is the grand-nephew of La Coeur's current president. He's an ambitious and intelligent man who had a grudge against my father. And very likely against my family. Every market share Giambelli's lost during these crises has been profit in La Coeur's pockets. As a family member, that's profit in Jerry's pocket, and personal satisfaction along with it."

DeMarco heard her out. "And I have no doubt that when presented with this information the proper authorities will want to question this Jeremy DeMorney. Obviously, as he's an American citizen residing in New York, I'm unable to do so. At this point, my main concern is the apprehension of Donato Giambelli."

"Who's eluded you for nearly a week," Sophia pointed out.

"We learned the identity of his traveling companion, or I should say the woman we believe to be traveling with him, only yesterday. *Signorina* Chezzo's credit card has several extensive charges. I am even now waiting for further information."

"Of course he used her credit card," Sophia said impatiently. "He's an idiot, but he's not a fool. He's certainly smart enough to cover his tracks there and to get out of Italy the quickest and easiest way. Over the border into Switzerland, I'd imagine. He contacted Jerry from the Como district. The Swiss border is minutes away. The guards there barely look at a passport."

"We're aware of this, and the Swiss authorities are assisting us. It's only a matter of time."

"Time is a valuable commodity. My family has suffered personally, emotionally and financially for months. Until Donato is apprehended and questioned, until we have the answers and assurances that no other sabotage is planned, we can't end it. My father was part of this, how much a part I don't yet know. Can you understand how this feels?"

"Yes, I believe I understand, *signorina*."

"My father is dead. I need to know who killed him, and why. If I have to hunt down Don myself, if I have to confront Jerry DeMorney personally and take on the entire La Coeur organization to get those answers, believe me, that's what I'll do."

"You're impatient."

"On the contrary, I've been remarkably patient." She got to her feet. "I need results."

He held up a finger as the phone rang. His expression changed slightly as he listened to the stream of information. When he hung up, he folded his hands. "You have your results. The Swiss police have just taken your cousin into custody."

It was an education to watch her in action. Tyler didn't say a word, wasn't sure he'd have gotten one in if he'd tried. She'd peppered DeMarco with demands, questions, scribbling down information in her notebook. When she'd marched out of DeMarco's office, Tyler had to lengthen his considerable stride just to keep up. She moved like a rocket with a cell phone attached to her ear.

He couldn't understand half of what she was saying anyway. She started in Italian, switched to French somewhere along the line and went back to Italian with a few short orders in English. She mowed her way through the tourists thronging the narrow streets, clipped busily over the pretty bridges and beelined across squares. And never stopped talking, never stopped moving, even when she had to cock the little phone between her ear and shoulder to drag out her Filofax and make more notes.

She passed shop windows without so much as a glance. He figured if she breezed by Armani without it putting a hitch in her stride, nothing was going to stop her.

At the main dock she jumped on a water taxi, and he caught the word for "airport" in her brisk stream of Italian. He figured it was a good thing he had his passport in his pocket, or he'd be left in her dust.

She didn't sit even then, but braced herself on the rail behind the driver and made still more calls. Fascinated, he wedged himself in on the other side and watched her. The wind teased her short cap of hair, the sun bounced off the dark lenses of her glasses. Venice washed by behind her, an ancient and exotic backdrop to a contemporary woman with places to go and people to see.

Small wonder he was crazy about her.

Tyler folded his arms, tipped back his head and let himself enjoy the last breezes of the city built on water. If he knew his woman, and he did, they were going to be spending some time in the Alps.

"Tyler!" He tuned back in when she snapped her fingers at him. "How much money do you have? Cash?"

"On me? I don't know. Couple hundred thousand in lire, maybe a hundred American."

"Good." She swung toward the stairs as the boat docked. "Pay the driver."

"Yes, ma'am."

She cut her way through the airport just as she had through the city streets. Per her orders, the corporate jet was waiting, fueled and cleared for the flight. Less than an hour after she'd received the news her cousin was in custody, she was strapped in for takeoff. And for the first time in that hour, she turned off her phone, shut her eyes and took a breath.

"Sophia?"

"*Che?* What?"

"You kick ass."

She opened her eyes again, and her smile came slow and sharp. "Damn straight."

He'd been taken from a tiny resort nestled in the mountains north of Chur and near the Austrian border. The farthest he'd thought ahead was perhaps getting over that border, or alternatively into Liechtenstein. The goal had been merely to put as many countries between him and Italy as possible.

But while looking north, Donato had failed to look at his own ground. His mistress wasn't as dim as he'd supposed, nor half as loyal. She'd seen a news report on the television while lounging in a bubble bath and had found his cache of cash in his traveling case.

She'd taken the money, booked a flight, placed a single anonymous call. And had been on her way, considerably richer, to the French Riviera when the efficient Swiss police had broken into Donato's room and plucked him out from under the bed-covers.

Now he was in a Swiss cell, bemoaning his fate and cursing all women as the bane of his existence.

He had no money to hire a lawyer and desperately needed one to fight extradition for as long as possible. For as long as it took, for God's sake, for him to think his way clear.

He would throw himself on the mercy of *La Signora.* He would escape and run to Bulgaria. He would convince the authorities he'd done nothing more than run off with his mistress.

He would rot in prison for the rest of his life.

With his thoughts circling this same loop, around and around, he looked up to see a guard on the other side of the bars. Informed he had a visitor, he got shakily to his feet. At least the Swiss had had the decency to let him dress, though he'd been allowed no tie, no belt, not even the laces in his Guccis.

He smoothed his hair with his hands as he was taken to the visiting area. He didn't care who'd come to see him, as long as someone would listen.

When he saw Sophia on the other side of the glass, his spirits soared. Family, he thought. Blood would listen to blood.

"Sophia! *Grazie a Dio.*" He fell into his chair, fumbled with the phone.

She let him ramble, the panic, the pleas, the denials, the despair. And the longer he did so, the thicker the shell grew around her heart.

"*Stai zitto.*"

He did indeed shut up at her quiet order. He must have seen that she stood for her grandmother now, and that her expression was cold and merciless.

"I'm not interested in excuses, Donato. I'm not here to listen to your pitiful claims that it's all been a horrible mistake. Don't ask for my help. I'm going to ask the questions, you'll give the answers. Then I'll decide what will be done. Is that clear?"

"Sophia, you have to listen—"

"No, I don't. I don't have to do anything. I can get up, walk away. You, on the other hand, can't. Did you kill my father?"

"No. *In nome di Dio!* You can't believe that."

"Under the circumstances, I find it easy to believe. You stole from the family."

He started to deny it and, reading his answer in his eyes, Sophia set the phone down, began to get to her feet. Panicked, Don slapped his palm on the glass, shouted. When the guards started forward, she coolly gestured them back, picked up the phone again.

"You were about to say?"

"Yes. Yes, I stole. I was wrong, I was stupid. Gina, she makes me crazy. She nags for more. More babies, more money, more things. I took money. I thought, what did it matter? Please, Sophia, *cara,* you won't let them keep me in prison over money."

"Think again. I would, yes. My grandmother might not. But it wasn't just money. You tampered with the wine. You killed an old, innocent man. For money, Don? How much was he worth to you?"

"It was a mistake, an accident. I swear it. It was only supposed to make him a little sick. He knew— He saw . . . I made a mistake." His hand shook as he rubbed it over his face.

"Knew what, Donato. Saw what?"

"In the vineyard. My lover. He disapproved, and might have spoken of it to *Zia Tereza*."

"If you continue to play me for a fool, I'll walk away and leave you to rot. Believe it. The truth, Don. All of it."

"It was a mistake, I swear it. I listened to poor advice. I was misled." Desperate, he dragged at his already loosened collar. His throat was closing, choking him. "I was to be paid, you see, and I needed money. If the company had some trouble, if there was bad press, lawsuits, I would be paid more. Baptista, he saw . . . people I spoke with. Sophia, please. I was angry, very angry. I've worked hard. My whole life. *La Signora* never valued me. A man has his pride. I wanted her to value me."

"And killing an innocent old man, attacking her reputation was the answer?"

"The first, that was an accident. And it was the company's reputation—"

"It's one in the same. How could you not know that?"

"I thought, if there's trouble, then I'll help fix it, and she'll see."

"And you'd get paid from both ends," Sophia finished. "It didn't work with *Signore* Baptista. He didn't get sick, he died. And they buried him believing his heart had just given out at last. How frustrating for you. How annoying. Then almost immediately *Nonna* reorganized the company."

"Yes, yes, and does she reward me for my years of service? No." Sincerely outraged, he thumped a fist on the counter. "She brings in an outsider, she promotes an American woman who then can question me."

"So you killed Margaret and tried to kill David."

"No, no. Margaret. An accident. I was desperate. She was looking at the accounts, at the invoices. I needed—wanted—only to delay her, a short time. How was I to know she would drink so much of the wine? A glass, even two, would only have made her ill."

"It was inconsiderate of her to spoil things. You sent bottles, poisoned wine, out on the market. You risked lives."

"I had no choice. No choice. You must believe me."

"Did my father know? About the wine? The tampering?"

"No. No, it was just a game to Tony. The business was his game. He didn't know about the dummy account because he never took time to look. He didn't know Baptista because he knew no one who worked in the fields. It wasn't his life. Sophia, it was my life."

She sat back briefly. Her father had been weak, a sad excuse for a husband, even for a man. But he'd had no part in murder, or in sabotage. It was, at least, some small comfort.

"You brought DeMorney to the *castello,* to the winery. You took money from him, didn't you? He paid you to betray your own blood."

"Listen to me." His voice dropped to a whisper. "Stay away from DeMorney. He's a dangerous man. You have to believe me. Whatever I've done, you have to believe I'd never want to hurt you. He'll stop at nothing."

"Murder? My father?"

"I don't know. I swear to you on my life, Sophia. I don't know. He wants to ruin the family. He used me for that. Listen to me," he repeated, laying his palm on the glass again. "I took money, I stole. I did what he told me to do to the wine. I was misled. Now he'll let me hang for it. I'm begging you to help me. I'm begging you to stay away from him. When I knew Cutter would expose me, I ran. I only ran, Sophia, I swear it to you. They're saying I hired someone, some thug from the streets to shoot him and steal the papers. It's a lie. Why would I? It was over already for me. It was done."

The twists of lies and truths had to be unknotted. It would take a cold and steady hand to do so, she thought. Even now, after all she knew of him, part of her wanted to reach out. She couldn't allow it. "You want my help, Don? Tell me everything you know about Jerry DeMorney. Everything. If I'm satisfied, I'll see to it Giambelli arranges for your legal needs, and that your children are cared for and protected."

When Sophia came back, Tyler thought she looked exhausted. Wilted. Before he could speak, she touched a hand to his. "Don't ask me yet. I'm going to arrange a conference call on the flight so I only have to say it all once."

"Okay. Let's try this instead." He pulled her in, held her.

"Thanks. Can you do without the things you took to the *castello* for a few days? I'll have them packed up and sent. We need to go home, Ty. I need to be home."

"Best news I've had in days." He kissed the top of her head. "Let's go."

"Do you believe him?"

Tyler waited until she'd completed the call, until all had been said. She was up now, pacing the cabin, sipping her third cup of coffee since takeoff.

"I believe he's a stupid man with a weak and selfish core. I believe he's convinced himself that *Signore* Baptista and Margaret were unfortunate accidents. He let himself be used for money, and for ego, by someone a great deal more clever. Now he's sorry, but sorriest for being caught. But I believe, absolutely, that he's afraid of Jerry. I don't think Don killed my father. I don't think he tried to kill David."

"You're looking at DeMorney."

"Who else? Proving it won't be so easy. Tying Jerry to any of this and making it hold won't be so easy."

Tyler rose, took the coffee from her hand. "You're revving yourself too high. Turn it off awhile."

"Can't. Who else, Ty? I could see you didn't agree when we were on the call. I can see it now."

"I'm not sure what I think just yet. I take longer than you to process things. But I can't figure out why your father'd have just met in your apartment with Jerry, or why after all this time, all this planning, Jerry would kill him. Would risk that, would bother. Doesn't ring for me. But I'm not a cop, and neither are you."

"They'll have to question him. Even on the word of someone like Donato, they'll have to. He'll slither and he'll slide, but . . ." She stopped, took a breath. "We'll be stopping in New York to refuel."

"Three countries in one day."

"Welcome to my world."

"You won't get anything out of him, Sophie."

"Just the chance to spit in his face."

"Yeah, there's that." And he'd get a charge out of watching her do it. "You know how to track him down? It's a big city."

She sat again and pulled out her Filofax. "Making connections is one of my best things. Thanks."

"Hey, I'm just along for the ride."

"Let me tell you something that didn't escape my notice today."

"Sophie, nothing does."

"Exactly. I was plowing my way through this mess, making calls, arrangements, pushing all the buttons, you never interrupted me, never asked me any questions, never patted my head and told me to step back so you could handle it."

"I don't happen to speak three languages."

"That wasn't it. It didn't occur to you to flex your muscles and take over, to show me you could handle things for me. Just like it didn't dent your ego that I knew what I had to do and how to do it. You don't have to flex your muscles because you know they're there. And so do I."

"Maybe I just like watching you flex yours."

She got up just to crawl into his lap, curl there. "All my life I've made certain to hook myself up with weak men. All show, no substance." With her head on his shoulder she could finally rest. "Now look what I've done."

. . .

Jerry made several calls himself. From pay phones. He didn't consider Donato much of a problem, but more of an inconvenience. And even that would be seen to before long. He'd accomplished what he'd set out to accomplish.

Giambelli was fighting its way out of yet another crisis, the family itself was in turmoil, consumer trust was diving toward an all-time low. And he was reaping the rewards, personally, professionally, financially.

Nothing he'd done—nothing he'd done that could be proved—had been illegal. He'd simply done his job, as an aggressive businessman would, and had seized opportunities that had come his way.

He was more amused than annoyed when lobby security announced he had visitors. Prepared to be entertained, he cleared them, then turned to his companion. "We have company. An old friend of yours."

"Jerry, we've got two solid hours of work to get through tonight." Kris uncurled her legs from the couch. "Who is it?"

"Your former boss. Why don't we open a bottle of the Pouilly-Fuissé? The '96."

"Sophia." Kris surged to her feet. "Here? Why?"

"We're about to find out," he said as the buzzer sounded. "Be a good girl, won't you? Fetch the wine."

He strolled to the door. "Isn't this a lovely surprise. I had no idea you were in town." He actually leaned forward to kiss Sophia's cheek. She was quick, but Tyler was quicker. His hand rammed sharply into Jerry's chest.

"Let's not start out being stupid," he advised.

"Sorry." Holding up both hands, Jerry stepped back. "Didn't realize things had changed between you. Come in. I was just about to open some wine. You both know Kris."

"Yes. How cozy," Sophia began. "We'll pass on the wine, thanks. We won't be here long. You appear to be enjoying all your new employee benefits, Kris."

"I much prefer the style of my new boss to the style of my old one."

"I'm sure you're a lot more friendly with your associates."

"Ladies, please," Jerry pleaded as he closed the door. "We're all pros here. And we know executives switch companies every day. That's business. I hope you're not here to scold me for snatching one of yours. After all, Giambelli wooed one of our best away just last year. How is David, by the way? I heard he had a close call in Venice recently."

"He's doing very well. Fortunately for Kris, Giambelli has a firm policy against trying to kill former employees."

"But apparently not a strong enough one against internal wars. I was shocked to hear about Donato." Jerry lowered to the arm of a sofa. "Absolutely shocked."

"We're not wired, DeMorney." Tyler ran an arm down Sophia's arm to calm her. "So you can save the act. We paid Don a visit before we left Europe. He had some interesting things to say about you. I don't think the police will be far behind us."

"Really?" He'd been fast, Jerry thought, but apparently not quite fast enough. "I have more faith in our system than to believe the police, or anyone else for that matter, will put much credence in the ravings of a man who'd steal from his own family. This is a difficult time for you, Sophia." He stood again. "If there's anything I can do—"

"You could go to hell, but I'm not sure they'd have you. You should've been more careful," she continued. "Both of you," she added with a nod toward Kris. "Spending time at the *castello,* the winery, the bottling plant."

"It's not illegal." Jerry shrugged. "In fact, it's not an uncommon practice for friendly competitors to visit each other that way. We were invited, after all. You, and any member of your family, are always welcome at any La Coeur operation."

"You used Donato."

"Guilty." Jerry spread his hands. "But again, nothing illegal about it. He approached me. I'm afraid he's been unhappy at Giambelli for quite some time. We discussed the possibility of him coming aboard at La Coeur."

"You told him to tamper with the wine. Told him how to do it."

"That's ridiculous and insulting. Be careful, Sophia. I understand you're upset, but trying to deflect your family's troubles onto me and mine isn't the answer."

"Here's how it was." Tyler had spent the hours in the air working it out in his head. Now he sat, made himself comfortable. "You wanted to cause trouble, serious trouble. Avano'd bounced on your wife.

Hard for a man to take that, even if the other guy's busy bouncing on every woman he can find. But trouble just slides right off Avano. Nothing sticks. He keeps his wife just where he wants her, which is out of his way but close enough to lock in his position with her family organization. That's a pisser for you."

"My ex-wife is none of your business, MacMillan."

"But she was yours, and so was Avano. Goddamn Giambellis gave the son of a bitch free rein. Now there ought to be a way to take that rein and hang all of them. Maybe you know Avano's skimming, maybe you don't. But you know enough to look at Don. He cheats on his wife, too, and he's pretty friendly with Avano. Don's a friendly guy. Wouldn't be hard for you to get close to him, hint that La Coeur would love to have him on the team. More money, more power. You'd play into his complaints, his ego, his needs. You find out about the dummy account, and now you've got something on him."

"You're fishing, MacMillan, and fishing bores me."

"It gets better. Avano's snuggling up to

Sophia's second in command. Isn't that interesting? Dangle a carrot under her nose and you get lots of inside information. Did he offer you money, Kris? Or just a corner office with a nice, shiny brass plaque?"

"I don't know what you're talking about." But she took a quick and careful step away from Jerry. "My relationship with Tony had nothing to do with my position at La Coeur."

"You keep thinking that," Ty said casually. "Meanwhile, DeMorney, you keep playing on Don, nudging him along. Deeper, deeper. He's got some money problems. Who doesn't? You lend him a little, just a friendly loan. And you string him along about the move to La Coeur. What else can he bring to the table? Inside information? Not good enough."

"My company doesn't require inside information."

"It's not your company." Ty inclined his head when he saw the fury spurt out of Jerry's eyes. "You just want it to be. You talk to Don about the tampering, just a few bottles. Show him what he should do, could do, then how he'd be able to step in and be a hero when the shit hits. Just like you'll be a hero at La Coeur because you're primed and ready to move when Giambelli takes the hit. Nobody's going to get really hurt, or that's what you tell that poor sap Don. But it'd shake up the company good."

"Pitiful." Beneath his precisely tailored shirt, a line of sweat ran down Jerry's back. "No one's going to believe this fairy tale."

"Oh, the police might be pretty entertained. Let's just finish it out," Ty suggested. "It goes wrong for Don, and an old man dies. No skin off your ass, of course. You've got Don by the short hairs now. He talks, he's up for murder. Meanwhile, Giambelli's moving right along. Avano's still sliding. And one of your own moves to the enemy camp."

"We've managed to bump along without the help of David Cutter." He wanted to pour wine, carelessly, but realized his hand was shaking. "And you've taken up enough of my time."

"Nearly done. You'd already started a second front, courting one of the brains in promotion, feeding her dissatisfaction, her jealousies. When the crisis hits, and you're going to make sure it does, the Giambelli spin is going to be off balance."

"I had nothing to do with this." Kris

grabbed her briefcase, began stuffing papers inside. "I don't know anything about this."

"Maybe not. Your style's more the backstabbing variety."

"I'm not interested in what you think or anything you have to say. I'm leaving."

She bolted to the door, slammed it behind her.

"Wouldn't count on too much company loyalty in that one," Ty commented. "You underestimated Sophia, DeMorney. Just like you overestimated yourself. You got your crisis, you spilled your blood, but it hasn't been enough for you. You want more, and that's what's going to choke you. Going after Cutter was stupid. Legal had copies of the paperwork, and Don knew it."

Kris didn't worry him. She could be sacrificed, like any pawn, if necessary. "Obviously Donato panicked. A man who's killed once doesn't scruple to kill again."

"That's right. Old Don, he doesn't figure he killed anybody. The wine did. And he was too busy running to worry about David. I wonder who clued you in to the meet in Venice, and Don's scramble to get the money out of his private account. The cops'll work on that angle, and they'll start tying you in. You're going to have a lot of questions to answer, and before too much longer you'll have your own public relations nightmare. La Coeur's going to prune you off, pal, just like they would a diseased cane."

Ty got to his feet. "You figure you've covered yourself, every inch. Nobody ever does. And when Don drowns, he's going to drag you under with him. Personally, I'm going to enjoy seeing you go under for the third time. I didn't care much for Avano. He was a selfish idiot who didn't appreciate what he had. Don falls in the same category, at a slightly higher level. But you, you're a dickless coward who pays people to do the dirty work you haven't got the guts for. Doesn't surprise me your wife went hunting elsewhere for someone with balls."

He stood where he was, hands at his sides as Jerry lunged. And he took the fist on the jaw without making a move to block it. He even allowed Jerry to knock him back against the door.

"Did you see that?" Tyler asked Sophia calmly. "He punched me, now he's laying hands on me. I'm going to ask him politely to stop. You hear that, DeMorney? I'm asking you, politely, to stop."

"Fuck you." Jerry bunched a fist and would have rammed it into Tyler's belly if it hadn't been stopped an inch from its mark. If it hadn't suddenly been crushed and the pain radiating up his arm hadn't dropped him breathless to his knees.

"You're going to want to have that hand X-rayed," Tyler told him as he gave him a light shove that sent Jerry the rest of the way to the floor in a curl of agony. "I think I heard a bone snap. Ready, Sophie?"

"Ah . . . yes." Slightly dazed, she let Tyler draw her out the door, toward the elevator. Inside, she let out the breath she hadn't been aware of holding. "I'd like to point something out."

"Go ahead." He punched lobby level, leaned back.

"I didn't interrupt, or ask any questions. I wasn't compelled to flex my muscles," she continued as Tyler's mouth twitched. "Or prove to you I could handle things. I just want to mention all that."

"Got it. You've got your areas of expertise and I've got mine." He slipped an arm around her shoulders. "Now let's go home."

CHAPTER TWENTY-SEVEN

"And then . .". *Sophia* dug into the leftover lasagna while the family gathered in the villa's kitchen. "Ty had his hand—I didn't even see it happen. It was like lightning. This big hand covering Jerry's pretty manicured one, which was probably still stinging from rapping against Ty's jaw. Anyway"— she gulped down some wine—"all of a sudden Jerry's gone white and his eyes are rolling back in his head and he's folding like, I don't know, an accordion toward the floor. And the big guy here's not even breaking a sweat. I'm goggling, I know I am, but who wouldn't, and Ty politely suggests that Jerry might want to get his hand X-rayed because he thinks he heard a bone snap."

"Good lord." Pilar helped herself to some wine. "Really?"

"Mmm." Sophia swallowed. She was starving. The minute she'd walked in the door, she'd been starving. "I heard this little sound, like when you step on a twig. Rather horrible, really. Then we just left. And I have to say . . . Here, Eli, your glass is empty. I have to say that it was so quietly vicious, and exciting. So exciting, I'm not ashamed to say that when we got back on the plane, I jumped him."

"Jesus, Sophie." Tyler felt heat rise up the back of his neck. "Shut up and eat."

"It didn't embarrass you at the time," she pointed out. "Whatever happens, however this all comes out, I'm always going to have the image of Jerry curled up on the floor like a cocktail shrimp. Nobody can take that away from me. Do we have any gelato?"

"I'll get it." Pilar got up from the table, then paused and kissed Ty on the top of the head. "You're a good boy."

Eli drew a breath, let it out. "He didn't leave much of a mark on your jaw there."

"Guy's got pussy hands," Ty said before he could think, then winced. "I beg your pardon, *La Signora.*"

"As you should. I don't approve of such

language at my table. But as I'm in your debt, I'll overlook it."

"You don't owe me anything."

"I know." She reached for his hand, held it tight. "That's why I'm in your debt. My own blood betrayed me and mine. For days knowing that opened a hole in me, made me doubt myself. Things I've done and things I haven't. Tonight I look and see the daughter of my daughter, and the boy Eli once brought to me. And that hole closes again. I regret nothing. I'm ashamed of nothing. How could I be? Whatever happens, we'll go on. We have a wedding to plan," she said, smiling as Pilar dished up ice cream. "A business to run, vines to tend." She lifted her glass. "*Per famiglia.*"

Sophia slept like a log and woke early. At six she was already closed in her office, refining a press release and making personal calls to key accounts in Europe. By seven, she'd worked her way across the Atlantic to the East Coast. She was careful, very careful not to mention Jerry's name, and not to accuse a competitor of shady practices. But she let the implication take root.

At eight, she judged it late enough to phone the Moores at home.

"Aunt Helen, I'm sorry to call so early."

"Not so early. I'd've been out the door in fifteen minutes. Are you still in Venice?"

"No, I'm home, and in need of a legal opinion. On several pesky matters actually. Some involve international law."

"Corporate or criminal?"

"Both. You know Donato's been taken into custody. He's being extradited to Italy today. He's not going to fight it. He's implicated someone, privately to me at this point, an American, a competitor. This person was at minimum aware of the tampering and the embezzlement, and very likely was more involved. Doesn't that make it conspiracy? Can he be charged? Margaret died here in the States, so—"

"Hold on, hold on. You're moving much too quickly, Sophie. The law's a slow wheel. First, you're going on something Don told you. He isn't very credible at the moment."

"He'll be more credible," she promised. "I just want a picture."

"I'm not an expert on international law. I'm not a criminal attorney, come to that. You need to talk to James, and I'll put him on in a minute. But I'm going to tell you this, as your friend. This is a matter for the police and the system. I don't want you to do anything, and I want you to be very careful what you say and what you print. Don't make any statements without running them by either me, James or Linc."

"I've drafted press releases for here and overseas. I'll fax them over if that's all right."

"You do that. You talk to James now. Don't do anything."

Sophia bit her lip. She wondered what her surrogate aunt, the judge, would have to say about the visit she and Ty had paid to Jerry the night before.

At mid-morning, David stood among the rows, among the young mustard plants, at the MacMillan vineyard. He felt useless, out of touch and more than a little panicked because his just-turned-seventeen-year-old son had driven off to school that morning behind the wheel of a secondhand convertible.

"Don't you have some papers to push?" Tyler asked him.

"Up yours."

"In that case I won't suggest you head over to the caves to check on the month's drawing. We're going to be testing the '93 Merlot for starters."

"I get to taste wine, you get to rumble."

"That's the breaks. Besides, it wasn't much of a rumble."

"Pilar said you flattened him one-handed." David tested his injured arm. "One hand's still about all I've got, though the sadist physical therapist says I'll be back to two in no time. I want to take a pop at him." David strode between the rows to work off some of the temper. "I worked for the son of a bltch. For years. Sat in meetings with him, had lunches, late-night strategy sessions. Some of them were about how to woo over some of Giambelli's accounts, some of yours. That's business."

"That's right."

"When La Coeur copped the exclusive on Allied flights to and from Europe, I went out and celebrated with him. We nudged Giambelli out on that one, barely. I patted myself on the back for days over that. Now I look at the timing, go through the steps and realize we copped it because he had the inside track. Don fed him Giambelli's bid before it was made."

"That's the way some people do business."

"I don't."

It was the tone that made Ty stop. He supposed somehow over the past months they'd become friends. Almost family. Near enough that he understood the guilt, and the frustration.

"Nobody's saying that, David. Nobody thinks that."

"No. But I remember how much I wanted that account." He started to jam his hands in his pockets, and his bad arm vibrated. "Goddamn it."

"You going to finish beating yourself up soon? Because I've got a lot of work to catch up on, seeing as I had to go to Italy to help wipe your blood off the street. You getting yourself shot really put a crimp in my schedule."

David turned back toward Tyler. "Did you use that same tone when you suggested that fucker DeMorney get an X ray?"

"Probably. It's the one I use when somebody's being annoyingly stupid."

The raw edges in David's stomach

smoothed away, and the first glint of humor sparked into his eyes. "I'd take a swing at you over that, but you're bigger than me."

"Younger, too."

"Bastard. Now that I think of it, I could take you down, but I'll give you a break because Sophia's heading this way. I'd hate for her to have to watch her future stepfather kick your ass."

"In your dreams."

"I'm going to go sulk in the caves." He started off, pausing as he passed Tyler. "Thanks."

"Anytime." He walked the opposite way until he met Sophia. "You're late. Again."

"Priorities. Where's David going? I wanted to ask how he was feeling."

"Do yourself a favor and don't. He's at the restless stage of his recovery. What priorities?"

"Oh, solidifying some shaky accounts, manipulating the press, consulting with legal. Just another quiet day for the wine heiress. How are we doing out here?"

"Nights've been cool and moist. Brings on mildew. We'll do the second sulfur spraying right after the grapes have set. I'm not worried."

"Good. I'll carve out some time for the vintner tomorrow, and you carve out some for the promotion whiz. Back to teamwork. Now, why haven't you kissed me hello?"

"Because I'm working. I want to check the new plantings, run by the old distillery and check on the fermentation vats. And we're testing today in the caves. Then we've got to move your stuff over to my place."

"I haven't said I was—"

"But since you're here anyway." He leaned down and kissed her.

"We're going to have to discuss this," she began, then pulled her ringing phone out of her pocket. "Very soon," she added. "Sophia Giambelli. *Chi? Sì, va bene.*" She angled the phone away. "It's Lieutenant De-Marco's office. Don was transferred to his custody today. Ah." She shifted the phone back in place. "*Sì, buon giorno. Ma che . . . scusi? No, no.*"

Still clutching the phone, she sank onto the ground. *"Come!"* she managed. Gripping Tyler's hand before he could take the phone from her, she shook her head fiercely. *"Donato."* She lifted her stunned gaze to Tyler's. *"E' morto."*

He didn't need her to translate the last. He

took the phone from her and, identifying himself, asked how Donato Giambelli had died.

"A heart attack. He wasn't yet forty." Sophia paced. "This is my doing. I pushed him, then I went to Jerry and pushed him. I might as well have drawn a target on Don's back."

"You didn't do it alone," Tyler reminded her. "I'm the one who yanked DeMorney's chain."

"Basta," Tereza ordered, but without heat. "If they find Donato died from drugs, if they find he was murdered while in the hands of the police, there's no fault here. Donato's choices put him where he was, and the police were obliged to protect as well as contain him. I won't have blame cast on my house."

And that, she determined, would end that. "He was a disappointment to me. But I remember he was once a sweet young boy with a pretty smile. I'll mourn the little boy."

She reached out, found Eli's hand, brought it to her lips in a gesture Sophia had never seen her make.

"*Nonna.* I'll go to Italy, to the funeral to represent the family."

"No, the time for you to stand in my place will come soon enough. Not yet. I need you here. Eli and I will go, and that's as it should be. I'll bring Francesca, Gina and the children back with me if they want it. God help us if they do," she finished with spirit and got to her feet.

Sophia studied Linc's office. No one, she decided, could accuse his father of preferential treatment. The room was little more than a glorified box, cramped, windowless and stacked with law books and files. She imagined there was a desk hiding under the mounds of paperwork.

"Welcome to my dungeon. It's not much," Linc said as he cleaned off a chair for her. "But . . . it's not much." He dumped the files and books on the floor.

"The nice thing about starting at the bottom is, you can't get any lower."

"If I'm a good boy, I'll get my own stapler." With a skill that told her he'd done so before, he wheeled his desk chair around the mountain. From somewhere under the mounds of papers and books a phone began to ring.

"Do you need to get that? Wherever it is."

"If I do, somebody'll just want to talk to me. I'd rather talk to you."

How anyone could work in such confusion and disorder was beyond her. She had to mentally sit on her hands to keep herself from digging in to organize. "Now I feel guilty about adding to your workload. But not guilty enough to stop me from asking if the papers I sent you are somewhere around, and if you had a chance to look them over."

"I've got a system." He reached under a stack on the left corner of his desk, pulled out a file.

"It's like the magician's tablecloth trick," she commented. "Nicely done."

"Want to see me pull a rabbit out of my hat?" Grinning at her, he sat. "You covered yourself here," he began. "I fiddled with the press releases a little, got to earn my inflated fee, after all." He passed the revised papers over. "I take it you're acting as spokesperson for Giambelli-MacMillan."

"I take it, too, at least as long as *Nonna*

and Eli are in Italy. Mama's not trained for this sort of thing. I am."

"David? Ty?"

"I'll see they have copies, just in case. But it's best that the media representative be someone from the Giambelli family. We're the ones getting kicked around."

"I'm sorry about Don."

"So am I." She looked down at the releases again, but she didn't see them. "Funeral's today. I keep thinking about the last time I spoke to him, how scared he was. I know what he did, and I can't forgive him for it. But I keep remembering how scared he was, and how cold I was to him."

"You can't slap yourself around for that, Sophie. Mom and Dad updated me on what went on, at least what we're sure of. He got greedy, and he got stupid. He was responsible for two deaths."

"Accidents, he called them. I know what he did, Linc. But who was responsible for him?"

"Which brings us around to DeMorney. You're going to have to be careful there. Keep his name out of your statements. Keep La Coeur out of them."

"Mmm-hmm." Idly, she studied her manicure. "It's leaked that the police are questioning him in connection with the tampering, the fraudulent account, even my father's murder. I can't imagine how the press got the information."

"You're a devious package, Sophie."

"Spoken as my friend or my lawyer?"

"Both. Just be careful. You don't want any leaks traced back to you. And if you're asked about DeMorney, and you're bound to be, go with no comment."

"I have plenty of comments."

"And the ones you're thinking of could dump you into a lawsuit. Let the system wind its tortuous way toward the end goal. If DeMorney was involved you don't have proof," he reminded her. "Let me be a lawyer. If he was involved, it's going to come out. But Don's word isn't enough."

"He pulled the strings. I'm sure of it, and that's enough for me. People are dead, and why? Because he wanted a bigger market share? For God's sake."

"People have killed for less, but I've got to say, that's the weak spot. He's a wealthy, respected businessman. It's going to be a rough road tying him to corporate espionage, embezzlement, product tampering, much less murder."

"He's opened it up, and the press is going to leap on the juicy morsel about his wife and my father. Humiliating him publicly. He hates us and will hate us more as this plays out. I felt that when I saw him in New York. It's not business, or not just business. It's very personal. Linc, have you seen our new ad?"

"The one with the couple on the porch? Sunset on the lake, wine and romance. Very slick, very attractive. It had your name all over it. Yours, I mean, not just the company."

"Thanks. My team put a lot of time and thought into it." She reached into her briefcase, pulled a photograph from a file folder. "Someone sent this to me yesterday."

He recognized the ad, though this copy had been computer-generated and altered. In this, the young woman's head was tipped back, her mouth open in a silent scream. A glass lay on the porch, the wine spilling out and bleeding from white to red. The header read:

IT'S YOUR MOMENT
TO DIE

"Jesus, Sophie. This is sick, and nasty. Where's the envelope?"

"I have it. No return address, naturally. Postmarked San Francisco. Initially I thought of Kris Drake. It's her style. But I don't think so."

She could study the doctored ad now without a shudder. "I think she's backing way off to keep herself clear of the fallout. I don't know if Jerry was on the West Coast, but he did this."

"You need to take this to the police."

"I took the original in this morning. This is a copy. I got the impression that while they'll look into it, they see it as another ugly little prank." She pushed to her feet. "I want the private detective you've hired to look into it, too. And I don't want you to say anything about it to anyone."

"I agree with the first part, but find the second stupid."

"It's not stupid. My mother's planning her wedding. *Nonna* and Eli have enough to deal with. So do Ty and David. Besides, this came to me. Personally. I want to deal with it personally."

"Even you can't always have what you want. This is a threat."

"Maybe. And believe me, I intend to be very careful. But I'm not going to have this time spoiled for my mother. She's waited too long to be happy. I'm not going to dump any more stress on my grandparents. And I'm not telling Ty, not just yet anyway, because he'll overreact. So it's you and me, Linc."

She reached down for his hand. "I'm counting on you."

"Here's what I'll do," he said after a moment. "I'll put the detective on it, and give him forty-eight hours to work before I say anything. If during that time you get another of these, you have to come to me right away."

"I can promise that. But forty-eight hours—"

"That's the deal." He got to his feet. "I'll give you that because I love you, and I know what you're feeling. I won't give any more because I love you, and I know what I'm feeling. Take it or leave it."

"Okay. Okay," she said again on a long breath. "I'm not being brave and stupid, Linc. Stubborn, maybe, but not stupid. He wants to scare me, and throw my family into more turmoil. He's not going to. Right now,

I'm going to meet my mother, and yours. We're going shopping for a wedding dress." She kissed his cheeks. "Thanks."

Maddy's idea of shopping was hanging around the mall, scoping out the boys who were hanging around the mall scoping out the girls, and spending her allowance on some junk food and new earrings. She expected to be terminally bored spending the day with three adults in fancy dress shops.

But she figured the points she'd earn with her father for agreeing to go would translate into the streaks she wanted to pul in her hair. And if she played her cards right, she could cop some pretty cool stuff out of Pilar.

A potential new stepmother was prime fruit for plucking. Guilt and nerves, by Maddy's calculations, equaled shopping bags.

She was supposed to call Ms. Giambelli Pilar now. Which was weird, but better than being expected to call her Mom or something.

First she had to get through the lunch deal with Pilar and the judge lady. A girl lunch,

Maddy thought with derision. Tiny portions of fancy, low-fat, tasteless food where you were expected to talk about clothes and your figure. It wouldn't have been so bad if Sophia had been with them. But Maddy's broad hints that she'd tag along with Sophia while she did her errands had fallen on barren ground.

She resigned herself to a miserable hour or two, more points, she decided. Then was surprised to find herself walking into a noisy Italian restaurant where the air was full of spice.

"I should get a salad. I should just get a salad," Helen repeated. "But I won't. I already hear the eggplant Parmesan calling my name."

"Fettuccine Alfredo."

"Sure, fine for you," Helen said to Pilar. "You never put on an ounce. You won't have to worry how you'll look naked on your wedding night."

"He's already seen her naked," Maddy said and had both women turning around to stare at her. She felt her back go up, her brows lower as she prepared for a lecture. Instead she got laughter, and Helen draped an arm around her shoulders. "Let's get a corner booth, then you can give me all the dirt on your father and Pilar I haven't been able to crowbar out of her."

"I think they did it outside last night. Dad had grass stains on his jeans."

"Can you be bought?" Pilar demanded.

Maddy slid into the booth, grinned. "Sure."

"Let's negotiate." Pilar sat down beside her.

She wasn't bored. She was surprised to find herself having fun, not being shushed for wisecracks or expected to sit quietly and behave. It was, she thought, a lot like hanging out with Theo and their father— only different. Good different. And she was smart enough to realize it was the first women's outing she'd ever had. Smart enough to understand Pilar knew it, too.

She didn't even mind being dragged into the dress shop, or having the conversation turn absolutely and completely to clothes and fabric and color and cut.

And when she watched Sophia dash in, windblown, flushed, happy, Maddy at not quite fifteen had a revelation. She wouldn't mind being like her, like Sophia Giambelli. She proved, didn't she, that a woman could be smart, really smart, do exactly what she wanted in the world, and how she wanted to do it, and look really amazing at the same time.

She didn't dress like she was craving attention, but she got it anyway.

"Tell me you haven't tried on anything yet."

"No, not yet. I wanted to wait for you. What do you think of this blue silk?"

"Hmm. A definite maybe. Hi, Maddy. Aunt Helen." She leaned over to kiss Helen's cheek, then let out a quick whoop. "Oh, Mama! Look at this. The lace is fabulous—romantic, elegant. And the color would be perfect on you."

"It's lovely, but don't you think it's a little young? More for you."

"No, no. It's for a bride. For you. You have to try it."

While she studied the dress, Pilar laid a hand on Sophia's shoulder. Sort of absentmindedly, Maddy thought. Just to touch. Her own mother had never touched her absentmindedly, not that she could remember.

They'd never had that connection. If they'd had it, she couldn't have left so easily.

"Try them both," Sophia insisted. "And this rose linen Helen's picked out."

"If she wasn't in such a rush to hook this guy, she could have something designed. And I could lose ten pounds before I have to wear the matron of honor gown. Do I have time for liposuction?"

"Oh stop. Okay. I'll start with these three."

When Pilar went off with the sales assistant to the dressing rooms, Sophia rubbed her hands together. "All right, your turn."

Surprised, Maddy blinked at her. "This is a grown-up shop."

"You're as tall as I am, probably about the same size," she added as she studied her target. "Mama's going for soft colors, so we'll stick with that. Though I'd like to put you in jewel tones."

"I like black," Maddy said for the hell of it.

"Yes, and you wear it well."

"I do?"

"Mmm, but we'll expand your horizons for this particular occasion."

"I'm not wearing pink." Maddy folded her arms.

"Aw, and I was imagining a pink organdy,"

Helen said, "with ruffles and little Mary Janes."

"What're Mary Janes?"

"Ouch. I'm old. I'm going over to daywear and sulk."

"Well, what are they?" Maddy demanded as Sophia went through the selections.

"Either shoes or pot—or both. I'm not entirely sure. I like this." She pulled out a full-length sleeveless gown in smoky blue.

"It'd look okay on you."

"Not for me, for you." Sophia turned, held the dress up in front of Maddy.

"Me? Really?"

"Yes, really. I want to see you in it with your hair up. Show off your neck and shoulders."

"What if I got it cut. My hair, I mean. Short."

"Hmmm." Lips pursed, Sophia mentally cut and restyled Maddy's straight mop. "Yes, short around the face, a little longer in the back. A few highlights."

"Streaks?" said Maddy, nearly speechless with joy.

"Highlights, subtle. Ask your father, and I'll take you to my guy."

"Why do I have to ask about having my hair cut? It's my hair."

"Good point. Go try this on. I'll give the salon a call, see if they can fit you in before we head back home." She started to hand Maddy the gown, then stopped. "Oh, Mama."

"What do you think?" She'd started with the peach, the ivory lace romancing the bodice, the skirt sweeping back into a gentle train. "Be brutal."

"Helen, come see," Sophia called out. "You look beautiful, Mama."

"Like a bride," Helen agreed and sniffled. "Damn, there goes the mascara."

"Okay." Half-dreaming, Pilar turned in a circle. "Maddy? What's your vote?"

"You look great. Dad's eyes are going to pop out."

Pilar beamed and turned in another circle. "We have a winner, first time out."

It wasn't as simple as that. There were hats, headdresses, shoes, jewelry, bags, even underwear. It was dark before they headed north, with the back of the SUV crammed with shopping bags and boxes. Which didn't include the dresses themselves, Maddy thought with wonder. Those had to be fitted and altered and fussed with.

But she'd ended up with a pile of new clothes, shoes, really cool earrings that she was now wearing. They showed off great with her awesome haircut. And highlights.

This new girl-family deal had definite high points.

"Men," Sophia was saying as she cruised north, "consider themselves the hunter. But they're not. See, they decide to go after a grizzly, and that's their whole focus. So while they track the big bear, they miss all the other game out of their narrowed vision. Women, on the other hand, may track the grizzly, but before, or even while, bagging it, they take down all the other game as well."

"Plus men shoot the first big bear they see," Maddy put in from the backseat. "They don't take into account the entire world of grizzlies."

"Exactly." Sophia tapped the steering wheel. "Mama, this girl has real potential."

"Agreed. But I'm not taking the rap for those shoes with the two-foot soles she's wearing. That one's on you."

"They're great. Funky."

"Yeah." Pleased with them, and herself, Maddy lifted her foot. "And the soles are only about four inches."

"I don't know why you'd want to clomp around in them."

Sophia met Maddy's gaze in the rearview mirror. "It's a Mom thing. She has to say that. You should've seen her face when I got my belly button pierced."

"You got your belly button pierced?" Fascinated, Maddy reached for the snap of her seat belt. "Can I see?"

"I let it grow back. Sorry," she said with a chuckle as Maddy sat back again in disgust. "It was irritating."

"And she was eighteen," Pilar pointed out, turning her head to give Maddy a warning stare. "So don't even think about it until you are."

"Is that a Mom thing, too?"

"You bet. But I will say the two of you were right about the hair. It looks great."

"So when Dad connips, you'll calm him all down, right?"

"Well, I'll . . ." She turned back as the car squealed around a curve. "Sophia, at the risk of saying another Mom thing, slow down."

"Tighten your seat belts." Grimly Sophia's hands vised on the wheel. "Something's wrong with the brakes."

"Oh God." Instinctively, Pilar turned back to Maddy. "Are you strapped in?"

"Yeah." She grabbed the seat to brace herself as the car shot around another turn. "I'm okay. Pull up the emergency brake."

"Mama, pull it up. I need both hands here." Those hands wanted to shake, but she didn't let them. Didn't let herself think about anything but maintaining control. The car squealed again, fishtailed around the next turn.

"It's up all the way, baby." And the car didn't slow. "What if we turned off the engine?"

"The steering'll lock." Maddy swallowed the heart that leaped into her throat. "She wouldn't be able to steer."

Gravel spit as Sophia fought to keep the car on the road. "Use my phone, call nine-one-one." She looked down briefly. A half tank of gas, she thought. No help there. And she wasn't going to be able to control the car around the upcoming S turns at this speed.

"Downshift!" Maddy shouted from the back. "Try downshifting."

"Mama, shove it into third when I tell you. It's going to give us one hell of a jolt, so brace yourselves. But it might work. I can't let go of the wheel."

"I've got it. It's going to be all right."

"Okay. Hold on." She pushed in the clutch, and the car seemed to gain more speed. "Now!"

The car jolted hard. Though Maddy bit her lip, she couldn't hold back the scream.

"Into second," Sophia ordered, wrenching the wheel from the shoulder of the road. A line of sweat ran cold down her back. "Now."

The car bucked, threw her forward, back again. She had a moment's panic that the airbags would deploy and leave her help-less.

"We've slowed down some. Good think-ing, Maddy."

"We're going to head downhill, around more turns." Sophia's voice was ice calm. "So the speed's going to pick up again some. I can handle it. Once we're through them, we go up a slope, and that should do it. Get my phone, Mama, just in case. And everybody hold on."

She didn't look at the speedometer. Her eyes were glued to the road now, her mind anticipating each turn. She'd driven the road countless times. The headlights cut through the dark, slashed across oncoming traffic. She heard the angry sound of horns blaring as she crossed the center line.

"Nearly there, nearly there." She whipped the wheel left, then right. It slicked in her hands as her palms sprang with damp.

She could see, could feel the ground begin to level. Just a little more, she thought. A little bit more. "Into first, Mama. Shove it into first."

There was a horrible noise, a tremendous shudder. Sophia felt as if an enormous fist punched into the hood of the car. Something shrieked, then clanged. And as the speed dropped, she pulled to the side of the road.

No one spoke when they stopped. A car whizzed by, then another.

"Is everyone all right?" Pilar reached for the latch of her seat belt and discovered her fingers were numb. "Is everyone okay?"

"Yeah." Maddy dashed tears from her

cheeks. "Okay. I think we should get out now."

"I think that's a good idea. Sophie, baby?"

"Yeah. Let's get the hell out."

She managed to get out, to get to the far side of the car before her legs buckled. Bracing her hands on the hood, she fought to get her breath back, and only managed to wheeze.

"That was really good driving," Maddy told her.

"Yeah, thanks."

"Here, baby. Here." Pilar turned her, held her when the shakes came. And, holding her, reached out for Maddy. "Here, baby," she said again. Maddy pressed herself into that circle of comfort and let the tears come.

CHAPTER TWENTY-EIGHT

Nearly blind with terror and relief, David bolted out of the house. Even as the police car braked, he scooped Maddy out, held her cradled in his arms as he would a baby.

"You're okay." He pressed his lips to her cheeks, her hair. Breathed her in, as the shakes he'd held off since the call took over. "You're okay." He said it a half dozen times as she curled into him.

"I'm all right. I'm not hurt or anything." But when she wrapped her arms around his neck, her world came all the way right again. "Sophie drove like one of those guys you and Theo like to watch on the raceway. It was kinda cool."

"Kinda cool. Yeah." Rocking now, calming himself, he kept his face buried in the curve of her throat while Theo awkwardly patted her back.

"Bet it was some ride." Theo manfully swallowed the prickly lump in his throat. There was a jittering inside his chest that came as much from seeing his father break apart as from anxiety over Maddy. "I'll haul her in, Dad. You're going to wreck your arm."

Unable to speak, David just shook his head and held on. His baby, was all he could think. His little girl might have been lost.

"It's okay, Dad," Maddy told him. "Everybody's okay now. I can walk. We got the shakes after, but we got over it. But Theo can haul in all the loot." She rubbed her cheek against her father's. "We kicked shopping butt, right, Pilar?"

"Right. I could use a hand, Theo."

"Theo and I'll get it." She wiggled until David set her down.

"What'd you do to your hair?" David ran his hand over the sassy crop of it, left his hand resting warm on the back of her neck.

"Got rid of most of it. What do you think?"

"I think it makes you look grown up. You're growing up on me. Damn, Maddy, I wish you wouldn't." He sighed, pressed his lips to the top of her head. "Just another minute, okay?"

"Sure."

"I love you so much. I'd appreciate it if you wouldn't scare me like that again anytime soon."

"I don't plan on it. Wait till you see the dress I got. It goes with the hair."

"Great. Go ahead, drag off your loot."

"You'll stay, won't you?" Maddy asked Pilar.

"Yes, if you want."

"I think you should stay." Since Theo had grabbed the bags, she clomped off after him in her funky new shoes.

"Oh, David, I'm so sorry."

"Don't say anything. Just let me look at you." He cupped her face, skimmed his hands back into her hair. Her skin was chilled, her eyes huge and full of worry. But she was here, she was whole. "Just let me look."

"I'm fine."

He drew her close, seemed to fold himself around her and rock. "Sophia?"

"She's fine." The taut wire that had held her straight and steady snapped as she burrowed into him. "God, David, God. Our babies. I've never been so scared, and all the time it was happening, they . . . they were amazing. I didn't like leaving Sophie back there, dealing with the police, but I didn't want Maddy coming home alone, so . . ."

"Ty's already on his way down."

She drew a ragged breath, then a second that came easier. "I thought he would be. That's all right then."

"Come inside." He shifted her, keeping her close to his side. "Tell me everything."

Tyler swung behind the police cruiser with a harsh scream of brakes. In the flashing lights, Sophia watched him stride over the road. She could see him well enough to recognize rage. As calmly as she could, she turned away from the cop who was interviewing her and walked toward him.

He grabbed her fast enough, hard enough to knock the breath out of her. Nothing had ever felt so safe.

"I was hoping you'd come. I was really hoping."

"Did you get banged up any?"

"No. The Jeep, on the other hand . . . I think I blew the transmission. Ty, I didn't have any brakes. They were just gone. I know they're going to tow it in and check it out, but I already know."

The words poured out of her, shaky at first, then gaining strength, gaining temper. "It wasn't an accident. It wasn't some mechanical failure. Somebody wanted to hurt me, and they didn't care if my mother and Maddy got hurt, too. Goddamn it, she's just a little girl. Tough, though. Tough and smart. She told me to downshift. She doesn't even know how to drive."

The rage would have to wait. He'd have to wait to break something in half, to plow his fist into something, anything. Sophia was trembling, and needed tending.

"Kid knows something about everything. Get in the car. Time for somebody else to take the wheel."

A little dazed now, she glanced behind her. "I think they still want to talk to me."

"They can talk to you tomorrow. I'm taking you home."

"Fine by me. I have some shopping bags."

He smiled, and his grip on her loosened to a caress. "Of course you do."

He meant what he'd said about taking her home. His home. When she didn't argue the point, he figured she was more shaken than she'd admitted. He dumped her shopping bags in the foyer, then wondered what the hell to do with her.

"You want, like, a hot bath, a drink?"

"How about a drink in a hot bath?"

"I'll take care of it. You ought to call your mother, let her know you're back. And you'll be staying here."

"All right, thanks."

He dumped half a tube of shower gel that had been around since Christmas into the tub. It smelled like pine, but it bubbled. He figured she'd want bubbles. He stuck a couple of candles on the counter. Women went for candlelit baths, for reasons he couldn't fathom. He poured her a glass of wine, set it on the lip of the tub and was standing back, trying to figure out what else to do when she stepped into the bathroom.

Her single huge sigh told him he'd already hit the mark.

"MacMillan, I love you."

"Yeah, so you said."

"No, no, at this moment—this exact moment, no one has ever, will ever love you more. Enough to let you get in with me."

In a tub full of bubbles? He didn't think so. And if he could overlook the mortification of that for the obvious benefits, she looked beat.

"I'll take a pass on this one. Strip and get in."

"You romantic bastard. A half hour in here and I'll feel human again."

He left her to it and went down to get her things. To his way of thinking, if he dumped her shopping loot in the bedroom, it would take her that much longer to run off again. As far as he was concerned, this was the first stage of her moving in.

He grabbed her purse, her briefcase, four—Jesus Christ—four loaded shopping bags, and started back up with them. As long as he kept busy, he told himself, did what came next, he wouldn't give in to the fury choking him.

"What'd you buy? Small slabs of granite?"

He tossed them on the bed, considered the job done, and her briefcase tumbled off. He grabbed for it, managed to snag the strap and, upending it, dumped out most of the contents.

Why did anyone need so much junk in a briefcase? Resigned, he crouched and began to gather it up again. Okay, he could see the bottle of water, her bulging Filofax, the electronic memo deal. The pens, though, God knew why she needed a half dozen of them. Lipstick.

Idly he uncapped it, swiveled the tube out. One sniff and he tasted her.

Travel scissors. Hmmm. Post-its, paper clips, aspirin, a powder-puff thing, a finger-nail thing, other assorted girl things that made him wonder why she bothered to carry a purse as well, and what the hell she put in it. Breath mints, a little bag of un-opened candy, a mini–tape recorder, Wet Naps, matches, a couple of floppy disks and some file folders, a pair of Hi-Liters and a bottle of clear nail polish.

Amazing, he decided. It was a wonder she didn't walk crooked once she strapped it over her shoulder. Just passing the time, he flipped through the file folders as he replaced them. She had a tear sheet of the first ad, a comp of the second, a ream of scribbled notes and a stack of typed ones.

He found the press releases, with the notes scribbled over them. Lips pursed, he read the English version and found it solid, strong and smart.

He'd expected nothing else.

Then he found the altered ad.

Holding it, and a copy of an envelope addressed to her, he came straight up. He was still holding them when he shoved open the bathroom door.

"What the hell is this?"

She'd nearly fallen asleep. When she blinked the first thing she saw was his furious face. And the second the sheets in his hands.

"What were you doing in my briefcase?"

"Never mind that. Where did you get this?"

"In the mail."

"When?"

A hesitation, brief but long enough to let him know she was considering a cover.

"Don't bother jiving me, Sophie. When did you get this?"

"Yesterday."

"And you were planning to show it to me . . . when?"

"In a couple of days. Look, would you mind if I finish up in here before we discuss this? I'm naked and covered with boy bubbles."

"A couple of days?"

"Yes, I wanted to think about it and I went to the police with it. To Linc just today so I could get a legal opinion. I can handle it, Ty."

"Yeah." He looked at her, up to her chin in froth, her face haunted by shadows of fatigue. "You're a real handler, Sophia. I guess I forgot that part."

"Ty—" She slapped a fist on the water when he walked out and closed the door. "Just wait a minute." She got out of the tub and, rather than drying off, just wrapped a towel around herself. She went after him, leaving a trail of water and bubbles.

She called him again, cursed him and heard the back door slam shut as she raced downstairs.

She slapped on the outside lights, saw that his long, angry strides were carrying him toward the vineyards. Tightening her grip on the knotted towel, she ran outside.

Her bare foot came down hard on a small stone, inspiring a fresh string of curses as she continued in a limping run.

"Tyler! Just wait a damn minute." She hurled insults at his back until she realized she was using Italian and they might as well have been promises of undying love to his ear. "Listen, you idiot, you coward. You stop where you are and fight like a man."

Because he stopped, whirled around, she all but plowed straight into him. She pulled up short, puffing like a steam engine and hopping to take the weight off her sore foot. "Where do you think you're going?" she demanded.

"You don't want to be near me now."

"Wrong." To prove it she tapped a fist on his chest. "You want to take a shot at me, fine." She angled her chin. "I'd rather somebody take an honest punch than walk away."

"As tempting as that is, and believe me I'm in the mood to punch something, I don't hit women. Go back in the house. You're wet and half-naked."

"I'll go back when you go back. In the meantime we can have this out right here. You're mad because I didn't come running to you over that nasty bit of business. Well, I'm sorry, I did what I thought best about it."

"You're half-right. You did what you thought best, but you're not sorry. I'm surprised you bothered to call me tonight just because somebody tried to kill you."

"Ty, it's not the same thing. It's just a stupid picture. I wasn't going to let it upset me, or you, or anyone."

"*You* weren't going to let. There you go. Teamwork, my ass."

He was shouting now, such a rare occurrence she could only stare up at him. A big, furious man who'd finally snapped his leash.

"You decide what you'll give, how much and when. Everyone's supposed to fall in line with your schedule, your plan. Well, fuck it, Sophie. Fuck that. I just stepped out of line. Goddamn it, I love you." He hauled her up on her toes, calloused hands against pampered skin. "You're it for me. If it's not the same on both sides, it's nothing. Do you get it? Nothing."

Furious with both of them, he dropped her back on her feet. "Now go inside and get dressed. I'll take you home."

"Please don't. Please," she said, touching

his arm as he started to walk by her. "Please, God. Don't walk away." The shakes were back, but had nothing to do with fear for her life. This was so much more. "I'm sorry. I'm so sorry that by not doing something I thought would worry you, I did something to hurt you. I'm used to taking care of myself, used to making my own decisions."

"That's not how it works anymore. If you can't deal with that, we're wasting our time."

"You're right. And you're scaring me because I understand this is important enough to make you walk away from me. I don't want that to happen. You're right and I was wrong. I wanted to handle it my way, and I was wrong. Yell at me, curse at me, but don't push me out."

His temper had peaked and ebbed and, as always, left him feeling annoyed with himself. "You're cold. Let's go inside."

"Wait." His voice was so final, so distant. It tied knots in her belly. "Just listen."

She gripped his arm, her fingers digging desperately into his shirt. If he turned away now, she knew she'd be alone as she'd never been alone before in her life.

"I'm listening."

"I was angry when it came. All I could think was that the bastard, I know it's Jerry, the bastard's using my own work to taunt me. To try to scare me, and I'm not going to let him. I'm not going to let him worry me, or my mother or anyone I care about. I thought I could handle it myself and protect you from the worry. And I realize standing here right now that if you'd done the same thing, I'd be just as hurt, just as angry as you are."

Her voice hitched, and she feared she'd sob. Unfair tactics, she reminded herself and bit down on grief. "I love you. Maybe that's the one thing I don't know how to handle. Not yet. Give me a chance to figure it out. I'm asking you not to walk away from me. It's the one thing I can't take. Needing someone, loving them and watching them walk away."

"I'm not your father." He cupped a hand under her chin. He saw the tears brimming, and her valiant attempt to hold them off. "And neither are you. My being there for you, taking some of the weight doesn't make you weak. It doesn't make you less, Sophie."

"He always let someone else deal with the

sticky parts." She drew in a breath, let it out shakily. "I know what I'm doing, Ty, when I push people back so I can deal with problems on my own. I know what I'm trying to prove. I even know it's stupid and self-serving. But I can't always seem to stop doing it."

"Practice." He took her hand. "I told you before I'd stick, didn't I?"

A shudder ran through her. "Yes, you did." To steady herself, she brought their joined hands to her cheek. "I've never been it for anyone before. No one's been it for me. Looks like you are."

"That works for me. We square now?"

"I guess we are." Her lips curved. He made things so simple, she thought. All she had to do was let him. "It's been a hell of a night so far."

"Let's go back, finish it off." He slid an arm around her to lead her back to the house, automatically taking her weight as she limped.

Served her right, he thought, riling him up the way she had. "Hurt your foot?"

The amused and satisfied tone didn't escape her notice. "I stepped on a rock while I was running after this big, stupid *culo*."

"Which would be me. I understand enough gutter Italian to know when the woman I love's calling me an asshole."

"But very affectionately. Since you're up on the language, why don't we finish the night off by . . ." She rose up to whisper in his ear, ending the provocative Italian with a quick nip on his lobe.

"Ummm." He didn't have a clue what she'd said, but the blood had cheerfully drained out of his head. "I think I'm going to need a translation on that one."

"Happy to," she said. "Once we're inside."

It surprised Pilar to see Tyler outside the kitchen door at what she imagined he'd consider the middle of the morning. It surprised her a great deal more to see the bouquet of flowers in his hand.

"Good morning."

"Hi." He stepped inside the Cutter kitchen, nearly shuffled his feet. "I didn't expect to see you here or I'd've . . ." Embarrassed, he shook the flowers in his hand. "You know, brought more."

"I see. You brought them for Maddy? Ty."

Delighted with him, she reached up, squeezed his cheeks. "You're so sweet."

"Yeah, right. Well. How're you feeling?"

"Fine. Lucky." She stepped toward the inside doorway and called for Maddy. "Sophia was amazing. Steady as a rock."

"Yeah, that's Sophie. I gave her a break, left her sleeping this morning." He looked over as Maddy came in. "Hi, kid."

"Hey. What're those?"

"I think they're flowers. For you."

Her eyebrows drew together in puzzlement. "Me?"

"I have to go. I'll just say goodbye to David and Theo." Pilar kissed Maddy lightly, absently on the cheek, and made the girl's color come up. "See you later."

"Yeah, okay. How come they're for me?" she asked Tyler.

"Because I hear you did good." He held them out. "You want them or not?"

"Yeah, I want them." She took them, noted the little flutter in her belly as she sniffed. A kind of muscle reflex, she supposed it was. A nice one. "Nobody ever gave me flowers before."

"They will. I figured I'd get you something for your brain, too, but I haven't come up with it yet. Anyway, what did you do to your hair?"

"I cut it. So?"

"So . . . just asking." He waited while she got out a vase. The new do made her look like a brainy pixie, Ty thought. Boys, he realized with a little tug of regret, were going to come sniffing at the door. "You want to hang with me today? I've got to check for mildew, then see how the work's going over at the old distillery. Start on the weeding."

"Yeah, that'd be good."

"Tell your dad."

When she was settled in the car beside Tyler, Maddy folded her hands on her lap. "I've got two things I want to ask you."

"Sure. Shoot."

"If I were, like, ten years older and had actual breasts, would you go for me?"

"Jesus, Maddy."

"I don't have a crush on you or anything. I sort of did when we first moved here, but I got over it. You're too old for me, and I'm not ready for a serious relationship, or sex."

"Damn right you're not."

"But when I am ready, I want to know if a guy would go for me. Theoretically."

Tyler ran a hand over his face. "Theoretically, and leaving out the breasts because that's not what a guy looks for, if you were ten years older, I'd've already gone for you. Okay?"

She smiled, slipped on her sunglasses. "Okay. But that's bull about breasts. Guys say how they look for personality and intelligence. Some of them say how they're leg men or whatever. But it's the breasts."

"And you know this because?"

"Because it's something we have you don't."

He opened his mouth, shut it again. This wasn't a debate he could comfortably enter into with a teenage girl. "You said you had a couple of questions."

"Yeah, well." She shifted in her seat to face him. "The other's an idea. Vino-therapy."

"Vino-therapy?"

"Yeah, I read about it. Grape seed–based skin creams and stuff. I was thinking we could start a line of products."

"We could?"

"I need to do more research, some experimenting. But this company's doing it in France. We could corner the American market. See, red wine contains antioxidants—polyphenols, and—"

"Maddy, I know about polyphenols."

"Okay, okay. But see the seeds—and you ditch them during wine production—they have antioxidants. And that's really good for the skin. Plus, I'm thinking we could do an herbal deal, internal, too. A whole health and beauty line."

Health and beauty. What next? "Look, kid, I make wine, not skin cream."

"But you could," she insisted. "If I could have the seeds when you harvest, and a place to experiment. You said you wanted to give me something for my brain. Give me this."

"I was thinking more like a chemistry set," he mumbled. "Let me mull on it."

He intended to let the mulling wait until after work, but Maddy had different ideas.

Sophia was in the vineyard, watching the cutters weed with their wedge-shaped blades. Maddy headed straight for her and started before Sophia could speak.

"I think we should move into vino-therapy like that French company."

"Really?" Sophia pursed her lips, a sure sign she was carefully considering. "That's interesting because I've had that idea on a back burner for a while now. I've tried the facial mask. It's marvelous."

"We're winemakers," Ty began.

"And will always be," Sophia agreed. "But that doesn't preclude addressing other areas. There's an enormous market for natural beauty products. I've had to table the idea because we've had a difficult year and other things demanded my attention. But maybe this is a good time to consider. Expansion rather than damage control," she mused, and was already playing on the spin. "I'll need to accumulate more data, of course."

"I can get it," Maddy said. "I'm good at research."

"You're hired. Once research moves toward research and development, we'll need a guinea pig."

As one, they turned to study Tyler.

He blanched. Actually felt the blood fall away from his face. "Forget it."

"Chicken." Sophia's amused expression faded as she spotted the two figures walking toward them. "The police are here.

Claremont and Maguire. It can't be good news."

Deliberate, Sophia thought as she sat in Tyler's living room. The four-wheel had been tampered with, as deliberately as the wine had been. Part of her had known it, but having it confirmed now with cold, hard facts brought a fresh chill to her skin.

"Yes, I use that vehicle often. Primarily I drive my car to and from the city, but it's a two-seater. The three of us were spending the day in San Francisco, shopping for my mother's wedding. We needed the bigger car."

"Who knew of your plans?" Maguire asked her.

"A number of people, I suppose. Family. We were meeting Judge Moore, so her family."

"Did you make appointments?"

"Not really. I stopped by to see Lincoln Moore before I met the others for lunch. The rest of the day was loose."

"And the last place you stopped, for any length of time?" Claremont asked.

"We had dinner. Moose's at Washington Square. The car was parked about ninety minutes. From around seven to eight-thirty or so. We left for home from there."

"Any idea, Ms. Giambelli, who would want to cause you harm?"

"Yes." She met Claremont's gaze levelly. "Jeremy DeMorney. He's involved in the product tampering, in the embezzlement, in every problem my family's had this year. I believe he's responsible for it, that he planned it and used my cousin and what-ever, whoever else came to hand. And as I've told him so personally, he's unlikely to be happy with me just now."

"Mr. DeMorney's been questioned."

"And I'm sure he had plenty of answers. He's responsible."

"You saw the ad he sent Sophia." Frus-trated, Tyler pushed to his feet. "It was a threat, and he made good on it."

"We can't prove DeMorney sent the ad." Maguire watched Ty prowl the room. Big hands, she noted. DeMorney must have crumbled like plaster under them. "We've confirmed he was in New York when the package was mailed from San Francisco."

"He had it sent, then. Find a way to prove it," Tyler shot back. "That's your job."

"I believe he killed my father." Sophia kept her voice calm. "I believe his hatred of my father is at the core of everything that's happened. He may tell himself, in some skewed way, that it's business. But it's personal."

"Basing that on the alleged affair between Avano and the former Mrs. DeMorney, it's a long time to wait for payback."

"No, it's not." Maddy spoke up. "Not if you want to do it right, pull everyone in on it."

Claremont took the interruption in stride, gave Maddy a quiet, go-ahead look.

"If he goes after Sophia's father right after the divorce, then everybody knows he's whacked out over it." She'd spent some time analyzing it, running theories. "Like if I want to get Theo for something, I sit back, wait, figure out how to hit him best. Then when I do, he's not expecting it and doesn't even know why he's getting it." She nodded. "It's scientific, and lots more satisfying."

"The kid's a genius," Ty commented.

. . .

"'*A dish best* served cold,'" Claremont mused on the drive back to the city. "It fits DeMorney's profile. He's cool, sophisticated, erudite. He's got money, position, impeccable taste. I can see that type waiting, planning things out, tuggling strings. But I can't get his type risking losing that position over a cracked marriage. How would you handle it if your man cheated on you?"

"Oh, I'd kick his ass, then scalp him in the divorce and do everything in my power to make the rest of his life a living hell, including sticking pins in the throat and balls of a doll made in his image. But then, I'm not sophisticated and erudite."

"And people wonder why I'm not married." Claremont flipped open his notebook. "Let's go talk to Kristin Drake again."

It was infuriating to have the police come to your place of business. People would be talking, speculating, snickering. There was nothing Kris hated more than people gossiping behind her back. And as she saw it, the blame of it was squarely on Sophia's shoulders.

"If you want my opinion, the problems Giambelli's been facing this year were brought on because Sophia's more interested in promoting her own agenda than in the company or the people who work for it."

"And that agenda is?" Claremont asked.

"Sophia is her own agenda."

"And her self-interest, as you see it, has resulted in no less than four deaths, a shooting and what might have been a fatal accident involving herself, her mother, a friend and a young girl."

She remembered the cold rage on Jerry's face when she'd been in New York and Sophia and her farmer had cornered him. "Obviously she's pissed somebody off."

Not her problem, Kris assured herself. Not her deal.

"Besides you, Ms. Drake?" Maguire said pleasantly.

"It's no secret that I left Giambelli on less than amicable terms, and the reason for it was Sophia. I don't like her, and I resent the fact that she was brought in over me when I clearly had seniority and more experience. And I intend to make her pay for it in the market."

"How long were you being courted by De-Morney and La Coeur while you were still drawing a salary from Giambelli?"

"There's no law against considering other offers while employed with another firm. It's business."

"How long?"

She shrugged. "I was first approached last fall."

"By Jeremy DeMorney?"

"Yes. He indicated that La Coeur would be pleased to have me on their team. He made an offer, and I took some time to consider it."

"What decided you?"

"I simply realized I wasn't going to be happy with Giambelli as things stood. I felt creatively stifled there."

"Yet you remained there, stifled, for months. During that period, were you and DeMorney in contact with each other?"

"There's no law against—"

"Ms. Drake," Claremont interrupted. "We're investigating murder. You'd simplify the process by giving us a clear picture. We simplify it for you by asking questions here, where you're comfortable, rather than bringing you into the station house where the atmosphere isn't nearly as pleasant. Were you and DeMorney in contact during that period?"

"So what if we were?"

"During those contacts did you give Mr. DeMorney confidential information about Giambelli—business practices, promotional campaigns, personal information that may have come into your hands regarding members of the family?"

Her palms went damp. Hot and damp. "I want to call a lawyer."

"That's your privilege. You can answer the question and help us out here, maybe cop to some unethical business practices we're not interested in using against you. Or you can hang tough and possibly end up charged with accessory to murder."

"I don't know anything about murder. I don't know anything about that! And if Jerry . . . Jesus. Jesus."

She was starting to sweat. How many times had she gone back over the scenario Tyler had painted in Jerry's apartment? How often had she wondered if what he'd said, even part of what he'd said, was true?

If it was, she'd be connected. It was time, she decided, to break the link.

"I'm willing to play hardball to get what I want, in business. I don't know anything about murder, about product tampering. I passed Jerry some information, yes. Gave him a heads-up on Sophia's big centennial plans, the scheduling. Maybe he asked about personal business, but it wasn't anything more than office gossip. If he had anything to do with Tony . . ."

She trailed off, and her eyes glimmered with oncoming tears. "I don't expect you to believe me. I don't care if you do. But Tony meant something to me. Maybe, at first, I started seeing him because I saw it as another slap at Sophia, but it changed."

"You were in love with him?" Maguire infused her voice with sympathy.

"He mattered to me. He made me promises, about my position at Giambelli. He'd have made good on them, I know it, if he'd lived. I told you before, I'd met him in Sophia's apartment a couple times. *Not,*" she added, "the night he was killed. We were cooling it awhile. I admit I was upset about that at first. Rene had her clutches in him deep."

"It hurt you when he married her?"

"It pissed me off." Kris pressed her lips to-

gether. "When he told me they were engaged, I was angry. I didn't want to marry
him, for God's sake. Who needs it? But I
liked his company, he was good in bed and
he appreciated my professional talents. I
didn't care about his money. I can make my
own. Rene's nothing but a gold-digging
whore."

"Which is what you called her when you
phoned her apartment last December,"
Maguire stated.

"Maybe I did. I'm not sorry for saying what
I think. Saying what I think's a long way
from having anything to do with killing
somebody. My relationship with Jerry's
been professional, right down the line. If he
had anything to do with Tony, or any of the
rest, it's on him. I'm not swinging with him. I
don't play the game that way."

"Some game." Maguire slid behind the
wheel. "Give me a nice, clean 'I killed him
because he cut me off on the freeway' any
day of the week."

"Drake's running scared. Shaking down to
the toes. She thinks DeMorney set all this
up and she's in line to take the fall."

"He's a slick son of a bitch."

"Yeah. Let's pump up the pressure on him. The slicker they are, the harder you squeeze."

CHAPTER TWENTY-NINE

He wasn't going to tolerate it. The idiot police were certainly on the Giambelli payroll. He had no doubt of it.

Of course they could prove nothing. But the muscle in Jerry's cheek twitched as doubts danced in his head. No, he was sure of that. Sure of it. He'd been very, very careful. But that was beside the point.

The Giambellis had publicly humiliated him once before. Avano's affair with his wife had put his name on wagging tongues, forced him to change his life, his lifestyle. He could hardly have remained married to the unfaithful slut—particularly when people knew.

It had cost him placement and prestige in the company. In his great-uncle's eyes, a man who lost a wife to a competitor could lose accounts to a competitor.

And Jerry, always considered the La Coeur heir apparent, particularly by himself, had been taken down a painful peg.

The Giambellis hadn't suffered because of it. The three Giambelli women had remained above it all. The talk of Pilar had been respectful sympathy, of Sophia quiet admiration. And there was never talk of the great *La Signora.*

Or hadn't been, Jerry reminded himself. Until he'd made it happen.

Years in the planning and stylish in its execution, his revenge had cut through to the core of Giambelli. It had sliced through the family, keen as a scalpel. Disgrace, scandal, mistrust, and all brought about by their own. Perfection.

Who'd been taken down a peg now?

Even with all his planning, his careful stages, they were turning it on him. They knew he'd bested them, and they were trying to drag him under. He wouldn't permit it.

Did they think he'd tolerate having his associates speculate about him—a DeMorney? The idea of it made him shake with black, bitter rage.

His own family had questioned him.

Questioned him on business practices. The hypocrites. Oh, they didn't mind seeing their market share increase. Had they asked questions then? But at the first sign there might be a ripple in the pond, they laid the groundwork to make him a scapegoat.

He didn't need them, either. Didn't need their sanctimonious questioning of his ethics, or his methods, or his personal agenda. He wouldn't wait for them to ask for his resignation, if they would dare to do so. He was financially comfortable. It might be time to take a break from business. An extended vacation, a complete relocation.

He'd move to Europe, and there his reputation alone would ensure him a top position with any company he selected. When he was ready to work again. When he was ready to pay La Coeur back for their disloyalty.

But before he restructured his life yet again, he would finish the job. Personally, this time. MacMillan thought he didn't have the guts to pull his own trigger? He'd learn differently, Jerry promised himself. They would all learn differently.

The Giambelli women were going to pay dearly for offending him.

• • •

Sophia zipped through her interoffice e-mail. She'd have preferred attending to the reports, the memos, the questions personally in her San Francisco office. But the law had been laid down. She didn't go to the city unaccompanied. Period.

Tyler refused to be pulled away from the fields. The weeding wasn't complete, the suckering was just begun, and there was a mild infestation of grape leafhoppers. Nothing very troublesome, she thought with a little twist of resentment as she answered an inquiry. The wasps fed on the leafhopper eggs. That's why blackberry bushes, which served as hosts for the predator, were planted throughout the vineyard.

Hardly a season passed without a slight infestation. But there were stories, and those who loved to tell them, of an entire crop being devastated by the little bastards.

She wouldn't budge Tyler until he was certain it was under control, and by that time, she'd be so busy with the last-minute details of her mother's wedding she wouldn't be able to spare a day to go into the office, much less out to the vineyards.

When the wedding was over, the harvest would begin. Then no one would have time for anything but the crush.

At least the demands, the tight schedule, helped keep her mind off Jerry and the police investigation. It had been two full weeks since she'd careened around turns with no brakes. As far as she could tell, the investigation was at a standstill.

Jerry DeMorney was a different matter.

She, too, had her sources. She was perfectly aware there was talk about him. Questions, not only by the police, but by his superiors. And the board members, led—mortifyingly, she hoped—by his own great-uncle.

It was some satisfaction to know he was being squeezed, as her family had been squeezed. Between the greedy fists of gossip and suspicion.

She brought up another e-mail, clicked to open the attached file.

As she watched it scroll on-screen, her heart stumbled, then began to race.

It was a copy of the next ad, one set to run in August.

A family picnic, a wash of sunlight, the dapple of shade from a huge old oak. A scatter of people at a long wooden table that was loaded with food and bottles of wine.

The image Sophia had hand-picked was of several generations, a mix of faces, expressions, movement. The young mother with a baby in her lap, the little boy wrestling with a puppy on the grass, a father with a young girl riding his shoulders.

At the head of the table, the model who'd reminded her of Eli sat, his glass lifted as if in a toast. There was laughter in the picture, continuity, family tradition.

This image had been altered. Subtly, slickly. Three of the models' faces had been replaced. Sophia studied her grandmother, her mother, herself. Her eyes were wide with horror, her mouth gaping with it. Stabbed into her chest, like a knife, was a bottle of wine.

It read:

THIS IS YOUR MOMENT

IT'LL BE THE DEATH OF YOU

AND YOURS

"You son of a bitch, you son of a bitch." She jabbed the keyboard, ordered the copy to print, saved the file, then closed it.

He wouldn't shake her, she promised herself. And he wouldn't threaten her family with impunity. She would deal with him. She would handle this.

She started to slap the hard copy of the ad in a file, hesitated.

You're a handler, Tyler had told her.

Suckering the vines was a pleasant way to spend a summer's day. The sun was warm, the breeze mild as a kiss. Under the brilliant blue cup of sky, the circling Vacas were upholstered with green, the hills rolling down lush with the promise of summer.

His grapes were protected from that streaming midday sun by a lovely verdant canopy of leaves. Nature's parasol, his grandfather called it.

The crop was more than half its mature size, and before long the black grape varieties would begin changing color, green berries miraculously going blue, then purple as they pushed toward that last spurt of maturity. And harvest.

Each stage of growth required tending, just as each stage brought the season to its inevitable promise.

When Sophia crouched beside him, he continued his work, and his pleasure.

"I thought you were going to hole up in your office all day, waste this sunshine. Hell of a way to make a living, if you ask me."

"I thought a big, important vintner like yourself would have more to do than suckering vines personally." She combed a hand through his hair, lavishly streaked by the sun. "Where's your hat, pal?"

"Around somewhere. These Pinot Noir are going to be our earliest to ripen. I've got a hundred down with Paulie on these babies. I say they're going to give us our best vintage in five years. His money's on the Chenin Blanc."

"I'll take a piece of that. Mine's on the Pinot Chardonnay."

"You ought to save your money. You're going to need it financing Maddy's brainstorm."

"It's an innovative, forward-thinking project. She's already buried me in data. We're putting together a proposal for *La Signora.*"

"You want to rub grape seeds all over your body, I could do it for you. No charge." He shifted, their knees bumped before he laid a hand on hers. "What's the matter, baby?"

"I got another message, another doctored ad. It came through a file attached to interoffice e-mail." As his hand tensed, she turned hers over so their fingers linked. "I've already called. It was sent under P.J.'s screen name. She hasn't sent me any posts today. Someone either used her computer or had her account information and password. It could've come from anywhere."

"Where is it?"

"Back home. I printed it out, locked it in a drawer. I'm going to send it to the police, add it to their pile. But I wanted to tell you first. As much as I hate the idea, I suppose the thing to do is call a summit meeting so everyone in the family's aware and on guard. But . . . I wanted to tell you first."

He stayed as he was, crouched, his hand dwarfing hers. Overhead a cloud teased the edges of the sun and filtered the light.

"Here's what I want to do. I want to hunt him down and peel the skin off his bones with a dull knife. Until that happy day, I want you to promise me something."

"If I can."

"No, Sophie, there's no if. You don't go

anywhere by yourself. Not even from the villa to here. Not even for a walk in the gardens or a quick trip to the goddamn minimart. I mean it."

"I understand how worried you are, but—"

"You can't understand, because it's unreasonable. It's indescribable." He tripped her heart by bringing her free hand up, pressing his lips to the palm. "If I wake up in the middle of the night and you're not there, I break out in a cold sweat."

"Ty."

"Shut up, just shut up." In one fast and fluid move, he got to his feet to walk off the nerves and the rage. "I've never loved anyone before. I didn't expect it to be you. But it is, and that's it. You're not doing anything to mess this up for me."

"Well, naturally, we can't have that."

He turned, gave her a look of profound frustration. "You know what I mean, Sophie."

"Fortunately for you, I do. I don't intend to mess this up for you, or me, either."

"Great. Let's go pack your things."

"I'm not moving in with you."

"Why the hell not?" Frustration had him dragging his hands through his hair. "You're there half the time anyway. And don't give me that lame excuse about needing to be home to help with the wedding."

"It's not a lame excuse, it's a reason. Potentially a lame reason. I don't want to live with you."

"Why? Just tell me why."

"Maybe I'm old-fashioned."

"Like hell you are."

"Maybe I'm old-fashioned," she repeated, "in this one area. I don't think we should live together. I think we should get married."

"That's just another . . ." The words sank in, momentarily dulled his brain. "Whoa."

"Yes, and with that scintillating response, I need to go back home and call the police."

"You know, one day you're actually going to let me work through a process at my own time and pace. But since that isn't the case on this one, at least you could ask me in a more traditional way."

"You want me to ask you? Fine. Will you marry me?"

"Sure. November's good for me." He cupped her elbows, lifted her a couple inches off the ground. "Which was when I was going to ask you—but you always have to be first. I figured we could get married, have a nice honeymoon and be back home before pruning time. Kind of a tidy and symbolic cycle, don't you think?"

"I don't know. I have to think about it. *Culo.*"

"Back at you, honey." He gave her a hard kiss, then dropped her back on her feet. "Let me finish this vine, then we'll go call the cops. And the family."

"Ty?"

"Mmm."

"Just because I did the proposing doesn't mean I don't want a ring."

"Yeah, yeah, I'll get to it."

"I'll pick it out."

"No, you won't."

"Why not? I'm the one who'll be wearing it."

"You're the one wearing your face, too, but you didn't pick that out, either."

On a sigh, she knelt beside him. "That makes absolutely no sense." But she tipped her head onto his shoulder as he worked. "When I came here I was scared and angry. Now I'm scared, angry and happy. It's better," she decided. "A lot better."

. . .

"*This is who* we are," Tereza stated, lifting her glass. "And who we choose to be."

They were dining alfresco, in a kind of Giambelli reflection of the ad. A purposeful choice, Sophia thought. Her grandmother would stand straight against a threat and kick it dead in the balls if need be.

The evening was warm, the sunlight still brilliant. In the vineyards beyond the lawns and gardens, the grapes were growing fat and the Pinot Noir, as Tyler had predicted, was just beginning to turn.

Forty days till harvest, Sophia thought. That was the old rule. When the grapes took color, harvest was forty days away. Her mother would be married by then, and just back from her honeymoon. Maddy and Theo would be her brother and sister, and back in school. She would be planning her own wedding, though she'd pressured Tyler not to announce their engagement yet.

Life could continue because, as *La Signora* said, this is who they were. And who they chose to be.

"When we have trouble," Tereza continued, "we band together. Family. Friends. This year has brought trouble, and changes and grief. But it's also brought joy. In a few weeks Eli and I will have a new son, and more grandchildren. And, it seems," she added, turning toward Maddy, "a new enterprise. In the meantime, we've been threatened. I've given considerable thought to what can and should be done. James? Your legal opinion of our options."

He set down his fork, gathered his thoughts. "While evidence indicates De-Morney was involved, even perhaps instrumental, in the embezzlement scheme, the tampering, there's no concrete proof. Donato's claims notwithstanding, there isn't enough to convince the district attorney to file charges on those matters, or Tony Avano's death. It's been confirmed that he was in New York when Sophia's car was tampered with."

"He would have hired someone," David began.

"Be that as it may, and I don't disagree, until the police have evidence against them, there's nothing they can do. And nothing," James added, "you can do. My best advice is to stay above it, let the system work."

"No offense intended to you or your system, Uncle James, but it hasn't been working very well to date. Donato was murdered while he was *in* the system," Sophia pointed out. "And David was shot on a public street."

"Those are matters for the Italian authorities, Sophie, and only tie our hands all the more."

"He's harassing Sophie with those ads." Tyler shoved at his plate. "Why can't they be traced back to him?"

"I wish I had the answers. This isn't a stupid man or, thus far, a careless one. If he's at the core of all of this, he's covered himself with layers of protection, alibis."

"He walked into my apartment, sat down and shot my father in cold blood. I'd consider that, at the very least, a careless act. He needs to be punished. He should be hounded and pursued and harassed, just as he's hounded, pursued and harassed the family."

"Sophia." Helen reached across the table. "I'm sorry. Sometimes justice isn't what we want it to be, or what we expect."

"He set out to ruin us." Tereza spoke calmly. "He hasn't done so. Damaged, yes, caused us loss. But he'll pay a price for it. Today he was asked to resign his position at La Coeur. I'm pleased to believe that discussions Eli and I had with certain members of their board, and discussions David had with key executives bore this particular fruit."

She sipped her wine, enjoyed the bouquet. "I'm told he didn't take it well. I'll use whatever influence I have at my disposal to see to it he finds no position at any reputable winemaker. Professionally, he's finished."

"It's not enough," Sophia began.

"It may be too much," Helen corrected. "If he's as dangerous as you believe, this sort of interference will push him into a corner, make it only more imperative that he strike back. As a lawyer, as your friend, I'm asking you . . . all of you, to leave it alone."

"Mom." Linc shook his head. "Could you?"

"Yes." The single syllable was a fierce declaration. "To protect what mattered most, I could. I would. Tereza, your daughter is about to be married. She's found happiness. She's weathered a storm, and so have all of you. This is a time for you to celebrate, to move on, not to focus on revenge and retribution."

"We each protect what matters most, Helen. In our own way. The sun's going," she said. "Tyler, light the candles. It's a pleasant evening. We should enjoy it. Tell me, do you still pit your Pinot Noir against my Chenin Blanc?"

"I do." He worked his way down the table, setting the candles to flame. "Of course, it's a win-win situation, as we're merged." When he reached the head of the table, he met her eyes. "Speaking of mergers, I'm going to marry Sophia."

"Damn it, Ty! I told you—"

"Quiet," he said so casually, Sophia sputtered into silence. "She's the one who asked me, but I thought it was a pretty good idea."

"Oh, Sophie." Pilar leaped up from the table and rushed to throw her arms around her daughter.

"I only wanted to wait until after your wedding to tell you, but big mouth here couldn't keep it shut."

"That part was her idea, too," Tyler agreed as he circled the table. "Sophie's not wrong that often, so it's hard to get it through her head when she is. The way I figure it, you just can't have enough good news. Here."

He grabbed her hand, holding it when she tugged. He took a ring out of his pocket and slipped the simple and spectacular square-cut diamond on her finger. "That makes it a deal."

"Why can't you just . . . It's beautiful."

"It was my grandmother's. MacMillan to Giambelli." He took her hand, lifted it and kissed it. "Giambelli to MacMillan. It works for me."

She sighed. "I really hate it when you're right."

Revenge, Jerry decided, made stranger bedfellows than politics. Not that they'd quite gotten to the bed yet. But they would. Rene was so much easier a mark than he'd have believed.

"I appreciate your seeing me like this. Listening. Hearing me out." He reached for Rene's hand. "I was afraid you believed those vicious rumors the Giambellis are circulating."

"I wouldn't believe any of them if they said the sun came up in the east." Rene settled back on the sofa, made herself cozy. Over and above her loathing for the Giambellis was a keen sense for a man with money. She was quickly running out of cash.

Tony, damn him, hadn't been honest with her. She'd already sold off some jewelry, and if she didn't land another fish soon, she'd have to go back to work.

"I'm not saying I didn't play hardball, that's my job. Believe me, La Coeur was behind me all the way. Until things got sticky."

"Sounds like the way the Giambellis treated Tony."

"Exactly." Oh, he'd use that, use that and her innate hatred to turn his tide. "Don offered me inside information; I took it. Of course, the Giambellis can't have that stand, can't abide people knowing they were undermined by their own. So it has to be me, I have to have coerced or finagled or bribed, or God knows. I took what was offered. It's not like I held a gun to their heads."

He broke off. Squeezed her hand. "Jesus, Rene, I'm so sorry. What a stupid thing to say."

"It's all right. If Tony hadn't lied to me, hadn't cheated and snuck around with that little tramp who worked with Sophia, he'd still be alive today." And she wouldn't be damn near broke.

"Kris Drake." For effect, he pressed a

hand to his brow. "I didn't know about her and Tony before I hired her. The idea that she might have had something to do with Tony's death . . ."

"If she did, she was still working for them. They're behind it. All of it."

Could she be more perfect? He only wished he'd thought of using Rene months before. "They've ruined my reputation. I guess I brought part of that on myself. I shouldn't have wanted to win so much."

"Winning's all there is."

He smiled at her. "And I'm a man who hates to lose. In anything. You know, when I first saw you, I didn't know you and Tony were an item, and I . . . Well, I never got the chance to compete there, so I suppose that doesn't qualify as losing. More wine?"

"Yes, thanks." She pursed her lips, considering how to play it while he reached over for the bottle. "I was swept away by Tony's charm," she began. "And I admired what I thought was his ambition. I'm very attracted to clever businessmen."

"Really? I used to be one," he said as he poured the wine.

"Now, Jerry, you're still a clever businessman. You'll land on your feet."

"I want to believe that. I'm thinking of moving to France. I have some offers there." Or would have, he thought grimly. Damn well would have. "Luckily I don't need the money. I can pick and choose, take my time. It might do me good to just travel awhile, enjoy the benefits of the years of hard work I've put in."

"I love traveling." She purred it.

"I don't feel I can leave until I've straightened all this out. Until I've dealt with the Giambellis, face-to-face. I'll be frank with you, Rene, because I think you'll understand. I want to pay them back for putting this smear on me."

"I do understand." In what could be taken for sympathy, or otherwise, she laid a hand over his heart. "They always treated me like something cheap that could be easily ignored." She worked tears into her eyes. "I hate them."

"Rene." He moved in slowly. "Maybe we can find a way to pay them back. For both of us."

Later, when she lay naked, her head pillowed on his shoulder, he smiled into the dark. Tony's widow was going to clear his

path straight into the heart of the Giambellis. And he would rip it out.

It was going to be fun. Rene dressed
carefully for the role she was about to play.
Dark, conservative suit, minimal makeup.
She and Jerry had worked it all out,
just what she'd say, just how she'd behave. He'd made her rehearse countless
times. The man was a little too demanding for her taste, but she figured she'd
bring him around. If she kept him long
enough.

For now he was useful, entertaining and a
means to an end. And he, as most did, underestimated her. He didn't realize she
knew he also considered *her* useful, entertaining and a means to an end.

But Rene Foxx was nobody's fool. Particularly no man's fool.

Jerry DeMorney was dirty up to the knot
of his Hermés tie. If he hadn't called the
shots in that whole product tampering business, she'd start wearing off-the-rack suits.
Gave those rotten Giambellis a good kick in
the ass with that one, she mused. As far as
she was concerned, a man smart and devi-

ous enough to pull that off was just what she was looking for.

She decided walking into the homicide division with the box in her hands was her first step into a very lucrative tomorrow.

"I need to see Detective Claremont or Maguire," she began, then spotted Claremont just rising from behind his desk. "Oh, Detective." She was pleased she'd tagged him first. She always did better with men. "I have to see you. Right away. It's urgent. Please, is there somewhere—"

"Take it easy, Mrs. Avano." He took her arm. "How about some coffee?"

"Oh, I couldn't. I couldn't keep anything down. I've been up half the night."

She was focused on the job at hand and missed his quick signal to his partner.

"We'll talk in the coffee room. Why don't you tell me what's upset you?"

"Yes, I . . . Detective Maguire. It's good you're here, too. I'm so confused, so upset." She set the safe box on the table, pushed it to the center as if she wanted distance, then sat. "I was going through some of Tony's things, his papers. I hadn't gotten to all of them yet. I couldn't before. I found this box on the top shelf of his closet. I couldn't imagine what might be in it. I'd already had to deal with all the insurance papers, the legal papers." She fluttered her hands. "There was a key in his jewelry case. I remembered coming across it before, but not knowing what it was for. This," she said, gesturing. "It was for this. Open it. Please. I don't want to look through it again."

"Records," she said when Claremont opened the box and began to sift through the paperwork. "Ledgers or whatever they're called from that false account the Giambellis set up. Tony, he must've known. And that's why they had him killed. I know he must have been gathering this evidence. Trying to do the right thing, and . . . it cost him his life."

Claremont glanced through the accounts and correspondence, passing the sheets on to Maguire. "You believe your husband was killed over these papers."

"Yes, yes!" What was he, Rene thought impatiently, an idiot? "I'm afraid I might be partially responsible. I'm afraid of what might happen to me. I know someone's been watching me," she said, dropping her voice. "It sounds paranoid, I know, but I'm sure of it. I snuck out of my own apartment like a thief to come here. I think they've hired someone to watch me."

"Who would do that?"

"The Giambellis." She reached out, gripped Claremont's hand. "They're wondering if I remember, but I didn't, I didn't until I found this. And if they know, they'll kill me."

"That you know what?"

"That Sophia killed my Tony." Rene covered her mouth with her hand and sacrificed her makeup to tears.

"That's a serious accusation." Maguire rose to grab some tissues. "Why are you making it?"

Rene's breath hitched, her hand trembled as she reached for the tissues. "When I found these I remembered. I'd come home. It was so long ago, a year ago. Sophia was there. She and Tony were arguing upstairs. She was furious, and he was trying to calm her down. They didn't even know I'd come in. I went into the kitchen. I could still hear her. She was shouting as she does when she's in that terrible temper of hers. She said she wasn't going to stand for it. That it was none of his business. I didn't hear what he said, because his voice was low."

She dabbed at tears again. "Tony never raised his voice to her. He adored her. But she . . . she detested him, because of me. The Cardianili account—she said the name, but I didn't think of it again. The Cardianili account would be left alone, and that would be the end of it. If he did anything with the ledgers, she would make him pay. She said, very clearly: 'If you don't leave this alone, I'll kill you.' I came out of the kitchen then because it made me angry. Almost at the same time she came flying down the stairs. She saw me, said something vicious in Italian, then stormed out."

She released a shuddering breath, sniffled delicately. "When I asked Tony about it, I could see he was shaken, but he brushed it off, said it was business and she was just blowing off steam. I let it go. Sophia often blew off steam that way. I never thought she meant what she said. But she did. He knew she'd been involved in embezzlement, and she killed him for it."

"So." Maguire tipped back her chair when she and her partner were alone. "You buy any of that?"

"For somebody who didn't sleep last night, she looked pretty alert. For somebody terrified and upset, she remembered to match her shoes to her purse and coordinate her hose."

"You're a real fashion cop, partner. No way she just came across these papers. She'd have been through every drawer, closet and cubbyhole within a day of his death, to make sure she had access to every penny."

"Maguire, I don't think you like the widow Avano."

"I don't like people who think I'm stupid. Question: if she had these papers all along, why turn them over now? If she didn't have them before, who passed them to her?"

"DeMorney's in San Francisco." Claremont tapped the tips of his fingers together. "Wonder how far he and the widow go back."

"One thing for certain, they've both got it in for the Giambellis, and that one wants to put the screws to Sophia G, and she wants it bad."

"Bad enough to give a false statement to the police."

"Oh hell, she enjoyed that. And she's

smart enough to know she didn't say anything we could hook her on. We can't prove if and when she found those papers. And if it came down to it, the argument scene would be her word against Sophia's, who's likely to have argued with her father at some point during the last year of his life. No way to cook her on that even if we wanted to bother."

"Never made sense for her to marry Avano and kill him the day after. She doesn't gel there for me. Doesn't gain her anything, and she's in it for what she can get."

"If we bought this, she could cop a little revenge. That's what she's after now."

"Yeah, and so's DeMorney." Claremont rose. "Let's see how tight we can link them."

CHAPTER THIRTY

Rene slithered onto the sofa beside Jerry and accepted the flute of champagne. "I got some very interesting information at the salon today."

"What might that be?"

"I'll tell you." She ran a fingertip down the center of his shirt. "But it'll cost you."

"Really?" He took her hand, lifted it to bite gently on her wrist.

"Oh, that's nice, too, but I want something a little different. Let's go out, lover. I'm so tired of staying in. Take me out to a club where there're people and music and wicked things going on."

"Honey, you know I'd love to. It's not smart for us to be seen together in public quite yet."

She pouted, nuzzled against him. "We'll

go somewhere nobody knows us. And even if they do, Tony's been dead for months and months. No one expects me to grieve alone forever."

From the reports that had winged back across the Atlantic, Rene hadn't grieved alone for a week. "Just a little while longer. I'll make it up to you. When we're finished here with everything and everyone, we'll go to Paris. Now what did you find out today?"

"To borrow from that slut Kris's lexicon, bitch number three is giving bitch number two a little party on Friday night—wedding eve. All females. She's setting up a damn spa in the villa for the night. Facials, body treatments, massages, the works."

"And what will the men be doing while the women are getting themselves scrubbed and rubbed?"

"Watching porno flicks and jerking off, I suppose. They're holding their bachelor-night deal at the MacMillan place. The bride and groom aren't allowed to do the dirty the night before the wedding. Hypocrites."

"This is interesting." And exactly what he'd been waiting for. "We'll know just where everyone is. And the timing couldn't be better, right before the happy event. Rene, you're a jewel."

"I don't want to be one. I just want to have them."

"A week from now, we'll be in Paris, and I'll take care of that. But first, you and I have a date on Friday night at Villa Giambelli."

She wanted it to be perfect, the kind of night they'd all remember and laugh about for years. She'd planned it, organized it, fine-tuned the details right down to the scent of the candles for the aromatherapy treatments. In twenty-four hours, Sophia thought, her mother would be dressing for her wedding, but for her last evening as a single woman, she was going to bask in a world of females.

"When we have our products, maybe we should sell direct to spas for a while." Maddy sniffed at the oils already arranged by the massage table. "Make them, like, exclusive so people are dying for them."

"You're a clever girl, Madeline. But no business tonight. Tonight is for female ritual. We're the handmaidens."

"Do we get to talk about sex?"

"Of course. This isn't about exchanging recipes. Ah, there's the woman of the hour."

"Sophie." Already in her long white wrap, Pilar circled the pool house. "I can't believe you went to all this trouble."

Various stations were set up, with lounging sofas and salon chairs. The evening light shimmered toward sunset while scents from the gardens clung to the air. Tables held abundant platters of fruit and chocolate, bottles of wine and sparkling water, baskets and bowls of flowers.

Along the wall, water spilled down the brass sculpture and into the pool to add sensuous music.

"I was shooting for a Roman bath thing. Do you like it, really?"

"It's wonderful. I feel like a queen."

"When you're finished, you'll feel like a goddess. Where are the others? We're wasting pampering time."

"Upstairs. I'll get them."

"No, you won't. Maddy, pour Mama some wine. She's not to lift a finger except to pick up a chocolate strawberry. I'll get everyone."

"What kind do you want?" Maddy asked her.

"Just water for now, honey, thanks. It's such a lovely evening." She wandered toward the open doors, then laughed lightly. "Massage tables on the patio. Only Sophie."

"I never had a massage before."

"Mmm. You'll love it."

As she spoke, as she looked out over the garden, Pilar ran a hand absently over Maddy's hair, left it lying on her shoulder. The gesture made everything inside the girl go warm. And made her sigh.

"What's wrong?"

"Nothing." Maddy passed Pilar the glass. "Nothing's wrong. I guess I'm looking forward to . . . everything."

"You're bluffing," David said around the cigar clamped in his teeth and tried to stare Eli down.

"Yeah? Put your money up, son, and call me."

"Go ahead, Dad." Theo had a cigar, unlit, in his teeth as well, and felt like a man. "No guts, no glory."

David tossed chips in the pot. "Call. Show 'em."

"Three little deuces," Eli began and watched David's eyes gleam. "Standing watch over two pretty ladies."

"Son of a bitch."

"A Scotsman doesn't bluff over money, son." Eli, jubilant, raked in his chips.

"The man's scalped me so many times over the years, I wear a helmet when we sit down to cards." James gestured with his glass. "You'll learn."

Linc's head came up at the knock on the door. "Somebody ordered a stripper, right? I knew you guy's wouldn't let me down."

"It's the pizza." Theo leaped up.

"More pizza? Theo, you can't possibly want more pizza."

"Sure I can," he shouted over his shoulder to his father. "Ty said I could."

"I said he could order it for me. He inhaled the last order."

Linc sent Tyler a sorrowful look. "You couldn't arrange for a stripper to deliver the pizza?"

"They were all out of strippers. Shriners' convention."

"Likely story. Well, I hope he got pepperoni at least."

· · ·

"*My God, Sophie,* this was a brilliant idea."

"Thanks, Aunt Helen." They sat side by side, tipped back with purifying masks thick and green covering their faces. "I wanted Mama to feel relaxed and completely female."

"This'll do it. Can you see Tereza and Maddy over there getting pedicures and arguing."

"Mmm," Sophia mused. "They disagree about the name for the beauty products we don't even have yet. I don't know if it's Maddy or the concept, but it's boosted *Nonna*'s morale."

"I'm glad to hear it. I've been worried about her, all of you, since we talked last. The idea of Rene trying to make Tony a hero and you a villain over the Cardianili business; it fries my cookies."

Sophia tensed, deliberately relaxed again. "It was a stupid move. DeMorney's behind it, and it's one of the first truly stupid moves he's made. He's cracking."

"That may be. But it caused more upset." She held up a hand. "And that's all I'm going to say about it. Tonight's not about problems. It's about indulgence. Where's Pilar?"

Don't think about it, Sophia ordered herself. Think pure thoughts. "Treatment Room B—otherwise known as the lower-level guest bath. Full-body facial. You need to be near a shower."

"Fabulous. I'm next."

"Champagne?"

"Maria." Sophia roused herself enough to sit up. "You're not to serve. You're a guest."

"My manicure's dry." She showed off her nails. "I have a pedicure next. You can bring me champagne then."

"That's a deal."

Maria glanced over as Pilar, looking soft and relaxed, came back in. "You've made your mama happy tonight. Everything's going to be all right now."

"You sure know how to show a woman a good time."

Jerry ran a hand over the butt of Rene's snug black pants. "You haven't seen anything yet. This is going to be a night to remember. For everyone."

They moved through the vineyard now. It

had been a long hike from the car, and the sack he carried seemed to gain weight with every step. Still, there was something to be said for doing the job himself that he hadn't experienced before. Not just the amused gratification he'd felt at other times, but a deep and personal excitement.

And if anything went wrong, he'd simply sacrifice Rene. But he didn't intend for anything to go wrong.

He knew the setup here. Between Don and Kris and his own observations, he was aware of the security setup, and how to avoid setting off alarms. It was simply a matter of patience and care. And a single driving ambition.

Before the night was over, Giambelli would, one way or another, be in ruins.

"Stay close," he told her.

"I am. Not to spoil the party, but I wish I was as sure as you are this is going to work."

"No second thoughts now. I know what I'm doing and how to do it. Once the winery's on fire, they'll come spilling out like ants at a picnic."

"I don't care if you burn the whole fucking vineyard to ashes." In fact, she got a thrill out of the image, and of her dancing at the edge of the flames. "I just don't want to get caught."

"Do what I tell you and you won't. Once they're out here busy trying to put out the fire, we go in, plant the package in Sophia's room, get out. We're in the car and heading back five minutes later. We call the cops from a pay phone, give them an anonymous tip, and we're back at your place popping champagne before the smoke clears."

"The old lady'll pay off the cops. She won't let her precious granddaughter go to prison."

"Maybe. Let her try, it won't matter. They'll be ruined. Sooner or later you find the right straw, and that's the one that breaks the back. Isn't that what you want?"

Something in his voice had a chill snaking up her spine, but she nodded. "It's exactly what I want."

When he reached the winery, he took out the keys. Don had been slick enough to make copies, and he'd been smart enough to duplicate those. "These get tossed in the bay when we're done." He slid the key into the first lock. "No one's going to need them after tonight. They'll have a hell of a time explaining how a fire started inside a locked building." With that statement, he opened the door.

Sophia lay on the massage table and looked up at the stars. "Mama, am I obsessive?"

"Yes."

"Is that a bad thing?"

Pilar glanced back from her stance at the edge of the patio. "No. Occasionally annoying, but not bad."

"Do I miss the big picture because I'm drilling on the details?"

"Rarely. Why do you ask?"

"I was wondering what I'd change about myself if I could. If I should."

"I wouldn't change anything."

"Because I'm perfect?" Sophia asked with a grin.

"No, because you're mine. Is this about Ty?"

"No, it's about me. Up until . . . well, I'm not exactly sure when, but up until I was sure I had everything figured out. Knew what I wanted and how I was going to get it."

"Not sure anymore?"

"Oh no, I'm still sure. I still know what I want and how I'm going to get it. But the things I want changed on me. I was wondering if they were there all along, and I was just missing the big picture. I . . . could you give us a minute," she said to the therapist. She sat up, holding the sheet to her breast when she was alone with Pilar. "Please don't get upset."

"I won't."

"Not that long ago I still wanted you and Dad to get back together. I wanted it because I didn't know how to want anything else, I think. Because I felt if you did, he'd be what I needed him to be. Not what you needed or what he was, but what *I* needed. That was the detail I kept obsessing over, and I missed the big picture. I'd change that if I could."

"I wouldn't. You would've been a good daughter to him if he'd let you. You were willing to be, you needed to be. No, I wouldn't change that."

"That helps." She took Pilar's wrist, turned it to check the time on her watch. "It's just midnight. Happy wedding day, Mama." She pressed Pilar's hand to her cheek, then started to lie back.

"What's that? It looks like . . . Oh my God. The winery! The winery's on fire. Maria! Maria, call nine-one-one. The winery's on fire."

She rolled off the table, and snagged her robe on the run.

As Jerry had predicted, they poured out of the house. Raised voices, running feet. From the shadows of the garden he counted the figures wrapped in white robes that raced down the path and out across the vineyard.

"In and out," he whispered to Rene. "Piece of cake. You lead the way."

She'd given him the location and setup of Sophia's room, but he wanted her going in first. She might have made a mistake. She claimed she'd only slipped into Sophia's room once, but that was once more than he'd managed.

He couldn't risk turning on the light, though he was sure his flashlight would be enough. He only needed to plant the package at the back of her closet where the police, even if they were idiots, would find it.

He moved up behind Rene, up the terrace steps, glancing over his shoulder. He could see the bright orange and gold of the fire against the night sky. A brilliant sight. It illuminated the figures rushing like frightened moths toward the flame.

They'd put it out, of course, but not quickly. It would take time for them to realize the water had been turned off for the sprinkler system, time for them to gather their wits, time for them to watch helplessly as precious bottles exploded, as equipment was ruined, as their god of tradition burned to hell.

So he didn't have the guts to do his own dirty work? Gingerly he flexed his hand. It still twinged now and then. They'd see who had the guts when the sun came up.

"Jerry, for God's sake." Rene hissed at him from the terrace outside Sophia's room. "This isn't a tourist attraction. You said we had to hurry."

"Always time for a moment of pleasure, darling." He stepped, swaggered, up to the terrace door. "Sure this is hers?"

"Yes, I'm sure."

"Well then." He pushed open the doors, stepped inside. And drew a deep, satisfied breath of her scent just as Sophia dashed through the opposite door and slapped on the lights.

The sudden glare slashed across his eyes, the shock froze his brain. Before he could recover from either, he was fighting off a hundred and ten pounds of enraged woman.

She leaped at him, blind fury catapulting her across the room. Even as she sank her teeth into him, the edges of her vision glowed red with blood lust. Her only clear thought was to inflict pain, monstrous pain. And when he howled, the feral thrill of it spurted through her like lava.

He struck out, caught her across the cheekbone, but she didn't even feel it. She went for his eyes, freshly manicured nails already tipped red, slashed out, missed by a breath and scored like the tongs of a rake down his cheek.

The burn of it maddened. With no goal but to free himself, he tossed her aside and sent her into a shrieking Rene. He could smell his own blood. Intolerable. She'd ruined all his careful plans. Unforgivable.

Even as she scrabbled to her feet, prepared to leap at him again, the gun was out of the pouch, in his hand, with his finger sweaty on the trigger.

He nearly ended it then, with one quick twitch of his nervous finger. Then her body jerked to a halt and her eyes cleared of rage and filled with shock and fear.

Finally, he thought, face-to-face. And he wanted more than survival. He wanted satisfaction.

"Now. Isn't this interesting? You should've run out with the others, Sophia. But maybe it's fate you end like your worthless father. With a bullet in the heart."

"Jerry, we have to get out of here. Just go." Rene pushed herself to her feet, stared at the gun. "My God! What're you doing? You can't just shoot her."

"Oh?" He thought he could, and that was a revelation. He didn't believe he'd have any trouble with it at all. "And why not?"

"That's crazy. It's murder. I'm not having any part of murder. I'm getting out. I'm getting out now. Give me the keys to the car. Give me the damn keys."

"Shut the fuck up." He said it coolly, and in an almost absent gesture smashed the gun into the side of her head. When she went down like a stone, he didn't even glance at her, but kept his eyes locked on Sophia's.

"She was a pain in the ass, on that we can agree. But she's useful. And this is perfect. You'll appreciate the spin on this, Sophia. Rene started the fire. She's had it in for you all along. She went to the cops a few days ago, tried to convince them you'd killed your father. And tonight, she came here, fired the winery and broke into your room to plant evidence against you. You caught her, you struggled, the gun went off. The gun," he added, "used to shoot David Cutter. I had it sent to me. Forward-thinking, which I'm sure you'll appreciate. You're dead, and she hangs for it. Very tidy."

"Why?"

"Because nobody screws with me and gets away with it. You Giambellis think you can have it all, and now you'll end up with nothing."

"Because of my father?" She could see the bright orange glow from the fire through the open doors behind him. "All of this because my father embarrassed you?"

"*Embarrassed?* He stole from me—my

wife, my pride, my life. And what did any of you lose? Nothing. Just another bump to you. I've taken my own back, and more. I'd have been satisfied to ruin you, but dead's better. You're the key. Tereza, well, she's not as young as she was. Your mother, she hasn't got what it takes to bring the company back. Without you, the heart and the brains are dead. Your father was a user, a liar and a cheat."

"Yes, he was." No one would come for her, she thought. There would be no one to race back from the fire to save her. She would face death on her own. "You're all that, and so much less."

"If there was time, we'd debate that. But I'm a little pressed so . . ." He brought the gun up another inch. "*Ciao, bella.*"

"*Vai a farti fottere.*" She cursed him in a steady voice. She wanted to close her eyes—to find a prayer, an image of something to take with her. But she kept them open. Waited. When the gun exploded, she stumbled back. And watched blood seep through the tiny hole in his shirt.

Baffled shock crossed his face, then another shot jerked his body to the side and dropped him. In the doorway, Helen lowered the gun to her side.

"Oh my God. Oh God. Aunt Helen." Her legs gave out. Sophia stumbled to the bed, lowered herself to it. "He was going to kill me."

"I know." Slowly, Helen came into the room, sat heavily on the bed beside Sophia. "I came back to tell you the men had come. I saw . . ."

"He was going to kill me. Just like he killed my father."

"No, honey. He didn't kill your father. I did. I did," she repeated, and dropped the gun she held to the floor. "I'm so sorry."

"No. That's crazy."

"I used that gun. It was my father's. It was never registered. I don't know why I took it that night. I don't think I planned to kill him. I . . . wasn't thinking at all. He wanted money. Again. It was never going to end."

"What are you talking about?" Sophia took her shoulders. She could smell gunpowder, and blood. "What are you saying?"

"Linc. He was using Linc against me. Linc, God help me. Linc is Tony's son."

"They've got it under control. It's—" Pilar

rushed in the terrace doors, stopped cold. "Oh dear God. Sophie!"

"No, wait." Sophia sprang to her feet. "Don't come in. Don't touch anything." Her breath came out in pants, but she was thinking, thinking fast. "Aunt Helen, come with me. Come with me now. We can't stay in here."

"It'll destroy James, and Linc. I've ruined them after all."

Moving quickly now, Sophia dragged Helen up, pulled her out onto the terrace. "Tell us. Tell us quickly, we can't have much time."

"I killed Tony. Pilar, I betrayed you. Myself. Everything I believe in."

"That's not possible. For God's sake, what happened here?"

"She saved my life," Sophia said. A blast rent the air as bottles exploded in the winery. She barely flinched. "He was going to kill me, with the gun that shot David. He'd sent for it, kept it like a souvenir. Helen, what happened with my father?"

"He wanted money. Over the years he'd contact me when he needed money. He never actually demanded, never actually threatened. He'd just mention Linc—what a

fine boy he was, what a bright and promising young man. Then he'd say he needed a
bit of a loan. I slept with Tony." She began
to weep then, silently. "All those years ago.
We were all so young. James and I were
having problems. I was so angry with him,
so confused. We separated for a few
weeks."

"I remember," Pilar murmured.

"I ran into Tony. He was so understanding, so sympathetic. You and he weren't
getting along, either. You were considering
a separation. He was charming, and he
paid attention. The way James hadn't
been. There's no excuse. I let it happen.
After, I was so ashamed, so disgusted with
myself. But it was done, and couldn't be
changed. I found out I was pregnant. It
wasn't James's because we hadn't been
together that way. So I made my second
hideous mistake, and I told Tony. I might as
well have told him I'd decided to change
my hairstyle. He could hardly be expected
to pay for one night's indiscretion, could
he? So I paid." Tears dripped down her
cheeks. "And I paid."

"Linc is Tony's child."

"He's James's." Helen looked pleadingly

at Pilar. "In every way but that one. He doesn't know, neither of them know. I did everything I could to make up for that night. To James, to Linc—God, Pilar, to you. I slept with my best friend's husband. I was young and angry and stupid, and I've never forgiven myself for it. But I did everything I could to make it up. I gave him money, every time he asked for it. I don't even know how much over the years."

"And you couldn't give any more," Pilar concurred.

"The night of the party, he told me he had to see me, told me when and where. I refused. It was the first time I'd done so. It made him angry, and that frightened me. If I didn't do as he said, he'd go inside, then and there, and tell James, tell Linc, tell you.

"I couldn't risk it, couldn't bear it. My baby, Pilar. My little boy with the loose shoelaces. When I went home, I got the gun out of the safe. It's been there for years, I don't know why I thought of it. Don't know why I took it. It was like a veil over my mind. He had music on in the apartment, and a good bottle of wine. He sat and told me his financial troubles. Charmingly, as if we were old, dear friends. I don't remember everything he said; I'm not even sure I heard him. He needed what he liked to call a loan. A quarter of a million this time. He'd be willing, of course, to take half by the end of the week, and give me another month for the rest. It wasn't too much to ask, after all. He'd given me such a fine son.

"I didn't know the gun was in my hand. I didn't know I'd used it until I saw the red against his white tuxedo shirt. He looked at me, so surprised, just a little annoyed. I could almost imagine him saying, 'Damn, Helen, you've ruined my shirt.' But he didn't, of course. He didn't say anything. I went home and tried to convince myself it had never happened. Never happened at all. I've carried the gun around with me ever since. Everywhere."

"You could have thrown it away," Pilar said quietly.

"How could I? What if one of you were arrested? I'd need it then to prove I'd done it myself. I couldn't let him hurt my baby, or James. I thought it could be over. And now . . . I need to tell James and Linc first. I need to tell them before I talk to the police."

Cycles, Sophia thought. Sometimes, they needed to be stopped. "If you hadn't used that gun to save my life tonight, you wouldn't have to tell them anything."

"I love you," Helen said simply.

"I know it. And this is what happened here tonight. Just exactly what happened." She took Helen by the shoulders. "Pay attention to me. You came back, saw Jerry holding me at gunpoint. He'd brought both guns with him—he'd intended to plant them in my room to implicate me. We'd struggled, and the other gun, the one that killed my father, was on the floor near the doorway. You picked it up, and you shot him before he shot me."

"Sophia."

"That's what happened." She took Helen's hand, squeezed it. Took her mother's. "Isn't it, Mama?"

"Yes. That's exactly what happened. You saved my child. Do you think I wouldn't save yours?"

"I can't."

"Yes, you can. You want to make it up to me?" Pilar demanded. "Then you'll do this. I don't care about what happened one night almost thirty years ago, but I care about what happened tonight. I care about what you've been to me most of my life. I'm not going to let someone I love be destroyed. Over what? Over money, over pride, over image? If you love me, if you want to make up for that mistake so long ago, you'll do exactly what Sophie's asking you to do. Tony was her father. Who has more right to decide than she?"

"Jerry's dead," Sophia said. "He killed, threatened, destroyed, all because of one selfish act by my father. And it ends here. I'm going to go call the police. Someone should take a look at Rene." She leaned forward, brushed her lips over Helen's cheek. "Thank you. For the rest of my life."

Late, late into the night, Sophia sat in the kitchen sipping tea laced with brandy. She'd given her statement, had sat, her hand holding Helen's, as Helen had given hers.

Justice, she thought, didn't always come as you expected. Helen had said that once. And here it was. Unexpected justice. It hadn't hurt that Rene had been hysterical, had babbled to everyone, including Claremont and Maguire when they'd arrived, that Jerry was a madman, a murderer, and had forced her at gunpoint to come with him.

Some snakes slithered through, Sophia supposed. Because life was a messy business.

Now at last, the police were gone, the house was quiet. She looked up as her mother and grandmother came in. "Aunt Helen?"

"She's finally sleeping." Pilar went to the cupboard, got two more cups. "We've talked. She'll be all right. She's going to resign her judgeship. I suppose she needs to." Pilar set the cups on the table. "I've told Mama everything, Sophia. I felt she had a right to know."

"*Nonna.*" Sophia reached for her hand. "Did I do the right thing?"

"You did the loving thing. That often matters more. It was brave of you, Sophia. Brave of both of you. It makes me proud." She sat down, sighed. "Helen took a life, and gave one back. That closes the circle. We won't speak of it again. Tomorrow my daughter's getting married, and we'll have joy in this house again. Soon, the harvest— the bounty. And another season ends. The next is yours," she said to Sophia. "Yours and Tyler's. Your life, your legacies. Eli and I are retiring the first of the year."

"*Nonna.*"

"Torches are meant to be passed. Take what I give you."

The faint irritation in her grandmother's voice made her smile. "I will. Thank you, *Nonna.*"

"Now, it's late. The bride needs her sleep, and so do I." She got to her feet, leaving her tea untouched. "Your young man went back to the winery. You don't need so much sleep."

True enough, Sophia thought as she raced across the grounds toward the winery. She had so much energy, so much life inside her, she didn't think she'd ever need to sleep again.

He'd set up lights, and the old building hulked under them. She could see the sparkle of broken glass from the windows, the smears from smoke, the chars from flame. But still, it stood.

It withstood.

Perhaps he sensed her. She liked to think so. He stepped out of the broken doorway as she ran up. And he caught her, held her close and tight and inches off the ground.

"There you are, Sophia. I figured you needed a little time with your mother, then I was coming to get you."

"I got you first. Hold on, okay? Just keep holding on."

"You can count on it." Even as he did, the ice skimmed through his belly again. He pressed his face to her hair. "God. God. When I think—"

"Don't think. Don't," she said and turned her mouth to his.

"I'm not going to be able to let you out of my sight for the next, oh, ten or fifteen years."

"Right now that suits me fine. You all alone here?"

"Yeah. David needed to get the kids home, and I sent Granddad back before he keeled over. He was exhausted. James was still pretty shaken, so Linc took him back to my place since your mom's with Helen."

"Good. Everything's as it should be." She rested her head on his shoulder, looked toward the winery. "It could have been worse."

He eased her back, touched his lips gently to the bruise on her cheek. "It could have been a hell of a lot worse."

"You should've seen the other guy."

He managed a strangled laugh as he held her tight again. "That's a little sick."

"Maybe, but it's the way I feel. He died with my mark on his face, and I'm glad of it. I'm glad I caused him some pain. And now I can put it away. All of it. Lock it away and everything starts now. Everything, Ty," she said. "We'll rebuild the winery, rebuild our lives. And make them ours. Giambelli-MacMillan is going to come back, bigger and better than ever. That's what I want."

"That's handy, because that's what I want, too. Let's go home, Sophie."

She tucked her hand in his and walked away from the damage and the scars. The first hints of dawn lightened the sky in the east. When the sun broke through, she thought, it was going to be a beautiful beginning.